Praise for Renee Collins's RELIC

"RELIC is like nothing else I've read—a historical fantasy teeming with ghost coyotes, duplicitous Haciendos, sexy cowboys, and dangerous relic magic. I loved spending time in Collins's magnificent reimagining of the Old West!"
—Jessica Spotswood, author of *Born Wicked*

"A magically romantic tale of how the West should've been won. Collins's debut drew me in and held me until the breathtaking end."
—Kasie West, author of *Pivot Point*

"Weaving the allure of the Old West with layers of magic, Collins's debut is an intriguing, enchanting ride."
—Kiersten White, author of *Paranormalcy*

RELIC

RELIC

RENEE COLLINS

This book is a work of fiction. Names, characters, places, and incidents are the product of the author's imagination or are used fictitiously. Any resemblance to actual events, locales, or persons, living or dead, is coincidental.

Entangled Publishing, LLC
2614 South Timberline Road
Suite 109
Fort Collins, CO 80525

Visit our website at www.entangledpublishing.com.

Edited by Stacy Abrams
Cover design by Alexandra Shostak

Ebook ISBN 978-1-62266-015-5
Print ISBN 978-1-62266-014-8

Manufactured in the United States of America

First Edition September 2013

The author acknowledges the copyrighted or trademarked status and trademark owners of the following wordmarks mentioned in this work of fiction: "The Red River Valley," Smith & Wesson.

To Diana: the best friend, sister, and Story Consultant a girl could ever ask for.

CHAPTER ONE

We were home alone the night that Haydenville burned. Mama and Papa had gone to a political meeting and left me in charge. I was sixteen, old enough to keep an eye on my younger brother and sister. Or so my folks figured. They had no way of knowing how I would be tested.

The evening started off so calm. Crickets were singing in the sagebrush, and the oppressive heat of daytime had been swept away by a velvety breeze, which drifted in through the open windows. Ella was playing with Sassy's new litter of kittens up in the loft, and Jeb sat by the fire, polishing the brand-new gun he'd gotten for his fourteenth birthday the week before. I was scraping a broom over the floor of our little one-room house, trying my best to banish the red-orange sand that seemed our constant companion. But my mind soon drifted from my chores.

I stood in the doorway, in the warm twilight, gazing at the

vast desert beyond. It stretched endlessly in either direction, with nothing but sage and rocks and the occasional rabbitbrush to break the monotony. The dark smudge of Haydenville sat on the horizon, a small spit of a town, not much more interesting than the cactus. It always made me feel lonesome to stare out at the stillness around us.

As I leaned my head against the doorframe and watched the first star pierce through the indigo sky, a reckless wish burned in my heart. I gazed up and let myself envision a sleek dragon diving out of the scrape of clouds, a creature long extinct, returned to breathe life back into this barren place. I pictured the ancient animal curling around the moon and soaring over the red-rock cliffs beyond our house. But as it swept downward, a strange glow on the horizon caught my attention.

I straightened, squinting in the direction of the wavering light. It was a wide line of orange spreading across the dark landscape in the distance, painting the night sky a deep amber. The breeze that drifted past my cheek carried the distinct scent of smoke. This was no figment of my imagination. This was fire.

And it was coming from Haydenville.

The broom slid out of my fingers and clattered to the floor.

"Maggie?"

I met my brother's gaze, and his brow furrowed. "What is it?" he asked, tightening his grip on the rifle as he stood. "A rock devil?"

"Fire." I pointed, my heart beating fast. "In the town."

Jeb raced to my side and gripped the doorframe. "God Almighty," he breathed. "The whole street's burning." Then he gave me a sharp look. "Mama and Papa."

"I'm sure they're okay," I said, more confidently than I felt.

"They would have seen the fire before it spread. They're probably on their way back right now."

Jeb squinted at the horizon, now rippling in the heat. "Someone *is* coming. A whole bunch of people..."

A row of separate flames undulated in the twilight. Torches. They moved across the desert toward us with a speed that could only mean they were carried on horseback.

"Maybe *most* people in the town got out," I said, but my voice faded away.

Jeb stared hard at the fast-moving torches. "I don't think so, Maggie."

We looked at each other, and the same thought came to us.

"Ella," I whispered.

I scrambled up the loft ladder, struggling to stay calm. I had to keep it together until Mama and Papa got home. I just wished they'd hurry.

Ella was lying on her back, holding a squirming kitten over her chest. "Look at this little orange one, Mags," she said. "Isn't she the sweetest thing you..."

As her large brown eyes fixed on me, the smile dropped from her face. "What's wrong?"

She was only seven, but she had a real knack for reading people's faces.

"You need to come down," I said, reaching for the kitten.

Ella pulled it out of my grasp. "Hey! I was holding her."

"You can have her back in a minute. Right now, we need to talk."

She held her pet close, scowling at me. I clenched my jaw. Sometimes that girl tried my patience like none other. "You come right now, or Mama's gonna hear about this." I grabbed the kitten and set it on the mattress.

"I want Jeb," she said, sitting up angrily.

Jeb was her favorite. Ever since she could walk, she'd followed him like a shadow. I wrapped my hand around her wrist. "You can talk to him when you come down. Now move it."

We climbed down the ladder steps swiftly. Jeb was standing in the doorway, watching the fire, his rifle poised. Ella ran up to him, hugging his pant leg. He stroked her hair absently but kept his gaze on the flames. I came up behind him, looking at the burning desert beyond us. Staring back at me was the undeniable reality: Mama and Papa weren't going to reach home before those torches did. Our safety now rested in my hands alone.

"We gotta get out of here," I said under my breath to Jeb.

"And go where?"

"To the hiding spot, just like we always talked about."

Jeb grimaced. "We don't need to do that. I can protect us here."

"Don't be a fool. You barely know how to use that gun."

"I do, too!"

"It doesn't matter. Mama and Papa put *me* in charge, and I'm sayin' we go to the hiding place."

Ella pulled on Jeb's arm. "What's goin' on?"

He hoisted her up against his hip. "It's nothing you need to worry about, baby girl."

It surprised me how calmly he spoke the lie. My anxiety was surely written all over my face.

I turned away from them, trying to mask my fear as busyness. "Help your brother grab some coats and blankets," I said. My gaze fell to the floor beneath Mama's and Papa's bed. "And some water…"

I bent down and lifted up the quilt. After feeling around a

moment, I located the loose floorboard and, beneath it, the small jewelry box. My heart quickened as I set the box on my lap. Our family's single relic lay inside on dark velvet. Kraken.

At first glance, it was little more than an almond-sized piece of bone, oval cut, which was one of the more popular styles. It had been polished a clouded blue-green color. Only exceedingly rare types were diamond clear. Papa had it set in a silver necklace, another common choice for relic wearing. My breath trembled as I lifted it into my palm. I'd dreamed of the day I would be allowed to use it for the first time. This remnant of the ancient world, live with magic.

"What are you taking that for?" Jeb asked, looking over my shoulder. "It's too small. That thing doesn't have enough magic to ward off a vampire scorpion, let alone whoever's coming."

"You got any better ideas?"

It was true that the relic wouldn't help much if those people with the torches meant to cause trouble. Kraken bone fossils possessed only water magic, and a pebble-sized piece like we had could barely contract or expand water as needed. Papa had spent our savings on it to help keep our animals and ourselves alive, should we ever have another drought like the one that had nearly killed us three years before.

I knew Jeb, like me, was wishing right now that Papa had bought a dragon claw or phoenix piece, or any of the other fire relics I'd read about. Not that we could ever even dream of affording such rare, potent ones, but still, I wished it. So many nights, I'd lie in my bed, turning the worn pages of Papa's relic almanac by candlelight. The more I learned about all the fierce and wonderful relics out there, the more keenly I felt that the day might come when we'd need something better.

And now, we were face-to-face with that day.

I clutched the kraken piece to my chest. "It's all we have."

Ella pulled the fabric of my worn calico skirt. "Someone's gotta tell me what's happening."

"Everything's going to be fine. Looks like there was some trouble in the town, that's all. We need to head to our hiding spot and wait for Mama and Papa."

"The hiding place?" Her expression went from shock to resolute fear. "No. I'm not goin'. There's rock devils up there!"

Every settler knew to stay away from the red-rock cliffs that cast their huge shadow over our little town. The rock devils, horse-sized lizards with endless teeth and claws like hunting knives, lived in the shadowed nooks and caves. Though not magical like their ancient relative, the dragon, rock devils were the most dangerous creature to haunt our desert lands. And with rattlers, vampire scorpions, and ghost coyotes behind every sagebrush, that was really saying something. But that was exactly why Papa said we should hide in the cliffs in case of trouble. Because no one would dare come after us.

"We don't have a choice," I told Ella. "We gotta go."

She ran into Jeb's arms. He held her and looked at me, his jaw clenched. I gave him my firmest look, and he sighed. "Fine. But I'm bringing my gun."

The three of us rushed into the warm night. The minute we were out, though, Ella slammed her little heels into the ground.

"The kittens!" She gasped. "We forgot Sassy and the kittens!"

Jeb gripped Ella's hand to keep her from running back. "They'll be fine. They'll get out in time."

But we all knew the kittens couldn't make it down the loft ladder on their own.

"I won't leave them!" Ella cried, tears springing to her eyes.

I rubbed my forehead. There was barely time to save ourselves, let alone the animals. But how could we leave them to die?

"You two go on ahead," I said.

"Maggie…"

"Go! I'll catch up."

Jeb hesitated, but then nodded once. Holding Ella's hand, he ran for the cliffs as I dove back into our house. Sassy hissed at the edge of the loft, surely sensing the danger.

"It's all right," I said, climbing up the ladder. "We'll get you out."

The kittens mewed loudly as I scooped them up into my apron. But when we got outside, I realized all I could do was release them and hope for the best.

"Run, Sassy girl," I said as they scampered into the darkness. "Get on out of here with those babies."

I had to get *myself* out of there. The burning line of torches on the horizon looked closer than ever, and it filled me with a wild, shaking panic. I turned to run, but then my gaze fell on Dusty, our horse, peacefully padding his hooves in the sand of the corral. He was a good horse, hard working and gentle with children. I couldn't leave him, either.

It wasn't until I reached the gate that I remembered the lock. Put there to keep horse thieves away. Papa always carried the key with him.

"No…"

I gripped the fence, but the realization struck that it stood too high for Dusty to jump, even if I did climb it. I shook the wooden planks, then threw myself against them. They hardly budged. I slammed into the fence once more, to no avail. I could hear Jeb calling my name in the distance; the raw fear in his voice only sharpened my own. I looked to the shadowy cliffs, to the approaching fire, and then back to Dusty. Choking down a lump in my throat, I patted his glossy neck and prayed he'd somehow make it out all right.

I ran hard all the way to the cliffs, sagebrush and scrub scraping against my legs. Jeb and Ella were waiting outside the mouth of the little cave. When they spotted me, they rushed up, and we hugged. "It's okay," I said. "We made it. We're gonna be okay."

I flopped to the ground of our hiding spot. We called it a cave, but it was little more than a crawl space. If anyone *did* come looking for us, we'd be done for.

Ella climbed into Jeb's lap, trembling. With his free hand, he gripped his gun, his eyes fixed in the direction of our house. "I should try to get help," he said, shaking his head.

"No," I said sharply. "We're staying right here until Mama and Papa find us."

But *would* they find us? Were they all right? Try as I might, I couldn't shake the thought of a raid we'd heard of not two weeks before. A tiny town called Buena—just a general store, bank, and livery—burned to the ground. No one survived. People blamed the Apaches—everyone knew they were ready to go to war over the relic mining in the hills and mountains. Likely that had been the first attack of many. I still hadn't made up my mind whether to believe the stories or not, but suddenly they didn't seem so far-fetched.

I stared at Ella and prayed inwardly for my parents. In this light, Ella and Jeb looked so much like Papa; they shared the same golden hair and big brown eyes. Even the same freckles on their noses and cheeks. Everyone said I was the spitting image of Mama, with my black hair, amber eyes, and a touch of copper to my skin. Josiah, our brother two years younger than Jeb, had looked a lot like Mama, too, when he was alive. The Good Lord took him when he was ten. Pneumonia.

In the distance, the sharp, panicked whinny of a horse cut through the air, and my spine straightened. Jeb's as well. We both recognized the sound.

Dusty.

Listening with my breath clenched in my throat, I could make out the low, rumbling sounds of men's voices. Then the repeated shatter of glass. Ella shot up.

"Our house!" Her voice sounded small and pained. I squeezed her hand.

Through the distance, Dusty's whinny came again. Louder. More panicked. Then the blast of gunshots.

And the whinnying stopped.

Jeb and I were on our feet. I couldn't breathe for the tension in my chest. "Why are they doing this?"

His eyes were distant with horror. "Mama..."

I grabbed his hand. I wanted to tell him that Mama and Papa were probably laying low somewhere or gathering a group of men to surround those attackers and put them to justice. But the words felt like sand in my mouth. All I could do was hold onto his hand as hard as possible.

An acrid wave of smoke blew against us, stinging my throat. In the distance, the glow of our burning home lit the sky. As I looked harder, I realized that the flames were moving, traveling over the rabbitbrush and sage that dotted the landscape. Heading this way.

They took the dry shrubs at terrifying speed, faster than any normal fire should. Men's voices rumbled on the air, so close that the hairs on my arms stood on end.

"They're coming," I whispered.

Jeb's brow lowered. "We gotta make a run for it."

The thought froze my very bones, but he was right. We couldn't stay in the cave. Either the fire or those men would reach this place in a matter of seconds. With a shaky nod to Jeb, I knelt down by Ella.

"We're gonna leave the hiding place now, okay, honey?"

Ella ran into Jeb's arms, breaking down into tears. "I want Mama," she sobbed.

He picked her up, stroking her hair. "Don't cry, baby girl. We'll be okay. I promise we'll be okay."

"Jeb's right," I said. "We'll be fine. But listen, we have to be real quiet. We all have to run as quiet as a little pack of deer."

She kept her face buried in Jeb's shoulder, so I kissed her head.

"Right," I said. "Let's go."

We tore out into the flickering darkness. The heat of the blaze immediately pressed against us as smoke filled our lungs, and we all started coughing. My eyes blurred from the fumes, but I kept running. I could hear Ella's sobs behind me, muffled as she pressed her head into Jeb's neck. I ran and ran, but part of me knew I had no idea where we were going. We could be headed right toward the mob.

Ahead, a huge rock formation blocked our path, and to the other side, a wall of fire. Coughing into my arm, I spun around, searching for a way out. There was only one. A tiny ravine to the left might provide just enough space for a person to squeeze through. With the billowing smoke, I couldn't see too far down that path, but there didn't seem to be any other choice.

"Down there," I called to Jeb over the roar of flames and

crackle of burning trees.

He examined the ravine, hesitating for a moment, but then nodded. Together, we climbed down into the little canyon of red-rock.

And I immediately saw what a terrible mistake it was.

Fire. Huge yellow tongues of it crawled toward us from the other end. A twisted, dead bristlecone pine blazed right in our path; the blast of heat made me stagger back. But when I turned to climb out of the ravine, I could see that the other flames had closed in, sealing off the entrance. We were surrounded. Trapped like animals.

Jeb and I stared at each other, ashen.

And then I remembered the relic. A flicker of hope lit within me, and I pulled the silver chain off.

"The water," I called to Jeb.

I knew we only had whatever drops were left in the canteen Jeb had grabbed on the way out of the house—but it still might do the trick.

With trembling hands, I twisted open the lid and held the kraken piece over the water. As much as I loved reading about relics, I'd only used one once before—my grandfather's kraken relic. He had taught me how close contact with the body was required to activate the magic, and that the more you concentrated, the more powerful the reaction was, but it was a skill most people had to practice to get good at.

I exhaled slowly. My fingers felt stiff and clammy with sweat. My head was pounding. I'd read that water magic supposedly had a calming effect on the user. Maybe I was just too worked up to feel it? I closed my eyes and forced a deep breath. *Come on. Expand. Please.*

I opened one eye to check. The water hadn't budged.

"Nothing's happening," Ella said, her voice high with panic.

"I told you it wasn't strong enough," Jeb said.

"Hush," I snapped. "I'm trying."

I swallowed a dry gulp and took a breath to calm down. *"Please,"* I whispered fiercely.

But the water in the canteen stayed at the exact level as before. I scraped a hand through my hair with a growl. "Why isn't this working?"

A horrible thought started to pound through me. *What if it's not working because it isn't real?* Forgeries were a serious problem in these parts, where the average family could hardly afford a single relic chip. Desperate miners and farmers were often swindled by a slick peddler with an irresistible price.

I stared at the beautiful relic in my hand. Beautiful, and useless as a piece of glass. I felt as though I'd been stabbed in the heart.

"Maggie…" Jeb's brown eyes were deep and sorrowful, even as they mirrored the approaching wall of flames.

Reading the emotion on his face, Ella hooked her little arms around his neck, and I knew she understood. I threw my arms around both of them and held on tight, stricken by my inability to save them. Stricken that I would never see another sunset on the desert. Never have my first kiss. Never be able to hug Mama and Papa good-bye.

A voice penetrated the crackling roar of fire. The sound of it shattered me.

They'd found us.

When I looked up above the ravine, I saw a dark face illuminated in the flames. It was a young man with black hair and black eyes. He was Apache. A warrior about my age—maybe a few years older.

A swell of terror rose up in me. But then, looking harder into those midnight-black eyes, a realization cracked through the fear, and memories flooded in.

I knew this boy.

Ages ago, when I was an awkward and gangly girl of nine, I'd gone to a year of schooling at the St. Ignacio Mission outside Burning Mesa. The friars taught any who came to read and write. But I didn't quite fit in there. Mama said it was because I asked too many silly questions. There was one boy who took kindly to me, though. Another misfit. An Apache boy with the darkest eyes I'd ever seen. He'd come to St. Ignacio to learn English. We both stuck out like weeds together.

We were friends until the day I made the mistake of telling Mama all about him. She refused to explain why, but after that, I never stepped foot in St. Ignacio again.

And now, there he stood before me. He looked the same in many ways but grown up in others. He was a warrior now. I could tell from the red band of cloth he wore tied over his forehead.

"Maggie Davis," he called, and he held out his hand.

I didn't move, stunned. He remembered my name?

"You stay away!" Jeb had his rifle aimed.

I pushed the barrel of the gun down. "Stop!" I cried. "I know him. He won't hurt us."

Jeb stared at me like I'd gone mad. "You know him?"

"You have to trust me, Jeb. There's no time to argue."

Fire choked the little ravine with startling speed. The Apache looked at the growing flames and held out his hand with more urgency. "You must come. I will help you."

I stood, and Jeb grabbed my arm. "No!"

"It'll be all right," I said, pressing my hand over his. "I promise."

I looked back at the Apache. I could see in his eyes that he wouldn't hurt us. I nodded once. He lay on his stomach on the rock face and reached his arms down.

"First the child," he said. "Hurry."

The flames pressed in. The entire ravine would be burning within a matter of minutes.

As I lifted Ella up into the warrior's hands, a smoldering branch of the nearby bristlecone pine snapped off and fell to the ground. Sparks scattered, spreading over the dry desert grasses spotting the ground. The grasses caught flame instantly. Fire joined with fire, spreading like floodwater. The heat rushed over us like a wave, stinging our eyes and singeing our throats. I turned to Jeb.

And I knew he could see it, too. There would only be time to lift one more person out before the fire engulfed the ravine completely. If even that.

As the angry yellow flames rushed toward us, roaring and crackling over the dry ground, we pressed our backs to the cliff wall.

"God Almighty," Jeb whispered.

I squeezed his hand, speechless with horror.

The Apache reached down again, and his eyes flashed with dismay.

"Hurry!" he cried.

"Can you lift us both at once?" I asked desperately. But then I felt Jeb's hand on my shoulder. He was looking up at the warrior, exchanging silent words. Then he looked back to me.

"Take care of Ella," he said softly.

"Don't you dare, Jeb."

The heat was blinding, oppressive. I could barely breathe or see in the onslaught of thick gray smoke, but I caught Jeb giving the Apache a nod.

"No!" I shouted, coughing, shaking my head violently.

Jeb grabbed my hand. He pressed a firm kiss to it, then yanked my fist up to the Apache.

"Jeb! No!"

The warrior's strong grip wrapped around my wrist, and he pulled me up with startling speed. I tried to kick, but he didn't release me. I stretched my free hand to Jeb, screaming. "No! No!"

Above me, Ella reached over the edge of the rock, shouting Jeb's name.

The flames below clawed at my shoes and bare ankles. They caught onto my skirt and seared my skin. Through the ruthless smoke below, I could just make out a final, mournful flash of Jeb's brown eyes. And then the Apache gave a big heave, pulling me over the ledge.

I crumbled to the high ground with an anguished cry. The Apache rushed to stamp out my burning skirt, but I wished he wouldn't. In that moment, I felt like dying right there on the hot sand.

But then I noticed Ella, still reaching for the flames, screaming for Jeb with raw anguish. I fell to her side. She resisted my embrace with all of her might, crying and sobbing for Jeb. I held her tight until she collapsed, her little body shaking with sobs, and I knew that even if I truly did want to die, I couldn't. And I couldn't break down, either, not here, not yet. For Ella, I had to be strong.

"It is not safe yet," the Apache said, crouching beside me, his voice gentle but tense. "We cannot stay here."

I felt the heat of the fire behind us. Tongues of flame curled up from the edge of the ravine. Thinking of Jeb down there hurt me more than any burn could have. A scream boiled in my throat, desperate to escape. It took all of my strength to keep myself together.

The Apache took my hand. "We must run."

He pulled us through a narrow path of red-rock. Smoke from the advancing inferno followed, relentless and cruel. The heat hung heavy on the air. When the rock widened, I spotted a black horse tied to a low pine.

Ella and I were too dazed with grief and fear to protest as the Apache lifted us onto the beast's back. He jumped on behind me, gave the animal one gentle kick, and we tore off across the wide desert.

The horse's hooves pounded fiercely against the moon-bleached sand, and the wind beat in our ears. We didn't speak. Finally, after what felt like hours, a settlement surfaced on the dark horizon. A wide adobe wall spread out before us as we drew closer. Behind it, a church dozed beneath the branches of shade trees and a large willow. I recognized the exposed bell tower and the run-down, crumbling wall. It was St. Ignacio.

We rode up the gates, and the warrior called for the horse to slow. The trauma had finally overwhelmed Ella, and she'd collapsed into sleep against me in spite of the long, pounding journey. Seeing this, the warrior hopped down from the horse. He gently lifted Ella, then reached for me with his free arm.

In the pale moonlight he looked tall and strong as an ox. His long black hair hung over his shoulders and blew gently in the wind like dark feathers. He wore thick pants, a vest over his bare chest. My face warmed to my ears as he lifted me effortlessly from the horse.

Stepping onto solid ground, my saddle-sore legs wobbled, but

I kept my composure. I quickly smoothed down my wind-blasted hair and wrinkled clothes. I probably looked as bedraggled as I felt.

Seeing a patch of singed fabric on my dress, the memories came flooding back in a river of fire. Mama. Papa. And Jeb. Oh, Jeb.

I scanned the dark, night-bathed surroundings of the mission. The quiet whistle of wind over the desert filled me with a consuming emptiness I couldn't escape.

Just then, I felt a hand on my arm. The warrior held Ella out to me, and I took her into my arms. The sight of her face, so sweet and utterly peaceful in sleep, only twisted the knife of sorrow deeper in my throat.

"You can stay here," the Apache said. "The fathers will protect you for a time."

"Thank you," I said softly. "For everything." Suddenly, words felt like little rocks in my mouth, but I forced myself on. "I… remember your face but not your name."

"Yahnuiyo," he said. "Yahn."

I didn't dare meet his gaze. "It's so strange to see you again. And under these circumstances…"

He turned his face in the direction of Haydenville. "My people did not burn your home," he said, somehow answering the very question I hadn't dared to ask. "Or your village."

"Then who did?" I asked quietly.

Yahn's gaze was firm on me. "May we never have to find out."

I flexed my grip over Ella. Something in his tone made me want her as close as possible.

"Leave if you can," he said. "Go far from these desert lands. Take your sister."

His words sent a shiver over me. Perhaps sensing this, he softened. "I am sorry," he said. "For the loss of your brother. I regret deeply that I could not save him." The sincerity in his voice stung my heart like a hot needle.

He sighed and took up his horse's reins. "Farewell."

"You're leaving us?"

"The fathers will take care of you. They are good men."

He mounted his horse. I took a halting step forward. "Will I ever see you again?" The words had tumbled out before I could stop them. I immediately snapped my gaze away, but then looked back.

"Perhaps, Maggie Davis. Perhaps."

The Catholic friars opened their gates warily, eyeing us in the faint candlelight. When I explained what had happened, they exchanged grim frowns. People had been uneasy enough after hearing about Buena. To find out that it had happened again sent a chill through the air. Some didn't want us to be allowed entrance, afraid the Apaches would follow to finish the job.

But the Father Superior stepped up from the shadows and spoke one phrase. "Suffer the little children to come unto me."

It was all he needed to say. The friars opened the gates.

When they had settled Ella and me into their spare quarters in the nuns' wing, I pulled Ella into my arms on the lumpy, straw-filled mattress. The room was barren, cold, and deathly quiet. So quiet, we had no choice but to face everything that had happened, everything we'd lost.

I was now all Ella had in the world. How could I possibly

take care of her? How could I be her mama and papa when I was practically a kid myself? Lying there with my sister, I'd never felt so small or helpless. I didn't want her to see my tears, but then I noticed that she was crying softly. She looked up into my eyes, trembling.

"Jeb," she said, her voice hoarse and weak with sorrow.

The sound of his name on her lips broke me. I took her into my arms, unable to stop the flood of grief. Clinging to each other on the little bed, Ella and I wept well into the night.

CHAPTER TWO

The first two weeks passed in a haze of sorrow. By the third week, however, I had to face the reality that Ella and I had relied on the generosity of St. Ignacio for long enough. The mission had barely enough to live on as it was. And while the Father Superior's kindness seemed to know no bounds, I couldn't ignore the resentful glances from the other friars. So, one hot spring morning, dressed in a too-big brown dress I'd been given from the mission's donation box, I made my way on foot into town.

The main hub of Burning Mesa spread around a crisscross of several long streets, with all the usual trimmings of these little bastions of civilization in the desert. Not the height of advancement one might expect in 1867, but they made do. I spotted hotels, a postal service, a smithy, general stores, laundry, ladies' shops. And of course, the local saloon. As I passed the crowded hall, laughter and the tinny strains of music wafted out into the dusty streets, almost welcoming. A flashy painted sign proclaimed the structure to be The Desert Rose and promised vittles, spirits, and entertainment. Judging from the woman standing in one of the open windows on the second floor, dressed in only a silk night-robe, I figured it offered a few other things as well.

I hurried down the street, not wanting to be seen lingering in front of a house of ill repute. I hadn't gone but a few paces when I saw it. Gleaming white and bathed in sunshine: a relic refinery. A bona fide relic refinery. My knees locked, and like a flash of light, I could see myself, so many nights, tucked in my chair by the flickering fire, my hands curled around Papa's worn relic almanac. I could see myself bent in the garden, my knees smudged with red dirt, pretending the carrots and radishes were relics, dusting them off and informing the lucky prospector of the finds he'd made. I recalled every time I'd stood in the windy shadow of our little farm and tried to imagine a fairy darting through the sage in a streak of shimmering light. Or a sphinx perched in the shadows of our sandy cliffs.

It made me truly sad to think they'd never come back. The mermaid, the behemoth, the griffin. Even the frightening ones, like the werewolf and the troll and the banshee. From the time I was barely old enough to flip through the pages of Papa's almanac, I'd mourned that I'd never have a chance to see one of those creatures alive.

Men of science said it was a star, blazing into our world and crashing to the earth centuries ago, that wiped them out. Pastor Abrams spoke of ancient days when humans and magical creatures lived together. Mankind envied the creatures' powers and relentlessly tried to steal the magic for themselves. They killed countless numbers in their quest, until God decided the whole earth had to be destroyed for the greed and envy it contained. But the noble magical creatures offered to sacrifice themselves instead. And so the Great Flood wiped away any remaining trace of magic, leaving only the bones buried under layers of sand and stone. Of course, no one *really* knew why the great creatures had left the earth. Only that they were gone for good.

That was why I loved the idea of relics so much. They were all we had left of a world that was young and vibrant and brimming with magic. And we were lucky to have them. These bones, still potent with the powers of their former owners, were a gift for us poor souls stuck in a mundane, aging land.

Mama, on the other hand, hated relics. I'd never understood why. She threw an awful fit when Papa bought the kraken amulet, and she'd scolded me whenever she caught me reading the almanac. She said a respectable lady cared nothing for relics. But I still dreamed of a job in the trade. Many women did. Everyone knew that a female's careful eye for detail and differentiation made her a welcome asset in refineries. Some of the best relic experts were women. And in the deepest shadows of my heart, I knew it was my calling.

There, on the dusty street of Burning Mesa, that calling took hold of me and moved my feet toward the refinery. It felt like a strange dream. My heartbeat pulsed in my ears, and my hands shook as I pulled back the smooth white doors. A little bell clinked in announcement of my arrival. Holding my breath, I stepped in.

My senses grasped for everything at once. The beam of sunshine that cut down from a high, round window, shimmering faintly with particles of dust. The metallic smell of soil and old books. The glints of multicolored light scattered around the room, reflecting off the relic elixir bottles of every size and shape and color that lined the shelves to the side of the main counter.

The room was large, but it felt smaller with the clutter of trinkets and wares for sale. Glass cases on the walls displayed blank rings, empty amulets, and weapons, all ready for relic enhancements. Paintings hung everywhere, showcasing some of the finest relic specimens that had been found in the surrounding areas. Water, fire, sky, earth—it seemed that every type of magic had passed through this refinery. There weren't any pictures of shadow relics, of course, seeing as how those were illegal, but it wouldn't have surprised me if a few had been exchanged, examined, or sold here under the cover of night.

I let out a trembling breath. I was really here. A genuine relic refinery. I moved farther into the room, wanting to examine every inch of it. With a little gasp of delight, I spotted the workstations behind the wide front counter. The gleam of the cogs and lenses and gears of the identification devices and polishing machines made my heart leap. I rushed up to the counter to get a closer look.

But something made me stop in my tracks. A pulse of energy, like the throb of some external heart, passed through my body. I blinked hard, startled by the strange sensation. And then I heard a sound. A rushing noise, like wind passing through the aspen trees in a forest. Whispers. Voices, not quite human. As if drawn by a magnet, my gaze rose to the end of the hallway behind the counter.

I couldn't see more than a dark line of iron, but I knew what stood there in the shadows. The vault. The secure safe where they stored every relic that passed through the refinery. They were there now. Rows of raw bone and polished pieces. Shards of antiquity, still pulsing with magic.

They were calling for me.

"Someone will be with you in a few minutes, miss."

The voice sliced into my awareness, and my thrumming thoughts popped like a soap bubble. All at once, I was snapped back to the sights and smells of the refinery. One of the experts waved at me from behind the counter and then moved into the back offices.

I nodded vaguely, blinking away the unsettling moment. I cast a glance around to see if anyone else in the room had heard what I heard. The only other person in there at the moment was a short, heavyset man standing in front of a room labeled *Consultation*. The man had ruddy cheeks and a wide nose, and he peered at me with small, calculating eyes. His arms were folded across his chest like a wary watchman, though I could tell he wasn't one of the refinery's guards. His expensive-looking silk vest and fine shoes gave that away.

Something about his vigilant manner piqued my curiosity. Perhaps he *did* know something. I strolled over to a public relic almanac displayed on the edge of the countertop. Pretending to be absorbed in the pages, I shot a swift glance into the consultation room.

There was a table, a few chairs, and a black case with its lid latched closed. I could see an aged hand resting on it. An expert, probably. His voice was a soft, cautious murmur. Another man sat across from him, saying nothing. All I could see was his hand, covered in a pristine white glove and folded casually around a decadent walking stick. I leaned in ever so slightly to catch a glimpse of the rest of him.

He was by far the most expensive-looking man I'd ever seen. And younger than I would have expected a wealthy relic buyer to be. He couldn't have been much older than his mid-twenties. He was tall and lean, with rich black hair that curled slightly around pale olive skin. Creole, I recognized that immediately. Probably a Haciendo.

The Spanish had settled in these regions more than two hundred years ago. I imagine they started out struggling to make a living in the barren land, but when they discovered relics in the mountains and hills, they'd become rich as kings. We didn't have much to do with the Hacienda folk in Haydenville, but I'd heard enough to know they owned pretty near every town from Texas to California.

I couldn't take my eyes off the Haciendo. He was so regal, like the paintings I'd seen of kings from distant lands. He motioned to the case, and with excruciating care, the expert clicked the silver latches open. One, then the other. His fingers hesitated for a moment at the crease of the lid. I held my breath. The expert lifted it slowly.

And then the door to the consultation room swept shut with a decisive *bang*.

Startled, I met the cold gaze of the heavyset man. He narrowed his eyes, and heat rushed to my face. I turned back to the almanac, flustered but trying not to show it. I was only looking. There wasn't any need for him to be so rude. Besides, I didn't quite like the idea of being alone in the room with him.

Luckily, at that moment, a tall, lanky woman in a smudged apron stepped up from behind the counter. I tensed, fearing she'd be sharp with me as well, but she had a warm smile.

"A rare beauty, isn't she?" the woman asked and shook her head wistfully. "We haven't seen one of those around here in many a year."

I realized she was talking about the page of the almanac I had been staring at blindly. Siren bone. There were several paragraphs describing the powers this relic retained, but I already knew it by heart. Siren was one of the rarest kinds of water relics because it also gave the wielder the ability to influence thoughts. To draw people to you like the tides.

The illustration in this almanac was lovely, dark blue with shimmers of crystal white. The artist had done a fine job capturing what must be a brilliant sparkle when fully polished. It was a much finer painting than the one in Papa's.

I brushed my fingertips over the picture and realized with a pang of sadness that I would never see my old relic almanac again. In that moment, I'd have given anything to trade this fine, detailed book for those worn pages.

The feelings were too painful to dwell on. And they reminded me of why I had come into Burning Mesa in the first place. It wasn't to daydream in the refinery.

"It is beautiful," I said in soft agreement, closing the book.

The expert smiled. "So what can I do for you? We charge a fair price for identification. And we've got competitive shipping to Denver or Wichita, if you're in the market for selling. Or are you perhaps looking to make a purchase?"

I swallowed a bitter laugh. One only had to glance at my ratty dress and rough, working-class hands to know how unlikely it was that I could even afford a relic chip. "No, I'm not here to buy anything."

The expert nodded, and I squirmed at her expectant pause. Suddenly, I felt foolish for coming to the refinery. I knew well the years of training that experts had to go through. It was folly to even approach the hope of working there.

My feet itched to turn away, but something in me refused to give up without at least asking. "I'm actually looking for work," I said, biting down the shame.

The expert's brow furrowed. "I—I'm real sorry, miss, but we aren't fixin' to hire— "

"I'm not asking much. I'd sweep floors and wipe your windows. I'd do anything, really."

"I'm sorry, but there's nothing." The expert sighed. "We've had to let all our apprentices go as it is."

"I see."

"It's tough here in Burning Mesa. Lots of folk are pulling up roots and heading east. There's just not enough work to go around."

I nodded through the pain. "Thanks, anyway."

"Grace?" A small man peeked his head out from one of the back rooms. "Can you spare a minute?"

"Coming," the expert called back. She turned and shot a final sympathetic glance my way. "Sorry again, miss."

After she'd left, I lingered for a moment at the counter, wanting to soak in as much of the magic as I could. Who knew when I would be this close to so many high-quality relics again? I peered down the hallway toward the safe, hoping to feel the pulsing energy or hear the windy, whispering voices. But there was nothing. Clearly it had been my imagination running away with me. I turned to the exit, a persistent lump squeezing at my throat.

A shadow fell over me, and I looked up. The heavyset man with the fancy vest and cruel eyes now stood between the door and me. He folded his arms across his chest. "I think you and I need to have a little talk."

CHAPTER THREE

My body stiffened. Did he mean to cause trouble? The man may have been finely dressed, but something about him seemed coarse and rough. I took a step back.

"I didn't mean any harm," I said. "I was only looking."

He smirked a little. "Oh, that? Never you mind that, miss. I'd like to speak with you on a different matter, if that's all right."

I frowned, unsure what he could possibly want to discuss.

"Name's Percy Connelly," the man said with a strange grin. "You see, I was just waitin' for my employer here to finish up, and I couldn't help but overhear your inquiry."

Was he going to mock me for seeking work in a refinery when I was so clearly unqualified? Warn me to leave town and not try to take any jobs? Something about this man made me uneasy.

"See, it just so happens that my employer has a job opening," he said, "and I think you could be the perfect gal for it."

I straightened.

"A fine job," Mr. Connelly went on. "Well payin'. Room and board included, with enough extra money for your needs, plus stylish clothes and other such things you women like. Why don't you and I take a walk, and I'll tell you all about it?"

I looked again at Mr. Connelly's rich apparel and for the first time noticed the jeweled rose pinned to his lapel. A desert rose…

"Where do you work?" I asked sharply.

"I'll be happy to explain as we walk."

I started to back up. "If you're offering what I think you're offering…"

Mr. Connelly chuckled, following me, closing in. "Come now, miss. You strike me as a real mature gal. Almost a woman. You understand the way things work. It's good for the men to have some pleasant company. These hot desert nights can be mighty lonely for a hard-working miner, and to have a pretty girl like you there to—"

"How *dare* you speak to me about such things!" I said. As hot blood rushed to my face, I was reminded just how alone I was in the world. That a man like this could approach me with an offer so degrading. Did I appear as desperate and forsaken as I felt inside? How many more lowlifes would close in to try and scavenge what little dignity I had left?

"Now now," Mr. Connelly said, his expression hardening. "Don't get all high and mighty. I'm offering you work. Didn't you say you needed it?"

My back was to the counter. He was so close, I could smell his bad cologne. Humiliation and despair blended with cold rage inside me.

"Get away!" I cried. "Now!"

Mr. Connelly's upper lip curled. "Let me tell you something, missy. This is the only job you're going to get in this dying town. And believe me when I say that there are plenty of girls who would welcome the opportunity. But go ahead, turn me down. You'll end up like them, sellin' your body in the shadows of the train depot, makin' one-tenth of what you'd earn at The Desert Ro—"

I slapped him. Hard.

He blinked, and his shock turned to fury. "Why, you little brat!" He grabbed my wrist, his grip frighteningly strong.

"Take your hands off me," I demanded, pulling back.

"I'll teach you to—"

"Stop!"

With a surge of energy, I tore my arm free. The tension of his grip broke, sending me stumbling backward.

Right into the aging relic expert and the elegant Haciendo exiting the consultation room.

My body collided with the black relic case in the Haciendo's arms. As I crashed to the ground, the case hurtled into the glass display on the wall behind us. A shattering sound filled the air.

Inside the broken display, the relic case's contents lay bare among the glittering shards of glass—the most incredible piece I had ever even dreamed of seeing. A shimmering unicorn relic. A full horn, all bright and polished and pure white. It glittered in the softly lit room like a beacon. Or a spear of sunlight.

For a moment, I could only stare at the relic in breathless awe. But then the Haciendo's gasp broke my trance. He dropped to his knees for his unicorn relic, frantic. My gaze shifted focus to the razor-sharp blades of glass on the broken display case, like jagged teeth. Mr. Connelly, the relic expert, and I all cried out in alarm.

But our warnings had come too late. The Haciendo grabbed

for his relic with blind desperation, scraping his hands on the serrated glass as he pulled it out of the shattered display case. Red marred the pure white of the unicorn horn. The Haciendo's fingers clawed with sudden pain, his gloves ribboned in blood. With a strained cry, he released his grip on the relic.

Gasping, I lunged to catch the piece before it crashed to the ground. I only wanted to prevent something so precious from being damaged, but the Haciendo's eyes flashed to me, bright with rage. In a daze, I looked down at my hands, tightly wrapped around his unicorn relic. I was about to release it when the air in the room shifted. Heaviness pulled at my very core, as if the whole earth were spreading within my chest.

And then the whisper returned to my ears, soft like a sigh. The distant whinny of a unicorn rushing through my mind on an ancient wind. Power surged down my arms, into my fingers. The iridescent shaft of the horn began to glow, shimmering white and gold and lavender.

I snapped my hand back, stunned. But the anger in the Haciendo's face had melted away. For a moment, no one moved. No one spoke. Then, slowly, he pulled his blood-stained gloves off and revealed perfectly unscathed hands.

His eyes flicked to me with an unreadable expression. Then he looked up at the expert.

The ancient Chinese man could pass for a laborer in his simple black pants and tunic. He had a thin white beard as long as I'd ever seen, and an equally long braid trailing down from the back of his head. His dark, almond-shaped eyes peered at me without expression.

I turned to the Haciendo, grasping for words. "I didn't mean to use it."

I stared back at the shimmering horn, still in a daze. I'd read a great deal about the gravitational forces that accompanied earth magic, but what about the whispers? The echo of the unicorn's voice in my head? It had to be my mind playing tricks on me. Or perhaps this was what powerful magic felt like. After all, I had healed the Haciendo without even trying. The experience was both frightening and thrilling at the same time.

I looked back up at him, heat coloring my cheeks. "Are you all right, sir?"

His face smoothed into a calm, almost charming smile. "It would appear so. Thanks to you."

"Thanks to the relic," I said. "I've never seen one so powerful."

The Haciendo and the expert exchanged a swift but meaningful glance. "Indeed."

"I'm sorry about the glass. I didn't—"

"No need for apologies, señorita." His voice was smooth and rich with a Spanish accent. "This was clearly an accident." He turned to the aging expert. "I shall send one of my men to pay for a new case at once, Moon John."

Then, carefully, the Haciendo lifted the unicorn relic from the glass, wiped the blood away, and laid it into its case. I noticed his hand tremble ever so slightly as he clicked the latches down.

The expert, Moon John, nodded. "I will clean up this mess."

He headed to the back rooms, but just before moving out of sight, he shot a single, piercing glance back at me. A look that made my breath catch.

The Haciendo held out his hand to help me up with the casual smile of a young man perfectly at ease with the opposite sex. "May I?"

"Thank you."

I stood on wobbly legs, my head still spinning at the rapid blur of the last few seconds.

When we had stepped away from the shattered glass, the Haciendo turned to Mr. Connelly. "Now," he said firmly, "what did you do to this girl to make her recoil so violently from you?"

It surprised me to hear the Haciendo address a much older man in such an authoritative tone, but Mr. Connelly only glowered.

"Nothing," he said. "She's a clumsy little fool, that's all."

"That's not true!" I said, outraged. "Your man here was speaking to me in a despicable way."

Mr. Connelly grimaced, and that seemed to be all the Haciendo needed to know what I meant. His jaw tightened. "You must forgive him, miss," he said. "Percy has all the tact of a mule."

Mr. Connelly snorted. I glared at him and brushed off my skirt.

"Yes, well, he hopelessly misunderstood what kind of a lady I am, sir."

"I have no doubt," the Haciendo said. "And you have my deepest apologies for that. Miss…"

"Davis," I said out of trained politeness.

"Miss Davis. Again, forgive my servant's poor treatment of you. Percy's a good man, though he has a nasty temper."

His genteel ways threw me off a bit, but I tried not to be too easily won over. He may have been rich and young and even handsome, with his raven hair and amber eyes, but I should not be associating with strange men without a proper introduction.

"Well, thank you for your apology, but since my answer is still a very emphatic no, I believe this conversation is over."

"Suit yourself." Mr. Connelly snorted. "I guess beggin' in the streets sounds better?"

"I'll find other work."

The Haciendo sighed a little.

I turned to him, the heat of fear creeping into me. "Surely there's other work. I may be only a girl, but I'll wash clothes or dishes. Clean rooms in the hotel. There has to be *something*."

"We are experiencing hard times here in Burning Mesa, Miss Davis. Indeed, there are many good men who would gladly take the jobs you describe, but alas."

"It can't be…"

"Might I accompany you back outside?" The Haciendo offered his arm, and I was so distracted by the bad news about work that I accepted it. We stepped back out into the heat and sand and sunshine of the street.

The Haciendo swept a brisk look at Mr. Connelly. "Fetch the carriage."

Mr. Connelly turned me a quick glare before stomping off, leaving us in silence. The Haciendo cast his gaze out over the town and shook his head. "I am sorry. These are hard times for all of us."

I broke away, dizzy with the disappointment the day had become. "I should go."

"Go where?"

"I apologize again for what happened in the refinery. If you'll excuse me."

I turned to leave, but he gently gripped my arm. "Wait." His eyes searched my face. I could see thoughts flickering behind them, but then a casual smile passed over his lips.

"You know," he finally said, "I think perhaps I *do* have a job for you. If you will take it."

I opened my mouth to chastise him again, but he set a preemptive hand on mine. "A most respectable one, I assure you. Complete with room and board."

"What kind of job? You said there were none."

"I'm creating a new one," he said with a smooth smile. "As you may be aware, The Desert Rose is, in fact, an establishment for food and drink. That is its primary purpose. We work our bartender too hard, and I've long wondered if we didn't need a hostess of sorts. Someone to serve drinks when needed, bring out food, clean a little. It's honest work. And I promise you double what any other job might pay."

"Why would you offer this to me? Do you think I'll give in after a while and become one of your *other* employees? Well, I won't. *Never*. I can tell you that right now."

The Haciendo smiled. "I believe you."

"Then why?"

"You have spirit," he said. "A quality I greatly admire."

His smile remained, but I noticed the faintest twitch in his gaze. There was more, something he wasn't saying.

I started to refuse, but something held me back. The offer was tempting. Honest work at double the wage I could earn anywhere else? If I could even *get* a job anywhere else.

But looking again at the Haciendo, I hesitated. I barely knew him. How could I trust him? Besides, I didn't like his employee, Mr. Connelly. Taking the offer was out of the question.

"I'm sorry. I'm not the kind of girl you're looking for."

He analyzed me, a smile curling the side of his mouth, then pulled a large ring from his coat pocket and slid it onto his pointer finger. My breath caught, and a hint of that same, strange heaviness of earth magic tugged inside me. Dryad bone could be polished spring green like that, but it wasn't usually found in these parts. It must have been purchased from a costly foreign market.

The Haciendo dug a small seed out of the pocket of his red

silk vest and held his ringed hand over it. On the palm of his hand, it trembled, then burst into a green coil. The coil stretched until a rose blossomed there in his hand. A desert rose. He smelled it, then tucked the stem in the hair above my ear so smoothly that I didn't have time to stop him.

"If you change your mind, do let me know."

It was a trick he'd doubtless charmed many girls with; he probably kept the seeds and ring in his pocket for just such a thing. But even still, color rushed into my cheeks. Noticing this, the young Haciendo flashed an easy smile.

At that moment, Mr. Connelly arrived with the carriage. The Haciendo stepped inside. "By the way, I don't believe I ever told you my name. How rude of me. I am Álvar Castilla."

He tapped his fist once on the inner wall of the coach, and the carriage drove off in a cloud of dust and sand.

I spent the entire day scouring Burning Mesa for a job. But again and again, I was turned back out on the streets with the same answer: no work.

When I dragged myself back to St. Ignacio's that night, Ella was already lying in bed, her back turned to me. She'd hardly spoken to me in the last three weeks. I sat down on the creaking little mattress and stroked her shoulder.

"When are we leaving this place?" she asked, still not looking at me. "I wanna go home."

"We can't go home. You know that."

I heard a little sniffle and realized she was crying. My heart sank.

"We'll start a new home," I said, squeezing her arm. "You'll see. I'll get some work and find us a nice new place to live."

Even as I spoke the words, they felt like an empty promise.

Ella sniffed again, pulling away from my touch. "Jeb wouldn't have us stay in this lonely old place." She was silent for a moment before adding in barely a whisper, "Why couldn't you pull him up?"

Her words were like a knife in the gut. We'd been through it before. I'd explained how Yahnuiyo, the Apache warrior, couldn't have lifted both of us, how Jeb made him take me instead. But I knew those explanations meant little to Ella. She wanted Jeb, not me. And it was my fault he was gone.

I stepped away from the bed. My vision blurred with tears as I stumbled blindly down the hall, the stuffy mission air suddenly seeming to choke me. I found my way out into the courtyard and pressed my back to the cool adobe wall. Staring up at the stars, I tried to breathe.

Ella was right. I wasn't as good as Jeb, and I certainly could never replace Mama and Papa. Maybe if I were older or skilled or smarter, I could give Ella the home she needed. Heavy-hearted, I twisted the rose Álvar Castilla had given me between my fingers. A warm night wind carried the flower's sweet scent across my face. It was time to accept my situation for what it was and do whatever it took to survive.

I sighed deeply. Tomorrow I would take the job.

CHAPTER FOUR

Late at night, The Desert Rose took on a solemn mood. Most of the men had either drifted home—drunk and broke—or had slid upstairs to lay down their money for a bit of "feminine company." A few stragglers played cheerless rounds of poker, sipping their whiskey with furrowed brows. The room smelled of men and alcohol and cheap perfume, but at least the crowds were gone.

I wiped the empty tables with a white cloth, reveling in the peace that had come at last. The only sound was "The Red River Valley" drifting from the saloon piano, jingling on the air like warm memories. Eddie, the piano player, was a dark, quiet man who didn't fit in here. We shared that in common. He played the popular ditties and tunes as he was paid to do, but once in a while he'd start making the most beautiful, sad music I'd ever heard. Music so sad it made me think of Mama and Papa and Jeb until I wept.

Leaning on the edge of the piano, I asked him to play me one of those.

Eddie glanced around the room. "There're still customers, Miss Maggie. I'd better give them some cheery tunes, seeing as how they're probably tired and broke."

"Please," I said. "It'll help me clean up this mess."

It had been an especially raucous night. Adelaide Price had starred in the musical revue, and she always drew a big crowd. Then a large group of railroad workers showed up to make an already full house even fuller. They were passing through town to replace the centaur relic in the engine of the locomotive, a task for which they demanded plenty of fanfare and special privileges. When their foreman commandeered the saloon's last three bottles of dragon whiskey, however, folks decided they'd had about enough, and a brawl broke out. Now, broken bottles and cards were scattered everywhere.

Eddie scratched the back of his neck but then smiled. "Okay. One song. Just for you."

He understood me. I figured he must have seen his share of sorrows, too.

As I bent and scrubbed the floors, the melancholy music filled me. I thought about my parents and my poor, sweet brother until I ached all over. It had been more than a month since they died, but the pain hadn't much gone away. If anything, it had only gotten worse, given my present circumstances: working long hours here at The Desert Rose, sleeping in the back room attached to the kitchens. It was no place for Ella, so the nuns at St. Ignacio had generously agreed to keep her there. I sent them all of the money I got from work and visited whenever I had the chance, but it still didn't feel like enough. The days in between passed in long stretches of quiet loneliness and drudgery. In those moments, I missed Mama and Papa and Jeb more than I could bear.

By the time I swept the final bits of broken glass into the dustpan, my eyes stung with tears. I carried the pan outside, hoping to hide my sorrows in the shadows behind the saloon. The sight of the night sky, so vast and shimmering with stars, did my heart some good. In a childish way, I liked to imagine my family up there, keeping an eye on me. But even still, as I gazed at the perfect sky, listening to Eddie's sad, beautiful music, I felt alone. So very alone.

"Lovely evenin'."

The voice jarred me out of my thoughts, nearly making me fling the pan of broken glass from my hand.

It was a male's voice. Sounded like a young buck, about my age. He stepped from the dark into a panel of orange light the windows had cast on the dirt. He was tall and lean with fair hair and a wide smile.

As he came closer, however, the smile faded. "Say, what's wrong?"

I realized that tears still wet my cheeks, and I swiftly wiped them away. "Nothing."

"You were crying. Are you hurt?"

"I'm fine."

He made a look of playful, exaggerated distress. "Did some varmint trample on your heart? Tell me where he is, and I'll give him a what for."

This made me laugh a little. "It's nothing like that. But thanks, anyway."

He grinned, and I felt a flicker of heat in my face. I didn't recognize him; he certainly wasn't one of the regulars. And I'd never seen him around town. He was probably one of those railroad workers and would be leaving for Tucson at first light.

"Did you break something important?" he asked, motioning to my pan. "Is that why you're upset?"

"You really want to figure this out, don't you?" I said, both amused and exasperated.

He stepped closer. "A man doesn't like the sight of a pretty girl crying."

I tried to laugh dismissively, though it sounded more like a cough.

"I'm Landon," he said, bending his head to try and meet my eye. "Landon Black. What's your name?"

His attention put me off sorts, and I shifted to the side. "I need to get to work."

"Now don't be like that," he said. "I only want your name."

I put my free hand on my hip. "What's it matter to you? I know you're one of those rail workers, only passing through for the night. What do you care what my name is or why I'm crying?"

"Does a man need a reason to talk to a pretty girl?"

"I'm not a pretty girl." I made a move to leave. "And you're no man."

"I'm eighteen," he said, stepping in my path. "A man by anyone's reckoning."

I raised an eyebrow, and he grinned, folding his arms.

"Tell you what," he said. "You give me two more guesses as to why you were crying. If I win, I get to know your name."

A smile pulled irrepressibly at my lips, and when I didn't refuse, Landon must have taken it as a yes. "Let's see now," he said, folding his arms and tapping his chin with one finger, analyzing me. "You say your heart wasn't broken, but maybe you broke a heart and you feel bad about it. That's it. A girl like you probably breaks three hearts a week."

I laughed, shaking my head. "Flattery is the devil's trick, stranger."

"Ah, so she's a Sunday School goer. A Sunday School goer working in a saloon? Aren't you a puzzle."

"I sweep the floors and wipe tables," I said defensively. "I ain't one of the girls, if that's what this is all about."

He held up his hands. "Didn't think it for a minute."

My pride was still ruffled. "I need to get back to work, now that you mention it."

"Wait," he said, jumping in front of the door to block me. "Don't leave. I've got the answer. I know why you were crying."

I folded my arms. "Oh, you do?"

The smirk faded from his face. This close, I could see sincerity suddenly pour into his pale blue eyes. Without a word, he took the pan full of glass from my hand and set it on the ground. Then he stood directly in front of me, looking straight into my eyes.

"You lost someone very close to you."

My stomach tightened, and I took a step back. "How did…?"

"It's easy to recognize a sorrow you've felt yourself."

His words halted me in place. I stared at him, trying to figure this boy out.

"Who did you lose?" he asked, filling the silence.

It wasn't proper to speak of such things, especially not to a stranger. But in spite of this, a reckless feeling flashed through me. I wanted to confide in Landon. Maybe it was because I knew I'd never see him again—he'd be gone forever on the morning train. Maybe it was sheer loneliness—I hadn't really talked with another person aside from Eddie since I came to Burning Mesa. And I certainly hadn't talked with anyone about my loss, about my guilt at having survived. The weight of it had been slowly crushing me from the inside.

My heart beat hard, sorrow rushing fresh into it. I set a hand on the outer wall of the saloon and sank onto one of the wood crates piled out back. "My parents and my brother. Two brothers, actually."

"I'm real sorry to hear that."

Somehow, just sharing that one thing made my burden feel a little lighter.

"And you?" I asked.

Landon scraped a hand through his sandy hair. I recognized the pain in his eyes. Coming to sit beside me on the crates, he sighed. "My ma. This last winter. It hit Pa real hard. He…he hasn't said but three words since."

"I'm so sorry."

He tried to smile, but he still looked mournful. He turned his eyes to the sky. "I thought I was the only one who tried to search for lost loved ones in the stars."

"Is that why you came out here?" I asked.

He shrugged. "Pastor said I can speak to her through prayers, but I haven't had much luck. Guess I'm not righteous enough."

"I don't believe that."

He smiled. "You don't know me very well."

"I have a pretty good sense of people."

He tilted his head slightly to the side. "I reckon you do."

I smiled, lowering my gaze. He bent his head down again to try and meet it. "So will you tell me your name now?"

At that moment, the back door was flung open, smacking against the wall. Landon and I both spun around with a start. Tom, the bouncer, appeared from the glow of the inside lights.

"What kind of riffraff—?" Then his eyes fell on me. "Maggie?"

Tom had a stern face and black hair, which he wore cropped short in an attempt to mask his Apache features. I suppose he couldn't get work anywhere else, given his race. And he only got his job here at The Rose because Connelly thought troublemakers would be more afraid of a big Apache man.

I jumped to my feet. "Tom—"

"What in the devil is going on out here?" he said. "I've been looking everywhere for you."

I motioned to the pan of broken glass on the floor. "I—I had to—"

"It's my fault," Landon said, rushing to his feet as well. "I kept her."

"You get on out of here, boy," Tom growled. "She ain't one of the gals. She earns her pay cleanin', not yappin' with the likes of you."

My face burned as I grabbed the pan and turned to go back inside.

"I meant no trouble," Landon insisted. "I only wanted to know her name."

"Find another gal," Tom snapped. "This one's busy."

As Tom pulled me back inside, I dared a look behind me. It seemed silly, but my heart sank a little, knowing I'd never see Landon Black again. He reached his arm out and seemed to say one last thing, some meaningful parting phrase, but the door swung shut behind us, and he was gone.

"You're in a *heap* of trouble," Tom said, still gripping my arm. He was usually kind to me, and so, seeing him this mad, I knew I was in for it.

"I didn't mean to stay out so long. I'm sorry, Tom."

"Don't try and apologize to me. Connelly's the one spittin' mad."

Connelly. My stomach knotted. He'd gotten no more polite or decent since I first clashed with him in the Relic Refinery—having him as my boss had been one of the biggest downsides of working at The Desert Rose. Gritting my teeth, I prepared for another dock to my wages, or perhaps extra hours of cleaning detail.

Just before we entered the main room of the saloon, however, we nearly collided with Adelaide Price.

She was dressed in a high-necked white blouse and a simple black skirt. But an evening cloak was draped over her shoulders, and for a moment, her eyes widened, as if caught in the act of something.

"Where do you think *you're* goin'?" Tom asked.

Quick as it had arrived, the panic slid from Adelaide's face. "Why, I was looking for Maggie," she said, smiling. "We'd planned to take a little stroll this evening, didn't we, Maggie?"

She shot me a look, and I caught the slightest hint of pleading in her eyes.

I had been working at The Desert Rose for almost a month and had made a point not to mingle with the less-than-savory characters—which was pretty much everyone except for Eddie—but Adelaide had been friendly to me from day one. I didn't know why. Not only was she the star of the weekend revue, but she was also the belle of the county. With her sapphire eyes and hair the color of corn silk, she had more men in love with her than I'd imagined possible.

All of the other dancer girls tried to get in good with her, figuring she had more political sway than even Mr. Connelly. I had mixed feelings about her friendliness to me. She seemed real nice, but I knew very well what she did in her upstairs suite. Mama would have called it disgraceful to associate with a person like her, and yet was I such a grand, important person to shun a friendly advance from anyone?

And so, in that moment, seeing her need, I found myself lying for her. "That's right," I said to Tom. "I was trying to tell you, but you didn't give me a chance."

"I already cleared it with Connelly," Adelaide said. "You know how he feels about us girls getting regular fresh air and exercise."

Tom twisted his lips to the side, unsure. Adelaide set a hand on Tom's arm and flashed him a coy look through her dark lashes. It was her trademark flirtation, a look I'd seen her bestow on many a gentleman caller.

"Aw, come on now, Tom. You know I'm innocent as a lamb. We'll take a turn around the block and be back before you can blink twice."

Tom had witnessed the charms of Adelaide Price for far longer than I had, and yet he still visibly softened. "Go on then," he said, trying to sound gruff but failing. "Make it quick."

"Sure thing," Adelaide said with a wink. She then linked her arm in mine. "Come along, Maggie."

We stepped out the back door. At a safe distance from The Desert Rose, Adelaide turned a smile on me. "Thanks a bunch, Mags. I knew you were a smart thing."

I shrugged. "I didn't want to see you punished by that awful Mr. Connelly."

"Oh, him? The old buzzard. I'm not afraid of him."

I laughed a little, wishing I could share her confidence. "Well," I said, "I guess I'll let you get on to wherever you were headed."

Adelaide pressed her arm, still laced with mine, against her side. "Stay. Why don't we take that walk, after all? I'd like to get to know you better."

I hesitated, but Adelaide led us on with a casual smile, and I didn't see any way of politely backing out. I supposed even I wasn't immune to her charm.

We headed along Main Street and down a back alley. After a while, the rushing sound of water and the damp, swampy smell revealed our destination. Adelaide led me down a wide, brushy bank, choked with sage and cattails, to a secluded alcove in the river where a round pool was tucked away from the main flow of water. Mesquite trees rustled gently in the wind, and crickets sang, hidden in the dark brush.

"Here now," she said, smiling. "The perfect place for a midnight swim."

"A swim?" I asked, taken aback. "It's so late."

"That's what makes it the perfect time."

"But I don't have a swimming costume."

"You don't need one," she said, her blue eyes glinting in the moonlight.

"What are you suggesting?"

Adelaide laughed. "Don't be so modest, Maggie. We're both girls."

She pulled her blouse over her head and dropped her skirt so quickly, I barely had time to look away.

"Please, Miss Adelaide. This isn't decent."

"Oh, come now," she said, "it's just a little swim. Aren't you hot on a night like this, after all that work you had to do? Think of it as a nice bath."

I *was* hot. The grit and grime of the saloon clung to my skin and the hair on the back of my neck. "Well…"

"We're perfectly safe here," she promised. "Everyone's asleep! And if it will make you feel better, I'll keep my camisole on."

She didn't look so terribly indecent in her white lace shift. I had seen her in less when she danced.

"Well, okay."

"Perfect," she said, shaking out her pale locks. "Now come on!"

As I nervously unbuttoned my blouse, Adelaide plunged into the water. She let out a cry and then laughed freely.

"It's wonderful! Hurry up!"

I kept on my camisole and petticoat, though I cringed, knowing that the thin white fabric would be mostly see-through when wet. At least it was dark out.

"You sure there aren't any water snakes?" I asked, inching toward the bank.

"None," Adelaide said. She smoothed her wet hair back and took a deep breath. "Oh, I needed this, Maggie. I certainly did."

The cold water felt like heaven on my feet.

"Isn't it marvelous?" Adelaide asked.

I nodded, breathing in the cool breeze that brushed over the river as I moved deeper.

She grinned mischievously. "You can't really appreciate it until you get all the way under."

"I don't think—"

But before I could finish my sentence, Adelaide lunged for me. I yelped once, and then I was under the water, the chill gripping my skin. I jumped up, gasping for air. Adelaide was laughing hard. Maybe it was the rush from being dunked into the cold water, but a surge of giddiness overtook me, and I splashed a wave in her face. She shrieked.

"Oh, you're in trouble now!"

She lunged for me, splashing handful after handful of water. A memory came to me of playing Catch the Mermaid with Papa when I was a little girl. With a grin, I plunged headfirst into the river. The pale gleam of Adelaide's legs stood out in the murky darkness. Wrapping my hands around her ankles, I pulled with all my strength. Adelaide's bubbly scream rippled through the water as she was dragged underneath. She kicked free and spun around to grab my arms. We wrestled beneath the cold, rushing river for a few moments before we both burst to the surface, laughing and coughing for air.

When the battle had subsided, Adelaide and I sat in the shallows, cupping water in our hands and letting it spill through our fingers in little trickles.

"How long you been here now?" Adelaide asked. "Two months? Three?"

"Not quite one."

She nodded, her eyes distant. "I always lose track of time in the spring."

"How long have you been here? At The Desert Rose, I mean."

She laughed shortly. "Too long."

"You don't look so old," I said. "If you don't mind my saying."

"Not at all." She grinned. "I'm only twenty. Not too terribly ancient, though I feel it sometimes." She got a somewhat sad look in her eyes. "I was only sixteen when I started."

"Oh…"

Adelaide shook her head with strained brightness. "That coyote Mr. Connelly snapped me up soon as he saw I didn't have a ring on my finger."

"Me, too! Him and Álvar Castilla?"

Adelaide looked taken aback. "Well, no. Just Connelly. I only wish it had been Señor Castilla."

"You do? Why?"

"He's the richest man in town. Owns most of it, too. I tell you, if I had a chance to impress him, I would. And then some."

"Isn't he married?" I asked, my face warming a little at her cheeky talk. "He looks old enough to be."

"He's only twenty-six." Adelaide laughed. "Anyway, I hear he has a long-standing betrothal to some rich, pampered Haciendella. Don't know why they haven't tied the knot yet. Fussing over their big wedding, I guess."

It would be nice to be so rich that my biggest problems were what I wanted at my wedding. I was so busy with trying to scrape out a living, I'd be lucky if I ever *met* a respectable gentleman, let alone married. And that was assuming he'd overlook my borderline scandalous job. Sighing, I let the river water slide from my palm and vanish into the dry desert soil.

Adelaide must have sensed my mood, and she tried to keep a pleasant conversation flowing. "So," she said, "how's your sister?"

"All right," I said. "She's being well taken care of. But I miss her a lot."

"I have a baby brother," Adelaide said, her voice soft. "I miss him something awful. He's with my father in Flagstaff."

"So far away? Do you get to see them much?"

She stared at the black river ahead. "No. They wouldn't see me anyway, even if I went."

I felt a sudden pang of guilt for having judged her. Clearly, plenty others did, too. Even her own kin.

"I'm sorry."

She put on a strained smile. "Doesn't matter. I'm too busy dancing for those varmints to think much about it. Quite a crowd tonight, wasn't there?"

"They come from all over the valley to see you perform. The girls were whispering tonight that a man from Green Springs brought you a relic shard just to have supper with him."

She smiled slyly. "You'd be surprised what a man will do for a woman he's in love with. You know, you're pretty enough to win a man or two, Maggie, with that dark, mysterious look you got goin'. You should try it."

I smiled, embarrassed. "I don't think so."

"Why?" She laughed. "You leave a boy back where you're from?"

The smile dropped from my lips.

Adelaide clapped a hand over her mouth. "Good Lord, I forgot. You're from Haydenville, aren't you?"

I said nothing.

"Oh, Maggie, I…I'm so sorry." She set her hand on my arm. "How horrible for you."

I nodded wordlessly.

She sighed. "All of Burning Mesa was up in arms when we got word of what happened. It was bad enough when we heard about Buena, but then to hear it happened right next door to us? No one could believe them Apaches would destroy whole towns."

"Apaches?"

"They're the ones who did it, of course. They're mad about the relic mining. Everyone knows that."

I pictured Yahnuiyo's honest expression as he told me his people weren't responsible. "Has anyone tried to talk with them?"

"What on earth for? To be killed on sight?"

I dug my toes into the cool mud of the river bottom. For some reason, I wanted to keep my moment with Yahn to myself.

"Maybe we don't understand," I said.

Adelaide shrugged and wrung out the golden twist of her hair. "Well, it makes sense to me. And frankly, I think we ought to do something about it before they strike again. The disputes over those mining sites aren't getting any calmer, you know." Her face became serious. "I talked with a miner two nights ago. He said he'd heard things."

The unmistakable fear in her eyes sent a chill down my spine. "What things?"

"He said he'd heard there was going to be another burning. Soon."

It felt like the air had been sucked out of my lungs. Maybe it was simply idle gossip or the bragging of a man trying to impress a pretty girl… But maybe it was true.

Just then, a rustle sounded in the nearby brush. I spun around. I was already on edge from the conversation, and the sound of movement sent me out of my skin.

"Adelaide!" I whispered. "I heard—"

"Shhh!"

We listened for a tense moment. Sure enough, over the gentle song of crickets, I could hear distinct footfalls. The soft mumble of voices. I gripped Adelaide so hard, my knuckles went white.

"We have to run."

"Wait…"

And then, pushing through the bushes, two men.

"Well, well, well," one of them said. "What have we here?"

CHAPTER FIVE

I screamed and flung myself into the water, away from them. "Adelaide! *Run!*"

She called my name, but I thrashed frantically through the river, trying to get to the other side.

"Maggie! Wait!"

I spun around. She stood on the banks, looking like a water nymph with her long, wet hair hanging around her and her curvaceous body draped in see-through linen.

"What are you— "

"It's okay," she said, exasperated. "These are my friends. Now settle down. You about near gave us all a heart attack."

I stared, speechless, as Adelaide turned to the two men. The dark-haired one with a black cowboy hat chuckled. "Didn't mean to interrupt you two water lilies."

I jerked my arms around my chest. Even though the water

mostly covered me, the awareness that I probably looked as visible as Adelaide in these wet clothes made me light-headed.

The dark-haired cowboy stepped up to Adelaide and swept her into an embrace. My heart stopped, but Adelaide giggled. She threw her arms around his neck, and they began to kiss in a most indecent way. I was frozen there in the river, completely stunned.

When they were done, Adelaide turned to me. "I want you to meet my beau. These two cowboys just rode into town, and I'm real happy to see them. Come on out and say hello."

I clung my arms tighter around my body. "I can't!"

Adelaide laughed as if I were being silly. "Landon, give Maggie her clothes."

Landon. The name shot through me like a bullet, and I whipped a look at the younger of the two men. In the chaos of my own fear, I hadn't noticed, but now I could clearly see the boy I'd spoken to outside The Desert Rose. He stepped forward, removing a light-colored cowboy hat he hadn't been wearing before.

"My, my," he said with an amused smirk. "Fancy meeting you here."

Words escaped me for a single frozen moment. Landon scooped up my blouse and skirt. "Forget something?"

"Don't touch those!" I shouted. Even in the cold river, I could feel my face heat with humiliation. I wanted to dive under the water and vanish downstream. "What are you doing here?"

"Just out for a stroll with my friend Bobby. Though seeing you two here, I have to say an evening swim sounds mighty refreshing."

It was definitely Landon there on the bank, and yet he seemed a wholly different person. Where was the lonely soul who searched for his mother in the stars? This smirking rogue bore almost no resemblance to him.

"Shall we all strip down and join you out there, *Maggie*?" Landon asked, reaching to take off his boots.

"Don't come any closer," I shouted. I looked to Adelaide. "Can't you send these ruffians away?"

"Ruffians?" Landon asked, laughing.

Adelaide stayed focused on her dark-haired cowboy, not even looking at me. A shiver passed over my skin. The temperature of the water was dropping by the second.

"Adelaide, *please.*"

"There's no need to be so ruffled," Landon said. "You come on out. I'll close my eyes, I swear."

"Somehow I don't believe you."

Adelaide began to kiss her cowboy again in a way so intense, I was surely sinning just *looking* at it. A flash of betrayal filled me. So *that's* why she wanted me to come along—to cover her tracks while she met up with her beau. I'd been played a fool. And apparently by more persons than one.

I glared at Landon, shame burning through me at the memory of our intimate conversation. He was clearly a liar and a no-good, probably looking to take advantage of me in my low moment. Well, he wouldn't succeed.

"Throw me my clothes," I called to Landon firmly.

He raised an eyebrow. "They'll get all wet."

"You throw me my clothes this second. I am *not* stepping out of the water in this state."

"Suit yourself."

My clothes landed on the water with a *plop*. I lunged to salvage them, but they were already soaked. Grimacing, I assessed the damage. The navy skirt would be fine, I supposed, provided it didn't cling to my legs too much. The pale blouse, on the other hand, was now as see-through as my camisole. I contemplated swimming to the other side of the river and dressing there, but I knew the current was too strong to risk it.

Closing my eyes, I rallied my courage and waded awkwardly to shore in my soaking clothes. When I reached him, Landon smiled a wide, shining smile and tipped his hat.

"Howdy," he said, and then he lowered his voice with words meant only for me. "Sure is a happy surprise to run into you out here."

I ignored him. "Adelaide, I want to go back now."

She broke away from whispering sweet nothings to Bobby and pouted. "Aw, Maggie, why don't we stay awhile? Landon here's real nice. And he's about your age, to boot. He'll keep you company."

"No, thanks. I'd really like to get home."

"Then go," she said, frowning. She turned a gaze of longing to her partner. "I so rarely get to have time alone with the people I actually want to be around."

She clearly wasn't leaving. In the cooling breeze, my clothes felt especially cold against my skin. I was shivering, though I tried not to show it.

"Fine, then. I'll go."

"Have Landon walk you back."

"No." I didn't want to be anywhere near him. I wasn't going to let him laugh at me one second longer.

"It ain't safe for a lady to walk alone at this time of night," Landon said, holding out his arm to escort me.

I kept my limbs tight at my sides. "Even so, I'd rather go alone than with a *complete stranger*."

Landon's brow lowered a little. I could see my words had stung him as I'd planned. But the realization came with an unexpected twinge of guilt.

"Or…if you like, you can walk along," I said, flustered. "What do I care?"

Without waiting for his reply, I lifted my drenched skirt and marched up the embankment. As I passed through the bushes, Landon came beside me. My pulse raced a little at him so near. I stepped away quickly, both from him and my foolish reaction.

"What's goin' on?" Landon asked. "Why are you so mad? Aren't you pleased at all to see me?"

"I've never seen *you* before. The person I spoke to outside The Desert Rose is not *you.*"

Landon let out a frustrated breath. "I can't very well go weeping about my dead mother every second, now can I?"

"If that's even true. You obviously have no scruples about lying."

He stepped forward, stopping me. "What are you talking about?"

"You lied about being a railroad worker to trick me into thinking I'd never see you again."

"I never claimed I was a railroad worker. You said that."

I opened my mouth to argue but then realized he was right. I folded my arms. "Well, you didn't try to correct me."

"I didn't see the need at the moment." His blue eyes lowered, and he sighed. "I just wanted to talk to you."

The sincerity in his voice silenced me. We walked along for a moment. Landon took off his hat and shuffled it in his hands, clearly frustrated. I pursed my lips. I knew I was being harsh; I could see that. And Papa always said everyone deserved a second chance.

"So you're a cowboy, huh?" I asked, shooting him a sidelong glance.

He perked up a little. "Yes, ma'am. One of Señor Castilla's finest. And a skilled fighter of rock devils, if I do say so myself."

I'd heard stories of cowboys but had never met one before. Ranchers hired them to move their cattle and horses and whatever other livestock they had to different grazing locations. But given that a pair of rock devils could wipe out half a herd of cattle in one night, and one organized pack of ghost coyotes could take out a whole one, the cowboys also had to be skilled warriors. I'd heard they carried infinitely growing behemoth rope, and that they had rare goblin bones, which could cause the user to blend into whatever landscape he was in, essentially giving him invisibility. Or giving invisibility to his herds. Very useful. And very expensive.

But the trademark weapon of the cowboy was the dragon-claw rifle. For most people, fire relics brought an agitating effect, which made them less than ideal in an intense situation, so ranchers hired men with not only physical strength but cool heads. The cowboys displayed their dragon-claw rifles as a proud badge of this composure.

It went without saying that for a man to be given the use of those relics, not to mention a rancher's entire livestock, he'd proved he had to be more than trustworthy. If Landon really was a cowboy, then I could count myself lucky indeed to have such an escort.

Though I wasn't about to tell him that.

When we reached The Desert Rose, Landon stood beside the closed doors, leaning against the wall. He studied me with a smile, and I couldn't help noticing how blue his eyes were even in the dim moonlight. My face heated a little under his gaze. Trying to look confident, I smoothed my damp hair out of my eyes.

"Well, thank you. I think I'm safe now."

For the second time that night, Tom broke up the moment. He pushed out the swinging double doors of the saloon.

"You again?" he said, eyeing Landon, his tone ripe with disapproval. His gaze then fixed on my wet clothes, and his dark brow furrowed. "What happened here? Are you all right, Maggie?"

As gruff as he could act sometimes, Tom had been like a protective big brother to me from the beginning. My first day at The Desert Rose, I caught him watching me real strange, like he knew something. I couldn't figure out what to make of it, but he'd treated me kindly every day after. I figured he just needed to get used to me.

"I'm fine," I said. "This gentleman was just leaving."

Tom frowned. "Where's Adelaide?"

The image of Adelaide, locked in an embrace with the darker cowboy, shot into my mind, and I was certain my face fell to match. Dropping my gaze from Tom's, I fingered the damp hem of my blouse. "She's coming. When…when I fell into the river, she ran for help. This cowboy here came to our aid, and…Adelaide is still talking with his friend. Letting him know I'm all right."

Tom's face betrayed nothing as to whether or not he believed my story. He gave Landon one final, piercing look, then turned back to his post.

I blew out a little sigh of relief.

"Nicely handled," Landon said, grinning. He had been watching me the entire time. He tipped his hat, not taking his eyes off me. "Good night, ma'am. It's been a pleasure."

I looked away, smoothing down my skirt again to show that I wasn't as ruffled by his words as I felt. "Yes, well… Good-bye."

When I glanced back, he was laughing quietly to himself.

I put my hands on my hips. "Did I say something that amused you?"

In response, he took a step closer, smiling. I knew I should smack him for being fresh, but instead my stomach fluttered like a caged bird. I couldn't look away from his gaze.

A distant scream shattered the moment like a hammer to glass. It was the sound of pure terror.

We both spun in the direction of the noise. A lone man sprinted toward us from up the otherwise dead-still street, screaming at the top of his lungs. Landon and I exchanged a look, and without saying a word, ran to meet him at the same time.

The screams didn't let up. Sudden patches of light illuminated windows all along the main street. A few people in nightclothes stepped out looking bleary-eyed but frightened. Tom and Mr. Connelly ran from the Desert Rose to see what the commotion was.

The man, a Chinese laborer covered with dirt, ran straight for us.

"Huo," he said in a frantic rasp. *"Huo!"* He gripped Landon by the shirt. *"Ta wen lai dau!"*

"Easy there," Landon said, prying him off. "Take it easy."

"What in the hell's got your goat?" Tom asked. "Wakin' up everybody in the town like that?"

"Huo!" the laborer said, eyes wide.

"How about you try telling us in *English,* boy," Connelly said. "We don't talk your damn Chinese gibber jabber."

The laborer trembled all over, pale as death. "Ah…pah…chey," he said, struggling to enunciate the words through his terror. "Ah pah chey!"

The small crowd that had gathered around exchanged confused looks. But his words struck me right in the chest.

"Apache," I whispered. Landon heard me, and our eyes met with a flash of fear.

His voice was louder. "Apache."

The word seemed to suck the air from the street. The laborer nodded frantically. *"Ta wen lai dau!"* He pointed to the flickering lantern that hung by the door outside a nearby shop. *"Huo!"*

I stared at his shaking, dirty hand, and all at once I could see it wasn't dirt. Of course it wasn't. I knew that color, that smell. Better than I wanted to. It was ash and smoke.

Huo. He meant fire.

CHAPTER SIX

The next few moments were a blur of sounds. Panic spread quickly. It was partly helped by the arrival of others rushing down Main Street, shouting for help. Within a few moments, everyone in Burning Mesa seemed to be awake and caught up in the fear.

"It's at the excavation camp!" someone shouted.

Less than a half mile out of town. The flames would arrive in a matter of minutes.

In my mind, all I saw was fire. Vast, angry orange flames, spreading with unnatural power. Devouring everything in their path. The fire that had destroyed my home. The fire that had killed my parents. Memories I had tried so hard to keep at bay now crashed down on me like a rockslide.

The commotion of the street pulled me back to the moment. Everywhere voices echoed together in the night like thunder.

"Run for your lives!"

"We won't go down like Haydenville! We'll fight!"

"Pray for God's mercy on our souls!"

Nausea rippled through me. I turned dizzily and would have tripped to the ground if a pair of strong arms hadn't caught me.

Landon.

"You all right, Maggie?"

"Ella." In spite of the chaos in my head and around me, the only thing that mattered sprang to my lips.

"Ella!" I said again.

Landon looked confused. "Who?"

"My little sister." I clung to his shirt. "You have to take me to her. Right now!"

"Take you where? I— "

"I'll run all the way there if I have to." I turned and broke into a dizzy sprint, but Landon caught up with me. He hooked his arm around my waist to slow me down.

"Maggie! Hang on."

"No!" I was gripped with horrible visions of the St. Ignacio mission engulfed with flame. "Let me go! I have to save her!"

"I'll take you," Landon said, holding my hands, trying to calm me down. "Of course I will. But you gotta relax. You're going to make yourself faint."

"I won't relax. Not until she's safe in my arms."

Landon's eyes met mine, his gaze so sincere that I was thrown off. "We'll get there in time," he said. "I give you my word. Just tell me where to go."

As we pushed through the confusion in the streets, I heard Adelaide shouting for me. I turned to see her and Bobby close behind.

"Thank God you're all right," she said, out of breath from

running. "We feared the worst."

"Where you heading?" Bobby asked Landon.

"I've got to get my sister," I said. "We have to hurry."

Bobby nodded. "We'll come with you."

We rode into the night, two horses galloping as fast as they could go. Landon and me astride his horse Titan, with Adelaide and Bobby close behind. I hesitated to put my arms around Landon's waist at first, but as we bounded over the sagebrush and red sand, I found myself holding tighter. I buried my head into his shirt and whispered again and again, "Please. Please let her be safe."

When the dim, moonlit outline of St. Ignacio's rose unscathed over the horizon, my heart nearly burst from my chest. We weren't safe yet, but at least I hadn't come too late. I jumped from the saddle before Landon had slowed Titan to a full stop, not even bothering to look back. I didn't greet any of the friars, who clustered in a panicked mass in the main courtyard. I didn't stop until I reached Ella. She was sitting on one of the benches in her nightclothes, afraid and alone—but safe.

She spotted me and let out a cry, jumping to her feet. We met halfway in a colliding embrace. With my arms tight around her, I dropped to my knees.

"I'm here," I whispered. "I'm here."

"I thought you'd been burned," she said, her tiny body shaking.

"No. Never. I'd never leave you."

I stroked her head, kissed her face. It felt like it had been weeks since she did so much as look at me. This newfound tenderness made my heart burst. "We'll be okay," I whispered. "I won't let anything happen to you."

She wiped her nose on her sleeve. "The fathers said Burning Mesa is going to be burned like Haydenville."

I didn't know what to say to this, so I pulled her back into my arms. "Whatever happens, we'll be okay."

Behind us, the chaos of the friars reminded me that St. Ignacio's was far from safe. We had to get out of there, head for the mountains or something. The fleeting thought came that I should try and find Yahnuiyo, the Apache brave who'd saved us the last time we'd faced these mysterious fires.

But then the idea seemed crazy. The Chinese man had said the Apaches were the attackers, like he'd seen them with his own eyes. Suddenly, I didn't know what to believe.

I looked up at Landon, who stood back with Bobby and Adelaide. They watched the doors, antsy to leave. Reluctantly, I broke out of my embrace with Ella.

"I have to talk with these folks here. But you stay right beside me."

Landon approached me as I stood. "One of the friars is saying the attack is already contained."

I frowned. "How can that be possible?"

Landon shook his head.

"I still say we get out of here," Adelaide argued. "You boys ought to know some places we can hide. Somewhere along your trail."

"It's too risky," Landon said. "Those Apaches know the mountains better than we do."

"Well, it beats staying here and being burned to death." Adelaide crossed her arms.

Beside me, Ella whimpered, and I pulled her closer. "No one is going to be burned," I said firmly. "We'll go on foot if we have to."

"We need to wait and see what's happening," Landon insisted. "The friars said they've sent a man into town to find out what's going on."

Bobby rubbed his forehead grimly. "I don't know…"

But at that moment, the decision was made for us. One of the younger friars burst into the courtyard, red-faced and dripping with sweat.

"It's over," he cried, panting. "It's all over."

"It's over?" I asked, filled with images of Burning Mesa as nothing but a smoldering pile.

Father Cortez stepped forward. "Tell us what you know, my son."

"Those Apaches attacked the Chinese excavator's camp. But Sheriff Leander got there before it spread to Burning Mesa. There's word they even caught a few of them."

"So we're safe, then?" Bobby asked, frowning. "How can we be sure?"

"I saw the camp with my own two eyes," the younger friar said. "It's nearly burned to the ground, to be sure, but the flames have been put out, and there's no sign of any more Apaches."

Father Cortez kissed his rosary. "Praise to God we have been spared."

I squeezed Ella's hand. "You see? We're safe."

Given it was such a late hour, and we were too jittery to leave anyhow, Father Cortez agreed to let us all stay the night in the nuns' wing.

As I tucked the blankets over Ella, I couldn't help but notice that she looked thinner. I knew the sisters were giving all they could, but it still wasn't enough. If only *I* could do more.

"Don't leave me," she whispered, gripping my hand.

"I won't, I promise." I kissed her soft, warm forehead.

"And I wanna keep the candle burnin'," she said.

I smiled. "Sure, baby girl."

It was the nickname Jeb always called her. Ella's eyes flicked to mine, but she didn't say anything. I knew I could never replace Jeb, but I had a mind to do everything in my power to at least be as good to her as he had been.

I stayed on the edge of the hard little bed as Ella drifted into sleep. Bobby and Adelaide sat up on the cot against the other wall, their hands entwined. Landon took a chair, though he barely sat on the edge, too tense to stay still. All of us were too shaken.

I glanced at Landon. I'd been too hard on him, that much was clear.

"Thank you," I said softly. "For taking me here. It was a real decent thing to do for a stranger."

He smiled. "We escaped death together. I wouldn't call us strangers anymore."

I couldn't help but smile back. "I guess you're right."

After a pause, Landon motioned to the one other cot in the sparse white room. "You should probably try and get some sleep. It's awful late."

"What about you?"

"I'll be fine." He fingered the rim of his hat. "Can't sleep, anyway."

"Neither can I."

Adelaide shivered, pulling the worn blanket closer. "I don't think I'll ever be able to sleep again. How can we, when we know those Apaches are out there, waiting to burn us in our beds?"

I winced at her words, though I wasn't sure if it was out of fear or some strange feeling of loyalty to Yahn.

Bobby put his arms around her. "I won't let that happen."

"How can you stop it?"

He traced a finger down the line of her jaw, stroked a loose, pale lock of her hair. "Maybe we should get out of this town once and for all. Get far away from here. You and me."

"Oh, Bobby." Adelaide gripped his neck. "I wish we could."

They began to kiss, and I looked into my lap, embarrassed.

Landon snorted. "And *I* wish I could get far away from you two and your lovemakin'."

They ignored him, if anything becoming more entangled in their passionate embrace. Landon and I exchanged an uncomfortable smile, shaking our heads. He scooted his chair in front of me. "At least I can block the lady from having to see such things."

Landon's knees brushed against mine, and I suddenly found it hard to meet his gaze. For a moment, we were quiet. Then Landon spoke.

"She's real sweet." He was looking at Ella, who was sleeping soundly now. I smiled and slid my hand down her cheek.

"I can tell you love her a lot," he said. "She's lucky to have you."

If only he knew that I'd nearly gotten her killed the night of the razing. That I'd let my brother stay behind in the flames and face a terrible death.

"No," I whispered.

"She is," he insisted. "You're giving her everything you can. You're not…shutting her out in your grief."

His words drifted off, and I didn't pursue it, remembering about his pa, who didn't speak to him.

"I just wish I could give her so much more." I picked at a stray thread on her blanket. "If I were smarter or clever with a craft, I could earn us enough money to live together somewhere nice. Be a proper family."

"You seem pretty sharp to me."

"I'm not. Trust me. My reading and letters are weak. I could never teach. And I can't sew a button for anything. All I know about are relics, and a lot of good that will do a girl like me, without two pennies to rub together."

Landon was quiet for a moment, shuffling his hat in his hands. "What happened to your parents?"

The words came slowly. "They died with everyone else in the Haydenville razing."

Landon exhaled and scraped a hand through his hair. "Aw, Maggie, I'm sorry."

I shook my head. The tenderness in his voice only sharpened my pain. His warm hand covered mine as he sat back, analyzing me in the dim candlelight. "You're a brave girl, Maggie. I'm awful glad I stepped out to see the stars tonight."

My stomach fluttered a little. "I should get some sleep," I said, too shy to meet his gaze.

"Sounds good."

I lay down on the stiff cot, turning my back to Landon. But somehow, as I drifted off to sleep, I knew he was watching me.

CHAPTER SEVEN

The tension from the night before still simmered in the streets of Burning Mesa the next day, thick as the smell of smoke that hung on the air. But Mr. Connelly insisted that was all the more reason for the show to go on. Adelaide's weekend revue would continue as planned. I thought it seemed a rotten thing to demand of her after the scare we'd all had, but as usual, the crowds flocked to see Miss Adelaide Price. Apparently a little diversion was just what they were after.

The saloon brimmed to overflowing with drunk miners and rowdy teenage boys. The alcohol flowed, and the poker games hummed. Adelaide's show was set to start around ten, but by nine the room was packed. I scurried from table to table, taking orders, mopping up spilled drinks, and delivering vittles.

The men, primed for a good time, watched me work with drunken smiles. Some even made lewd comments as I passed.

A table of relic polish salesmen from across the Mexican border whistled and called me *bonita*. As I poured them more dragon whiskey, they insisted I was a señorita they'd known back in Nogales.

I shook my head, smiling. "Don't let this dark hair trick you. I've never even been out of the Territory."

"A shame, *bonita*," a handsome older man in the group said. "One day, you must see the Hermosillo Relic Fields. They are a sight to behold."

I nodded, smiling, but inside felt a twinge of sadness that I surely never would. I'd be lucky if I ever got to a new town, let alone a new country.

At that moment, the house lights fell, snuffed out by a gust of wind from Mr. Connelly's griffin relic. The little three-man-band rattled out a chord of heralding music. Cheers erupted from the audience as the red velvet curtains opened.

But the stage was empty. The murmuring fell quiet as the crowd waited. And waited. Until somebody finally yelled, "Bring her out!"

"Yeah, we want Adelaide!" another cried.

The calls grew louder, and the suspense among the men heightened, until suddenly a single flame, the size of a candle's flicker, appeared on the empty stage.

"Look!" someone said.

The little flame rippled for a moment, and then, with a flash of orange light, it exploded into an enormous blaze. Gasps of wonder erupted from the audience. And then, with a flourish of the band, Adelaide suddenly burst from the center, her arms flung out.

The crowd went wild.

The flames dropped to a small ring of fire around her. She

stood in the center, beaming and bowing. After the cheering had died down a bit, the music started up. Adelaide began to sway her hips. She was draped in a long, fireproof cape, which she slowly began to shimmy out of. First, she revealed her bare shoulders. Then she pulled it up a little to show her legs. The men were howling by now, jumping up from their chairs. Adelaide turned her back to them. Eddie ran his hands up the piano keys in a dramatic glissando, and Adelaide tossed the robe in the air. It burst into a flash of white flames and was gone. Naturally, this only made the men crazier.

Adelaide spun around, dressed in a crimson corset with a skirt only a few inches long in the front that swept back to a fashionable bustle. The whole outfit was styled to suggest the form of a phoenix. Her blond hair was piled high on her head with a red ostrich feather gleaming in it and a red choker wrapped around her slender neck.

A plum-sized oval of gold gleamed from the center of her bodice. A relic. Phoenix bone, sewn right into her costume. Adelaide stroked the mirror-like piece and winked at the audience, looking scandalous but undeniably beautiful. The other girls came on behind her, kicking their legs in the air, and the number went on. I smiled and shook my head as I turned back to my work. Adelaide certainly knew how to put on a show.

Tom passed me, cradling a tray of empty dishes on his arm. "Them high rollers need more dragon whiskey."

I looked over at the secluded table tucked into a shadowy corner of the saloon, the usual haunt of the wealthy and powerful in the valley. Immediately, I could tell something was amiss. For starters, not a single man there was watching Adelaide's dance. And while there were cards and poker chips on the tabletop, no one was playing. Instead, they all bent in to speak over the noise, their faces stone serious. And none other than Álvar Castilla sat at the head of the table.

Usually when he came into the saloon, it was with a raucous group of young Haciendos like himself. They drank and laughed and flirted with the prettiest of the dancers. Tonight, however, Álvar seemed all business.

"Whiskey," Tom snapped, breaking my reverie. He was grouchier than usual tonight.

"Easy now," I said. "I'm goin'." Tom snorted and tromped off to the back room.

I smoothed the sweaty strands of hair from my face and surveyed the high rollers' table again. Álvar spoke to the men with intensity, making tight gestures with his hands. He looked a little more ruffled than I'd seen him last. His black hair was damp with sweat. He'd rolled up the sleeves of his white silk shirt, and his vest was unbuttoned.

A stranger seated beside him caught my eye. He was stroking his bearded face and eyeing Álvar with unease. He was older, mid-fifties perhaps, and he was huge—tall and bulky as a bear. He wasn't from Burning Mesa, that much I knew. The man reeked of money. It gleamed on his countenance. From the rich, beaver fur–lined coat to the sparkling diamond cuff links on his sleeve to the oiled perfection of his brown hair.

But more than any of that, I noticed the egg-sized relic that topped his walking cane. It gleamed pale yellow, like a piece of moon. Werewolf bone. Not only dazzlingly rare and expensive, but highly illegal. They had once been used by soldiers for the surge of strength and speed they created within the wielder, but the viciousness and bloodlust that inevitably took over proved too hard to keep under control. And too dangerous in the hands of the wrong kind of people. As shadow relics, they had not only been banned, but the government had confiscated most of them long ago. Though I was learning that if you were rich enough, nothing was off-limits.

Keeping an eye on the wealthy stranger, I got the top-shelf dragon whiskey from our bartender.

"Smits," I asked as he laid the glistening amber bottle in my hand, "who's that man with Álvar? The filthy rich one."

Smits adjusted his spectacles and peered over at the high rollers' table. "Oh, him? That's Emerson Bolger. He's some big relic tycoon. Owns half of the mining companies in the Colorado Territory."

"Does he own the mines here?"

"No, but he sure as hell wants to."

Smits went back to his work, and I cautiously approached the high rollers. Álvar's voice drifted toward me over the noise in the saloon.

"The sheriff is unwilling to do what must be done. This is unacceptable to me—to all of us. I say, if he will not do his job to protect this city, then I must."

My ears burned. I knew I wasn't meant to hear these words. Luckily, the moment I stepped into the alcove, Álvar looked up, and a smile spread over his face.

"Why, good evening, Miss Davis. It is a pleasure to see you again."

It seemed strange to have such a handsome and wealthy young man pay any attention to me. I did my best not to act flustered. "Pleasure to see you as well, sir."

"Please call me Álvar."

I noticed a few of the men glance at me, half smirking.

"I'd better stick with 'sir,'" I said, trying to ignore them. "Seein' as how you're my boss."

I poured the dragon whiskey into his goblet. As any good fire relic vintage would, it hissed as it touched the glass, and a slender wisp of smoke curled up. Álvar watched me pour, grinning. I'd never seen such straight white teeth. "And how do you like working here at my fine establishment?" he asked when I'd finished.

"It's very good, sir. Thank you."

Álvar laughed. "Señor Bolger," he said, turning to address the large, opulent stranger who sat beside him. "This is my new employee, Maggie Davis. Maggie, I would like you to meet Emerson Bolger. He is a fellow businessman and investor."

"Charmed," Mr. Bolger said, not looking up as he pulled a fat cigar from a gold tin case he carried in his inner pocket.

I bowed my head, and at that moment, a roar went up from the crowd. It was the big finale of Adelaide's act. She was bursting into flames and reappearing in different places in the saloon. The men loved it and begged for her to show up on their table. When she indulged their pleas, they'd go wild, grabbing for her and throwing their money.

Emerson Bolger took a meditative puff of his cigar. "What about the Apaches who were captured?" His voice was rich and deep as a canyon. "Shouldn't we interrogate them first?"

I kept my face expressionless and tried to move inconspicuously around the table to fill the rest of the whiskey glasses, listening to every word.

"The prisoners will not speak," Álvar said. "But there is no need to hear their words. Every man in this room knows why they did it. They made their intention clear last night, attacking our excavators as they slept. The *excavators*, not the miners. Because miners simply dig into the mountain, but without the specially trained excavators, it is impossible to successfully extract the relics from the rock. What more proof do you need, Señor Bolger?"

"I don't want proof. I want assurance that this kind of thing doesn't spread to my town, to the other towns where my miners work."

"Indeed," Álvar said. "This thought compels all of us."

I poured slower, staring at the flicker of light on the rim of the glass and reciting the facts again to myself. It *did* seem like proof. Another town. Another fire. Only this time, they'd been caught at the scene of the crime. Come to think of it, the Apaches had been found at the scene of my home's burning as well.

Why had Yahnuiyo been there in the first place? Everything seemed to add up to one conclusion: it really *was* the Apaches who were burning towns.

But a part of me couldn't shake the sincerity on Yahn's face as he insisted on his people's innocence. Why should I doubt him? He was the reason I still had breath in my body, still had Ella.

"Hey!"

I looked up, startled. A puddle of whiskey shimmered on the floor. Lost in my thoughts, I'd missed the final man's glass altogether.

"So sorry, sir."

I bent quickly to sop up the mess. But once I was on my knees, my hand slowed, my focus remaining on the conversation at the table. With the ruckus of Adelaide's performance ending and the crowd roaring their approval, it was difficult to hear, but I could just make out the voices.

"So what are we supposed to do, then?" one of the men asked.

"No one knows where they're camped. I 'spect they got a mess of goblin relics hiding 'em."

"Or worse," Álvar said, letting the ominous words hang in the silence.

An older man at the table cleared his throat. "I thought the Apaches shunned the use of relics. Isn't that why they're attacking?"

Álvar snorted. "What they *say* and what they *do* can differ greatly."

A man with fancy shoes beside him spat on the floor angrily. "Everyone knows them greedy Apaches only say that to throw us off their trail. They want the relics all to themselves. That's why they're fightin' us so hard!"

The men at the table murmured in agreement. I dabbed the rag mindlessly on the ground, my head spinning.

"Miss Davis."

I sprang to my feet, wide-eyed, but Álvar wore a casual smile with no trace of suspicion or anger. "Would you please find Señor Connelly and ask him to join me here?"

"Of course."

"Thank you." He lifted his glass and winked. "And thank you for the good whiskey."

I took that as a subtle cue that Mr. Connelly alone was to return. After delivering the summons, I got back to my usual chores. I needed time to think, to collect the crush of thoughts in my head. As I cleared some plates and cups away, however, my eyes fell on a distracting face.

Landon Black.

He sat a few tables away, laughing with Adelaide's dark-haired cowboy. Drinking. Gambling. One of the upstairs girls, a curvy redhead named Dora, stood behind his chair with her hands on his shoulders. As I watched, she leaned closer to whisper something in his ear, and they both laughed. I grabbed for a stack of dirty glasses. I'd heard cowboys kept a gal in every town. Appeared the rumors were true.

I didn't want to see any more, and I certainly didn't want him to spot me. I worked fast as I could, but as I reached for the final glass on the table, Landon glanced to his side, and our eyes met.

I straightened with a snap. The cup slipped from my hands, and though I fumbled to catch it, whiskey splashed over the freshly cleaned table. Landon rose from his chair and made a move toward me, but I pivoted, lunging in the opposite direction, and crashed right into a patron. The man staggered back, flailing his arms. Then with a shout, he tumbled onto the table behind him, sending drinks flying everywhere and glass crashing to the floor.

Tom pushed his way over. "What in the hell's goin' on here?"

"Nothing," I said, my face heating up all the way to my ears. "I've got it."

"Jeez, Maggie, we got a full house tonight. You need to watch where you're going."

"I know. I'm sorry."

He shook his head, walking away. I bent to clean up the mess, my breath tight with frustration.

"Need some help there, ma'am?"

Landon's voice sent a cringe through me. "No," I said, not looking up. "No, thank you."

He started to gather some broken glasses anyway. "I didn't mean to put you out of sorts."

"Yes, well, you shouldn't…" I caught my mistake. "I mean, you didn't put me out of sorts. I didn't even see you. My hand slipped, that's all."

Landon failed miserably at suppressing a smile. I should have wanted to shove him, and yet, a smiled twitched at my own lips. To cover it, I elbowed his arm.

He laughed. "Hey, don't blame me if you've got butterfingers."

I searched for a witty reply but found myself struck dumb by the way he smiled. Looking me over that way, like a man who knew what he wanted and knew how to get it. I blinked hard and stood, cradling my apron, which was filled with pieces of glass. With my hand, I nudged a strand of hair from my eyes. "I'd better put these away."

I headed over to empty the glass in a mop bucket. Landon followed.

"What are you gonna do after that?" he asked, watching me.

I gave my apron a quick shake. "I have work to do. In case you didn't notice, we're a tad busy tonight."

He frowned. "Can't you take a little break? Surely Connelly gives you one."

"Well—"

"Tell you what, you come and sit at our table with Bobby and me and take a load off. I'll even buy you a drink, so Connelly will make some money off your break."

I'd never had a drink in my life and didn't feel like giving him another reason to laugh at me. "I don't think so," I said. "You seem a little *busy* over there."

Dora had moved on to sit beside a gambler at another table, but she watched Landon, betrayal gleaming in her eyes.

Landon smiled at me, oblivious to her looks. "Not as busy as you. See? You're the one who should be kicking back, not me."

Darn it if he wasn't handsome, with that sandy blond hair and dark brow. He was young but had a worldly glint in his eyes that suggested he was in on the joke, whatever that joke might be.

He was trouble. No doubt about it.

"I'm sorry, Mr. Black, but I'd better—"

"Mr. Black?" Landon laughed loudly.

Setting my jaw, I turned away, but he grabbed my arm.

"Come on, Maggie. Just a few minutes."

Without waiting for a reply, he started to lead me over to his table. Adelaide had just joined Bobby there. She still wore her dance costume and looked a little worn, but she was beaming nonetheless.

"Hi there, honey," she said to me brightly. "Joining us for a drink?"

I felt keenly out of place, standing there in my oversized mission dress, sweaty and red-faced from work. These were a different kind of people from me. A savvy, older crowd. I was only a sixteen-year-old hostess, who until two months ago had lived in the same one-room house my entire life, hoeing carrots and baking bread. I didn't belong there.

"Have a seat," Landon said, pulling out a chair. "I'm tired just *watching* you clean this place."

He pressed on my shoulders, gently lowering me into the chair. "You've earned a break."

I'll stay for five minutes, I told myself. *Five minutes only.*

Connelly and Tom were occupied, but I still felt uneasy. I shot a glance at the high rollers' table. The men in the group looked serious as ever. Their whispered words rang in my ears.

Landon scraped the playing cards and multicolored poker chips away from the center of the table and stashed a half dozen empty shot glasses under his chair.

"Come on, Bobby. Get your vices off the table. We have a lady present."

Bobby snorted. "*My* vices?"

Swatting a hand through the air, Landon went to fetch a round of drinks. Whiskey for all of them and a glass of strawberry soda water for me. I wasn't sure whether to feel embarrassed or pleased that he had me pegged.

"You sure gave a great show tonight," Landon said to Adelaide, raising his glass in a toast.

She smiled. "Did you like the new opener, then?"

"Sure. You had us all going for a minute."

She gazed at Bobby, the longing clear in her eyes. "I was thinking of you the whole time."

Bobby tossed a quick look around, then planted a kiss on her neck.

"Careful," she said, somewhat sadly, pulling back.

I sipped my soda water, wondering what they had to be careful of.

"What'd you think of the show, Maggie?" Adelaide asked.

I'd barely watched it. I was too busy tracking the clandestine meeting taking place at the high rollers' table. "It was good."

Adelaide pursed her lips. "Aw, Mags, you still mad at me about last week?"

I squirmed. It hardly seemed appropriate to bring that up right in front of the men. The last thing I wanted was to conjure the image of me in my dripping-wet underclothes.

"I'm not angry," I said. "I—"

"I only wanted you to meet Bobby. Him and Landon just barely arrived. These boys only come into town for a few weeks in the spring. You understand, don't you?"

"I guess so."

"Look on the bright side," Bobby said, chuckling. "It made for a *very* memorable first meeting."

My face flushed with heat, and Adelaide gave him a pinch. "Oh, hush, you. Don't you mind these teasing fools, Maggie. Bobby really is a good man. Honest."

"I'll take your word on it," I said.

Landon laughed. "Take mine. Bobby Lopez is the biggest lush in three counties."

Bobby smacked his hat at Landon. "You're a fine one to talk. He may be just a kid, Maggie, but he drinks like a world-weary old man."

Adelaide laughed. "You see? These two roughnecks need some feminine charm to set 'em right."

I couldn't help but smile. Perhaps they were a little rough around the edges, but they certainly seemed like good people. And wasn't that what really mattered?

Adelaide called Smits over for another round of drinks.

"It's on me," she said, pulling a dollar from her garter belt. Bobby watched with raised eyebrows, and she winked at him. They laughed conspiratorially, their hands clasped under the table.

Just then, Mr. Connelly appeared out of nowhere. "What in the hell do you think you're doing?"

A jolt of ice passed through me until I realized he was talking to Adelaide. He ripped her hand out of Bobby's, yanking her to her feet.

"Take it easy," she said, trying to pull away.

Bobby had his hand on his gun in an instant, tense as a rattrap in his chair. Landon gripped Bobby's shoulder and shook his head once. Mr. Connelly stabbed his two cigar-pinching fingers at Adelaide, nearly poking her in the face.

"Unless this buck's payin', you'd better get your fancy little behind over to our *real* clients." He motioned to a table of well-dressed middle-aged men positively dripping with wealth. Connelly had set Adelaide's price far above the other girls at The Desert Rose. Only the high-end customers could afford her.

"I just sold you a full house with my dance back there," she said, glaring. "I think I've earned the right to a few drinks."

"There are plenty of men who'll buy you drinks, but not if they see you fawning all over this idiot. They're not paying to sleep with someone who's givin' it out for free." He lifted the black notebook with a tense hand. "In case you haven't noticed, we don't have money to throw away right now."

"I'm your biggest draw," Adelaide said, lifting her chin. "If it weren't for me, you'd *really* be broke. Think about that."

Mr. Connelly snorted. "And if it weren't for *me*, you'd still be a two-bit whore down at the depot."

I stared at him, stunned at the accusation. Only…Adelaide didn't deny it. She glared at him, furious, but a sheen of tears glinted in her eyes.

"You're a bastard."

"A bastard who's paying you to work," he said. "If you want a break, take one upstairs, on your back where you belong."

Bobby sprang from his chair, his eyes ablaze. He made a lunge for Mr. Connelly, but Landon pulled him back.

"Let go of me, you son of a— "

"Think who you're about to clobber," Landon whispered sharply.

And he was right. Connelly was essentially their boss. He had Álvar Castilla's ear and therefore the power to punish anyone who relied on the Haciendo for work. And these days, none of us could risk losing our jobs.

Connelly turned a look of disgust on Bobby and Landon. "If you boys want to spend time with one of my girls, you have to pay for it like everyone else." He then glared at me. "And last time I checked, I didn't hire you to sit around. This place is a pigsty. Get movin'."

Anger burned through me from my head to my toes. I stood sharply, not looking away from his gaze. He spoke again in a slow, threatening tone. "I said, get movin'."

I was about to give him a chunk of my mind to chew on when the doors to The Desert Rose flew open and a single gunshot blasted into the air. Silence tumbled through the room. The sheriff of Burning Mesa, James Leander, stepped onto the saloon's polished wood floors, accompanied by three of his rangers.

He lowered his pistol, which still smoked.

"Nobody move," he said, his voice loud but calm. "You're all under arrest."

CHAPTER EIGHT

Silence prevailed for a moment. Sheriff Leander was a thick, sun-baked man with white hair and a bushy white mustache that hung over his top lip. He looked every inch the kind of man you didn't trifle with. No one in the saloon moved, and yet everyone looked confused about what was going on. Everyone but me.

I darted a wide-eyed glance at the high rollers' table. Álvar was already off his chair, gliding over with casual charm, as if he were about to receive the sheriff in his sitting room.

"Ah, Sheriff Leander," he said. "What a pleasant surprise."

The sheriff's gaze swept over the confused faces, the innocent rounds of poker halted on tables. His brow furrowed as he looked back to Señor Castilla. "No games tonight, Álvar. I have it on good authority that a meeting of vigilantes is taking place in this very saloon, at this moment."

A soft murmur of voices rippled through the room. Glances

were exchanged. Álvar put a hand to his lips.

"This is most perplexing, Jim. As you can see, it's been a fairly typical weekend evening for us. Our star, Miss Price, gave an excellent performance—ask any man here. You should have seen it yourself."

Sheriff Leander glanced at Adelaide, still decked out in her costume. He looked again at the typical crowd of drunks and lonely miners. I wasn't sure what he'd been expecting to see here, but this wasn't it.

"Please come in." Álvar motioned to the table. "Have a bit of refreshment. We can discuss this source of yours, and why he or she might have misinformed you."

Sheriff Leander set his jaw but took a step farther in. Álvar turned back to the crowd, smiling in a reassuring way.

"The sheriff and I will have a talk. There is no reason you all cannot go back to your entertainments."

He turned to Eddie at the piano. "Edison," he said, "some lively music."

Eddie hit the keys, and the strains of "Three Gals in the Corn Crib" jingled in the air. Men scraped back into their chairs, and the hum of conversation slowly returned. As the sheriff took a cautious seat at a nearby table, Álvar motioned to me. "Miss Davis, why don't you bring our fine sheriff some of that excellent whiskey you served us earlier, hmm?"

Sheriff Leander gave me a long look. I was sure he could hear my pounding heartbeat, that he could tell I knew what was really going on here, could read it plain as day on my face. Heat crawled up my neck, tickling my hairline, but I didn't dare scratch. I tried to hold his gaze but couldn't.

"Young lady," he began. "May I have a word with—"

At that moment, Tom clanged a whiskey bottle on the tabletop. "For the sheriff." His eyes flashed at me. "And you. How many times do I have to tell you to get back there and finish those dishes?"

"I'm coming," I said, grateful for an exit.

I ran all the way to the kitchen and didn't look back. Tom followed, carrying his tray of dirty plates.

"Thanks," I said, when I was safe behind the door.

He dumped the dishes onto the pile. "I didn't do it for you."

He started arranging clean, empty shot glasses onto trays for Smits, clunking them down so hard, I was sure they'd shatter. It dawned on me all at once why he was so out of sorts. Tom had left the Apache camp as a young teenager, but still, it had to hurt deeply to see the war with his people unfolding.

"I'm sorry," I said softly.

"Sorry for what?" he snapped, clanging more glasses down.

"The fires. The captured Apaches. It can't be easy for you."

Silence. Then he swung around. "I'm not one of them anymore. Understand? Haven't been for years. So none of it matters to me."

I rolled up my sleeves and reached into the wash bucket. For a few moments, we worked in dense silence. I knew he didn't want to talk about it, but it mattered to me. I had to know.

"Tom, do you think they really are the ones burning the towns?"

"You don't?"

I dipped the soapy pan into the rinse bucket. "I think we need to find out more information. Maybe it isn't what it looks like."

Tom snorted. "Or maybe it is." He lifted the trays to carry out to the bar. "They're nothing like these folks here, Maggie."

"I don't believe they're all cold-blooded killers."

"Don't be swayed by your—" He stopped abruptly and pulled his gaze away from me.

"Swayed by my what?"

Tom set his jaw. "No more questions. I don't have nothing to do with the Apaches anymore. If you want answers, go ask them yourself. Ask the high and mighty Yahnuiyo."

The pan clattered to the floor. I blinked, scooped it back up, and then turned to Tom. "What did you say?"

"The Tribe Mother's oldest son," he said in a matter-of-fact tone.

I struggled for words. Could he possibly know about how Yahn had saved me?

Tom's eyes narrowed slightly, as if he were trying to read my face. It wasn't clear what he might know or not know. Finally he looked away from me and very slowly set the final shot glass on the tray. "He was one of the Apaches Sheriff Leander captured last night."

It took everything in me to wait until quitting time to sneak out. All I could think of was Yahn. When Connelly finally sent me to bed, I wasted no time pulling my shawl over my shoulders and slipping out my window.

The sheriff's office had a single lantern hanging in one window. Most of the deputies had either gone home or were out on the new heightened patrol. Only one man stood on guard. Everything hinged on that man being Sheriff Leander.

I breathed a sigh of relief to see him sitting at his desk, pouring over a map of the mining areas in the nearby Alkali Mountains.

"Evening, ma'am," he said, sitting up with surprise. "How can I help you at such an hour?"

My pulse throbbed in anticipation of what I was about to ask. "My name is Maggie Davis," I said, forestalling the inevitable.

"Pleasure to meet you." He waited for me to state my business.

I tried to swallow, but my throat felt dry as sand. "I come to offer a trade."

He was quiet, looking confused.

"You were right to try and single me out at the saloon earlier. I have the information you want."

Sheriff Leander frowned. "I'm listening."

I took a step closer, gripping my shawl tightly at my chest to keep myself together. "I can tell you what went on at The Desert Rose tonight."

Sheriff Leander looked at me a long time before speaking. "A meeting of vigilantes?"

I nodded. "With Álvar Castilla at the head."

He exhaled, rubbing the bridge of his nose wearily. Not the reaction I'd expected.

"Did you actually hear them discuss mob actions, Miss Davis?"

"Well..."

Apparently, that was the answer *he* expected. "Unless you have specifics, I'm afraid you're no more help to me than my previous source."

"But I heard them talking."

Sheriff Leander tried to smile. "Yes, and I appreciate you telling me. That's a real honest thing to do."

Panic gripped me. "But what about our trade? Will you still honor it?"

"What was it you wanted in exchange?"

My legs felt wobbly as a colt's. I took a slow breath. "I need to talk with one of your prisoners. An Apache you captured last night."

The room would have been silent if not for the throbbing of blood in my ears. Sheriff Leander frowned. "Miss, I'm not sure what on God's green earth you'd have to say to those Apaches, but regardless, it's out of the question."

"Please. I have to. It's very important."

"Would you mind telling me why?"

I pressed my lips together. Would he use the information about Yahn against him? Would it even make a difference? Regardless, there was no other choice but to share my story. "I'm a survivor of the Haydenville fire."

He stared at me. I definitely had his attention. So I told him about the night of the razing. I told him how Yahn had saved Ella and me and how he'd brought us to Burning Mesa. That he'd told me the Apaches had nothing to do with the fire.

When I finished, Sheriff Leander's expression was inscrutable. "I don't know exactly what happened that night, Miss Davis. But after yesterday's attack, how can any of us doubt their hand is behind these burnings?"

"That's exactly why I need to speak with him. I need to understand. Please, Sheriff. Give me the chance to understand what happened to my parents, to my home."

This seemed to hit a soft spot in him. He puffed out a breath, rubbed his face, and then stood. "You have five minutes. *Five*. And stay good and far back from the bars of that cell. I'm not going to be responsible for some kind of hostage situation."

I exhaled with relief. "Thank you, Sir. Truly."

I didn't breathe as I walked down the dark, narrow corridor

toward the holding cell. Maybe because I didn't know how I really felt. Nervous? Scared? Or excited? And then there it was ahead of me, lit by a single lantern.

Seeing Yahn again, behind the dark iron bars, made my stomach clench. All at once, I saw the little boy who'd been my only friend in the dusty schoolhouse. The young man who'd saved my life, Ella's life. Prison was the last place on Earth he should be.

The two other Apaches slept on the cell's benches, but Yahn sat awake, leaning forward, deep in thought. He looked tired. His clothes were singed, and his long hair had been pulled back behind his head, though strands of it hung down in his face. But even within the walls of a prison, there was a quiet dignity and strength about him.

As I stepped into the light, Yahn's face snapped up. Shock flashed in his eyes. He sprang to his feet, his body seeming to act of its own accord. "Maggie Davis."

I took a step closer to him, my heart pulsing in my throat.

"Why did you come?" Yahn asked. He stood against the edge of the cell, gripping the bars with both hands. "How did you know I was here?"

"I need to understand what's happening. I need you to be honest with me."

A shadow fell over his face. "I have been honest."

"Then how is it you were caught burning the excavators' camp last night? You were riding in to save *them*, too? And what about those others with you?"

He sighed. "It is as it seems."

"What do you mean?"

"My people wish to stop the mining of the Sacred Mountains, the desecration of the ancient sleeping bodies of the Sacred Ones.

To my people, it is the greatest of defilements to break apart the ancients' bones and sell them off. And it is blasphemy for a man to carry them about as if he owned them, to steal the sacred powers within for base, human uses. Some in our tribe would go to war to protect the Sacred Ones. They would be fierce and strong in fighting for our cause. It was these men who attacked the diggers' camp."

I stepped back, the breath taken from my lungs. "So it's true, then?"

"Only the attack last night," Yahn said, clenching his fists with frustration. "Kuruk and his men had no plan to attack the rest of your village. Only the fire at the diggers' camp. A warning."

"A warning that killed five excavators."

Yahn shook his head. "I told them not to do it, but the council agreed stronger action should be taken."

"And my home?" I asked, my voice choked. "Was that 'stronger action,' too?"

"My people were not responsible for the tragedy in Haydenville."

"Then why were you there both times?"

"I was out riding when I saw the flames. It was too late to save anyone in Haydenville, but I saw your home, still untouched, and I felt in my heart that I must act."

His words tore open the barely healed scars inside me. I took a shaky step backward.

Yahn gripped the bars again, his eyes intense. "Maggie. If I could have saved your family…"

"Who did it?" I asked, strained. "And why?"

He shook his head. "I do not know." But in his eyes, it looked like he might.

"How do you know it wasn't your men? How can you be *sure*?"

"The fire that burned your home was started with a great and terrible magic."

I could see the flames cutting across the sage and pine around our home, the fire destroying all in its path with unnatural speed.

"Not only would my people never use the bones of the Sacred Ones for our purposes, we would certainly never use ones that could wield a power so dark and consuming."

I backed away again. I had no words. My head felt numb and heavy.

Yahn reached his arm through the bars. "Please. You must believe me."

I said nothing, couldn't even if I'd wanted to.

"Maggie. My people are innocent. Do you not feel the truth burning inside of you?"

I looked into the liquid dark of his eyes. I knew almost nothing about him, only that he came from an entirely different world than I did, and yet I felt connected to him somehow. It went beyond the depth of my gratitude for his saving Ella and me. There was something more. Something I could barely grasp with the reaches of my mind. But I *did* feel the truth of his words burning inside me. That much was clear.

"I believe you," I said, my voice barely above a whisper.

Yahn exhaled, closing his eyes. "If only the rest of Burning Mesa did as well."

"No one even acknowledges the possibility that anyone else could be to blame."

"And we are partially responsible for this. Our actions have made us look guilty. It is something I wish Kuruk and his men would understand."

A dark thought came to me. "But while everyone is busy blaming the Apaches, the real villains walk free."

Yahn nodded grimly. "No one is safe until we find out who is truly responsible and stop them."

"But how do we do that?"

He shook his head.

"You were there the night my home burned," I insisted. "You must have seen something."

"Only the shadows of men. Nothing more."

I had no clues. No leads. The men could be anyone. Anywhere.

The scuff of Sheriff Leander's boots startled me like a shot. I wasn't ready; there was still so much more I needed to know. I grabbed the bars of the cell. "Yahn."

He gazed at me, helpless.

"Time's up, Miss Davis," Sheriff Leander said. He folded his arms across his chest, eyeing Yahn warily.

"I need a few more minutes, sir."

"Sorry, Maggie. It was a stretch to let you talk at all. These men are set to hang soon as we get the judge from Durango."

The words slammed against my chest, knocking the air from my lungs. "Hang?"

I looked to Yahn. He wasn't shocked. He met my gaze stoically, with maybe the slightest tinge of sadness. But for me, the room was spinning.

"No. No! You can't!"

"Miss Davis—"

"He's innocent! He had nothing to do with the burnings! He saved my life!"

Sheriff Leander had me by the arm. "You need to leave now."

"Let go of me!" I wrenched free and ran to Yahn. "They can't do this!"

"Miss Davis, I don't want to have to charge you for disorderly conduct."

Yahn closed his hand over mine. He shot a look at Sheriff Leander, then leaned close, speaking in a soft voice. "Go to the ruins of Haydenville. To your home. There must be proof there that my people are innocent."

Sheriff Leander grabbed my arm with force. "That's enough." His brow bent with anger as he dragged me down the corridor. "You crossed the line. And I was doing you a favor."

"You're not doing anyone a favor by hanging the wrong men."

"That's for the judge to decide."

The sheriff walked me all the way to the door before releasing his grip. He studied me with narrowed eyes. He was angry, yes, but he also looked concerned. "These are dangerous times, Miss Davis. I have the feeling this town is headed for big trouble, and I don't mean a razing. My advice to you is to stop poking around the rattler's nest. Keep to your work and stay away from trouble."

I struggled to appear calm in spite of the roiling emotions inside me. "Good evening, Sheriff. I apologize if I caused you any distress."

He gave me the same look Papa used to when I went riding on our horse Dusty alone. Perhaps Sheriff Leander wished I *were* his daughter, who he could order to stay at home and be safe. But I wasn't, and he couldn't. He may have thought it best that I kept my head down and stayed out of the way, but I knew differently. Yahn was right. As long as every lawman and vigilante in this town was focused on the Apaches, the *real* villains behind the burnings would be free to plan their next attack. I wasn't going to let that happen.

"Good night," I said again.

I stepped out into the moon-bathed street, heading back to The Desert Rose. Sheriff Leander stood in the lit doorway, a dark outline watching me. I couldn't tell if he would be my friend or foe in all of this, but it didn't much matter. I had made up my mind.

As I approached the window of my room to sneak in again, I spotted the shadowy figure of a man leaning against the wall. His horse pawed a hoof in the dust near my window. I froze in place, but it was too late. I'd been noticed.

Landon pushed back his hat. "Maggie."

"What are you doing here?" I asked.

"Looking for you. You plumb vanished after the sheriff showed up." A smirk crept onto his face. "Where'd you sneak off to so late?"

"That's none of your business," I said, tugging my shawl closer.

He laughed. "I wondered if there wasn't a little devil inside you, waiting to come out."

"It's nothing like that." I wasn't in the mood for his teasing. I had too much on my mind.

"Easy now. I only came to talk. That is, if you're finished with all your midnight shenanigans."

I strode past him haughtily. "If you're finished, I believe I'll go back to my room now."

He caught me by the arm. "Aw, don't be mad." Our faces were close. Too close. I struggled to get a grip of myself.

Mama hadn't taught me much in the way of courting and

accepting suitors; scraping out a living in the desert soil had taken all of our time. My experience with boys my age had been limited to a few clumsy two-steps at the various barn dances and spring flings or an occasional walk home from Sunday lessons. Jake DeMint had taken me for a ride to see his pa's new twin colts once, and I'd sat next to Harvey Bjornson at the talent show. All innocent moments between a boy and girl. But the way Landon looked at me was something else entirely. One part of me demanded I do whatever it took to discourage the advances of a boy like him. The other part of me…

Heat pulsed on the back of my neck. I looked away, determined not to let Landon see me blush.

"I can't figure you out," he said softly. "Sometimes you seem to want nothing to do with me, but then…the first time I met you…I saw a tiny glimpse behind that hard shell you wear."

I couldn't understand him, either. Was Landon really the roguish, flirting cowboy or the young man who searched for his dead mother in the stars? And would my heart be broken by the time I figured him out?

"I'm going now," I said, gently breaking away from his grip.

Landon let me go but stayed by my window, leaning against the wall. "I've been waiting here so long because I want to call on you tomorrow."

"You want to call on me?"

He nodded, smiling. I realized I must have sounded rather shocked and pleased, so I turned away. "I can't."

"Tomorrow is your day off, isn't it?"

"Yes, but I've already made plans."

"With that secret beau you've been sneaking off to see?"

"No!" I saw the laugh in his eyes and grimaced. "No. I have

something very important to do. That's all you need know."

Why was I refusing him? If I knew the *real* Landon would call on me, I did want to see him again. I scraped for words, something, anything to fill the pulsing silence. And then Landon reached for my shawl, which had slipped down on one side, and pulled it up around my shoulder. His hand lingered there. His fingers brushed through my hair for the smallest moment, just long enough to send a ripple of heat through me.

"Let me spend one day with you," he said softly. "Please?"

I exhaled a trembling breath. "All right."

"It's settled, then." Landon smiled. "I'll come by around nine."

He climbed on Titan's back. His gaze swept my face, and a smile pulled at his mouth. He tipped his hat. "Ma'am."

CHAPTER NINE

Landon arrived exactly on time. He'd combed his hair in a neat part. He wore his whitest shirt. And as he helped me into the front seat of his wagon, I smelled the spicy scent of nickel cologne from the general store.

I blushed, wishing dearly I hadn't worn my new dress, which the dancers' seamstress at The Desert Rose had sewn for me under Mr. Connelly's command. Apparently he was tired of seeing me walk around in "that darn ugly potato sack."

The new dress was a beautiful dark-wine color, and it fit the way a garment should, but the seamstress had cut the neckline in a deep square, and it certainly wasn't a dress I'd feel comfortable speaking to the pastor in. That was Mama's gauge for modesty. I swore I'd never wear the thing. I didn't need to offer those buzzards at the saloon another inch of my flesh to ogle.

And yet there I sat beside Landon, offering a fine display of myself. What on earth had possessed me to even think to put it on? But then Landon lashed the reins, and we lurched off at a fast clip.

As we rode along, the hot desert wind rushing past us, I remembered I had bigger things to worry about. Like how I was going to tell Ella that I wouldn't be spending my day with her. It was bad enough I could only visit once a week, and I knew how lonely she was at the mission. It broke my heart. But I simply didn't see how she could possibly be ready to go back to Haydenville. *I* wasn't even ready.

As I expected, Ella didn't take my abandonment too kindly. When I told her I was visiting Haydenville and she couldn't come along, she stared at me with a look of utter betrayal. Tears welled up in her eyes, and she ran off to fling herself on her bed. I tried to reason with her, but she wouldn't speak. Even when Landon made a joke, she only sniffled and shook her head. Just when I thought she and I were making progress, she seemed as heartbroken as she'd ever been.

I left the mission hurt and frustrated—not the best way to begin what would likely be an emotionally taxing afternoon. As we drew closer to the red-rock cliffs, my palms started sweating, and my head beat with dizziness. What would it feel like to walk on the charred ruins of my home? To know I could be stepping on the very place Mama or Papa or Jeb had died?

I was glad Ella had stayed back at the mission, safe from these memories. Mad at me or not, she shouldn't have to face this. Not yet.

When we came within a dozen yards from my home, I put my hand on Landon's arm. He pulled on the reins, bringing Titan to a stop.

"It's right down that hill," I said, staring at the sage-dotted red terrain, so familiar to me.

"You sure you want to do this?" Landon asked.

"No. But I have to."

Landon climbed out of the wagon, then held his hand out to help me down. I said nothing, just started to walk in the direction of home. Landon followed a few steps behind. It was a walk I'd taken a hundred times, though now it felt like foreign soil. My feet were iron weights. Every step shot through me like pain.

As I came around a gnarled old bristlecone pine, I could see it.

The house where I was born, where I'd taken my first steps, ridden my first horse, and read my first book. The place I played cowboy warriors with my brothers and sister, where I'd baked tart apple pies with Mama and picked strawberries with Papa, sneaking bites of the tastiest ones. It was gone. A vast patch of burned black. Nothing remained, not even a piece of framing or foundation. Everything had been destroyed.

I walked for a bit over the ruins, my vision a blur of charred darkness. I didn't know what I thought I'd find, and suddenly I wasn't sure why I'd come at all. I wanted to run away, but my body was heavy like a stone. Overcome by the awful silence, I could only stare at the scorched earth.

Then a warm, gentle arm came around my shoulders. The gesture forced a few tears from my eyes, though I tried to gulp them back. Without a word, Landon pulled me softly against his chest. We stayed in the tender embrace for a long time.

After a while, he coaxed me to sit on a boulder in the shade of a nearby pine and offered me a sip from his canteen. "It's awful," he said softly as I drank.

I wiped my lips on the edge of my sleeve and handed him back the canteen.

He shook his head. "Never seen anything like it."

The vastness of the destruction overwhelmed me. Nothing I'd read about compared to it. Not even the stories Papa would bring home from the Haydenville market during the Civil War days. They told of fire that burned groups of men, not entire towns.

I looked out at the ruins of my home. Whatever burned it clearly wasn't simple dragon bones. Most folks around here could barely afford the smallest relics. Who could possibly have one that powerful?

Landon ran a hand through his hair, deep in thought. "It's strange," he said. "I thought the whole reason we were fightin' those Apaches was because they don't believe in digging up and using relics."

"That is the reason," I replied quietly.

"It doesn't make sense."

My pulse quickened. I knew I should tell him about Yahn. I should tell him the Apaches were innocent. Somehow in that moment, I knew he would believe me.

"Landon, there's something you need to know." I told him everything. About the night of the razing. About Yahn. About my conversation with him in the jail cell. When I had finished, Landon was quiet for a while, staring at the ground.

"If that's true, then who burned Haydenville?"

"That's why I had to come back here. I have to find out who's *really* responsible before they strike again. Before they target Burning Mesa."

Landon cast a long look out at the ruins of my home. He didn't have to speak; I knew he agreed.

He shook his head. "Why Haydenville? Seemed like such a

quiet little town."

"It was. Mostly just farmers and miners." I scraped a toe in the sand, trying to put the vague pieces together in my mind. "We did have a spot of trouble about a year ago. A rival company of miners wanted to excavate our red-rock. They tried to sabotage the Haydenville miners. Lured a pack of ghost coyotes into their camp at night with fresh horse meat. My papa said twelve men were killed."

"Did they use fire relics?" Landon asked.

"I don't think so, but that doesn't mean they couldn't in a different attack. Maybe they came back to finish them off." Thoughts came rapidly. "Maybe that Mr. Bolger person is behind it."

Landon frowned. "Who?"

"Emerson Bolger. He's some kind of relic tycoon. Smits says he owns half the mining companies in the Territory."

"And?"

"Maybe he wanted the rights to our mining area, and when he couldn't get it, he used stronger force."

"And burned the entire town, killing dozens of innocent men and women in the process?"

"Maybe."

Landon sighed. "I don't know, Maggie."

We fell silent, both knowing it was a far-fetched idea. I stared out at the black smudge of ruin before us, feeling spent.

After a long pause, Landon spoke. "You know, now that I think of it, this fire reminds me of a bank robbery I saw in Durango last year." His gaze was far away. "You ever heard of the Chimera Gang?"

A cold shiver crawled over me. "Who hasn't?"

As soon as I spoke the words, the possibility in Landon's suggestion struck me like a rod. The Chimera Gang was the largest, most ruthless group of bandits, drifters, and outlaws in the entire Territory. Feared by the innocent. Hunted in vain by the authorities. They got their start robbing a train transporting a rare full chimera skeleton to the National Relic Depository in Washington. Needless to say, the attack went well for them. And since that day, with the chimera magic giving them the power to breathe fire, they had become the terror of the West. Exactly the kind of people who would burn an entire town.

"I can't believe I hadn't thought of them before," I said. I exhaled as snippets of stories and whispered rumors about the Chimera Gang swirled in my head. "It makes perfect sense!"

A grin pulled at his lips. "I can be useful from time to time."

"I suppose you can," I said, nudging him lightly with my shoulder. He chuckled, and in that moment, I had the strongest desire to kiss him. I contained the urge, figuring it was probably just the relief talking. No need to get carried away.

A strange cry suddenly echoed over the open desert. It was throaty and harsh, the sound of a wild animal. I jumped to my feet.

"Did you hear that?"

"It came from the cliffs," Landon said, standing, his pistols already out.

I stuck close to his side, my heart racing. "I think I know that call."

The growl came again, this time accompanied by the high whinny of a horse. And then a human scream. The sound cut through my body like a spear. I knew that voice.

It was Ella.

CHAPTER TEN

It couldn't be—she was safe back at the mission. And yet... I knew my sister's voice. I ran, one foot pounding after the next. Dodging around bushes and jumping over cactus and boulders. I could hear Landon calling my name, racing after me, but I couldn't stop. The sound of Ella's scream rang in my ears.

Landon's arms hooked around my waist, jerking me to a halt, nearly making us both tumble to the ground. "What in the devil are you doing?"

"Let go of me!" I shouted. "It's Ella; I heard her! She's in trouble!"

"Maggie, calm—"

The scream came again, undeniably that of a child. Landon's face went pale.

I pulled away and scrambled for the cliffs, nearly tripping on an embedded rock. The world around me blurred and shook. All I could hear was my own ragged breathing.

And then I saw her. Ella. She stood close to our old hiding cave, in a clearing that opened before the massive red-rock cliffs. She was struggling to hold on to the reins of a skinny brown mare, roughly saddled. And surrounding her on either side were two rock devils. The huge, spiny creatures slowly closed in, snapping their wide mouths open and shut.

It was like I had stepped into one of my own nightmares. For a blinding moment, I was frozen in place.

Landon slammed to a stop behind me. "Good Lord Almighty."

The two rock devils circled, sizing up their prey. In the white afternoon sun, they were barely visible. Their mottled, sand-colored skin blended into the landscape around them. One of the rock devils scratched forward a step, making a loud hiss with his rancid purple tongue.

I felt faint. Dizzy, I lurched toward my sister, but Landon grabbed my arm. With one hand he whipped his belt off and pressed the buckle into my hand. A polished gray-green stone gleamed in the center of the belt. Goblin bone. The heaviness of the earth relic pulled at me.

"You know how to use this?" he asked. I hesitated, but Landon was already squinting with one eye through the sights on his dragon-claw rifle. He held it with complete confidence, with his left hand resting against the gleaming curl of the embedded dragon relic. I couldn't help but marvel for a moment.

A panicked whinny pulled my attention back to Ella. The mare had reared up on her hind legs, terrified, and the rock devils hissed with rage, a burst of black spit flying from one of their mouths. The horse barely missed the acid-like poison, and Ella screamed. The sound of it wrenched my heart out. I had to go to her.

"Ella!"

In the same moment I screamed, Landon fired his rifle. The fireball scorched through the air, blinding, deafening. But my scream had alerted the rock devils, and they twisted around, enraged. The fireball exploded on the face of the red-rock. The sheer power of the rifle's shot paralyzed me.

"The belt!" Landon shouted. "Go now!"

Clinging to the goblin relic, I squeezed my eyes shut. *Be invisible. Please, be invisible.* A lurch pulsed through my legs, settling in my gut, as if I were gathering energy from the ground I stood on, from the very core of the earth. My skin tingled. When I opened my eyes and held up my hand, all I saw were the cliffs in front of me. It worked.

I ran to Ella. One rock devil scratched its claws toward Landon, but the other stayed back, creeping closer to my sister. I held my breath. The creature couldn't see me, but that didn't mean I wasn't scared out of my wits to run right past him.

Landon's gun blasted again, shooting the other rock devil. The burst of light and heat from the fireball nearly knocked me over, and Ella screamed again. The mare reared up, screeching out a raw, terrified whinny. But Ella held onto the reins, which only worked the animal up more. I couldn't get past her unless I wanted a kick to the head from its wild hooves.

"Let the mare go," I shouted.

Ella shot a frantic look around, trying to find my disembodied voice. But the rock devil heard me as well. He spit his black poison, missing me by less than a foot, and then crawled closer to Ella with a whip of his tail.

"NO!" I flung myself against the rock devil. His spiny skin scratched me, but in the moment, all that mattered was that I'd shoved the beast out of the path of my sister.

A garbled roar scraped through the air. Landon had the other rock devil's neck lassoed in his behemoth rope. He flung himself at a nearby tree, winding his end of the rope around the trunk. The snared rock devil flailed and roared like death. After a quick wipe of his face with his sleeve, Landon got on one knee and aimed his rifle.

Gripping the goblin belt with a trembling hand, I lunged toward my sister. We tumbled to the ground as the scorching flames blasted overhead. Ella cried out, feeling me but not seeing me. I'd probably scared her more than the rock devil, but there was no time to explain. All that mattered was she was invisible as well now.

Ella's fall broke her grip on the mare's reins. The horse flung her head around and began to tramp on the closest thing to her—the rock devil. He let out an enraged roar. His spiny tail lashed up like a whip, and a sharp animal shriek tore through the air. The blood from the mare's torn side sprayed all the way to my cheek. I pulled Ella's face against me to hide her eyes.

"Maggie!" Landon called. "Are you safe?" He scrambled down from the side of the hill. When he spotted the massacred mare, he skidded to a stop.

"Take cover," he shouted. "I'm gonna shoot!"

Cold surged through my veins. We were directly in the path of Landon's gun, and he couldn't see it. I scrambled to my feet, pulling my sister up with me. "We have to run!"

Ella spotted the torn-open mare and screamed in horror. The rock devil snapped his head in our direction and charged right at us. He opened his hideous, bloody jaws.

I grabbed Ella and lunged out of the way. We crashed to the

ground, tumbling apart on impact, and the belt flew from my hand. My head smacked against a rock. When my vision stopped spinning, my eyes fixed on the rock devil leaping in the air. His target: Ella, sprawled helpless on the sand.

My voice tore out of me. "Landon!"

The shot echoed against the red cliffs, shaking the ground, and a flash of fire burst in my eyes. I covered my face with my arms, turning away from the blast of heat. The wind from the explosion drove sand into my skin. After a moment of my heart pounding in my ears, I lifted my head.

The rock devil lay on the ground, weakly scraping his legs and making a garbled hissing noise. Black blood and smoke oozed from the gaping wound in his throat, which sizzled red hot. I blinked several times, hardly able to gather my thoughts together. My arms trembled as I pushed myself up, and a shot of pain seared through my side from where I'd rammed into the beast. I set my hand over the spot…and when I pulled it away, my fingers were smeared with blood. I swallowed hard, wiping them on my skirt. My legs shook, but I staggered forward.

"Ella? Ella, baby, you okay?"

Silence.

I cast my gaze in every direction of the smoldering ravine. "Where are you?"

Wind blew my hair across my face, but I didn't brush it away. "Ella?"

Then I heard Landon call my name.

Something caught in his voice. Something that sent a cold spear through me. Somehow I knew what it meant. I shot to my feet and found his gaze—his eyes were red, wide with anguish.

My voice faltered. "No."

Landon squeezed his eyes shut, and I stumbled over to him. "No," I said again, more firmly.

He knelt, partially hidden, behind a large crop of red-rock and brush. As I drew closer, I could see what he held in his arms.

Ella. Covered in blood. Her body still.

CHAPTER ELEVEN

"Give her to me," I demanded.

"Maggie—"

"Give her to me!"

I dropped down by Landon's side and pulled Ella's bloody body from his arms.

"Give her to me!" I screamed again, even though she was already in my lap.

Landon gripped my shoulder, his head hanging down. "I tried to save her."

"She's not dead," I said sharply. "Stop talking like that." I stared at Ella, a frantic energy overpowering me. It couldn't be. It couldn't. I'd promised her I would never let anything happen to her. She *had* to be all right.

Stubborn, *stubborn* Ella. I should have guessed she'd do something like this. If only I'd taken her with us. If only I hadn't left her at that barren mission, unsupervised and alone.

I pressed my fingers to Ella's throat beneath her chin. *Please, please, please.* But the beating of my own pulse made it too hard to distinguish anything. Trying to calm my throbbing head, I pulled Ella's body up and set my ear against her chest.

A few seconds passed. I held my breath. I squeezed my eyes shut.

Then I heard it: a faint beat, weak but still there.

"She's alive!" I shot up. "I can hear her heartbeat."

Landon's eyes lit with shock. "Are you sure?"

I nodded. Huge, sharp sobs filled my chest, and I held Ella to me. Landon released a gasping breath and pulled us both into an embrace. We held each other, the tension and terror of everything that had happened releasing in laughter.

When we broke apart, I saw tears on Landon's cheek. He tried to wipe them away, but I put my hand on his face. My heart burst to see him so touched.

"We need to get her back fast," I said, looking down at my sister.

Landon nodded. "I'll fetch the wagon." He set his dragon-claw rifle in my lap. When I blanched, he squeezed my hand.

"I'll be back before you can blink."

It was a relief to have Ella safe inside the grounds of St. Ignacio's, but at the same time, as she lay there in her worn little bed, I could see just how bad off she was. The nuns had given her a tiny bit of laudanum to ease the pain, and though she'd drifted into a fitful sleep, she was drenched with sweat, moaning and thrashing weakly on the sheets. I dabbed her head with a cool, damp cloth, but it didn't seem to help. Landon had left us to fetch a doctor, and it was just as well. Worry rested on me like a great rock, making it hard to breathe, let alone think straight.

My mood lightened a bit, however, when I heard Landon's footsteps coming down the hall. Before he entered, Adelaide burst in. She threw her arms around my neck, a gesture that surprised me but touched me all the same.

"Oh, Maggie. We came as soon as we heard."

Bobby stepped in, taking off his dark hat. He gazed at Ella with the pale, pained look of a man who'd seen one of his own family members lying wounded on a table.

Landon followed close behind. "Hope you don't mind these two tagging along. They were so worried when I told them."

"I'm glad you did," I said, squeezing Adelaide's hand.

"We came with help," she said.

Landon motioned to the door. "Maggie, this here's Moon John."

It was the expert from the refinery. The wrinkled old Chinese man and I shared a look of recognition.

"Thanks for coming," I managed in spite of my surprise. I wasn't sure whether his presence was a relief of not. Because as powerful as relic healing could be, I knew that it came at a steep price.

Moon John set his battered traveling case on the table beside Ella's bed. "The wound," he said, his voice soft. "Show me."

My hands shook as I pulled the sheet down to reveal the gashes in Ella's side. Adelaide stifled a gasp with her hand. Bobby put his arm around her, but he looked no better.

"It was a rock devil," I said, stroking Ella's forehead. "Attacked her this afternoon."

Moon John examined the wounds wordlessly. "The cuts go

deep," he finally said.

Landon paced, shuffling his hat back and forth between his hands, about near bending it in half. Watching him made me even tenser. When Moon John opened his case, I peered inside, where it was lined with a few dozen small glass bottles. The liquids glowed faintly in every color imaginable. I stared at them with fascination. "Medicine?"

"Relic elixirs," he said, his fingers brushing over the vials. "They mix two types of magic, using chips and tiny remnants left over from polishing and refinings. But they are not as strong as a solid piece."

"Are they very expensive?"

Moon John examined me again with his dark, penetrating gaze. "Yes."

My heart sank a little. "Please, sir, I'll give you everything I have."

Trembling inside, I ran for the tiny savings I'd put aside in the jar I kept in the sparse monastic cell. The money made a pathetic pile on the sheet.

"I know it's not enough. Not even close, but—"

Moon John set his wrinkled hand on mine and gave me a small smile. "There is more to this world than money."

I watched speechlessly as he selected a shimmering white bottle from his case, uncorked it, and tipped the liquid into Ella's parched mouth.

For the next five solid minutes, the room was so dead silent, you could have heard a mouse crawl across the floor. All eyes were fixed on Ella. No one dared to breathe too loudly. Or blink. Or move.

We all flinched with a start when Moon John clicked his case shut.

"Well?" Landon asked, gripping his crumpled hat with both hands. "Did it work?"

Moon John still watched Ella. He nodded slowly. "Perhaps."

Landon set his jaw. *"Perhaps?"*

"I told you relic elixirs might not be strong enough for this kind of healing."

His words send a cold stab through me. "But they usually work? They must work."

"Give the magic more time," the old man said, in what was probably an attempt to be reassuring.

"Sure," Adelaide said. "She'll be right as rain come morning, won't she, Moon John?"

He didn't meet my gaze. "Let us hope."

"She will be," Adelaide affirmed. "Thank goodness you came."

Her bright outlook felt strained, and the tension in her face read louder than her words. Maybe only because I felt that same desperation inside of me. I watched Moon John latch his case as if he were latching my final hope away with it.

He sensed my gaze. "Give the magic some time," he said again. "I will come back in the morning."

I nodded and took my sister's tiny hand in mine. She moaned softly, almost a whimper, and I kissed her clammy little palm. She had to be okay. She just had to be. I would never forgive myself otherwise.

I was partially aware of the others thanking Moon John and saying good-bye, but a dark haze seemed to shroud my head. I watched the aging man go, a slight limp in his left leg. As he reached the door, his eyes flicked to mine for a single moment, and then he left.

The rest of the evening passed in a numb haze. Landon, Adelaide, and Bobby stayed with me in the room, though few words were spoken. They dabbed Ella's head with wet rags and watched and waited. But nothing improved.

After Adelaide and Bobby bid a cautious good-bye, the room fell deathly still. Landon had drifted off to sleep, sitting in a chair on the other side of Ella's bed, his chin dipping into his chest. The candles burned low. Watching Ella's rattled breathing, the cold truth settled on me. The elixir hadn't worked. Ella wasn't getting better.

I brushed a sweaty lock of hair away from her forehead. There had to be something more we could do. But what?

The empty elixir bottle stared up at me from the nightstand by Ella's bed. All my life, I had been certain that relics could solve everything. I gripped the small glass bottle in my hand, wanting to crush it.

Then in my mind, I saw another relic. A gleaming spike of white and gold and lavender lying on the carpet of broken glass at the refinery. I remembered the warm, thrumming power it had sent rushing through me. There *was* a relic that could heal Ella, even if the elixir couldn't. And it was here in Burning Mesa.

I was on my feet, my pulse racing. All at once, I could see clearly what I needed to do. I would seek out the assistance of the only person who could save Ella.

Álvar Castilla.

CHAPTER TWELVE

Landon awoke early the next morning. The sun hadn't even risen yet, but pale blue light filtered in through the tiny window. He sat up with a sharp breath, as if he were startled to have fallen asleep. "Maggie?" he asked groggily.

"I'm here."

I was standing at the washbasin, pulling my hair into a long, dark braid. I hadn't slept a wink, but I didn't want him to know that.

Landon rubbed the sleep from his face. "Ella any better?"

I didn't look at him as I smoothed a stray lock of hair behind my ear. "I think so."

I had already decided I wouldn't tell Landon about my plans to throw myself at Señor Castilla's feet. He'd only feel angry or betrayed. Landon had done all he could, and I was deeply grateful, but it was time to take matters into my own hands.

"Are you going out?" he asked.

Still avoiding his gaze, I picked up a ratty shawl from the top of the bureau. Landon lifted to his feet. "Maggie."

"I'm going into town," I said, tightening my bootlaces. "The nuns will watch after Ella."

"What's in town?"

"Nothing you need to worry about." I turned for the door, but Landon grabbed my hand and pulled me to face him.

"Maggie."

"What?" I said, with more bite than I'd intended.

His soft blue eyes scanned my face, his expression so tender it made my throat choke up. He could see the pain. I think he knew I was about to do something rash. "Let me help you," he said softly.

"You have helped. But I can't ask you to do everything."

"Yes, you can."

"No." I pulled away from his grip. "There are some things you simply can't do."

His eyes darkened. "What things?"

"Oh, leave me be." I turned to the door, but it felt as if someone were making a fist around my throat. I paused with my back to Landon. "She's getting worse. Look at her."

In the dim sunlight, Ella looked as pale as the sheets she was covered with. Her little chest rose and fell with each strained breath.

Landon brushed his hand along her forehead. "There has to be some way to help her."

"There is," I said. "And that's why I have to leave." I turned my eyes on him. "Don't follow me."

He caught me by the waist, and with strong hands, he pulled me closer. Our faces only a breath apart, I could feel his heat on my skin. His lips hovered over my temples; his breath on my hair and skin sent tingles down my spine. I could feel his face tilt down, and I knew he was likely to try and kiss me.

My heart started to beat hard in my chest. I was so tired. So tired and afraid. And Landon's arms around me felt strong and safe. I turned my face into his warm neck. I wanted to stay there and hide from the whole world.

But the ache in my gut was still there. The worry still weighed in my chest. And somehow it felt wrong to ignore that.

"Good-bye," I whispered and ran from the room before he could stop me.

I left the Mission with only the flimsiest of plans. I didn't know how to find the famous Hacienda Señor Castilla called home, and I also knew visitors were almost never allowed past the Hacienda gates, especially not a nobody like me. But I knew someone who *did* know where the Hacienda was, and who *was* allowed past the gates.

As much as I cringed at the idea of asking Mr. Connelly for help, I didn't have many alternatives. My only hope was that my savings, tucked into my apron pocket, would entice him enough to help me out.

Wild black clouds brewed in the sky as I headed toward Burning Mesa, the wind picking up, sending tumbleweeds dancing across the open desert. There would be an afternoon thunderstorm for sure. I pulled my shawl tighter around me and picked up my pace. But as I entered the outskirts of town, I could see a different kind of tempest brewing.

The walkways were emptier than usual, and the housewives and old folks peeked down into the street from behind curtains, afraid. The raised voices of a crowd led me into the center of town.

And then I saw them. A mob of people, mostly men, teemed outside the sheriff's office. They waved their rifles and pistols in the air. A few had torches, even though it was morning. Their harsh voices rose in a single chant. "Justice! Justice! Justice!"

All at once, I remembered Sheriff's Leander's words. Yahn was set to hang.

My plan came crashing down like broken glass.

Hang.

I'd seen one public execution in my life, and at that moment, I relived it in my mind. Only this time, it was Yahn, not some faceless horse thief who'd been stealing Haydenville's best mares. Yahn's kind eyes watching me as the men led him onto the scaffolding, as they pulled the noose around his neck. Yahn's body dropping and jolting with shock as they released the trapdoor beneath his feet. In my mind, I watched Yahn die. Yahn, who had saved my life and Ella's, would die for a crime he never committed.

I couldn't let it happen.

Frantic, I dove into the heaving crowd. I had to stop them, had to get Sheriff Leander to call it off. This was no justice. This wouldn't save Burning Mesa. I had to tell the sheriff about the Chimera Gang—it was a lead, at least. Anything to make him see the Apaches might not be responsible.

As I drew closer to the sheriff's office, my eyes fell on a figure standing in shadow, watching at a distance from the crowd.

Álvar Castilla.

I stopped in my tracks, the noise and commotion of the crowd muting and blurring to nothing. All I could see was Ella, struggling for breath, clammy in her little bed. It didn't matter what level of humiliation or disgrace I would bring on myself in begging—I'd do it. Whatever it took to save my sister.

But then the noise of the mob seeped back into my consciousness like poison. Yahn. They would bring him out any moment. Bring him out to hang. Maybe I could quickly talk to Sheriff Leander, and then…

I looked back to Álvar. As if I were watching in slow motion, he turned away from the crowd and spoke a few words to his servant. Then they started to walk back toward his elegant carriage. He was leaving. I knew well how rarely he came into town—if I wanted to talk with him, I'd have to do so right then, before he left.

Again, I looked back to the sheriff's office, to the cruel mob chanting for justice, hungry for death.

I had to choose, and I had to choose right then. Yahn's life or Ella's.

My stomach roiled at the prospect. But as I closed my eyes, I knew there was really only one answer. I swallowed down the burn of tears and hoped that somehow, if Yahn's soul watched this moment later, he'd understand.

"Señor Castilla!" I shouted, rushing into the crowd. "Wait!"

But the noise of the mob drowned out my cry. They pushed against me as I tried to run to him, shouldering me aside, shoving me away. I thrashed my arms against them. "Let me past, you fools!"

Álvar stepped up into his carriage, clicking the little door shut behind him.

"No! Señor Castilla! Wait!"

I was almost to his carriage. Pushing a big brute of a man aside, I leapt for it. But the driver lashed his whip. "Hyah!"

"No!" I shouted. The driver didn't hear me. Or maybe he did, but he chose to ignore my cry. Álvar Castilla probably attracted desperate beggars on a daily basis. But I didn't want his money—I wanted something so much more important.

The clatter of horse hooves stirred up a cloud of red dust in my face. A burst of sandy wind choked my lungs. Coughing, I ran blindly after the carriage, my arm outstretched, the wheels spinning just in front of my fingertips. Blinking back sand, I noticed a little ledge made for luggage, tucked near the gilded thoroughbrace. I could reach it if I gave one good leap. But once the carriage moved beyond these crowded city streets, it would speed up, too fast for me to keep pace. It was now or never.

The rim of the wheel whirred before me. It was crazy to even *think* about doing this. I could fall on my face or trap my hands in the spokes of the wheel and be dragged across the desert. I could be caught, thrown into prison. Or worse.

But this was my last chance to save my sister, and anything was worth it for Ella. Drawing in a sharp breath, I kicked my feet off the ground and threw my body at the carriage.

My hands closed around the gilded rod attached to the ledge. For a blinding moment, I was hanging in midair, my feet scraping wildly beneath me. Then, with a burst of determination, I kicked them under me, and my shoes came down on the metal of the thoroughbrace.

My heart was pounding, my head spinning. I was sure my sweaty palms would slip right off the rod. As we pulled out of Burning Mesa and onto the dusty roads that stretched along the river, the carriage picked up speed until it shook and barreled down the path like a wild pig. My shawl slipped from my shoulders and flew off in a gust of wind. But I held on.

For my very life, I held on.

A flash of lightning lit the sky above me, followed by a rumbling *boom*. I looked up at the angry sky, then back at the bulge on the horizon that was Burning Mesa. Maybe the rain would postpone Yahn's hanging. If only.

Squeezing my eyes shut, I turned away. I couldn't think about that, not until I'd dealt with saving Ella. Then I would face the consequences of my choice.

A cool wind picked up, and then, sure as sunrise, the rain followed. It broke from the black clouds above, falling with a breath of wind, smelling of wet desert grass and dust. A hearty downpour to make up for the dry weeks we'd had. As I clung to the bounding carriage, rain streaking down my neck and back, I marveled at how far my desperation had taken me.

By the time the carriage driver called for the horses to slow, I was soaked through. My arms trembled from gripping the rod so long, and my legs were weak. I tried to peer through the workings of the carriage to get a glimpse of the Hacienda. All I could see was a flash of green treetops and a tall outer gate.

The carriage driver called out in Spanish. A few responses drifted through the air, and the gate creaked open with a low groan. My heart was beating in my throat, and I pressed as close to the carriage as I could. *Please, please, please.* The carriage slowed even more. Then the horses' hooves clicked on a stone pathway. We were entering the grounds.

The fence passed by. I was frozen, trembling. But the two guards were occupied with pulling the wide gateway shut as fast as possible and getting out of the downpour. They didn't so much as glance back at the carriage.

The driver pulled to a stop in a vast, tree-dotted courtyard.

Bushes with bright, sweet-smelling flowers colored the brick pathway, which probably led to the house, but I couldn't see much from where I sat. Two men ran up with umbrellas, and the weight of the carriage shifted as Álvar Castilla stepped out.

I had to act quickly. But by the time I'd pried myself off the ledge and jumped down, Álvar and the two men holding their umbrellas over his head were already rushing through the rain to the glorious scene. The walls of the Hacienda surrounded more than a single home—it looked more like a village, with a gleaming white mansion at the center. For a single moment, the grandeur of the scene stopped me cold. But then my eyes fell on Álvar, getting farther away in his dash from the rain. I made a run for him.

That was, until a pair of rough hands grabbed me by the shoulders and spun me around.

"Gotcha!" It was the carriage driver.

"I can explain," I said, breathlessly, my heart racing from being startled.

"I'm sure," he said. He was a rough-looking man with small, pitiless eyes.

"Please, I need to talk with Señor Castilla right away. It's urgent."

"That's what they all say, sister." He tugged my arm. "Save it for the Captain of the Guard."

CHAPTER THIRTEEN

Nightfall found me still in the holding cell of the Hacienda's guard station. I had spoken with neither the Captain of the Guard nor Álvar Castilla. I was cold and hungry and worried sick about Ella, plus wracked with guilt that I might have sacrificed Yahn's life for nothing. That thought, more than anything else, knotted in me like a great, tough root, fiercely cutting through the soft flesh of my insides.

Errant rain slid down the bars and dripped from one spot in the ceiling. A puddle of water had carved its place in the ground where the drip landed. The guard had finally grown tired of hearing me holler about why I needed to talk with Señor Castilla, and he'd gone to go smoke with the others by the doorway.

I couldn't sit on the dirt floor—the last thing I needed was to look a muddy mess. It was bad enough that I was wet as a river rat. So I paced the cell.

A laugh from the guards drew my attention. They were looking at me, smirking. One spoke a few words in Spanish, and they all laughed again. I turned my face away from their mockery.

"Do not be mad," the guard said, his brown eyes filled with false innocence. "We only wanted to know if you'd like to get out of those wet clothes."

I stiffened but didn't look up as they laughed. Out of the corner of my eye, I could see the guard step closer.

"Miguel thinks you might have Creolla blood in you, so we want to give you a proper inspection."

"What do you say, señorita?" another guard said, grinning. "We'll let you go if we confirm you're one of us."

"You leave me alone," I said, mustering all the venom I could manage when my insides were quaking like a leaf. "I'm not one of your kind."

"You sure? With that dark hair, and that shade to your skin… you don't look like the other whores at The Desert Rose."

"I'm no whore."

"So she's not a Creolla, eh?" the guard said, smirking. "Then she must be a stinking Apache!"

The men all laughed, goading him on.

"She ought to hang!"

"I'll see you arrested by the sheriff if you so much as come near me," I shouted.

The biggest of the guards smiled. "The sheriff has no power at the Hacienda. *We* are in charge here. What a shame you are not one of us."

The bigger guard pulled his iron key ring from his pocket and dangled it in the air. I backed up slowly, not that there was far to go in that tiny cell.

"I think a full inspection is in order. Just to make sure."

My back was to the wall, my heart rattling inside my chest. "Leave me be!"

He pushed the key into the lock. "I'm afraid not, señorita."

"Norega."

The voice of Álvar Castilla shot through the room like a Smith & Wesson. Everyone spun around to see him in the doorway, illuminated by lamplight.

The bigger guard, Norega, went stiff as a pole. "Señor Castilla."

Álvar stepped into the room, his elegant face bent more sternly than I'd ever seen. He pulled the keys from Norega's hand. "Get these no-accounts out of here," he said to the guards who followed behind him. "I want them on suspension without pay."

My heart was still pounding when Álvar turned his attention back to me. He hurried to unlock the cell door and pull it open. "My deepest apologies, Miss Davis. I had no idea it was you my carriage driver apprehended. Had I known, I would have come much sooner. And I certainly wouldn't have allowed you to be treated this way."

Maybe it was the tension from the guard's threat or exhaustion and despair from the last forty-eight hours—or maybe it was relief at finally being face-to-face with him—but that small show of kindness pushed the tears from my eyes. I swallowed down a sob like a rock in my throat and quickly wiped the tears away.

"Dios mio," Álvar said, sounding genuinely sorrowful. "This distresses me greatly, Miss Davis. But I shall make it up to you, I swear it. Come. Let me show you the full hospitality of my estate. I will get you a warm meal, some dry clothes—"

"No, señor," I said. "Please, I came because I *must* speak with you."

He looked surprised. "But of course."

"It's my sister. My baby sister, Ella. She was attacked by a rock devil yesterday. We tried everything, but she's dying, you see, and there's only one thing that can save her." I fell to my knees, clutching the leg of Álvar's pants with one hand. "I beg of you, señor. Your unicorn relic is the only way she'll live."

"Miss Davis," Álvar said, trying to get me to stand.

"I'll give you all of my money," I said, squeezing my eyes shut, unable to see him refuse. "I'll work for a year without pay. I'll do anything! Anything you ask!"

He lifted me by my shoulders, forcing me to stand before him. "Miss Davis. Please."

Pain surged through my chest. I couldn't bear to look at him as he turned me away. But then his hand set under my chin, and when I looked up, his gaze was warm.

"I saw from the first day I met you that you had spirit. And knowing that you rode on the back of my carriage in a lightning storm to speak with me only confirms this."

I blinked, not breathing.

Álvar nodded to his two men. "Go fetch Miss Davis's sister."

"You'll help me?"

He flashed an easy smile. "What use is all the money and power in the world if it can't be used to save one small girl?"

Ella looked like she walked in the shadow of Death himself as they laid her on the table in the Grand Hall. All the color had slid from her cheeks; the only hue to break the paper paleness of her face was the red that rimmed her eyes. Damp hair clung to her skin, and her limbs hung limp, as if she were already dead. I fell down by her side, gripping her hand.

"Uncover the wound," Álvar said, coming to her other side.

My fingers trembled as they pulled the bloodied bandages away. The three gashes had swollen on Ella's small belly. The skin around it was a sickly purplish-red, tinged with white pus. *Please help her,* I thought, over and over. *Please, God, let her be saved.*

Álvar removed his fine red-and-gold jacket and rolled up the sleeves of his white undershirt. All the while, his eyes stayed on Ella. Then he held out a hand, and one of his servants laid the unicorn horn in his palm. The polished bone gleamed with iridescent shimmers of lavender and gold. A true sight to behold.

Álvar lowered the tip of the horn over Ella's bare torso. He hesitated for a single moment, then looked up. "Miss Davis."

His hand was stretched out to mine. Trembling and unsure what he wanted, I didn't move. He nodded once, as if to say it would be okay, and took my hand. The weight of the earth magic settled over me, stronger than anything I'd felt before. Álvar gave me a sidelong, analyzing look, as if he could somehow sense my reaction to it. Then his eyes closed.

The tip set against Ella's skin. As Álvar and I concentrated, the horn began to glow like the sun slowly cresting over a mountain. It gleamed tenfold times brighter than when I'd seen it the first time, a brilliant blaze of pure light.

I held my breath, my eyes moving from the glittering relic to Ella's wound. Silence prevailed. I counted ten pulsing seconds, but nothing happened. Ella didn't budge, and her injury looked as bad as ever. Despair crashed into me. It had gone too far. She was beyond help.

Then her body twitched.

The movement sent a current of raw hope through me. Álvar pushed the tip of the horn harder against her, and suddenly Ella drew in a huge gasp, like someone who had been held underwater too long. Her back arched, and her head snapped back. Watching in horror, I had a flash of a thought that he'd somehow killed her. But then she exhaled deeply, and her body straightened back to normal. It was as if she were letting all the injury out of her with that breath. It ended in a shudder, and then she was still.

No one in the room moved or spoke. No one even blinked. We all stared at the wound on Ella's frail little body. Perhaps my weary mind had started to play tricks on me, but as I watched, a healthy color started to seep into the skin. Ella's breathing steadied, and her cheeks looked flushed. She was healing.

Relief could be a strange thing. In spite of everything that had happened to me in the past two days, I'd never felt more drained than in that moment, watching her heal. I slunk back and would have lost my footing if a servant hadn't been there to prop me up.

Álvar set his hand on Ella's head with a satisfied nod. I could barely stand, let alone form the words in my mouth.

"Señor…" I fell to my knees before him and pressed my lips to his hand, again and again. "Thank you." My voice was little more than a whisper.

"Please," he said. He lifted me to my feet and put a hand on my cheek. "I insist that you and your sister stay as my guests tonight to recover."

They put us on one of the most comfortable beds I had ever set a hand to, in one of the most beautiful rooms I'd ever seen, but I didn't dare sleep. I sat up, watching Ella in the candlelight. It filled me with unspeakable relief to know she was safe now, but heaviness still hung over my heart.

I knew that I owed Ella's life not just to Álvar but also to another. I owed it to Yahn.

The brave man who'd brought us through the flames that killed my parents. He'd taken a risk to save us. And when the moment came to repay that debt, I'd chosen differently.

I didn't allow myself to envision his unjust death. I pushed any vision of it away before it even formed in my mind. But the awareness still burned a hole in me.

If there had been any other way, any other choice.

Forgive me, Yahn. Forgive me.

I gazed at Ella, stroking her forehead. If only I knew for certain that Yahn's sacrifice would purchase Ella a long, happy life. But doubts and fears still clouded my heart.

I had come so close to losing her. Who was to say it wouldn't happen again?

Even now, with Ella finally healed and no chance of any rock devils creeping about in this spacious room, I didn't want to stop watching her. I could see plainly how fragile it all was. How in a single, flashing moment, everything you love could be taken from you. Tomorrow I could lose her again. Or the next day. She could fall off a horse and snap her neck in an instant. Or catch pneumonia like Josiah. Or burn in a town razing.

I pressed my face against the soft white pillow. I knew that I would die to protect my sister, but what if she died because I *couldn't*? The heaviness of my task weighed upon me. Tomorrow we would return to the mission, to uncertainty. I should have been elated with Ella's recovery, but instead, I drifted off to a fitful sleep wondering what the next danger would be, when it would come, and if I would be able to save my sister when it did.

CHAPTER FOURTEEN

A small hand on my cheek awoke me. My eyes shot open with a start, then immediately fell on Ella's face. Her large brown eyes watched me. She looked pale, but the pained grimace was gone.

"Maggie?" she whispered. "Where are we?"

I sat up, my heart bursting to see her well again. "It's good to see you awake. How are you feeling?"

"Better." She looked around the room with an awed grin. "Do we get to stay here for a while? I hope so."

A soft knock came at the door. "Breakfast, miss," the voice behind it said.

I suddenly felt a little sheepish. I didn't belong here, in this elegant white nightgown, sleeping in this fine room, and now they were bringing me breakfast in bed. The servant didn't wait for my reply, which was good, since I probably would have politely refused. She carried in a silver tray with two lidded plates, tea service, and a twist of blue and yellow flowers. The sharp floral fragrance drifted over the savory smells of breakfast.

Ella eagerly grabbed for her plates, lifting the lid with a gush of bacon-scented steam. I picked the intricate bunch of flowers from the tray. The petals shimmered like gems and danced, as if on a breeze of their own making. They had to have been created by relic magic. My mind went to Álvar's dryad ring. Had he made this with his own hand?

The servant girl gave me a single swift glance, then dropped her gaze. "Can I get you anything else, miss?"

I put the flowers down. "No. Thank you, though. My sister and I will be leaving as soon as we dress."

The girl slipped a crisp white envelope from her front apron pocket. "From Señor Castilla, miss."

"What is it?"

"I don't know, miss." The servant girl curtsied. "Good day, miss."

"Good day."

I turned the envelope over. Ella gave me a look, her mouth full of eggs and buttered bread.

"Well, aren't you gonna open it?"

A quick slip of my breakfast knife along the rim, and the envelope flapped open. The paper inside felt expensive. The ink had a slight sheen of gold. I didn't breathe as I read the elegantly written words.

Miss Davis,

I still feel deeply ashamed of the way you were treated last night on my own estate. While helping your young sister pleased me greatly, I wish to offer more. Please accept my invitation to stay here in my family's home until you and your sister are fully rested and recovered.

Also, I would like to beg the pleasure of your company at a little soiree I'm having here tonight with some of my close friends. You have been through a great ordeal, and you deserve some enjoyment.

With warmest regards,

Álvar

I read the letter three more times. Me? Invited to some party with these rich Hacienda folk? I was as likely to fit in there as a cow in the sheep herd. Why would Álvar even ask me? Besides, after everything that had happened, it didn't feel right to go dance the night away.

Another fist rapped against the door, and again, a strange woman entered without waiting for a response. She was a plump and sharp-looking Haciendella with raven hair pulled in a tight bun.

"I'm Flora," she said, her skirt swishing as she swept into the room. "I'm here to measure you for your gown."

I blinked. "My gown?"

"For tonight. Señor has requested one be made specially for you."

Heat rushed to my cheeks. I felt Ella looking at me, and I pressed my hand harder over Álvar's letter.

"I don't think I'll be attending, ma'am. You see, my sister and I have been through a lot. I think we should be leaving as soon as—"

"Señor Castilla desires your presence at the party tonight."

"And I appreciate that, but I need to take care of my family first, and—"

"One would think a girl of your station would not only accept such an invitation, but would be deeply honored as well."

A snap of anger flared within me. "A girl of my station?"

"Come, come, I don't have all day. And I must say," Flora said, her eyes flickering with disapproval, "I am shocked you are being so fussy. After the service señor rendered to you last night?"

"I am very grateful to him, ma'am. And I plan to repay him with every penny I earn—"

"Señor Castilla does not need your money, you stupid girl. For whatever reason, which I am sure is lost on me, he wishes for you to be among his many fine and important guests tonight. If you are truly grateful, you would not even think of insulting him with a refusal."

My face burned to my ears. I didn't want to go, and I didn't understand why he wished me there, either, but I certainly didn't want to insult him. Not when I owed him so very much.

"I'm sorry," I said, lowering my gaze. "I didn't think of it that way. Please tell Señor Castilla that I will attend tonight."

"I don't need to tell him—he never assumed anything less. That's the way these great men are, miss, and you'd do well to remember that. Now stand up and let me get your measurements."

Shortly after we'd finished our breakfast, two nurses came in to tend to Ella, while Flora and her crew whisked me off. I would have refused to part with her, but they brought a small, happy gaggle of Hacienda children with them, and Ella's face lit up so brightly at the sight of other kids her age that my heart nearly broke. She turned a pleading look on me, and I couldn't deny her a day in their laughing, easy company. It would be so much more pleasant than the nuns at St. Ignacio's could offer, generous as they were.

As soon as they'd gone, a team of female Hacienda servants swept in. They eyed me grimly and discussed what a task they had on their hands right in front of me. The grooming regimen lasted several hours and included a long soak in a rosewater bath, where my hair and body were scrubbed clean. They dried me, lathered me in perfumed powders and oils, and then brushed my dark hair by an open fire until it shone like ink. Not at all accustomed to such luxury and relaxation, I dozed off more than once, awakening as the maids giggled into their hands.

In the late afternoon, Flora returned with my gown. When I laid eyes on it, I drew in an involuntary gasp. Flowing chiffon of silver, white, and gold glittered to the floor like a cloud. And behind the corseted top, attached to the thin sleeves, two ruffles of luxurious taffeta—the faintest suggestion of fairy wings.

It was the height of fashion to wear a gown designed to emulate the ancient fantasy creatures; all the women in Paris and New York City owned one. Mama said it was for vain, upper-crust types who wanted to fancy themselves a walking relic. I stroked the shimmering fabric. I'd never so much as come near a dress that grand, let alone put one on. It was a gown for a woman—a fine, wealthy woman. It didn't belong on a no-account girl like me.

"It's beautiful," I said in a hushed voice.

Flora shrugged as if she didn't care, but I saw a glint of pride in her eyes. "Señor requested the design." She laid the dress on the bed and stood back to examine me. "You'll need proper petticoats. And a corset is a must."

When I looked hesitant, Flora snorted.

"I don't suppose a girl of your station has ever worn one before, but no matter. We'll get some curves out of you tonight."

By dark, they had squeezed me into the corset, poked and prodded and pulled at my hair, powdered my face, rouged my lips and cheeks, and generally fussed over me. I tried to relish the moment, seeing as how such pampering would likely never happen to me again, but a distressing image had begun to gnaw a hole in me—the picture of myself tromping into that Grand Ballroom. What would I say? Where would I stand? How on earth was I going to avoid looking like the biggest bumpkin ever to step foot through the Hacienda's gates?

But then Flora marched me over to the tall oval mirror that stood in the corner of the room. I hadn't caught so much as a glimpse of myself all day. I wasn't prepared to see the young woman peering back at me in the glass.

The dress really did the magic—I almost wondered if there were some kind of actual relic sewn into the fabric. It shone slightly in the golden lamplight and hugged the new hourglass curves of my body. The little lace sleeves hung down, leaving my shoulders bare, and the neckline scooped elegantly to reveal more bosom than I ever imagined I'd show. And yet, with the perfume and delicate jewel choker around my throat, I didn't mind.

My hair had been pulled up into an elegant curled style, though a few strategic tendrils hung down around my neck. Three pins of white crystal were tucked into my piled hair, bringing a flash of shimmer and beauty. With white gloves to complete the look, I could almost imagine myself as an ethereal fairy, soaring on the wind. I stared at my reflection with hushed amazement. This wasn't me. This couldn't be me.

"You clean up well," Flora said, scrutinizing me with folded arms. "Almost like a Haciendella. I think señor will be pleased."

The mention of Álvar pulled me away from the fantasy of fancy dresses and brought me back to reality. "Oh, Miss Flora," I said, turning away from the mirror, "I do love the dress, I really do. And you all worked so hard to make me look pretty. But I don't see how I won't make a darn fool of myself tonight. I don't know anything about this sort of party! Or these people."

Flora smiled a little and patted my cheek once. "There, there. It is simple. Just be charming and sparkling and witty, and you will come out fine."

"Should be a simple task for a girl of my station."

Flora raised an eyebrow at my retort, but at that moment, a male servant dressed in finery stepped through the door.

"I am to take Miss Davis down to the ballroom now."

I was sure the color drained right from my face. Flora smirked. "Have a wonderful time."

The servant motioned to the hallway, and I suddenly reckoned I knew just how the lamb felt as she was being led to the slaughter.

CHAPTER FIFTEEN

The music from the Grand Ballroom wafted through the hallway like perfume, mingled with muffled laughter and conversation. It sounded like there were a great deal of people at the party, which was good. The bigger the crowd, the more easily I could sink into the background unnoticed.

I caught my servant escort giving me a sidelong glance, and he snapped his gaze away. With every step, the magic of that moment in front of the mirror dissolved, leaving me to see exactly what I'd gotten myself into. I'd been primped and painted and dolled up like a fine horse on display. The dress was far too gaudy and *far* too revealing. Mama would have taken a lash to my behind if she'd ever seen me showing so much skin. I had half a mind to march right back to that room and take it all off when the servant paused before two enormous, elaborate double doors.

"Right in here, miss."

The doors swung open, and I was powerless to stop them. All at once, a flash of color and a swirl of music and voices gushed against me like a blast of wind.

The Grand Ballroom.

Grand, indeed. I'd never seen a finer room. It was round and two stories high, with coral-colored marble columns rising from various points, each one carved in the massive, breathtaking form of an ancient creature. Here a dragon with stone wings folded high. There a watery siren with arms stretched as if holding up the ceiling. And of course, a unicorn eternally rearing up on his massive hind legs.

A mezzanine ran around the expanse of the entire room, where guests mingled and danced. The walls around the outside of the room weren't actually walls but enormous windows that displayed a star-glittered sky. Rich red silk draped over everything, and elegant greenery bloomed from marble vases. There were tables upon tables of fine food and benches where ladies sat in conversation, cooling themselves with elaborate lace fans that probably cost more than I made in a month. The orchestra sat near the back, playing an airy Spanish tune. And in the center of the room, elegant men and women dressed in splashes of color and finery danced together.

For a moment, my feet were nailed to the marble floor. I could have watched from right there all night, but the servant cleared his throat and motioned me in with a white-gloved hand. "Señorita?"

"Yes. Thank you." I stepped in. My heart was pounding hard against my chest, no doubt accentuated because that awful corset pressed it down. I darted my eyes around me as I walked, not knowing where to go or what I was supposed to do.

Then I spotted Álvar, surrounded by a crowd of people. He

looked dashing and elegant, as always. He wasn't wearing his usual Spanish regalia—a high-collared red coat with gold-rope trim—but instead a pair of sleek black pants and a coat with tails, a white shirt, and a crisp white tie. The people around him, beautiful Haciendellas and handsome young Haciendos, laughed easily at his words and sipped champagne from fluted crystal glasses, already tipsy. There were many older, distinguished Haciendo folk there, but I could see at once that the young would set the tone for the evening.

I admired the glamorous, exciting company around Álvar. The Haciendellas wore gowns that were even more beautiful and lavish than mine with an air that anything less wouldn't be worthy of them. Their raven hair and sparkling brown eyes set off the lovely olive tone of their skin. I had heard of the beauty of the Hacienda's women before, but they so rarely ventured into Burning Mesa that I had never seen one.

Álvar stroked the bejeweled throat of one particularly beautiful Haciendella, whispering in her ear. His wealthy fiancée, perhaps? But even as I wondered this, another of the young Haciendellas flung herself at his side with a laugh. He hooked his arm around her waist and kissed her cheek. No one seemed ruffled by his casual promiscuity.

I was about to stop gawking when Álvar looked up, and his eyes connected with mine. He appraised me, a smile spreading over his face, then lifted his champagne glass in a little toast. I supposed the dress pleased him. I smiled and gave an awkward curtsy. Álvar clearly knew how to throw a girl off sorts.

At that moment, a spindly man in all white stepped onto the center of the dance floor. "Choose your partners for the *vals vuelo de España*!" he announced.

The audience cheered. I didn't know what the *vals vuelo de España* was, but my two left feet weren't about to find out. As I made my way to the sidelines, however, a bearded Haciendo with streaks of silver in his black hair stepped into my path.

"I do not believe we have met, señorita." He bowed low gallantly. "I am Señor Ernaldo Vasquez."

"Maggie Davis," I said, dipping in another curtsy and wishing dearly I'd had more training in ladylike conduct.

"Encantado," Señor Vasquez said, kissing my hand once.

"Thank you."

"Miss Davis, would you do me the honor of dancing the *vals vuelo*?"

Darn it if I couldn't feel my face turning red yet again. "Thank you, sir, but I'm afraid I can't."

"Why ever not?"

"Well, for starters, I don't know this dance at all, but also—"

"There is nothing to it," he said, grinning. "I shall do all the leading. Besides, you are dressed for the part."

"Sir, I—"

But he was already walking me into the center of the room. I remembered what Flora the dressmaker said about "great men" and realized I didn't have much of a choice.

I felt people watching as we stepped into place among the other dancers. Probably wondering who on earth I was and what I was doing at such a swanky Hacienda affair. Álvar swept a gorgeous Haciendella in a red-and-black dragon gown to the center of the floor. Just *walking* they looked graceful. *These* were the kind of people who should be dancing some fancy Spanish dance, not me.

Señor Vasquez gave me an amused smile, and I knew I was

wearing my discomfort on my face. "Relax, señorita," he said. "It is quite enjoyable."

"We'll see if you still say that after I've stepped on your feet half a dozen times."

Señor Vasquez laughed heartily. "You have indeed never danced this before. Trust me when I say stepping on my feet shall not be a problem."

Before I could ask what he meant, the violins struck a fierce chord. A line of suited servants glided out with trays held at eye level. The audience, apparently knowing what to expect, applauded with delight. For some reason, this made me very uneasy.

A servant stopped before each couple on the dance floor and lowered his tray. On each one sat a small glass case filled with shimmering rainbow-hued powder.

"¿Con permiso?" the servant before us asked, bowing low.

I shot an uncertain look at Señor Vasquez, and he nodded with a smile.

The servant opened the case and, with a gloved hand, grabbed a pinch of the shimmering powder. Before I could blink, the dust was a puff in the air around Señor Vasquez and me. My arms and dress and hair twinkled like sunlight on the surface of a lake. A light, flickering sensation blew through my insides. All at once, my surroundings seemed sharper, more clearly drawn, as if every detail in the room tingled through me.

It was sky magic.

A faint chime rang in my ears, something both musical and almost human. Like singing and wind and sunshine.

"What is this?" I whispered to Señor Vasquez, not sure whether I was excited or terrified.

"Fairy relic powder. Very rare. Very expensive."

Now I could see why he said I was dressed for the part. I twisted my shimmering hand in front of me. "What will it do?"

A second herald of the violins drowned out my question. The dance had begun.

Señor Vasquez winked once, and suddenly, I felt my feet lifting from the floor.

Exhilaration. Terror. Disbelief. My body shifted through the emotions with rapid speed as Señor Vasquez gently pulled us higher into the air along with the other couples. I clung to his hands, white-knuckled, sure my life depended on it.

He laughed at my expression. "Do not worry, señorita. You will not fall."

Below us, the applauding guests blurred and doubled in my eyes. My feet dangled in the air, and I felt as if I weighed no more than a snowflake. I let out a shaky breath. "I'm trusting you, sir."

"Try to enjoy it," he said. "Look. See how beautiful."

Indeed, it was a sight to see. The gorgeously dressed Hacienda couples swirled around in the air like elegant birds. The music glided around us, softer than a spring wind. And everywhere the shimmer of the fairy relic sparkled on the light.

I loosened my grip a bit and took a breath. It wasn't likely I'd see this sight again in my life, let alone be able to experience such a thing, so I figured I'd be a fool not to enjoy it.

Just as I was finally starting to relish the inexplicable sensation of dancing on the air, however, I noticed a pair of sharp blue eyes watching me from a balcony on the mezzanine.

Landon.

My arms locked. Señor Vasquez swung me out in a spin, and I would have performed a spectacular slow-motion backflip if he hadn't swiftly tugged me back.

"I'm sorry!" I said, my face going hot.

"*¡Está bien!* You are doing fine."

Señor Vasquez carried on with the dance, but I looked back at Landon. He gripped the polished marble of the balcony railing, dressed finer than I'd ever seen him in a coat with tails and silk cravat of dark blue, his hair slick and sharp. He looked like a true gentleman.

I expected him to be laughing at my pathetic attempt at dancing, but he wasn't. His eyes stayed on mine as Señor Vasquez led me gliding through the air. There was something different in his gaze. A fire. A hunger. He seemed to be taking in every inch of me with that gaze. I felt very aware of how exposed I looked in my dress, and it made my heart quicken. It was all wrong, but somehow, instead of feeling ashamed, I *wanted* him to look at me that way.

Señor Vasquez unfurled me out in another spin. My hand slipped from his, and I nearly careened into the couple behind us, but Señor Vasquez only smiled patiently. I forced myself to look away from Landon. I knew I wouldn't fall, but a midair collision seemed only a single glance away.

We slid higher into the dancing crowd. Landon wove through the sidelines to follow, peering over and around heads to see us. Then Señor Vasquez turned me, my back against his chest, our left arms flung dramatically in the air. His other hand flattened against my stomach. Landon tensed. He stared at the señor's hand on me, sliding over to my waist. I wanted it to be Landon's hand there. The thought made my breath catch.

Señor Vasquez turned me back around for a final spin, dipped me, and then, at last, the power streamed from us. The dancers all dropped slowly to the floor, like petals, the ladies' gowns flowing behind them. By the time my feet touched solid ground again, the music had ended. The audience cheered again, and Señor Vasquez gave my hand a peck.

"You did very well, Miss Davis."

"Thank you, señor."

He smiled. "I do suggest you go out on the veranda and get some fresh air, though. Your face is rather flushed."

I touched my cheek, self-conscious. "Is it?"

"From the dancing, I am sure. It is quite an experience the first time."

"Yes, the dancing. Of course." I smiled, though I wondered if he was simply too polite to mention that he'd noticed me staring at another man while we danced.

"It was a pleasure to meet you," he said, bowing. "Now if you will excuse me, I must go speak with a dear friend of mine."

"Of course," I said, curtsying. "And thank you again."

I fanned myself with my hand as Señor Vasquez ambled off into the mingling crowd. Then a voice sent tingles down my spine.

"Good Lord Almighty, Maggie."

I spun around, my heart leaping. "Landon."

CHAPTER SIXTEEN

For a breathless moment, he took in every inch of me with his eyes. Then he shook his head, laughing a little.

"Dammit, Maggie, what are you trying to do to me?"

I smiled, but my face was surely beet red. "I think I need some air," I said, fanning myself. "That dance was a bit overwhelming."

"Of course," Landon said. He pointed to the large, sprawling veranda that hugged the outer curve of the ballroom. We walked there in silence—I'd never felt so tongue-tied in all my life. And every time I glanced up at Landon, he was staring at me with that look, which only made it worse.

I felt instantly better as we stepped out onto the veranda. A cool breeze blew off the adjacent gardens, bringing the softness of a summer night and the delicate scent of gardenias. I took in a slow breath and folded my arms on top of the thick marble railing. A few other couples strolled by, chatting in the night air, but Landon and I were mostly alone. He leaned against the rail, facing me.

I shook my head. "What on earth are you doing here?"

"I actually have an invitation to this shindig, seeing as how I'm one of Señor Castilla's *vaqueros*. And I'm the one who should be asking that question."

"I was invited, too!"

"I know." He laughed, and his smile softened. "I heard about your sister's recovery."

My throat caught. "Did you?"

"Word got around The Desert Rose that Álvar had used his unicorn relic to heal a child. I reckoned it must be Ella."

"Oh, Landon, I wanted to tell you. I tried to make it into Burning Mesa, but I've been trapped here all day, being primped like a poodle."

My thoughts pulled me back to Yahn. The truth was, the last thing I'd wanted to do was go back to Burning Mesa. To face the idle drunks in The Desert Rose laughing and chatting about the hanging, regaling anyone who'd listen with every gory detail. I remembered how I was going to atone for my selfishness by being solemn and respectful of his memory tonight. *Not* by feeling all jittery at the sight of a handsome cowboy.

Landon must have seen my countenance fall. "What's wrong?"

I gripped the railing of the veranda, looking down at my hands. "It's nothing. I just wish I could have done something to save those Apaches."

"The Apaches?"

"The ones they…" It hurt to even say the words. "The ones they hanged yesterday."

"They didn't hang."

I spun around. "What?"

Landon shook his head. "I'm surprised you didn't hear about it."

"But the mob. Outside the sheriff's office. I thought…"

"The mob was stopped."

I grabbed Landon's arm. "Tell me what happened."

He looked a little sheepish. "Well…I followed you into town yesterday. I wanted to help you somehow, even if you said you didn't need me. Then I saw the mob. I gather it all started when that judge from Durango sent a telegraph saying he wouldn't be coming for a week or so on account of illness. Which, of course, meant the trial would be postponed a week, and the hanging was delayed, too. Well, a bunch of men got mad and wanted to take justice into their own hands." Landon shrugged. "I remembered what you'd told me about the Apache who saved you and your sister. I knew the sheriff had to guard the prisoners, and the rangers were likely gone on patrol."

I was hanging on his every word, my heart pounding. "And so?"

"And so I got Bobby and a few other cowboys, and we cleared the mob out."

My head was spinning. I could only open my mouth, but the words died on my lips.

"They didn't go quietly, but when we pulled out our dragon-claw rifles, they disbanded pretty quick."

"So they're alive? Yahn and the others? They're okay?"

"Well, they're still prisoners, but I guess being alive in a cell beats hanging any day."

I gripped his sleeves. "You're certain of this? You're *positive*?"

"Yes." He laughed, amused by the passion of my question.

I stepped back, breathing hard. "He's alive," I whispered,

dazed. "And you saved him."

And then it was as if warm light suddenly burst inside me, lifting me up like a shimmer of wind. Shock and happiness and relief collided in a blaze in my head. I shook Landon's arms. "He's alive!"

For the first time that day, the air in my lungs didn't feel heavy with guilt. I found myself laughing freely, throwing my arms around Landon's neck. "This is wonderful!"

"Gosh, Maggie." He chuckled. "You sure are happy about this."

We both laughed. As the sound of it faded, our gazes set on each other, and only then did I realize I still had my arms around his neck. Only then did I notice how close our bodies were, radiating each other's warmth. Landon's hands were pressed to the small of my back, his face just a touch away from mine. We studied each other in the dim glow of lights, quiet, breathing softly.

"I don't think I can ever thank you enough for saving Yahn," I said, my throat choked with gratitude.

Landon smiled. "I'm glad I could please you. It makes you look even prettier than you already do tonight."

I turned my eyes down, blushing with pleasure, unable to hold the intensity of his gaze. "It's just this fancy fairy dress."

"No. It's you." He stroked his hands up my back, holding me closer. "You're a beautiful woman, Maggie."

My lungs suddenly seemed incapable of taking in air. Being in his arms like this made me dizzy and excited and nervous all at once.

"When I laid eyes on you tonight," he said softly, "I thought I'd never seen anything so perfect."

The blue of his gaze shone, even in the starlight. A power

surged between us, like the tingling in the air before a lightning storm, pulling us to an inevitable moment.

Landon seemed to feel it as well. "I'd like to kiss you, Maggie. May I?"

The light from the ballroom behind us seemed to blur. There were only those eyes. And maybe it was crazy. Maybe it wasn't right to kiss a boy who hadn't formally courted me yet. But I felt light as a cloud about Yahn being alive. My sister was alive. Everything was going my way. Breathless, I nodded.

Landon hooked me against him and pressed his lips to mine. His mouth was hot, like a cattle brander on my skin. His fingers curled against my back, pressing me to him.

My head swam. I'd thought some about kissing, wondered what it would feel like, but I never imagined this fire surging through me.

Landon's hand slid up to the nape of my neck as he swiveled me around against the marble rail, tipping my head back. His kisses pulsed with hunger, with longing. The awareness excited me. I gripped his shirt, not wanting him to stop, and, sensing my encouragement, Landon pressed me even closer. His embrace pinned me between his body and the railing. I couldn't breathe, couldn't think. It felt like I was tumbling backward in darkness, and suddenly it was all too much.

I pushed away, gasping for air. The corset squeezed my lungs like a fist, and I pressed my hand to my chest.

"You okay?" Landon asked, touching my arm.

"I'm fine, I…"

"You look a little pale."

I set my hands on the railing and pulled in a breath. "I'm fine."

We were quiet for a few moments, standing there in the glow of the party inside. Then a tiny smile pulled at the corner of Landon's mouth. I narrowed my eyes but felt one tugging on my lips as well.

"First kiss?" Landon said.

I elbowed him. "Don't you fancy yourself some Casanova. It's this darn corset. It's crushing my lungs."

"I see."

I glared at him, but he beamed and wrapped his arms around me.

"Aw, don't be mad. It's my fault, really. I should have controlled myself."

"I'll say," I sniffed, trying to pull out of his grip.

He held me fast. "You only have yourself to blame. You look too beautiful tonight. I'm under your spell, Maggie. What relic are you hiding in that dress?"

"Don't you wish you knew."

Landon lifted an eyebrow. "Maybe I should search for it, then?"

"You, sir, are a no-good coyote!" I whacked him on the arm, but it secretly pleased me to flirt with him like this. I knew it was improper, to be out here alone, talking of such things. It wasn't the kind of behavior a girl of my age and good breeding should engage in. Maybe Adelaide was rubbing off on me.

"I'm going back inside," I announced, marching away from him.

Landon grabbed my hand. "Don't! Let's stay out here."

"I won't kiss you again, if that's what you're after."

"No kissing," he promised. "We'll only talk." Then a thought seemed to come to him. He placed a hand over his vest. "Actually, I have something I need to show you. I've been waiting all day to tell you about it." His expression became more serious. "Something about the Chimera Gang."

I froze. "What is it?"

"You gotta see for yourself." He reached into his vest pocket and pulled out a yellowed clipping from the Burning Mesa newsletter. "Now, you read this and tell me if I'm not onto something." He held up the clipping. "Five months ago, Petey McCoy, one of the original founders of the Chimera Gang, was hanged in Durango for the crimes of train hijacking, bank robbery, and murder."

I took the creased paper in my hand. Landon pointed to the smeared words at the end of the article. "Look at this. Judge Harper Walsh passed the sentence."

I met Landon's gaze, stunned. "I know that name."

He nodded. "Judge Harper Walsh lived his entire life in Haydenville." Landon filled my shocked silence. "I did a little digging on him today at the hall of records. But that's not all. Look here. One of the jury members they interviewed, Pedro Morales—I looked him up, too. He was from Buena."

"Buena… The other town that was razed."

"Exactly."

I pressed a hand to my forehead. "Could it be a coincidence?"

"I don't think so," Landon said. "It all adds up, Maggie. The judge from Haydenville. Jurors from Buena. Those razings were revenge for the hanging of Petey McCoy. I think the Chimera Gang is going after the people who convicted him. They're sending a message that no one will ever forget."

I felt dizzy. "So they *will* strike again."

Landon nodded grimly. "Now I just need to find out who the other jurors were and where they came from."

"You did all this for me?"

His gaze softened. "You ought to know by now how I feel about you, Maggie."

My heart fluttered. Landon touched my chin, then nodded firmly. "Besides, we need to stop those bandits before they get to Burning Mesa."

"And we will stop them. With this information, Sheriff Leander will *have* to see that the Apaches aren't responsible for the razings."

The night just seemed to keep getting better. Bursting inside, I slid my arms around Landon's neck. "You may get that second kiss, after all, Mr. Black."

At that moment, the doors to the Grand Ballroom opened, and a shadow fell over us. I pulled back with a start. But it was Bobby stepping out onto the veranda, dressed as dapper as Landon.

"There you are," he said. He glanced at me, and then did a double take. "Maggie?"

I smiled. "Hey, Bobby."

"You look different."

"Thanks. I think."

Bobby grinned, then hit Landon on the shoulder. "Porter's looking for you. Wants all the cowboys together for a little powwow, I guess."

Landon grimaced. "Now? At a party? Tell him I'm busy."

Bobby snorted. "Nice try. Come on."

Landon sighed, then turned to me. "Don't go far. I'll find you quick as I can."

"Don't worry about me. I've had my eye on those fancy vittles since I came in. I can keep myself occupied." I followed Bobby and Landon back into the ballroom, but we parted ways in the thick of the crowd.

The party was still in full swing. Couples danced and laughed and drank even more champagne. I found myself a quiet bench and sipped on some spiced punch. I didn't have much of a stomach for the food, after all. Too much going on in my head to eat.

I brushed my finger along my bottom lip. It might have been my imagination, but I could still feel the heat of Landon's mouth there. It traveled through my blood, sending shivers over my skin. I still didn't know what I was leading myself into, getting tangled up with a wild young cowboy. I only knew that I didn't want to stop.

Besides, he was more than some good-looking beau. He was my friend.

I still couldn't believe Yahn was alive, and that I had Landon to thank for it. I had him to thank for saving Ella from those rock devils, too. Not to mention all this work he was doing to try and help me get the Chimera Gang. He had the biggest heart of any boy I'd ever known—that had to count for something. In fact, the more I thought about it, the more ashamed I became of my initial hesitation. I'd judged people like Landon and Bobby and Adelaide too quickly. I'd pegged them as shady characters, when it turned out they were the ones I'd most like to call friends.

By the time I'd finished my punch and watched three or four dances, I felt anxious to see Landon again. I wanted to tell him how grateful I was, how much he meant to me. Maybe it was crazy to talk seriously with a boy unless we were officially courting, but I wanted to tell Landon that I cared for him. Unfortunately, he was nowhere to be seen.

A half hour ticked by. Then an hour. At that point, I had gotten up from my bench and was walking in a wide circle around the ballroom, looking for him. I passed throngs of elegant people, but no sign of Landon.

Just as I was beginning to get upset, a finely dressed servant approached. He bowed and handed me a rolled piece of paper. "For the lady."

I pulled open the little scroll as soon as he walked away.

Sorry to keep you waiting. Meet me in the gardens.

My heart leapt. I tightened my fist around the note and held it to my chest. I couldn't get there fast enough. With an irrepressible smile, I wove through the crowds, taking the fastest route to the outer doors. To the far end of the veranda, a set of stone steps led down into the gardens. My feet danced over the pebbled path.

The gardens spread over a massive expanse filled with flowering bushes, well-trimmed hedge rows, and long lines of flower beds. Strings of lanterns hung above, providing a faint golden glow to the darkness. Out here, crickets sang louder than the orchestra and the hum of voices from the party, which grew fainter with every step. I imagined kissing Landon again, and my heartbeat raced.

"Where are you?" I laughed, turning in the center of a manicured sitting area. "Don't you try and scare me." The crunch of footsteps filled my insides with fluttering birds. I spun around. "There you are!"

But it wasn't Landon approaching through the shadows. It was Álvar Castilla.

CHAPTER SEVENTEEN

"Good evening, Maggie," he said with a casual smile.

"Good evening." I curtsied, because there didn't seem to be anything else to do at the moment.

Álvar raised two glistening champagne glasses. "Have a drink?"

I tossed a glance around the shadowed gardens. No sign of Landon.

Álvar set the drink in my hand and clinked his glass against the rim of mine. And then it struck me. The note. It wasn't from Landon.

Álvar swirled his drink, inhaling the aroma.

"I have my champagne shipped cold from the French vineyards, packed with yeti relic ice from the Siberia. It's the only way to capture the sparkle of the grape, I find."

He looked down, seeming to have noticed I hadn't moved. "Go on. Drink."

"Actually, I should be—"

"Try it, Maggie."

My jaw tightened, but it would be the fastest way to get out of there and find Landon. I lifted the polished glass to my lips and tipped the smallest bit of the drink into my mouth. The liquid tingled on my tongue like sunlight on a gem. I blinked with surprise, and Álvar smiled.

"I trust you are enjoying yourself tonight?"

"Yes, it's a lovely party. That relic waltz was simply amazing."

"Ah yes. Wasn't it? Nothing but the best here at the Hacienda."

A silence settled, but Álvar kept his eyes on me. His gaze made me uneasy. I wasn't keen to waste any more time on pleasantries.

"Well, thank you again. I really ought to—"

"You received my note, I trust," Álvar said. I paused. "Of course you did," he said with a casual laugh. "Otherwise you would not be wandering alone in these gardens."

Álvar circled slowly, examining me like a farmer sizing up a new horse. I didn't move. He fingered the fabric on the sleeve of my dress.

"The gown is exquisite," he said.

"It is."

"I knew you would be quite beautiful in worthy apparel."

His fingertips grazed against my bare shoulder. The feel of it sent a cold creeping in my stomach.

"You know, Maggie, a beautiful woman is much like the fruit of the vine. If it grows wild and uncared for, the grape will never live up to its ultimate potential. But with the right pruning, the proper trellis, with good soil, enriched with dryad relic, the grape will blossom into something transcendent."

I stepped back, pulling my shoulder away from his touch. "I

have to go."

He moved into my path. "Off to see your cowboy friend?"

My legs stiffened. He knew about Landon and me?

Álvar took a slow sip of his champagne. A hot, tingling feeling crawled up my throat. "It has brought me great pleasure to help you," he said. "And I would like to help you more. You and your charming sister."

I searched again for Landon, even though I knew now that he hadn't called me here. He was probably inside, walking around the crowded ballroom. Looking for me.

"I appreciate that, sir, but— "

"Nothing would please me more than for you to stay here at the Hacienda as long as you wish."

The invitation took me off guard, but Álvar filled the silence. "I will be frank with you. As I should have from the first day, when you healed my hands in the relic refinery."

"I-It was mostly that relic," I said. "No special skill of mine."

"No." His gaze fixed on me. "It was more than that. I felt it."

I wanted to protest, but then I remembered the strange, rustling whispers as I touched the unicorn horn, and the words died on my lips.

"What I am trying to say is that you are special, Maggie. You have a gift. I sensed this right away. It is why I wanted to hire you at The Desert Rose. I wished to observe you, to see if it were true."

I stared at him. "You think I have a gift?"

"With relics. Yes."

Just like with singing or painting or riding a horse, some folks had more of a knack for harnessing relic magic than others. I had read of certain individuals born with unique prowess, but it seemed highly unlikely that I could be one of them. I'd handled relics all of three times in my whole life.

"I don't know…"

"But I do. I saw it. Something about you made that unicorn relic stronger. I wish to study your gifts more closely, which is why I would like you to stay here. Let your young sister enjoy the finest tutors in the county, good food, the happy company of children her own age. And for you, no more scrubbing floors at The Desert Rose. You shall have the training you deserve. To become the woman you ought to be."

For a moment, I entertained the shining vision of it. No more moonlight reading of relic almanacs. No more out-of-reach dreams. I could get the actual training, study with real relic experts. I would be that much closer to becoming one myself. The thought seemed almost too good to be true. Álvar certainly knew how to paint a tempting picture.

But then again, even a naive farm girl like me knew that temptation came naturally to wealthy, powerful men. Especially ones as handsome as Álvar. Perhaps he'd "observed" me long enough to find my weakness. I couldn't be blinded by dreamy visions. He was up to something, wanted something from me. But what?

"I would love nothing more, sir. And I would love that for Ella—of course—but I simply couldn't afford such a thing."

"It would be my pleasure," Álvar said with a little smile. "As I said, your rare talents with relics are something that could be a great benefit to society one day."

I didn't know what to say to this. I still didn't trust him. People rarely gave something for nothing, even someone as rich as Álvar Castilla.

"I insist," he said, taking my hand.

I had to tread carefully here. I knew I'd seem an awful ingrate to turn him down after he'd saved my sister's life and welcomed me into his beautiful home. And I would gladly spend the rest of my days repaying him for what he had done for Ella. But he was slowly backing me into a place I wasn't sure I wanted to go. "It's a truly kind offer, but—"

"My men told me of the conditions at St. Ignacio," Álvar said, his voice cold. "Barren rooms. Sparse food. Surely it is not the place for young children."

His words burned like a hot poker, and he seemed to sense this, because he went on. "Would you send her back to languish in the crumbling mission? Without school? Without proper nourishment?"

It was as if he knew my exact weakest point. Guilt coiled around my heart like a silent desert snake. "I would do *anything* for my sister, sir."

"Anything but accept a freely given offer of assistance?"

He had finally backed me against an invisible corner with his words. The edges of it closed in around me—one side from his insistence, and one side from my own guilt. Of course, I wanted Ella to live like a little princess here at the Hacienda. Of course, I wanted her to have friends and tutors and a full belly. How could I deny her that?

Would I *really* do anything for her?

Álvar gripped my hand in both of his. "Maggie, please. Let me help you. If you both come to live here, you will never have to worry about harm coming to your sister again."

The final wall to his trap, boxing me in. I knew it was foolish to try and play Álvar's game without knowing the true cost, but I was willing to try for Ella. I bowed my head. "I would be very grateful to accept your offer."

"You will stay here, then?"

I nodded.

Álvar beamed, then lifted my hand. He pressed his lips to it. I could feel their heat through my glove.

"I am so glad," he said. "We shall move you into your own quarters at once. Your sister can room with the other children in the—"

"I'd like her to stay with me. If that's all right."

"Ah." He hesitated for only the slightest moment before nodding. "But of course."

"Thank you, sir."

"Álvar."

"Álvar," I repeated.

His eyes swept over me, my shoulders, my waist, my bosom. My heartbeat stalled. I was trembling inside, but I managed a little curtsy. "I should let you get back to your party."

"Indeed," he said, his expression flicking once again to his easy charm. "My guests will wonder where I am." He set his hand under my chin, lifting my face to look at him. "I hope I shall see you very soon, Maggie."

I could barely nod. As I watched Álvar dissolve into the shadows of the garden, a heavy question pressed down on me. What had I done?

It took me awhile to get the courage to go back into the ballroom. I was afraid Álvar would try and make some kind of fuss, draw some untoward attention to me as his new protégée. I wanted to find Landon, though I didn't know how I would explain what had happened. I didn't know if I should even *try* to explain. But lingering in the shadows outside only made me feel more nervous. Drawing in a breath for courage, I turned the corner.

My face collided directly with a broad shoulder in an oily, expensive coat. The musky smell of fancy cologne and cigar smoke filled my nose.

"What the devil?" the man barked.

I recognized that deep voice at once. Emerson Bolger, the relic baron with the werewolf cane, stood before me.

"I'm sorry," I said quickly. "I didn't mean—"

In a blink, three men surrounded me. Mr. Bolger jabbed a thick finger in my face. "How long have you been standing there?"

"What?"

"Sneaking around in the shadows like some kind of… What are you doing out here anyway? Who sent you?"

His beady eyes slid over me, searching. The two men on either side mirrored his stance. The cigar Mr. Bolger had been smoking smoldered silently on the grass. I squirmed back, unsure whether the strange intensity of his discomfort made me angry or afraid.

"I was out for some fresh air," I said, trying to move away from them. "On my way back into the ballroom. Now, if you'll let me past?"

His gaze stayed clamped on me, but he took a step aside. "Of course. You must excuse me."

I hesitated for only a moment, eyeing him warily, before one of the other men gestured for me to move along. I didn't dare look behind me as I rushed away, but my mind lingered. What was such a wealthy, powerful man doing out there in the hushed shadows?

I stepped into the crush of noise and music in the ballroom. As

I pressed through the crowd, I felt the sting of eyes on me. Was it possible they somehow knew about my new "arrangement" with the master of the house? Maybe they could spot his next conquest from a mile away. Maybe they'd pegged me the minute I showed up at the soiree.

Heat from the masses of bodies pressed against me. The heavy smell of perfume and alcohol singed my nostrils. I suddenly wanted to get out of there as quickly as possible. When a hand set on my shoulder, I spun around like a cracking whip.

"Good lands, Maggie!"

It was Adelaide, decked out in a sparkling blue gown with a skirt that suggested a mermaid's tail splashing through waves of organza ocean. She'd fixed swirls of tulle and seashell in her golden upswept hair and a string of pearls around her neck to finish the ensemble.

"You look beautiful," I said.

She laughed, pulling me into a hug. "You're sweet. I won't dare tell you how long I saved to order the pattern for this thing." She held me at arm's length and appraised me. "But look at you! Land's sake, I knew these Haciendellas made some gorgeous dresses."

"To tell the truth, I'm about ready to cut this darn thing off."

Adelaide frowned. "What's going on?"

"I honestly don't know where to start."

She nodded thoughtfully. "You want to go back to your room? I'll take you. Bobby's gone off with Landon and the other cowboys somewhere."

"Would you mind? I don't think I can get out of this thing without help."

Adelaide linked her arm in mine. "Of course I will."

Back in my room, I couldn't shimmy out of the gown fast

enough. As Adelaide loosened the laces on my corset, and I slipped into a loose, billowy nightgown that had been left on the bed for me, I felt like I was breathing for the first time that night. I checked on Ella, who was sleeping soundly in the little adjacent room in my quarters, then collapsed on my bed. Adelaide flopped down beside me. She looked around the room and whistled softly. "Well, you sure did something right."

I sat up. "What do you mean? What have you heard?"

She laughed a little. "Take it easy, Maggie. I've heard nothing. I just assumed you'd caught Álvar's eye, seein' as how he helped your sister and let you sleep in his house, and then invited you to his fancy shindig."

It must have looked so obvious to everyone else. Shame blossomed hot over my face. Surely now my reputation would be tainted, no matter why I told them Álvar wanted me there. And Landon. Would I lose him forever?

"What are you so worked up about?" Adelaide asked, setting her hand on mine. "Did I embarrass you? I'm sorry, honey. My mouth runs away from me sometimes."

I shook my head. "No. It's not you. It's the whole situation."

She nodded, prompting me to continue.

I rubbed my temples. "It all happened so fast. I just wanted to talk with him. I hoped he could save Ella. And before I knew it, I was here being measured for a dress, and then Álvar was…"

It didn't seem decent to say what had happened in the gardens. But Adelaide sat up, her eyes intense with curiosity.

"Well, don't keep me on tenterhooks. What did he say?"

I sighed. "You *know* what he said. Only he never came right out and said it. He gave me some line about my having a talent with relics and said that he was gonna train me and…" I sighed. "I don't know what to believe. He said he was willing to help Ella. At the time, that seemed to be all that mattered. He's going to give her the life I never could."

Adelaide put her arm around me. "Aw, cheer up. You look like somebody's died."

"Maybe someone *has* died."

"Oh, hush. You're a lucky girl. There's a dozen girls that would kill to be in your place right now. To have the attentions of Álvar Castilla? The richest, most powerful man in the county, who also happens to be charming and damn good looking. Don't you realize what you've got here?"

"I don't love him," I said fiercely. "And I'll never be some man's kept woman, living out my days in dishonor. Never knowing if the meal ticket will come to a sudden end."

"Well, what's the arrangement, then?"

"I told you. He said he wanted to train me, help hone my 'gifts' with relics. For the good of society, he said."

Adelaide pursed her lips, but I could tell at once what she thought. I hung my head in my hands. "What have I gotten myself into?"

"It ain't as bad as you'd think. I'm telling you, Maggie. Besides, you could still have Landon. I've got Bobby."

I snapped my face up. "And some freedom you have there. Sneaking around in the shadows, hoping no one notices."

Her hand slid from my back. I mentally kicked myself for offending her. "I'm sorry."

"Sorry for what? For telling the truth?"

This made me feel even worse. "I think you and Bobby have a wonderful relationship. Truly. You two are more in love than anyone I've ever seen."

She tried to smile, but the sorrow dangled over her expression like a dark cloud. "I do love him. So dearly." She flopped back on the bed with a sigh. "Oh, Maggie, what a world it is for us."

I lay beside her. "It shouldn't be like this. We shouldn't have to fight and scrape for every small happiness."

She took my hand. "Our time will come. One day, we'll be happy as a couple of birds on the wind. And no one will be able to take it away from us."

We stayed like that, lying side by side on my bed, our hands laced together, until the shadows in the room had stretched long across the ceiling and we drifted off to sleep.

CHAPTER EIGHTEEN

The next morning, anxiety about my arrangement with Álvar awoke me. The last thing on earth I wanted to do was face it, so I insisted on escorting Adelaide back into Burning Mesa. It was the least I could do after making her miss her ride the night before. Thankfully, the servant I spoke with procured one of Álvar's posh carriages for us without so much as a blink.

Adelaide and I spoke little on the ride—there was too much on our minds and too little we could do about it. I pressed my head to the cool glass of the carriage window and watched the red desert landscape whir by.

The sight of Sheriff Leander's office ahead made me shoot up straight as a board. Yahn. I'd been so preoccupied with the sudden turn of events that I'd nearly forgotten. I had to see him, had to make sure he was okay.

I rapped on the inner wall of the cab. "Driver! Stop the

carriage."

Adelaide gripped the windowsill as we tumbled to a jerky stop. "What on earth?"

I was already half out the door. "There's something I need to do," I called back.

My pulse raced as I ran past the rangers outside the office and burst through the doors. "Sheriff— "

But it wasn't him I saw leaning in the chair at the desk—it was one of the rangers. I'd seen him around before. A tall man with piercing eyes and a shaven head. He looked me up and down as if I were something the cat dragged in.

"Can I help you?"

"Is Sheriff Leander here?"

"It would appear not, now wouldn't it?"

I bristled. Adelaide came in behind me, one hand on her hip. "What is going on, Maggie?"

"Nothing. I have to talk with the sheriff, that's all."

Adelaide glanced at the bald ranger, then at me. "Well, guess we can go home, then."

"No." I stepped closer to the desk. "It's very important."

"He ain't here," the bald ranger said, sitting up. "How much clearer do I need to be?"

"I'll talk with you, then. It's about the town burnings. I know who's responsible."

The bald ranger snorted softly and leaned back in his chair. "That right?"

"Yes." I pulled the newspaper clippings Landon gave me from my pocket and pressed them to the desktop. "These burnings all have a direct connection to the Chimera Gang."

"Uh-huh." The bald ranger pulled a cigarette paper from his

vest pocket and began rolling himself a smoke.

I looked to Adelaide, but she only shrugged.

"Did you hear me?" I said, turning back to the ranger. "You people are going after the wrong men. The Apaches have nothing to do with these burnings. It's the Chimera Gang. The proof's right here in this paper."

The bald ranger struck a match against his boot and lit his cigarette. He puffed in a breath, then exhaled a column of smoke into the room. "I'll be sure to pass that information along to the sheriff, miss."

I envisioned myself taking that cigarette right out of his mouth and stamping it on the desktop. Instead, I adopted the most authoritative stance I could. "I'd like a word with the prisoners, please."

The bald ranger gave a half laugh, half choke on his cigarette smoke. "You'd like *what*?"

"Sheriff Leander lets me talk with them whenever I like."

"Listen, girlie, I suggest you march your fancy little—"

Adelaide suddenly pressed her hand over her chest. "My word. Is that a troll relic you got there on your hat?"

I recognized the slightly exaggerated drawl in her voice at once. It was the flirty way she spoke when she was trying to secure the high rollers at the saloon for the night.

The bald ranger blinked at her. "Why, yes, it is."

"How *fascinatin'*," she said, moving forward. She perched herself coyly on the edge of the desk. "I've never seen one of them up close before. Are they awful powerful?"

He shifted in his chair, startled at her sudden attentions. "Well, yes, ma'am. They are."

"I'm scared just lookin' at it." She batted her eyes once. I'd never seen a girl with such a knack for grabbing a man's attention. She bit her bottom lip and leaned over to look at it, showing just enough bosom to entice him.

"Just *fascinatin',*" she said again. "Say, why don't you let Maggie go talk with those prisoners? They aren't goin' anywhere. And while she's talking, you can tell me how that relic works. Only don't try and scare me, or I'm liable to scream."

The bald ranger chuckled, already under her spell. His smile faded a little when he looked back at me. But after a playful, pleading look from Adelaide, the ranger snapped his head toward the cell. "Two minutes."

I owed Adelaide big.

My heart pulsed with anticipation as I rushed down the little hallway that led to the cell. The one tiny window in the room had been blocked with a plank of wood, so at first, all I could see were shadows. Then one of them stood. The single strand of light that pushed in past the blockade cut across his face.

"Maggie?"

The sight of Yahn, alive and safe, filled me with white sunshine as I rushed to the cell. Breath caught in my throat, and I felt the strange urge to reach through the bars that separated us and touch him.

I resisted. It didn't seem right. But I couldn't stop the words that flowed from my heart. "I thought they hanged you," I said, my voice choked. "I would never have forgiven myself if they had."

"We are safe. For now."

"I was so afraid. I saw the mob outside, and I thought for sure—"

"Maggie."

The sadness in his tone silenced me.

"My people," he said. "Are they safe? Do you know if they have been attacked?"

"Not yet, but I fear it's only a matter of time."

Yahn's face lowered, and he exhaled shakily.

I gripped one of the bars. "Listen to me, Yahn. I know who's responsible for the burnings. And as soon as I see the sheriff again, I'm going to make things right."

He nodded, not looking up, not speaking. I swallowed the twist in my throat and brushed my palm against his fingers. His skin was warm, soft. "I will get you out of here. I swear it."

"Don't put yourself in danger."

"I'll do whatever it takes."

"Maggie—" Yahn halted, and he looked beyond me. I spun around. It was only Adelaide.

"You better come on," she said softly. "I bought you all the time I could."

I looked back to Yahn. My heart burst with so many more things I wanted to say to him. I didn't want to leave his side. Not yet.

"Go," he whispered.

I searched for the perfect words, the perfect way to give him hope at my parting. But nothing came, and when Adelaide urged me to come even more insistently, I silently obeyed.

I said nothing until we were back in Álvar's carriage. Adelaide sat across from me and folded her arms across her chest. Her left eyebrow arched.

"You gonna explain what just happened?"

I sighed. My chest still ached from seeing Yahn, but I knew I'd have to explain sooner or later.

"There's something you need to know about the night my home was burned."

When we showed up at The Desert Rose, both pensive and quiet, I still wasn't ready to go back to the Hacienda. A part of me longed to tie my apron around my waist and get back to wiping tabletops.

"Want to stick around for a while?" Adelaide asked as we got out of the carriage.

"I can't. I should get back to Ella." I glanced at the carriage, but the thought of facing Álvar again made my legs go stiff.

"I'm sure she's fine," Adelaide said, sensing my distress. "They've got a whole army of nurses over there to look after her. Why don't you come up and relax for a bit?"

"Well, maybe just a few minutes."

Adelaide smiled at the carriage driver. "You mind waiting around a spell? Havin' a drink on the house while Miss Davis and I visit?"

The driver tipped his hat, blushing at her attentions. "Not a bit, señorita. Take all the time you need."

I gave Adelaide a wry, sidelong smile as we went into The Desert Rose, arm in arm. Was there no man she couldn't win over?

Only one.

Mr. Connelly was sitting at an empty table near the stairs as we walked in, sharpening his big bowie knife on a wet stone. He didn't looked up as we passed. A bad sign.

"Morning," he said. "Have a good time at the ball, Miss Cinderella?"

He slowly turned his eyes up to Adelaide, who was still wearing her gown from last night. I noticed a small flame of hatred flicker in her gaze. She smirked and gave him an exaggerated curtsy. "A fine time. Thanks for askin'."

Connelly stood with force, his chair falling backward to the floor. Adelaide's body tensed, but her face still wore a defiant expression.

"I need rest for the show tonight," she announced, sweeping toward her room.

She made it to the hallway at the top of the stairs before Mr. Connelly flew up after her and grabbed her wrist. I rushed toward them, fearing he was going to strike her, but he only growled in her face.

"What in the hell kind of game do you think you're playin'?"

"I was invited to that party," she said, pulling to release her arm. "Now let me go, you mangy coyote."

He grabbed her face, pressing his fingers into her chin, and pushed her against the wood paneling of her doorway.

"Mr. Connelly!" I shouted, horrified.

He ignored me. "You know the rules," he said, his face in Adelaide's. "Tell me the rules."

"No."

He must have tightened his grip even more, because she drew in a sharp, pained breath. I grabbed Connelly's arm.

"Let go! She was with me! She was helping me! Let her go!"

He shoved me off with a flick of his arm, and I crashed into the hallway wall. "You stay out of this," he snapped.

By now, some of the other girls had stirred from their rooms, watching from narrow openings in their doors. Connelly pulled Adelaide's face close to his, so close she could probably feel his spit as he talked.

"If I see you throwing yourself at that worthless cowboy one more time, I will kick you out of here for good. And if you so much as step foot out of this house again without my permission, I will make sure every door in this town is slammed in your face. Do I make myself clear?"

She winced, breathing hard.

"You wanna wind up a two-bit whore at the depot again? 'Cause that's what would happen if I kicked you out. Hell, you'd probably end up dead in a month. You're *nothing* without me. You understand?"

She wouldn't look at him. "Yes."

"Yes, what?"

"Yes, sir."

"Don't you forget it."

Connelly pushed her away, and she stumbled back against the wall. He brushed off his coat briskly, then examined her with a smirk.

"Nice dress." His fingers stroked along the neckline of her gown. "You'll wear it tonight. I have a rancher from El Dorado coming into town on business. He likes to see a well-made woman."

Connelly tugged the front of Adelaide's bodice down, which pressed her bosom up farther. She flinched only slightly.

"That's more like it," he said. "That's the way a whore oughta look." Satisfied, he patted her cheek. "Now get in there and freshen up." He then glared down the hall. "All of ya."

Doors clicked shut quickly. Adelaide tried to keep a look of dignity as she turned into her room, but I saw the shine of tears forming in her eyes. I balled my fists, ready to give Mr. Connelly a taste of my rage, when he whirled around.

"You," he snarled.

My resolve cracked a little, though I tried to stand strong. "How dare you treat a lady that way!"

"Her? A lady?" He laughed.

"She *is,* and she deserves to be treated with respect."

"I'm not here to talk about this with you. You have no say in the matter. Don't you dare start putting on airs already."

I stiffened. So he knew about my arrangement with Álvar. Mr. Connelly read my expression and snorted with a mixture of amusement and disdain. "Ain't you a sly little hussy."

Hatred coursed through me, but no sharp words came to my rescue.

"I knew," he went on. "From the first day I met you. The second you turned down my offer, I knew you had bigger fish to fry. Pretty smart to refuse to be any old whore, with the plan to whore yourself after the source himself."

I wanted to slap him. No, worse, I wanted to beat him with a cattle prod. There wasn't any violence that seemed fitting enough for him at the moment.

My voice shook slightly as I addressed him. "Not only have you insulted me, sir, but you are most sorely mistaken as to the nature of my understanding with Señor Castilla."

He snorted. "That right?"

"Yes. Señor Castilla has been generous enough to offer room and board to my sister and me. However, his intentions are purely scholarly. I have a special talent with relics, and so he wishes to see me trained."

Mr. Connelly barked out a laugh, and I could smell the brandy on his foul breath. "And you believed that?"

"Just because you are low and base doesn't mean every man is."

Connelly shook his head, still laughing. "Well, if that doesn't take the cake. You're gonna whore yourself out, and you don't even know it yet."

My face was hot, my fists so tight I could barely feel any blood flowing through them. "I'm not going to be any kind of whore."

"Sure," he said, smirking. "Speaking of which, what the hell are you doing here? Get on back to the Hacienda. Álvar must be looking for you." His brow arched up suggestively, and once again I had to restrain myself from lashing out at him. Grinding my teeth, I turned away.

But then a threat trembled inside of me along with the rage. I shot a look over my shoulder. "You're not the only one with the ear of Álvar Castilla now. If I were you, I'd be a little more careful how you treated me."

Exhilarated and mildly shocked by my own boldness, I started to walk away. But Mr. Connelly grabbed my arm and spun me around hard. His face was even redder in his rage.

"Why, you little…" He clenched his jaw, trying to calm his breath, and released his grip. I backed away, my heart pounding in my chest.

Mr. Connelly pointed a tense finger. "I'm onto you. Oh, yes, ma'am, I am. You think you're pretty smart. You think you can play Castilla for a fool."

"I don't know what you're talking about."

"Don't play dumb. I know you've been messin' around with that cowboy."

I froze, and a satisfied smile crossed Connelly's face. "And we can't have that, now can we? Protégée or conquest, either way, you're accepting a meal ticket from Álvar Castilla, and so you have to play by his rules."

"We're just friends," I said, my voice weaker than I wanted it to be.

"Not anymore, you ain't. I don't want to see you so much as

breathe near that buck. And I've got eyes everywhere, so don't think your being up there at the Hacienda will hide it. I'm gonna be watching like a hawk. Waiting for you to slip up, 'cause I know you will. And when you do..." He snapped his fingers once. "Just like that, you'll be mine."

CHAPTER NINETEEN

My heart quivered as I reentered the Hacienda. It took me half the day to work up the courage to go back. If Ella hadn't been there, I probably wouldn't have gone at all. With trembling legs, I stepped out of the carriage in the main courtyard.

A neatly dressed maid waited for me, her hands folded primly in front. "Señorita," she said, curtsying.

"Maggie. Just call me Maggie."

Her eyes shifted at the suggestion, but she said nothing of it. "I am to show you to your new quarters, if it pleases you."

A warning shot off in my heart. "New quarters?"

"Why yes, miss. Señor Castilla has requested you be moved to one of the larger suites in the Hacienda."

"Where's my sister?" I asked, trying to appear calm. "I'd like to see my sister."

"I would assume she's in your suite."

She turned without any further explanation and headed toward the grand, gleaming spectacle of the main house. I'd hoped for a more discreet entrance, but the Hacienda grounds bustled with people and life.

Servants came and went, carrying baskets of clean laundry, bundles of dried chili peppers, and bolts of expensive green silks. To my right, three stable workers trained a shining black mare in the corral, calling orders to her in Spanish as they led her over a wooden jump. From her speed and the spectacular height of her leaps, I reckoned she was a sky steed, a rare equine breed descended from the ancient Pegasus. They were rare and very expensive, so I shouldn't have been surprised that Álvar owned one.

A group of well-dressed Haciendos watched the progress of the sky steed and discussed intently. The Haciendellas accompanying them stood chatting in the shade of the massive oak, their colorful parasols spread for decorative purposes only.

I followed close behind the maid, keenly aware of all the watchful eyes. But no one seemed shocked at my presence. Word had probably gotten around. The knowledge made my stomach churn.

My new quarters were located on the far west side of the house, tucked into the end of a long maze of carpeted hallways. The gaudy suite was lit with ornate glass lanterns and wide windows draped in airy curtains. Real wallpaper hung on the walls, with dark wood paneling. A silk comforter was flung lavishly over the bed, and a fresh bouquet of roses waited in a vase on the vanity.

"Are the accommodations satisfactory to you, miss?"

"It's beautiful," I said, dazed. I stepped into the room, looking around. "What about my sister?"

"Here is where she will sleep," the maid said, motioning to a doorway toward the back of the suite. "This room was originally designed for the ill or elderly. That connected sleeping room could be used for a nurse to be in close proximity. The señor thought it would be pleasing for you to have your sister as close as possible."

"Yes," I said, surprised at his thoughtfulness. "That's perfect." I looked into the little room, but it was empty. "Where's Ella?"

"I am not sure, miss. Perhaps with the nurses?" The maid curtsied again. "I am to help you dress now."

I glanced down at my maroon work frock from The Desert Rose. "I'm already dressed."

The maid's eyes flicked to the massive armoire wardrobe that stood in the corner of the room. Hesitant, I moved toward it. The doors, made of glossy, polished cherry wood, swung open smoothly. As the light fell on the inside, I gasped.

Dresses. At least two dozen of them. They hung in a thick row inside the wardrobe like an expensive rainbow. Rich fabrics and ribbons and lace in every color imaginable. Bewildered, I pulled one down. It was black velvet with white satin ribbons and intricate beading. The neckline scooped deep, trimmed with thin lace. I held the gown up to me. It was my size.

"Señor Castilla wishes to see his guests dressed in only the finest, miss."

I shut the doors of the wardrobe, Mr. Connelly's mocking words ringing in my ears. Gritting my teeth, I pulled open every drawer of the bureau. Each one overflowed with fine handkerchiefs and pristine lace underclothes.

Then came the nightclothes drawer. It was filled with expensive sleeping gowns, every single one of which had wide necks and thin, see-through fabrics. A velvet-trimmed robe in deep red lay folded at the bottom.

I pushed the drawer shut. "I will wear what I have on, thank you. Please send for my sister *at once*."

The maid studied me for the briefest of moments, then curtsied. "As you wish."

When she'd gone, I flopped onto the bed, distraught. I couldn't accept that I had become Álvar's mistress. Maybe I *had* been a fool to believe all his talk about talents and training with relics. But on the other hand, it seemed ridiculous to believe otherwise. That someone as wealthy and charming as Álvar would go to lengths to seduce a no-name like me.

I think I just *wanted* it to be true. So very badly. I thought of what he offered—the relics, the training I'd always dreamed of—and my heart ached.

At that moment, Ella burst in the door, her cheeks flushed from running. She was dressed in a pristine pink frock, with her blond hair curled in ringlets like a china doll. She looked beautiful. And happy.

A smile lit her face when she saw me. "Maggie!" She ran up and spun around in a twirl, as if to display her pretty new dress. "Isn't this the greatest place?"

I laughed. "Are you having a good time?"

"Oh, yes," she said. "We're playin' Blind Basilisk." Acting out the game for me, she ran in a circle with her eyes closed and her arms outstretched. "I'm the best at it, but this boy named Alfonso is pretty good, too."

"It's real nice that they're taking care of you like that."

Ella nodded. "It's much better than that stuffy old mission. I want to stay here forever."

My heart sank a little. I looked at my hands, trying to find the words. "Ella…"

She kept playing out her game of Blind Basilisk. "Yeah?"

"Ella, baby, I'm not sure we're going to stay here much longer."

Her eyes shot open. "What?"

"We need to be careful about what we accept from these people. I know it might be hard for you to understand."

"No!" she said, frantic. "We can't go! You can't make me!"

"Try to be reasonable—"

"No, *you* try!" Tears sprang to Ella's eyes. She flew to my side and grabbed my arm, squeezing it to her. "Please don't make me go back to the mission, Maggie. *Please*."

I felt like I'd been kicked in the heart. "Oh, Ella."

"I'll be good. I promise. I'll do anything you say. Just please, *please* don't make me go back."

I couldn't bear the sight of her like this. Taking her into my arms, I stroked her head and shushed her softly. "Don't cry, baby girl. Please don't cry."

"I can't go back," she sobbed. "I hate it there. I'll never be happy if we go back. I'd rather die."

I squeezed her tightly. "Don't even speak of such things!" I closed my eyes, exhaling in defeat. "If it means that much to you, we'll stay."

Ella looked up at me, wiping her eyes. "Promise?"

I nodded. I couldn't say no. For the first time since I took Jeb away from her, I felt like I'd actually made her happy, bringing her here. Besides, until I'd figured out for sure what Álvar's intentions were, we might as well stay anyway. No sense leaving what could be the best thing that happened to both of us just because a lowlife like Connelly tried to scare me.

But when two days passed without the slightest whiff of

training, the pit in my stomach returned. The first day, after a quiet breakfast with Ella in our room, the maid, Esperanza, came to help me dress. She called the cream taffeta gown with luxurious bustle and black lace trim a "day dress," even though it was fancier than anything I'd ever owned back on the farm.

Señora Duarte, the Hacienda's school mistress, came to collect Ella, who offered me a quick, guilty hug before running off with her. Then, dressed up in my borrowed finery, I followed Esperanza to the sitting room, where the Haciendellas were playing Liar's Dice. But when no one had spoken to me for two hours, I slipped out to wander the halls alone. It felt strange not to have an endless list of chores to do. Before that moment, I'd had no idea how little rich folks actually did.

The second day was no better. I had been invited to an afternoon of croquet with a small party of the Hacienda's other various guests, mostly wealthy businessmen and visiting Creole nobles from other states. The same pack of laughing, beautiful Haciendellas I'd seen at the ball joined them.

I missed Adelaide and Landon and Bobby, and I worried about what was happening with Yahn. I hadn't come to the Hacienda to act like some spoiled princess with nothing to do but amuse herself. No, not a princess—according to Connelly, I was little better than a pampered courtesan.

Still, if Álvar's intentions were to woo me, he had a mighty funny way of going about it. I hadn't caught so much as a glimpse of him yet. But I obviously hadn't had a glimpse of a relic or a relic almanac yet, either. How was I to know what to expect? I decided I'd had enough fretting in darkness. I was going to do something about it.

After a quiet supper in our room that second night, Ella was whisked off to be bathed and put to bed. I tried to insist on doing the job myself, but the maids only looked at me blankly and carried on with their task. With no other excuse to drag my feet, I had Esperanza help me into one of the "fine" gowns that apparently pleased Álvar so much—a butter-yellow satin with delicate black velvet patterns of flowers. Feeling a little lightheaded, I made my way to the library. If Esperanza was right, he would be there having drinks with his other guests.

I was thrumming with nerves as I stepped into the room. Ceiling-high bookshelves lined the walls, and a marble-framed fireplace glowed with heat and flickering light. A group of men sat on the red velvet sofas in the center of the room, talking in low, stern voices. They all looked so old and serious, with Álvar at the center, so young and charming, that it seemed a mismatch. My eyes shot to Emerson Bolger beside him. He looked up, and his eyes narrowed.

But it was too late to turn back. Face-to-face with my benefactor, the words I'd prepared caught in my throat.

"Why, Miss Davis, what a pleasure to see you." Álvar stepped over and kissed my hand. "You look lovely this evening, as always."

I felt the eyes of the other men on me, and my face flushed with heat. "I didn't want to disturb your conversation. I only wondered if I might have a moment of your time."

"But of course. Come, let us talk in the study."

The men watched me as I followed Álvar to the connected study. I suddenly wished I hadn't come.

"Please," he said, motioning to a cushioned chair.

I obeyed, caught up in my own thoughts. Álvar sat across from me, his dark eyes searching my face. I felt childish and irrational. Foolish. This was a gentleman, surely, and the master of an expansive, busy household. The reason I hadn't started any training certainly had more to do with his full schedule than his secret plans to make a mistress of me.

"You look distressed," Álvar said. "Please, tell me what is on your mind."

"I probably shouldn't have bothered you. Thinking about it now, I feel rather silly." I swallowed dryly. "I was simply wondering when I might begin with my training."

I prepared for his offense at my impudence, but he only nodded.

"Of course. How ungentlemanly of me, Maggie. I have been so busy that I have left you to wonder and doubt." He took my hand. "Please forgive my rudeness. Tomorrow morning I shall send for my finest relic expert to begin your training."

I looked up. "Do you mean it?"

"It is why I asked you to stay here at my Hacienda, is it not?" he asked, smiling.

I blushed. "Yes, of course. Thank you. It will mean a great deal to me."

He stroked his thumb once over the back of my hand, and for a moment, I caught the slightest glint of something behind his eyes. Something I couldn't quite grasp. But then, quick as it had come, it vanished behind his smile.

CHAPTER TWENTY

"What you are about to see, Maggie, only few in my entire household have ever laid eyes upon."

Álvar, dressed casually in tan pants and a white shirt rolled up to the elbows, led me through a narrow corridor tucked in the back of the Hacienda. It was lit only with flickering lanterns, and was so shadowy and empty that a momentary pang of hesitation struck me. But curiosity pushed me on. I'd barely slept the night before, preoccupied by dreams of what I would see the next day. So I followed Álvar through the dim quiet of the hallway.

As we rounded the corner, a pulsing passed through me, parallel with my heartbeat, and my steps faltered a bit. That sound I'd heard in the relic refinery returned: a rushing of wind. Whispers—ancient, faint, and echoing.

"Maggie?"

Álvar waited for me a few steps ahead. I blinked and rushed

up to join him. He gave me only the smallest curious look before leading me on.

A large doorway finally appeared ahead. Two guards stood at our arrival and saluted Álvar.

"*Está bien*," he said. "Is my guest already in the vault?"

"*Sí*, señor," one of the guards said, twisting the safe-like handle on the door.

"The relic vault," Álvar said, setting his hand on the steel frame. His eyes shone slightly as he gazed into the room. "This is where I store my greatest treasures."

My insides fluttered like a wild bird as I peered through the large, round doorway. It was a small room, almost barren on the inside, save a large wooden table in the middle. But I could see the rows of cases that lined the walls. My throat was dry with anticipation, my palms sweaty.

I spotted a man sitting on a small chair that had been brought in. Even from the back, I recognized him. "Moon John?"

He turned and offered me a small smile. "Miss Davis. Good morning."

"I take it you know each other?" Álvar said. "How perfect."

He motioned me into the vault. "I will leave you to it, then. Just tap for the guards to let you out when you're through."

He shot Moon John a glance, one so swift I was certain he intended for me to miss it. But I didn't.

I stepped in, stiff with nerves. The door shut securely behind me with a little rush of wind, and the sensation seemed to pass through my heart. I didn't move, but I allowed myself a swift glance at the cases that lined the walls. Perhaps it was only my imagination, though I could hear the whispers again, pulsating through the room.

Moon John reclined in his chair, folding his hands across his stomach. He apparently heard nothing. "You look tense, Miss Davis. Do not be afraid. You won't break anything."

I took a slow breath. I had to calm down. The last thing I wanted to do was somehow ruin my chance at this opportunity by acting like a mad woman. I stepped farther into the room and even managed a weak smile.

"I had a feeling you would find your way to the Hacienda before long," Moon John said. "Señor Castilla's unicorn relic is an incredible piece."

I nodded. "It surely is."

"And how is your young sister?"

"She's well. Thank you."

Moon John nodded. "I apologize that my elixir could not help her."

"That's all right. It worked out in the end."

Moon John nodded, but his smile looked strained. "Yes, I suppose it did."

A silence settled. Moon John pressed his fingers together, deep in thought. "I imagine you must have many questions, Miss Davis."

I edged deeper into the room. "Well, yes, sir, I do."

"I imagine you are wondering why you are here. If it's true that you have a special talent with relics. What that means."

I nodded.

With his slight limp, Moon John moved slowly to the table in the center of the vault. I noticed the lumps under the burlap that had been draped over it, and my stomach tensed. I didn't breathe as Moon John pulled away the cover.

Five relics lay beneath. Five pieces of antiquity. They had all been cut from the rough, fossilized skeletons into perfect, varied shapes and polished to bring out their brilliant colors. But none had been embedded into any kind of setting or device for use. They were solitary pieces of glistening bone, glorious in their simple power.

"Go ahead," Moon John said, the hint of a smile on his lips. "You can touch them."

Every nerve in my body shivered as I set my fingertips to the nearest piece, a brilliant blue siren relic, sparkling with white iridescence. Only then did I release a shaky breath. "They're beautiful."

"They are. Castilla has quite the collection."

I dared to take the siren relic into my hand. The blue shard was no bigger than my thumb, but it shone like a piece of the ocean on my palm and felt cool as a mountain stream. The sensation slid through my body like a current and slowed my racing pulse.

"You feel the calming effect?" Moon John asked.

I nodded, savoring it.

"The great generals and military leaders are known to carry water relics into battle to keep their hearts calm in the face of danger."

Holding that siren piece, I could understand why. I stroked the smooth, cold surface, losing myself in the depth of its blue. As I did, a faint voice began to tone in my ears, haunting and beguiling. The voice of a siren calling to me.

I set the piece down, shooting Moon John a quick look, but he didn't seem to have heard what I had. I knew those voices must mean something. The nagging feeling that I should tell Moon John about them tugged at me, but before I could decide, he spoke again, drawing me from my thoughts.

"And do you know what the siren magic accomplishes?"

"It gives the wielder influence over the minds of others," I said. "Pulling their thoughts like a tide."

When Moon John looked impressed, I shrugged a little. "Studying my papa's relic almanac used to be something of a hobby of mine."

Moon John smiled. "Good. And can you classify these by magic category?"

A thrill passed through me as I examined the pieces. I'd take any reason to stay close to them, to touch them. "This one's water," I said. "But that's an easy one." I ran my finger along the relics remaining on the table. "Looks like griffin relic here. That's sky. I'm thinking this one is troll—earth. That's dragon. Another easy one—fire. And..."

I went to lift the final relic, a pebble-sized piece as black as obsidian, into my hand. But as my fingertip touched it, a deep, angry breath cut through my mind. A stab of hunger reached into my chest, hot and lustful. Startled, I jerked my hand back as if the relic were red hot. I shot a look up to Moon John. "Is that what I think it is?" I asked, my pulse racing.

"Vampire," Moon John confirmed matter-of-factly.

"Álvar has shadow relics?"

Moon John smiled a little. "As you become more familiar with this world, Miss Davis, you will come to see that the government's ban on relics such as this one are merely a front to feed the ignorant masses an illusion of security. I've never met a relic expert west of the Mississippi who didn't peddle a little vampire or banshee."

It certainly didn't comfort me any to hear that shadow relics were common. I loved magic, sure, but not magic that dealt out death or pain.

"It's fitting that we be exposed to all the types of magic that exist in our world. There must be balance, as there always has been." Moon John pulled a small globe-like device from the ground and set it on the table. A dark metal orb, about the size of a fist, hung suspended between the ends of an inverted metal arc. The surface was punctured with what looked like hundreds of tiny holes, and I could just make out the glint of something glittering inside.

"Tell me, Maggie. You are sixteen?"

"That's right," I said, still staring at the odd globe.

"Then you were born in the year of the unicorn. How fitting."

"What do you mean?"

He drew a thin orange vial from his pocket. "I will show you," he said, and he tipped the liquid into his mouth.

Closing his eyes, he pointed to the three lanterns hanging in the vault. The flames were snuffed out, leaving us in utter darkness. I tensed, but just as quickly, he set his hand on the globe, and it was illuminated. Pinpricks of light burst out, filling the room with infinite glowing specks.

"The stars," Moon John said.

I exhaled with awe, turning slowly to take in the twinkling sight. It was as if Moon John had snatched the night sky and set it right there in the vault.

He stepped over to one cluster of light specks and traced his finger along a constellation. "This is *Zang Tu*, the unicorn. The first bringer of earth magic. Those born under her sign are often gifted with earth relics."

Maybe it was my imagination, but if I looked hard enough, I could see the majestic white creature galloping across the sky, her horn gleaming like a spike of light. It was thrilling to learn the old legends of Moon John's people. I didn't know if they were true or just ancient stories passed down through generations, but it didn't matter much. I relished every morsel. I'd have given anything to hear such stories as a girl. But with Mama so opposed to relics, all discussions remained limited to absolute necessity.

"Here is *Lóng*, the dragon," Moon John went on, sliding his finger along the glittering clusters of light. "Here, the sign of the mermaid. And here, *Fenghuang*, the great bird, bringer of sky magic."

"They're beautiful," I said softly.

"Indeed. In many ways, the stars are relics unto themselves. They teach us our history, our present, and our future, if we only care to learn."

I wanted him to go on, but he set his hand back on the globe, and the stars vanished. With a *snap*, the lanterns relit. I blinked the brightness from my eyes, still seeing the constellations behind my closed lids.

"I suppose I should test you, as Castilla wishes," Moon John said. "Though I think your birth in the year of the unicorn explains everything."

"You *should* test me. Just to make sure."

Moon John gave me a wry smile. "As you wish." He motioned to the relics. "Shall we begin with the dragon bone?"

My fingers itched to snap the piece up, but I controlled myself.

"Go on, Maggie," Moon John said. "See if you can produce a small flame here on this table."

I plucked the smooth piece of opaque amber, about the size and shape of a walnut, into my palm. Instantly, a current of warmth spread up my arm and into my core. The heat flickered out across my chest, swarming like ornery bees. The sensation made my breath catch in my throat, and I staggered back a little.

"Fire relics have an agitating effect on the nerves," Moon John said. "The feeling will subside."

"I've never used one before," I said, holding up the bright piece with trembling hands.

Moon John motioned to the table. "Try. Most can create at least a spark their first time."

I curled my fingers around the relic. That darn antsy feeling made it hard to focus, but as I did, a faint growl, like a whispered roar, pierced the dull hum. The sound sent chills up my neck. I squeezed my eyes shut.

And the next thing I knew, an exploding burst filled the room.

I ripped my eyes open in time to see a flash of orange light—flames spraying across the little table. In an instant, every inch of it was ablaze. I gasped. Moon John jumped for me, pushing me away from the fire, but as we slammed against the vault wall, all I could think of were those beautiful relics, tucked away in their boxes on the shelves.

"We have to put it out!" I screamed.

"We can't!"

I twisted away from his grip. I wouldn't let the relics burn. My gaze fell to the burlap crumpled on the floor; it was the only chance. Grabbing it, I flung the thick cloth over the burning table. By this time, the vault door had swung open and the guards had run in, shouting in frantic Spanish.

The four of us jumped at the table, stamping out the flames furiously. And with all of us working together, the blaze was quickly smothered. Coughing at the smoke, we pulled back the burlap. Miraculously, the fire hadn't had time to cause any great amount of damage. I spotted the five relics unscathed, and my heart leapt with relief. Before I could reach for them, however, Moon John snatched them up. He gripped my arm, his face tight with masked emotion. Something about the subtle intensity thrumming beneath the surface of his calm made the hair on my arms prickle.

"Come," he said.

"Shouldn't we—"

"Now."

I didn't know what to make of his reaction. Was he angry that I'd burned the table? Had I failed some unspoken test I didn't even know about? I cast a look at the guards, but they were busy examining the rest of the vault for damage, coughing into their arms, and waving away the smoke. But then Moon John headed for the door and turned a look so piercing on me, I followed with no further resistance.

We were silent as we headed back down the winding corridor. Moon John's limp seemed worse with his agitation. I offered him my arm, but he was so absorbed in his thoughts, he didn't even notice. He didn't break his intent expression until we had moved completely out of the main house and into the gardens. When we reached the little duck pond on the grounds, Moon John finally stopped.

He eased himself onto the grass with a grunt, his aged body resisting. I dropped to my knees beside him, my throat tight. "I didn't mean to burn that table," I said. "I swear to you. I only wanted to make a spark, like you told me to. Honest."

"I believe you," he said quietly, his gaze fixed on the glittering surface of the pond.

"I would never have wanted any damage to come to those relics. Never. I didn't even want to use the dragon piece, only you told me—"

"I said I believe you." He met my distressed gaze. I could see the racing thoughts behind his. "But clearly, your intentions and your actions are two different things."

I had no words. Shame gripped me, and I looked away.

Moon John pulled the five testing relics from his pocket. "Your gifts are not what I had thought. You must test the others." He lifted the tiny vampire relic between his thumb and index finger. In the bare sunlight, it looked like a frozen bead of night. I stared at it, and then at him, breathless.

"No."

"You must, Maggie. There is something I need to see."

"I can't. Not that one."

Moon John motioned to a fat white duck that was paddling happily in the water near us. "Drain his life."

I was too horrified to speak.

Moon John took my hand. "You do not understand how important it is that I see this."

"You're right. I don't."

"Trust me when I say, it is *vital*. I must test you with *all* relics."

"I won't!"

His grip tightened, and his eyes flashed. "Then I will have to tell Castilla of your insubordination."

Cornered and panicking, I stared at the shining vampire relic. But then the whisper of a song drifted through my mind. My gaze fell to the cobalt siren piece sitting in Moon John's lap. Impulse took over. I lunged for the relic and jumped to my feet before the old man could react.

"You won't make me test the shadow magic," I said, focusing all my energy on the power of the siren. The cold, calm tide coursed through me. I could see Moon John taken over by the magic, even against his own will. "Our test is over," I added. "And you won't tell Álvar any of this."

Moon John nodded jerkily, as if he were trying with all his might to fight it.

"Do you give your word?" I pressed.

His voice was soft, weak. "Yes."

A wave of exhaustion pressed on me, and I dropped the siren bone. I felt drained, frightened. I sank down to my knees, staring out at the little duck nibbling at the water plants on the bank.

There was a moment of silence, and then the last thing I expected to hear: Moon John's deep chuckle. I whipped around to see a smile brightening his face.

"My, my," he said. "I must say, you continue to surprise me, Maggie Davis."

That night, after putting Ella to bed, I sat at the window and gazed out at the dark blur of night. I couldn't stop thinking about the relic test. I still wasn't any closer to understanding my gift or what Álvar wanted with it, and apparently, neither was Moon John.

"I have theories," he had said, when I begged him to tell me what it all meant. "A dozen theories, but no facts. I need to think on this more. But in the meantime, be cautious, Maggie. You've seen now how Castilla collects and hoards relics. Do not let him collect and hoard you."

His words echoed in my mind as I stared blankly out the window. The prospect of having a gift with relics had been so exciting at first, but now it frightened me.

A knock came at the door, and Esperanza slipped in with a small package in her hands. She wouldn't meet my gaze as she set it on my bed and curtsied. When she'd gone, I grabbed for it, frowning. The paper looked slightly mussed, as if the package had been opened and rewrapped. My eyes narrowed and shifted to the door where Esperanza had just left.

With a swipe, I ripped the fold of the package open and upended it. Two small vials, blue as cobalt, fell into my hand. I held one up to the light, gazing with amazement. White shimmers told me what I needed to know. These were relic elixirs. Siren relic, to be exact. Those two vials alone were worth more money than the average man made in a year.

My pulse raced as I searched the package for some indication of the sender. But no note had been stuffed in the package with the elixirs, nor any name scrawled on the front. I unfolded the paper completely, searching every inch in the hopes of finding some clue.

The effort paid off. There, written on the inside edge of the paper wrapping, were a few scrawled words.

Perhaps these will help us obtain the answers we seek.

CHAPTER TWENTY-ONE

The next morning, the nurses had swept Ella off before I'd even finished dressing. A male servant then escorted me to a rich breakfast of quiche and pastries and fruit. As I sipped the strong Spanish coffee, all I could think of were the siren elixirs. Moon John's message was clear: the siren magic would make Álvar trust me, open up to me. Exactly what I needed.

Breakfast that morning was served in the sunny inner courtyard, a usual haunt of the lower-ranking Haciendos and Haciendellas as well as the constant stream of guests who ebbed and flowed into the estate. So when Álvar himself breezed in unexpectedly, right as I was plotting to use magic against him, I was certain the color drained from my cheeks. I stood with the other guests and prayed that my thoughts weren't somehow painted plainly on my face.

"Good morning, Maggie," he said with his casual charm, as always. "I'm glad I caught you before they swept you off to that garden party."

I curtsied. "Good morning."

Álvar motioned for me to sit, and as I did, he took the empty seat beside me. The others at the table went back to their murmur of conversations, but I caught their gazes darting to me, tinged with everything from curiosity to resentment.

"I have something special planned for tonight," he said, leaning in a bit to confine the conversation to just us. "A very small number of us are taking an excursion to the Harpy Caverns."

I blinked, uncertain if he were joking. "Last I heard, they were overrun with ghost coyotes."

Álvar smiled, a glint of mischief in his eyes. "You heard correctly."

"Is flirting with death your idea of amusement, sir?"

He laughed. "No, but hunting a deadly beast with relic magic is. Believe me, nothing compares to the thrill of seeking a foe far more dangerous than you, and fighting him on his own terms, come what may."

I gave him a sidelong look, unsold, and Álvar patted my arm.

"You will enjoy it. Besides, there is something in those caves I wish for you to see." He swept out of the courtyard, surrounded by his entourage, leaving thoughts swimming in my head. Hunting ghost coyote sounded like a fool idea if ever I'd heard one, though I knew I should be grateful. Álvar had unwittingly provided me with the perfect opportunity to use that siren elixir.

The night was particularly dark. The moon hung in a thin, pale crescent, and even the stars seemed dimmed by a strange haze.

The party exited the carriages at the foot of the towering red-rock cliffs, chattering in nervous, excited whispers. A chill breeze rustled past, making the pinyon bushes nearby shiver. I cast a nervous look around, but part of me knew that even if there *were* ghost coyotes nearby, we wouldn't see them until too late.

I set a hand to my bodice, feeling terribly aware of the elixir vial, which I'd slid beneath the fabric and tucked into my corset. The tube of glass lay cool against my breast, making my heart race a little every time I thought about it. I only needed a moment alone to slip it out and drink it, but I had to time it right. I didn't want the magic to wear off before I had a chance to speak with Álvar.

Señor Torres, the Captain of the Guard at the Hacienda, hefted his rifle over his arm and stepped in front of us. "Everyone stay close to me," he said firmly. "Stray from the group, and you may well find yourself in the jaws of the alpha male."

An excited murmur rippled through the air. Álvar's idea of a "small" group consisted of his two personal guards, six Haciendo nobles with their servants, Señor Torres, and a small entourage of beautiful Haciendellas. I guess they saw no point in being brave and reckless without someone to be impressed by it.

"I thought the women would each have a goblin relic," one of the younger Haciendellas said, her dark eyes wide.

"Of course, Granada," Álvar said soothingly. "We shall pass them around now."

Granada gave him of look of demure gratitude. Well practiced, no doubt. Of all the social climbers I'd observed in my time at the Hacienda, she seemed the most intent on catching Álvar's eye.

Señor Torres frowned. "Even goblin bone cannot conceal your thoughts from the probing minds of the ghost coyotes. Only my sphinx relic will do that, so stay close. Understand?"

Granada nodded, her pretty face painted with appealing fear. She reminded me so much of Adelaide at that moment that I had to smile a little.

As the servants passed out the goblin relics, an eerie howl sliced through the air. It was distant, but the sound made everyone in the group freeze. The ghost coyote was easily one of the most dangerous animals in these parts. I'd only heard stories about them, never seen one. Papa said they could speak to one another with their minds, and that was how they attacked so silently, suddenly, and with such accuracy. I thought of Ella, sleeping in her little bed back at the Hacienda, and wondered again what on earth had possessed me to come on this mad mission.

Álvar, however, looked alive with excitement. "Come," he said, motioning to the men. "Head for the cave."

The entrance to the Harpy Caverns looked even more ominous than I'd feared. It was a jagged mouth, waiting to consume us in its depths. A chill gust of wind whistled past, eerie and low, making me almost turn back. But the rest of the group pressed on, so I did as well.

The Haciendellas twittered nervously as Álvar led us into the pitch-black tunnel. He gripped Granada's hand with a comforting smile, and in that moment, I felt a pang of longing for Landon by my side, to soothe my fears, to confide in. Getting the information I need from Álvar wouldn't feel nearly so daunting if I had Landon here to help me through. I decided right then that I'd write him a letter as soon as I got back.

The group moved forward, sticking as close as possible to Señor Torres. A rope had been tied around his stone-gray sphinx relic ring, and we all clung tightly to it. I may have been invisible, but somehow that thought didn't comfort me at all.

When we reached the pure darkness of the caverns, the servants lit green-painted lamps and lifted them on sticks to light our path.

"Coyotes are colorblind," Álvar said, as if sensing me gaze up at the strange emerald light. "They have trouble seeing green."

I nodded, grateful to have some light, but the otherworldly color spilled onto the spear-like stalactites, stretching bizarre shadows across our path, and the mournful whistle of wind through the tunnels sent a shiver over me. I stayed as close as possible to the Haciendo in front of me.

The group moved in a swift, silent pack for what felt like an eternity. Around every corner, we found more green shadows and jagged cave formations, but no sign of ghost coyotes. The longer we walked, the more the energy that had first electrified the group disintegrated. The women took off their goblin relics, and some were starting to complain in grumbling whispers of the cold or their tired feet. Even skittish Granada was looking bored.

After a long, dark stretch of cavern, as we squeezed through one narrow pass, a strange awareness tugged in my chest. At first, I almost didn't notice it, but the farther we walked through the pass, the more I felt it. It was a dull ache, a wanting. It grew stronger until finally the sensation made me stop in my tracks. My hand drifted away from the rope as I turned to search my dim surroundings.

In the faint green darkness, a hidden tunnel peeked out from behind a cluster of stalagmites. Something about its bent, gaping maw made my breath catch. I didn't quite know how, but a sureness settled deep within my gut that something important lay beyond those cool shadows. Something powerful. Something magical.

I walked closer. I could just make out a worn wood frame around the entrance. Was this once a mining tunnel? The closer

I drew to it, the darker my surroundings became. I stopped and looked back over my shoulder—the group, the light, was pressing on without me. I shot a regretful glance at the tunnel, but the last thing I needed was to get lost here in the pitch black.

I turned back to the others. The faint green glow ahead proved they hadn't gone too far. I jogged toward them.

And then, like white lightning, something stabbed into my mind.

Heat, paralyzing me. I tried to blink the feeling away, but it persisted. Like a pair of hands wrapping around my mind, searching, probing. It was almost as if I could see myself standing alone in the passage of the cavern. So vulnerable.

Only then did I realize what was going on. And before I could react, or even think, a series of pale flashes streaked across my path and around me. And then I saw him right before me—the white face of a ghost coyote, his eyes the color of silver moons. I'd never seen anything so beautiful…or so terrifying.

I wanted to scream, but the alpha coyote still had his grip on my mind, and I could do nothing. The pack surrounded me in a circle. I couldn't take my eyes off the alpha's steel gaze—it was calm but piercing. Almost human. In that moment, I felt the strangest connection to him. Somehow facing death in his jaws didn't seem so unbearable.

But then a shot echoed through the cave, and men's shouts ricocheted off the arched stone above. With yips and growls of rage, the pack scattered to attack. The alpha snapped his large head to the side, and his grasp on my mind released. I staggered back, dizzy and nauseated. I could hear Álvar sounding the charge.

"I'm here!" I screamed. "Help!"

Green light burst around the corner. Men spilled out as well.

Everywhere gunshots reverberated through the cavern. Señor Torres grabbed me by the arm and pulled me to the side with the rest of the women. They were still invisible, thanks to the goblin relics, but I could hear their frightened whimpers.

"Get your relic out, foolish girl," he snapped.

He didn't have to tell me twice.

After a while, the chaos of shouts and growls and gunshots subsided. The Haciendellas and I waited in tense silence. But then we heard whoops and laughter deep in the cave.

"They got something!" Granada, the social climber, said, her face materializing as she put away her goblin relic.

Sure enough, a servant appeared to guide us back to the central cavern and partake of the victory. A fire had been built in the center of the largest space and a fruit-and-cheese platter arranged on a makeshift table. The Haciendellas, exhilarated by the danger and excitement of the hunt, raced up to the nobles to chatter and laugh delightedly. The coyote had been laid out on display, a lean white mass of fur. I stepped over to check its face. For some reason, I hoped fiercely that it wasn't the alpha.

A quick look confirmed it wasn't.

"Quite the adventure, wasn't it, Maggie?" Álvar looked immensely pleased as I turned to face him, and I took that to assume he'd made the kill shot that brought down the prey. I looked back at the beautiful animal, graceful even in death.

"I can't say I'd be game to try it again, but it was definitely an experience," I said.

Álvar laughed. "Indeed it was. You had us all worried for a moment there."

My face flushed. "I'm sorry. I didn't mean to stray off."

"I think I know why you did."

I frowned, and Álvar offered me his arm. "Come. Do you remember that I wished to show you something?"

Taking a green lamp with us, we delved back into the depths of the cave. Very quickly, I realized that we were headed once again to the strange tunnel that had gotten me into all the trouble. I cast a sidelong look at Álvar. Did he feel the same power coming from within? Did he know what it meant? Deep down, Mama's voice in my head scolded me for going off into a dark cave alone with him like this. But my curiosity burned stronger.

When we stood in front of the tunnel once again, shivers prickled my skin. That same *awareness* thrummed inside of me.

"Is this what you fell behind to see?" Álvar asked, holding up his lamp.

Spears of green light shot into the crooked opening, but only darkness peered back at us.

"Yes," I said. "What is it?"

"A relic mining tunnel. A very important one." Álvar had a casual expression on his face, but an intensity trembled at the edge of his voice. "Tell me, do you feel anything strange?"

"Yes. Is that normal?"

His eyes gleamed in the green light. "No."

"What does it mean?"

"That you have a gift," he said, smiling, but I felt strongly that he was concealing something. I thought of the siren relic against my bosom. If I could just sneak away for a single moment…

"There is a man I would like to introduce you to," Álvar said, breaking my train of thought. "An expert on the study of relics. A genius, really. I've known him for many years. I studied his writings on relics first and then, over time, built up a correspondence with him. You will never meet a man more well versed in all things pertaining to the ancient beasts that ruled this earth." His expression looked guarded. "I told him of your unique gifts, and he seemed very eager to meet you."

I'd never heard Álvar speak with such enthusiasm for learning about relics. I assumed he gathered them like treasures, but it appeared he had a genuine interest in the study of them.

"I'd be happy to meet this expert," I said. "I imagine that would be very enlightening."

Álvar nodded. "Yes. Good. He lives on the East Coast, of course, but he may be visiting soon."

"You must meet so many interesting people with all these guests coming and going from who knows where."

He chuckled, but I noticed a lack of mirth in his laugh. "Yes. I wish they were all as pleasant company as you, Maggie, but alas, they are not."

"No trouble, I hope?"

He didn't speak for a moment. Then a strained smile pulled at his lips. "Of course not."

My jaw tightened. More lies. More secrets.

"Shall we walk back?" he said brightly, leading me away by the arm.

"That was all you wanted to show me? A mining tunnel?" I peered back into the black depths. The ache to investigate hadn't gone away. And now, with Álvar's secrecy, I wondered if there weren't some dark truth connected to it. A shiver rushed over me.

"You must be cold," Álvar said, removing his coat. "These caverns can get quite drafty." He draped his thick coat gently around my shoulders. "Better?"

"Yes. Thank you."

He continued to lead me away from the tunnel and back to the others. I turned a regretful glance over my shoulder but followed along.

"So, Maggie," Álvar said after a pause. "Are you liking it here? At my home, I mean."

"My sister is very happy, sir. And that makes me happy."

A sad smile colored his face. "It is my great regret that I was never close to a brother or sister."

Only then did I realize that I'd never seen any immediate family at the Hacienda. "I didn't realize you even had siblings."

"Yes. I had one brother. He died very young of the same pneumonia that took my mother."

"My brother Josiah died of pneumonia," I said, surprised and saddened to have such a thing in common.

"A terrible illness," Álvar said grimly. He sighed. "And then my father died five years ago. Fell from a horse."

"I'm so sorry," I said.

"It was difficult to lose him. As the only heir to the Castilla line, I inherited everything at twenty-one. A man, but many thought me not ready to take on the responsibilities required to manage the Hacienda. Sometimes I wonder if they weren't right."

His words surprised me. It was the first crack in the calm, confident persona Álvar always presented. But more than that, it surprised me to see that I had something so profound in common with a man I'd always imagined to be worlds apart from me.

"I worry all the time that I'm not fit to take care of Ella," I said softly, fingering the hem of Álvar's jacket.

He gave me a sidelong glance. "But you do well; I see that. You are as good to her as any mother could be."

My face rushed with heat. "Thank you, sir."

"Álvar," he said.

"Álvar," I repeated.

A twitter of voices echoed toward us through the pathway. We were nearing the others. I could hear one of the Haciendellas complaining loudly, and I recognized it as Granada's voice. "If he does not come back soon, I will go look for him myself."

Álvar smiled. "I should rejoin my other guests."

I turned to him, blocking his path. "Wait."

His eyebrows rose with surprise.

"What was in the tunnel?" I asked, holding his gaze. "I know you didn't bring me here just to tell me something I already knew."

He analyzed me for a moment, indecision shading his gaze. "I cannot tell you everything. Not yet."

"Tell me *something*, then." I knew I didn't have the power of the siren relic to help me, but perhaps I didn't need it. "Please."

"I will say only this: the world has much to learn about relics, about how they came to be. But there are theories. And there are some who would do anything, *anything* to possess the truth."

I waited for him to elaborate, but he caught himself and stopped.

"We will talk more later," he said, his voice heavy with meaning. "I promise you."

CHAPTER TWENTY-TWO

Álvar stayed true to his word. He summoned me to meet him three times over the next three days. We met in his relic vault, examining his different specimens and testing out their magic. On the afternoon of the third day, we spent hours flipping through his beautiful, gilded relic almanac, discussing the different magic types.

"Ah," Álvar said, tapping a page bearing the illustration of a gleaming green relic. "This is a good example of what I mean. Wyvern. From the shores of England."

We were seated side by side at the small table at the center, sharing the single, large almanac. I peered at the smaller drawing of the creature beneath it.

"Wyvern? Looks a lot like a dragon to me."

"To most, it does," Álvar agreed. "And yet there are subtle variances in appearance, and dramatic changes in the type of magic."

I studied the picture a moment, noticing the lack of front legs, the strange barb on the tail, and the slight difference in wing shape.

"You see, the essence of fire magic is consumption," Álvar continued. "Physical fire consumes whatever it comes in contact with, but relic fire can consume anything. While dragon relic magic produces normal fire, wyvern fire burns green. And instead of destroying with heat and flame, it consumes with a poison that kills living things with sickness."

"Fascinating," I murmured, transfixed.

Álvar cocked his head to the side a little, watching me. He then went to one of the black boxes on his upper shelf. I perked up.

"You have a piece?"

"A very small one," he said, smiling. "I've always been especially drawn to fire relics. Moon John says it's because I was born under the sign of the dragon."

My pulse increased as Álvar set the box on the table and sat beside me again. I wanted to snatch it and rip the lid off to get a peek, but I restrained myself. Álvar drew a small, corked vial from the box. Inside, a tiny shard of emerald green wyvern relic glinted through the glass.

"Amazing," I breathed.

"One of my favorite pieces."

I analyzed Álvar as he examined the relic. He continued to surprise me. There was more to him than the rich playboy and womanizer.

He flipped to a page in the almanac featuring a different species of wyvern. As he spoke, I realized how close we were standing together. I could feel the warmth of his arm touching mine. The flicker of a daydream slid into my mind: Álvar and me traveling the world to study relics. The things we would see, the things we would learn together! There could be worse fates than being on the arm of a handsome, wealthy man like him, even only as his mistress. It could almost be worth it. No more scraping out a barely acceptable living for Ella and me. No more watching my dreams drift away as I scrubbed floors.

I felt Álvar's dark gaze and snapped back to the present, back to the real world. My cheeks flushed. I pretended to be absorbed in the almanac page but scolded myself inwardly. It was ridiculous to entertain such whims, even as a passing fancy. Not only would I never think so poorly of myself as to be a kept woman, it seemed more and more clear to me that Álvar had no intention of making me one. We'd spent hours alone together here in his vault. He'd had more than enough opportunities to try and seduce me if he'd wanted. It appeared he truly did only have interest in helping me develop my talent for relics.

I fumbled to fill the awkward silence. "You have quite the collection," I said, motioning to the wyvern piece. "All these different relics, they could buy a king's ransom."

Álvar's hand gripped around the little bottle, his eyes cutting to mine. "They are more than expensive treasures, Maggie."

"Yes, I agree. I was only saying—"

"They are the key to understanding our world," Álvar said, his expression both earnest and intense. "They are the last clues we have as to the dawn of the world and the creation of magic." He went on, taken by his own thoughts. "Knowledge is power. And you cannot put a price on power."

He fell quiet and, not wanting to upset him further, I carefully shifted the subject. "So this expert, this relic scholar you want me to meet, does he have theories about the creation of magic?"

But Álvar's gaze was still distant. "He does." Then he turned to me. "Have you read anything about the alchemists, Maggie?"

"A little." I strained to remember. "They believed they could extract the magic from relics, right? And make that magic part of themselves?"

"Yes. Imagine, to no longer need an amulet or ring or weapon. To have the magic within your very being." He looked back down at the vial and tenderly stroked the glass. "To become a living relic."

I frowned. "But alchemy is just a myth. No one's ever actually been able to internalize magic."

"Only because mankind still does not understand enough about it. Some believe that if we only understood the origins of how magic came to the earth and why it left, we would be able to truly harness it at last."

"Do you believe that, Álvar?"

His eyes snapped to me. "I never said that I did."

With startling speed, he set the relic back in its box, snapped the lid down, and placed the box on the shelf.

It wasn't the first time I'd seen Álvar react oddly to an offhand remark. Every once in a while, a strange, sudden mood seemed to take hold of him. A gleam in his eye. An obsession. He used his charm and charisma to mask these moods, but I noticed nonetheless.

The next morning, the Haciendellas were buzzing with plans for a grand play they intended to give that night—a tableau, as they called it. It would be a performance that, with dancing and song, would tell the story of the first magical creatures. Somehow, in spite of my firm protestations otherwise, they roped me into playing a small role.

"We need a full group of sea sirens to accompany the First Mermaid," one of the Haciendellas explained to me, as if I were being silly not to understand. Outnumbered, outranked, and outsmarted, I yielded, and evening found me preparing for the tableau. A makeshift stage had been built of red velvet cloth, forming a kind of open-faced tent in the center of the inner courtyard. Servants rushed to bring in chairs for the audience and light the lanterns that would illuminate our performance. Maids rushed to and fro, carrying armfuls of shimmering muslin to create seafoam, or large potted trees for the First Unicorn's forest. I felt bad watching them work so hard for something that was little more than the idle whim of the Haciendellas.

I sat on a stool in the curtained backstage, getting the finishing touches on my costume. Esperanza powdered my face as pale as she could make it with a large pink puff. My costume, if you could call it that, consisted of a sleeveless white undershift, wrapped with pale blue organza that twinkled in the light.

As I sat still for my maid to fix a few glittering silver starfish into my loose hair, Granada stalked up. She looked dramatic in a long red gown and robe to match her ruby lips. Black paper wings draped in red tulle had been fixed on her back. Her raven hair was twisted up in an elaborate style, interwoven with shimmering red ribbons. Even as a dragon, she managed to appear effortlessly beautiful.

She examined me for a moment, then shot a pointed look at Esperanza. "Leave us."

Esperanza obeyed immediately. I tightened a little in my seat.

"Hello."

Granada strolled over and picked up one of the starfish Esperanza had left behind. "So," she said, circling around me to place it in my hair, "I understand you have been spending some time with Señor Castilla."

"Yes. He's helping me, training—"

"You must feel rather pleased with yourself." She tugged a pinch of my hair and started to tie the starfish to it. "You think that because you have caught his eye for a fleeting moment that you can crawl your way to the top. You think you can bring yourself out of the pathetic station you were born to."

I tried to turn to face her. "I don't think that at all—"

She jerked my head forward and continued to tangle the starfish in my hair with increasing intensity. "He is not himself lately, that is all. He has been thinking strangely, saying strange things. The fact that he speaks of you so much is of no consequence."

"Granada, please."

She gripped my shoulders and spun me around to face her. To my shock, I saw the gleam of tears in her eyes, though her expression was still one of hard disdain.

"He will forget about you in a moment," she said, her breath short with anger. "You mean nothing to him."

She started to back away, but I grabbed her hand, stopping her. "I don't *want* to mean anything to him," I said earnestly. "And I don't think I do. His interest in me is nothing more than a mutual appreciation of studying relics."

Granada pulled her hand free. Tear still shone in her eyes, but the hardness in her expression softened slightly.

At that moment, Isabel, the Haciendella who would narrate the tableau, swept up, looking rather frazzled. "Sea sirens need to be in place right now. Hurry, *niña*!"

I jumped up from my seat and rushed toward the stage. I could feel Granada's eyes burning into my back as I went, her words echoing in my ears. But she had to be wrong. She was simply jealous of the time I was spending with Álvar.

At that moment, a herald of violins struck the air. I'd save my worry for later. At the moment, I had to focus, lest I make an absolute fool of myself.

A pretty Haciendella named Olinda, glittering in a silver-and-green fish tail, pranced out as the First Mermaid. The chime of a harp heralded her arrival from the blue silk waves, which servants holding the ends offstage fluttered gently. Olinda moved with the grace of a dancer, spinning once, her arms in a smooth arc over her head. The sea sirens followed close behind, walking in step with the music and tossing handfuls of shimmering powder out into the rapt audience.

We posed in a half circle around Olinda as the other First Creatures made their entrances. When we were all displayed, the "humans" came out and fell before our feet. The First Creatures lifted the humans up, one by one, and then danced around them to their delight. Then came the big dance number of the tableau where all of the First Creatures and their accompanying entourage performed displays of magic for the humans, earning their worship and love.

But then, with a dramatic crash of cymbals, a troupe of male dancers in all black leapt out from behind the curtain. They represented the greedy humans who hungered for powers of their own, who longed to steal them from the First Creatures and become magical themselves. The crowd booed appropriately. I, however, was relieved, because it meant the sea sirens could "flee" offstage. My part in the performance was thankfully over, and I could take a much more comfortable place beside Ella in the audience.

In true Hacienda fashion, there was a party to celebrate our little performance. A small, informal affair in the sitting room, more an excuse to drink and dance than anything else. The wine flowed freely, and soon that room looked an awful lot like The Desert Rose, with drunken men and women eager to take advantage of the moment.

Most of the Haciendellas had paired off with a noble, sitting in their laps and giggling or talking. Isabel leaned on the piano while an older gentleman played, singing sad, beautiful songs from Spain.

I tried to leave the party early, but the Haciendellas insisted I stay. And the only thing that surprised me more than them wanting me around was how pleased I felt to be included. They'd ignored me for the most part since I'd come to the Hacienda. I suppose my participation in the tableau had been a turning point.

The party wore on, and I became swept up in the singing and dancing and general merriment. Before I knew it, dawn approached. Mama would have taken a switch to my back if I'd tried to sneak home at this hour. Feeling groggy and properly shamed, I forced myself to head back to my quarters.

The network of rooms proved more maze-like than I remembered. Maybe I was too tired. Opening doors and looking for a familiar hallway, I slipped inside one room to find a small, dark office. Standing in the doorway, I saw a beam of light spread across the room, exposing a couple locked in a passionate embrace. The man sat on the writing desk, and the woman straddled him. Her skirt was pulled up completely, and the man's hands gripped her bare thighs. She clawed at the back of his neck, her fingers twined in his dark hair.

Eyes wide, I turned to go. "Sorry—"

But at the same time, the woman spun around. It was Granada. Her red dragon gown was disheveled, almost completely falling off on the top. The man she straddled sat up a little.

Álvar, his shirt unbuttoned, his coat flung somewhere on the ground.

Heat burst across my face. I was frozen with embarrassment.

"Ah, Maggie." Álvar slid Granada off his lap and stood. He smoothed his shirt a little and nudged a stray lock from his eyes. "I was hoping I would run into you before you left."

I shot a tense look to Granada. Sure enough, she looked as mad as a wet hornet.

"I have a very special guest coming into town tomorrow," Álvar continued, as if it were nothing at all that I'd stumbled upon them in such a state. "We are holding an event to welcome him. I do hope you plan to be there. He has something you very much need to see."

"Of course," I said, trying not to stammer stupidly or meet Granada's enraged gaze. "I'll be there."

"Excellent. I shall be looking for you."

I forced a little smile, curtsied, and turned to leave as quickly as I could.

CHAPTER TWENTY-THREE

The next day, all of the Hacienda was buzzing about the party. Apparently, the new guest had arrived with full fanfare and entourage. I had wondered last night if Álvar wasn't talking about the East Coast relic scholar, but it appeared not. It was disappointing news, but my mood brightened significantly when Esperanza mentioned that Álvar had invited his *vaqueros* to the event.

Landon. I hadn't seen him since the night of our kiss, which seemed ages ago. Night couldn't come soon enough.

On account of the glorious weather, Álvar called for the reception to be held out in the gardens. Hundreds of multicolored paper lanterns had been strung along the trellis that stretched above. The servants also strung rope after rope of glittering beads to catch the light. Round tables of food and drink had been placed in strategic locations for the guests who wandered the flowered paths.

I stepped into the modest crowd, searching for this new guest who warranted all the commotion. A pair of men watched me as I passed, grinning with approval, and I suppressed a smile. For this party, I'd picked out a dark rose satin with black crystal beading that shimmered in the lamplight. During my time at the Hacienda, I'd grown more and more accustomed to being dressed up like a princess and admired. In fact, I couldn't deny I was starting to rather enjoy it.

As I crossed into the main mingling area in the open, brightly lit courtyard, I searched for familiar faces, for Landon. But my gaze fell on Adelaide, striking as always in a deep blue gown with a gleaming sapphire necklace. It seemed like forever since our last meeting, and I'd never been happier to see her. I was about to run over when I noticed the man standing beside her.

I wondered if it were the rancher from El Dorado, the one Adelaide was expected to entertain at Connelly's command. He was a tall, rough-faced man, probably in his late fifties, with long silver hair in a ponytail. The way he stood, both feet planted firmly on the ground, the way he cast a commanding gaze around the crowd, you could see he had money and power, and that he'd come about it through sheer grit. His arm was tucked around Adelaide's slender waist like a proclamation of ownership.

Adelaide caught my gaze. I must have looked as sorry as I felt, because she shrugged one of her shoulders and gave me a half smile as if to say she was fine. I knew better. Perhaps once she hadn't minded the forced caresses of other men, but now, with her heart so completely given to Bobby, I knew she hated every minute with her clients. And Bobby would be here tonight, too, just out of reach, while Adelaide would be paraded around like a prize steer. The injustice of it all coiled in my chest. I wanted to march over there and rip that man's arm away from my friend. If only I could.

"Ah, Miss Davis. Excellent to see you."

I spun around. Álvar stood behind me, dashing in his Spanish regalia. A dolled-up Granada, dripping with jewels, clung possessively to his arm. The men with Álvar all had a Haciendella as their own dates for the evening, and the three women appraised me as they would a rat crawling into their home.

"Surely you remember my colleague, Señor Bolger?" Álvar said, motioning to the huge man beside him.

Emerson Bolger's eyes narrowed ever so slightly as I curtsied. Apparently, he hadn't forgotten our encounter outside the fairy ball, either. "Charmed," he said, sounding anything but.

Álvar set his hand on the shoulder of the other man standing beside him. "And this is my most distinguished guest, Sheik Nadir Ibrahim."

The man bowed low, and I tried to curtsy to match. Sheik Nadir Ibrahim had black hair and dark olive skin, though his eyes were a striking hazel green. In his black suit and white tie, I'd assumed at first glance that he was a Haciendo. The only thing that hinted at his distant homeland was a rich emerald cap, embroidered with red and gold, that he wore at the crown of his head.

"This is Maggie Davis," Álvar said. "The girl I was telling you about."

Sheik Nadir nodded slowly with recognition. "It is indeed a pleasure to meet you," he said, his voice heavy with a strange but alluring accent.

"Pleasure's mine," I said.

"Stay close, Maggie," Álvar said with a twinkle in his smile.

"The main event of the evening begins very soon."

"I will, certainly."

As they walked away, Granada whispered something in his ear, and they both laughed as he slid his arm along her slim waist and gave her hand a quick kiss. I watched them for a moment. *Of course* it was silly to ever imagine a man as distinguished and wealthy as Álvar would ever bother with a sixteen-year-old nobody like me. The past few days had proved his interest in me to be purely relic related. Clearly Granada had been wrong. And in this case, I was sure she was happy to agree.

A flourish of the trumpets called everyone's attention to the wide platform that had been set up in the center of the garden's courtyard. Álvar and Sheik Nadir stepped to the middle of it, beside a small pedestal draped with velvet cloth. Álvar raised his hands to silence the crowd.

"My friends," he announced. "As you know, I have called you here for a very special treat. Most of you already know the esteemed Sheik Nadir Ibrahim."

The crowd applauded politely.

"From the far-flung desert of Arabia to our own humble desert, he has brought with him an item so rare that many have doubted its existence. But no longer. Señors and señoritas, I present to you the main event of the evening."

With dramatic flair, he pulled the velvet cloth from the pedestal.

"I present the rare and amazing Djinn relic."

A shocked murmur rippled through the crowd. My mind raced through the pages of Papa's almanac—no djinn. In fact, I'd never even heard of it in stories or gossip. Álvar must not have been exaggerating about its scarcity. I lifted on my toes to try and get a better look.

"A lucky number of you will get the chance to experience the magic of this relic," Álvar said, "and I assure you, it will be an experience like none other. The only payment is that you must share your tales with the other guests, so we might all take part. But in the meantime, perhaps we can enjoy the fine champagne and some excellent entertainment."

On cue, a line of extravagantly dressed flamenco dancers glided out into the courtyard, and the crowd cheered as the music began. I wanted very much to catch a closer look at that relic, but Isabel and Olinda, two of the kinder Haciendellas, ran up to me and insisted I join a game of Ghost Coyote.

We ran to hide, and the "ghost coyotes" were supposed to sense our thoughts and find us. It wasn't really a game, more an excuse for the nobles and Haciendellas to pair off in the dark corners of the gardens. Not particularly wanting to be "found," I bent behind a large trellis, covered in purple lilac blossoms, deep in the hedge maze. I could hear Olinda giggling somewhere nearby, followed by the deeper laugh of one of the nobles. I bent even farther behind the trellis.

A pair of hands slid around my waist. "Surprise."

I spun with a start, only to come face-to-face with Landon. It was as if my pulse had been struck by lightning.

Taking advantage of my shock, he pulled me close. "Where have you been, Maggie Davis? I about thought I'd scared you off forever."

"No," I said, breathless. "I've just been...busy."

Landon ran his hand up my back, curling his fingers in my hair. "Busy, huh?"

He pressed his lips to my temples, then slowly moved them

down my cheek. "When are you coming back?" he asked between kisses. "Isn't Ella better yet?"

For some reason, I'd dreaded having to explain this to Landon, even now knowing that Álvar had no interest in me as his mistress. I tried to avoid answering, but Landon pulled away a little to meet my gaze.

"It's complicated," I said, lowering my eyes.

"How is it complicated? If Ella's better, you just come home."

"Ella doesn't want to leave, for one thing."

"And?" Landon asked.

"And I've been given an…opportunity. Álvar thinks I have a talent with relics. He's been training me. Him and Moon John."

Landon was quiet. I set my hand to his cheek. "I missed you, though. I meant to write to you, but…"

My voice trailed off. Landon moved closer and pressed his lips hesitantly against mine. The kiss sent a hot shiver over my skin. I tilted my head back to enjoy it, but in the corner of my mind, I remembered that Connelly was here, probably patrolling the grounds with those beady eyes. He'd make trouble if he caught me with Landon.

"We'd better be careful," I said, turning my head away.

Landon pulled back abruptly. "Why? Who would care?" There was an edge in his voice. "Álvar?"

"Excuse me?"

He released his hold on me with a frustrated sigh but, stung, I pursued it further. "What are you trying to say, Landon?"

"I'm not saying anything that hasn't been said and laughed about ten times over by the folks back at The Desert Rose."

I felt like I'd been slapped. "And you believe them?"

"No…"

"You obviously do."

"I'm not sure what I think," Landon admitted angrily. "But can you blame me? Everyone knows what he's like. And maybe you feel like you owe him, since he saved your sister."

"I can't believe what I'm hearing," I said, turning away from him. Hot tears pricked at my eyes. "From *you,* of all people."

Landon let out a frustrated sigh. "Well, how was I supposed to know any different? I haven't heard from you in a week. Not one letter. Not one word. You didn't even look for me tonight at the party—I had to track *you* down. You were too busy playin' around with the Haciendellas."

"I did look for you," I said, but a knot of guilt twisted inside me. I'd meant to write him. Why hadn't I?

"And whatever happened to you trying to free that Apache?" Landon went on, ignoring my weak defense. "Or finding out who started those fires? The fires that killed your family. I suppose now that you're some pampered Hacienda princess, you just don't care anymore."

"How dare you," I said, hot tears pricking at my eyes. "How *dare* you bring up my family in such a way?" I turned and stumbled away from him, but I could hear him running up behind me.

"Maggie, wait."

"Leave me alone!" I cried. I pushed through the nearby hedgerow to escape. The bushes and tangled vines scratched my arms, but I ran as fast as I could. My heart was aching, my head spinning.

Back in the loud crush of people and merriment, I should have felt relieved, but I didn't. My skin pulsed where Landon's hands had gripped me, and his words burned in my ears. I tried to catch my breath, but it felt as if the pain was sitting against my chest.

Then I noticed Álvar approaching. Given Landon's words, he was the *last* person I wanted to talk to.

"Are you ready?" he asked with a sly smile as he came to my side.

I tensed a little. "Ready?"

"For the Djinn relic, Maggie. I wish for you to have a turn."

CHAPTER TWENTY-FOUR

Álvar led me into another secluded area of the garden, an ivy draped pavilion surrounded by hedgerows and huge ceramic pots of rose bushes. Several nobles, Haciendellas, and curious onlookers filled in the gaps, watching. Sheik Nadir Ibrahim waited beside an empty chair, holding an elaborate lidded box, inside of which I assumed the Djinn relic lay. When I didn't move from the entrance to the pavilion, Sheik Nadir smiled and motioned to the chair. I looked to Álvar.

He nodded. "Go on, Maggie."

My breath trembled as I lowered into the chair. I was still upset about my conversation with Landon, but curiosity was rapidly taking over.

Sheik Nadir came before me, and slowly he opened the lid of his carved box. Inside, the relic, no bigger than a silver dollar, gleamed on the muslin lining. It was an iridescent violet, a color unlike anything I'd seen. I wanted to touch it, to hold it close to me.

"I understand you have a gift with relics," Sheik Nadir said.

A little rush of pride filled my chest. "I suppose so."

"Have you heard of the sacred Djinn before?"

I shook my head, unable to take my eyes from the gleaming piece.

"It is rare, indeed. Powerful and dangerous."

"What does it do?" I asked, my voice little above a whisper.

Sheik Nadir's green eyes flickered with a strange reverence. "When you hold the sacred Djinn in the palm of your hand, it will show you the deepest wishes of your heart."

I started to reach for the glistening relic, but the Sheik grabbed my hand.

"A word of caution. The Djinn will show you these things on its own terms. Wide is its vision and clear its sight."

I had no idea what he meant, but his words made me hesitate.

"Go on, Maggie," Álvar said softly. He was standing behind me, and his breath tickled the back of my ear.

"Have you tried it?" I asked.

"Not yet," Álvar said. "I suppose I, too, fear what I will see." His eyes were shadowed with distant thoughts, a vague hunger.

Sheik Nadir moved the box closer to me. "Take it. Fearful you may be, but it's unlikely that the chance to use such a relic will come your way again."

He was right. I lifted the Djinn into my hand; it felt cool and smooth as a pebble on a river bottom. An energy pulsed through me, full of hunger and desire. Was it a shadow relic, then? I realized it didn't matter. I wouldn't let the piece go. A whisper of longing rustled through my mind—not so much a voice, but a call just the same. Drawing in a breath, I closed my eyes and bid the magic to do what it would.

Pale shadows, like white smoke, drifted over my vision, and flashes of gold light rippled in the background. In my ears, a wind rushed by, low and constant and hollow. My body seemed to dissolve into the gentle nothingness around me.

And then I saw them. Mama and Papa. Jeb. Josiah. They stood in the distance, surrounded by red, sun-drenched desert. Their images wavered in the heat, but they were calling to me. Reaching out and calling for me to come. Come and be with them forever.

Ella ran past me toward them. I tried to reach out to her—I wanted to run like Ella. I wanted to be with them, but I was nothing, less than sunshine or wind.

Landon appeared before me, closer than the others, but still out of reach. He beckoned for me, his eyes like blue flames. I wanted him to come and hold me. I wanted to feel his lips on mine.

But I was only made of want, with no body to act on it. If I could have screamed, I would have. I made one final attempt to go to them before a swift, blinding darkness took over. It blotted out the sun, poured down from the sky like pitch, filling the earth around me. It swept away Landon and my parents and Ella and Jeb.

And then, there was silence.

Smoke.

The smell of it cut into my being. I wanted to go far, far away from that smell. Because even in this black, endless expanse of nothingness, I knew that smoke heralded…

Fire.

First came the softest of orange glow. Then the heat. The glint of flames cast my shadow into the darkness before me, and I realized I had a body again. Though as I examined my hand before me, it looked different in a way my mind was incapable of understanding.

I could run away now, but instead, I turned slowly to face the flames.

Yahn stood in the middle of them. *Maggie.* His voice echoed in my being. *Have you forgotten?*

He reached out his strong hand. In the flickering shadows, I saw the images of others like him. Apaches. Standing in the midst of the blazing fire, they called for me. Their voices mingled with the roar of flames to make a deafening blur. Again and again, they spoke a single word.

Sitsi.

I didn't know what the word meant, but something deep inside me was certain it was important. It mattered. I had to remember.

I'm coming, I shouted.

The fire raged, ready to consume me. Only Yahn's dark eyes cut through the flames. I tried to reach for him. I screamed over the endless cries of, *Sitsi, Sitsi, Sitsi.*

I'm coming!

A hand gently slapped my cheek; the contact stirred me from the vision of fire. From somewhere beyond, I heard a man speaking my name.

Another slap, and I realized it was reality. Somehow, I could feel that the Djinn relic was no longer in my hand. My eyelids fluttered open.

"Maggie?" Álvar sounded more nervous than I'd ever heard him.

I looked up through blurry eyes.

"She's waking."

"Can you hear me? Are you all right?"

I blinked hard.

"Forgive me, Maggie," Álvar said, brushing the sweat-pasted hair from my forehead. "I should have known that with your talents, the Djinn would be too overpowering."

"Help her up, Álvar."

He and Sheik Nadir lifted me gently from the ground, where I had somehow ended up.

"Are you all right?" Álvar asked again, studying my face.

I released a slow, shaking breath. The images still flashed in my mind, so vivid it was as if I saw them with my waking eye. The fire. My family. Yahn. I couldn't escape them, how I'd failed them. I sat up.

Álvar set a cautious hand on my arm. "Are you quite well?"

"I'm okay," I said, standing on wobbly legs.

"Perhaps you should sit for a moment longer—"

"No. Please. I have to go."

Without another word, I staggered away from the pavilion, away from the party. Away from this sparkling, empty world.

Midnight found me curled up in Ella's bed, wide awake. After leaving the party, I had retreated immediately to her little attached room, crawled in beside her, and held her close. Ella's warm, sweet breath fanned against my cheek. I squeezed her small hand, never wanting to let go.

Since coming to the Hacienda, I had barely seen Ella awake. Yes, we shared the same suite, but the chief nurse, Señora Duarte, kept her on a rigid schedule of studies and outings. And that, combined with my own constant parade of mindless teatimes and pampering, meant we rarely crossed paths.

It was good to be with my sister, but the vision I'd had under the magic of the Djinn relic haunted me. Yahn's words, *Have you forgotten?* echoed more than anything else—maybe because I *had* forgotten. Landon was right. I had allowed myself to be swept up in the glamour and opulence of the Hacienda. Of Álvar and his relics. I had allowed myself to forget what really mattered.

But not anymore. With a determined clench to my jaw, I crawled out of Ella's bed and sat down at the writing desk in our quarters. I would compose a letter to Sheriff Leander, insisting that he examine Landon's findings about the Chimera Gang. I would demand that he begin a full investigation into the matter and, in the meantime, offer his most capable protection to the Apaches and to Yahn.

After five different drafts, I'd written a version of the letter that satisfied me. I read it over again, wishing I had better penmanship, and wondering if it wasn't too brash. But did it matter? We had to get to the bottom of this, and Sheriff Leander needed to know the truth. Who cared if he thought I was too presumptuous? Besides, for all he knew, I had the ear of Álvar Castilla. And that alone gave me some small power.

I enclosed the letter in a gilded Hacienda envelope. It had to go out immediately, that night. With a firm nod, I pulled on my robe and tucked the envelope into my pocket.

The dim hallways stretched out with nothing but carpet and low-burning lamps. Most servants were probably out tending to the last guests at the party or starting the huge task of cleaning up. I searched for a single maid or valet but found only empty rooms.

Then, just as I approached a T intersection in the hall, men's voices drifted into my hearing. Rough, agitated voices.

I halted where I stood. I recognized one of them all too well. Few men had a more unpleasant way of talking than Mr. Percy Connelly.

I flattened my back to the wall of the corridor. Part of me knew I should run back to my quarters as fast as possible, and yet the rest of me begged to stay. The clandestine tone in Mr. Connelly's voice hinted at dirty dealings and some ripe, important thing.

"He's a damn fool, I say. Having that ruddy Sheik shipped in with his gibberish relic. And all for what? For show."

A second voice came. "I want to know how he's paying for this. His family's good name, no doubt? Or perhaps Hacienda bonds?"

Both men laughed. I strained to recall how I recognized the other voice.

"Castilla thinks relics are going to save him," Connelly sneered. "He thinks that stupid girl is going to save him."

I flattened even closer to the wall, squeezing in my breath.

"Nothing will save him from what I have in store," the other man said.

I finally placed his voice. It was Emerson Bolger.

"I tell you this," Emerson continued. "If Castilla doesn't cooperate, he has reason to fear. He knows now what I am capable of. I will do exactly what we have discussed."

"Careful what you say," Connelly hissed. "These walls have a way of listenin'." He sighed. "We'd better get back to that party before someone notices. Leave those in your room. We'll talk more later."

I heard the sound of a door closing, and then their footsteps growing more and more faint. My pulse throbbed in my head, beating out the sound of my own whirling thoughts.

I didn't know exactly what to make of what I'd just heard. But it was clearly important. I peered around the edge of the wall. The hallway stretched out in both directions, completely empty. The only door close enough to be the one Bolger had closed was right in front of me.

My heart beating hard, I looked in the direction they'd gone. My mind hollered to me in two voices. One shouted to run back to my room; the other asked me what I would find behind that door. What *was* Bolger up to? The cruel way he spoke of Álvar caused a tug of loyalty within me. For all of his flaws, Álvar had been nothing but generous to Ella and me since we arrived. I'd hate to see men like Connelly and Bolger try and hurt his good name.

I stepped to his door and set my hand on it, the beating sound in my head drowning out all other noise. But I had to know. With a trembling hand, I twisted open the brass doorknob and stepped into Emerson Bolger's room.

A stack of papers had been set on the desk right by the door. I bit my lip. What if I found something in those papers? Some incriminating tidbit, some way to solve the mystery that literally haunted my dreams? I tossed a glance at the open door. Surely I'd hear if Mr. Bolger was coming. I just needed one quick peek.

As gingerly as possible, I lifted the papers to the light. The writing on the first page had been hastily scribbled. Something about the Alkalie Mountains. Mining companies.

> THE BORDER ALONG THE NORTH RIDGE OF ALDO'S PEAK HAS PROVEN HIGHLY LUCRATIVE IN PROCURING MERMAID RELICS.

I bit my lip and flipped to the second page. More random notes beneath it. I perked up slightly at what looked like the description of a relic.

MAIN COLOR: RED. ACCENTED WITH BLACK MARBLING. STRANGE DARK GLOW. WILL HAVE S. PRITCHARD EXAMINE.

Frowning, I flipped through the rest of the pages. There were receipts and hand-scrawled notes about various mining ventures in other counties. Nothing I could use to directly incriminate Bolger, but they still got my mind humming. I couldn't help thinking of my conversations with Álvar, of his words in the Harpy Caverns when he spoke of some men who would do anything to find the truth about the origins of relics. Was Bolger a man like that?

I set down the papers and backed out of the room, closing Mr. Bolger's door quietly behind me. But as I turned to go back to my room, my eyes fell on the figure of a man rounding the corner at the end of the hall.

Emerson Bolger.

The sight of him shot through me like a bullet. My knees locked, and I suddenly felt as if I were made of stone. Mr. Bolger approached, massive, powerful, nearly a foot taller than me. "What are you doing here?" he demanded.

I was still as a statue.

"Why aren't you at that silly party?"

Had he seen me in his room or not? His cold gaze betrayed nothing.

I scraped for a semblance of calm. "I was tired."

Mr. Bolger frowned. "Indeed." His eyes appraised me, and he snorted again. "You have no idea who you're tangling with."

"I'm not tangling with anyone. Señor Castilla and I have worked out a business arrangement, where—"

"A *business arrangement*? That makes it even worse. Trust me, my dear, you don't want to be doing business with the likes of

Álvar Castilla."

"You're a fine one to talk."

He snorted. "I'm here to buy him out. And at the price I'm askin', it's a damn right act of charity."

I narrowed my eyes. Was this what he had been talking about with Connelly?

Mr. Bolger smirked. "Doubtless you've been wooed and won by the fine gifts and lavish parties. Maybe you're as foolish as you look." One of his dark, thick brows rose. "Álvar Castilla is *deep* in debt, Miss. Consuming, irreparable debt."

I was silent, and his eyes gleamed with satisfaction. "It's all a big cover-up. A cover-up by him and his pampered Hacienda snobs. See, not only has he squandered his father's entire treasury, but he's buried himself so deeply in credit and bad investments that the entire town of Burning Mesa belongs to others in distant counties. It's all tied up in a mess of collateral and liens and back payments." He laughed. "If he has any sense at all, he'll do business with me, on my terms."

I stared at Mr. Bolger, trying to piece it all together in a way that made sense. "So you've come to either buy him out or ruin him?"

Mr. Bolger's mouth twitched with a smile. "You catch on quick."

I took a step back, my pulse racing. What kind of villain was standing before me? "And how will you ruin him? What kind of retaliation are you capable of?"

He seemed to sense the suggestion buried deep in my words. His thick brow knitted, shadowing his eyes. "If I were you, I'd watch out for your own hide and not poke around in matters that don't concern you."

I said nothing, and Mr. Bolger grimaced. “I have work to do.”

“Yes. I should go back to my room, anyway.”

“Good. I suggest you stay there. Bad things can happen when little girls start snooping around.”

CHAPTER TWENTY-FIVE

By dawn the next morning, I was on one of the stallions from the Hacienda's stables, galloping at full speed toward Burning Mesa, the letter I'd written still sitting on my desk. The situation had become much more pressing. New suspects had entered the picture. I needed to speak with Sheriff Leander myself.

As I rode, I noticed a strange color to the sky, an off scent in the breeze. I couldn't put my finger on what it could be, but my mind was too occupied to dwell on it much. In town, the streets were mostly empty. The smithy's fire was just starting to cough up smoke; a farmer woman arranged fresh vegetables on her cart for the day's business.

And yet I could sense the change the moment I got into town. It was *too* empty. I pulled on my horse's reins to halt him. Perking up my ears, I listened. And then I heard it.

Raised voices. Chanting. It was the same sound the lynching

mob had made when they gathered outside the sheriff's office.

Yahn.

I jabbed my heels into the horse's side, and he took off down the street. The buildings and storefronts blurred past me; all I could think was, *Please don't let me be too late. Please, please, don't let them hang him.*

Like before, the mob of men seethed outside the sheriff's office, raising their torches and weapons. At least the rangers lined along the deck sidewalk in front were preventing any kind of violence. But that could change at any moment.

After tying my horse, I pushed right into the center of the mob. I wasn't afraid of these men with their tight fists and loud, angry words. I elbowed through them, ignoring their irritation. Jake, one of the rangers on the deck outside the sheriff's office, recognized me. He was among Adelaide's many admirers as well as a regular I'd served at The Desert Rose. He knew me well enough to know the sheriff and I were on friendly terms.

"Maggie," he called, leaning forward to hold out a hand. I grabbed it, and he lifted me up onto the walkway. "You shouldn't be here," he said, shouting over the roar of the mob. "It's not safe."

"What's happening? Is it the judge from Durango again?"

Jake looked hesitant to speak.

"What is it?" I asked. "Please."

"Another town was burned last night, twenty miles from here. There were no survivors."

All at once, I realized that it was smoke I smelled on the wind this morning. Smoke that colored the sky. The scent of it filled my nostrils now, choking me like poison. Unbidden, the flames that consumed my home burned in my eyes, and I could hear Dusty whinny in terror. I could see Jeb watching me as the smoke engulfed him. "Another town."

Jake set his hand on my arm. "You should go."

I blinked hard. I couldn't just walk away. *Because* the flames still burned in my eyes, I couldn't walk away.

"No. I have to talk with Sheriff Leander."

"You know I can't let you do that. He has a prisoner in there for questioning."

"Please. It's very important. It's about the razings."

Jake pursed his lips. "I can't."

"*Please*, Jake." I set a hand on his arm.

He exhaled and nudged his head to the door. "Make it quick, Maggie."

"Thank you."

I slipped through the door, shutting out the anger of the mob behind me.

The sight that met me inside made my heart stop. Yahn sat in a chair in the center of the office, chains pinning his wrists behind his back, and a ball and chain had been strapped around his left ankle. Sheriff Leander leaned against the edge of his desk, rubbing his eyes wearily. When I stepped into the room, they both looked up with a start.

Sheriff Leander stood. "How did you get in here?"

I couldn't take my eyes off Yahn. The sight of him bound like that tore at me. He looked so tired, so worn down, with dark circles under his eyes and his black hair limp. It pained me to think of him sitting in that barren cell, waiting for his possible death. Wondering if his people would be attacked.

I felt an unexpected longing to throw my arms around his neck, to hold him and tell him I would do anything to help.

"Maggie, are you listening to me?"

I looked up and forced myself to remember why I'd come. "The Apaches aren't responsible for the razings."

"What?"

"It wasn't them. There's plenty of proof it was someone else. I tried to tell you before. I explained it to one of your rangers." I pulled out the newspaper clipping and practically shoved it into the sheriff's hands. "Look at this for starters. Ever thought about it being the Chimera Gang? It all makes sense, Sheriff. Their leader was hanged, and they want revenge. Everyone knows they use fire relics, that they're capable of terrible violence. And revenge seems right up their alley—"

"Maggie."

"No, listen. The judge who passed the death sentence on Petey McCoy was from Haydenville. And then Haydenville burns! How can that be a coincidence?"

"Maggie—"

"But that's not all. One of the jurors on the case was from Buena. Buena's gone. And—"

Sheriff Leander gripped my shoulders. "Maggie, listen to me."

My heart was beating fast from finally being able to talk to him. "What?"

"The Chimera Gang isn't responsible."

"They are. I'm sure of it."

He sighed. "It's a good theory. It really is. But it can't be true."

"What are you talking about? Look at this article!"

"The Chimera Gang was captured in the California Territories three months ago. Didn't you hear about it?"

I stared at him, struck silent. He released his grip on me and went to slump wearily in the chair behind his desk. "I'm sorry to disappoint you. I wish you were right. I wish it were that simple."

"No," I said softly. "No. It can't be true. Maybe they busted out of prison or…or…"

"I'm afraid we're going to have to face the facts that are staring us in the face, Maggie. I don't want to. I know *you* don't want to. But it's getting hard to dispute."

"What are you talking about?"

Sheriff Leander sighed, but his trailing glance to Yahn revealed everything.

I shook my head. "You can't honestly think—"

"There's no one else it could be. The evidence is right there. Motive and a proven tendency to violence. Come on now. Be reasonable."

I looked to Yahn, my heart breaking. His gaze was fixed on the floor.

"No!" I cried. "He saved my life. I know he didn't do this!"

"Maybe not him," Sheriff Leander said. "I'm willing to believe his personal innocence. But the Apaches in general *are* responsible. There's no other way around it."

"You're wrong!"

Sheriff Leander pounded his desk with a fist. "If you care so much about this Injun here, then why don't you convince him to talk? I can lessen his sentence if he tells us where to find the Apache camp."

"Never," I said fiercely.

He rubbed his brow. "Then we have nothing further to discuss, Miss Davis. I'd appreciate if you'd leave the way you came."

"No, wait! I have more. What about Emerson Bolger? He's a shady type if I ever saw one. He has powerful relics, and I just *know* he's up to something, Sheriff. I—"

"We're not discussing this, Maggie."

"But you have to at least *listen*—"

"I said leave!"

The ferocity of his tone stunned me into silence.

The sheriff let out a frustrated sigh. "Dammit, Maggie. I told you not to get involved in this. It's dangerous and far too complicated for a young girl such as yourself. You leave this to the professionals. I'm sorry, but if I see you prodding into this matter again, I'll have to cite you for interference with the law. And that means jail time if you can't pay the hefty fine. Understand?"

I could barely breathe with the frustration in my chest. "Sheriff."

"*Good-bye*, Miss Davis."

Stung, I turned to the door. I passed a final glance over my shoulder at Yahn, knowing he wouldn't look up. Then, without a word, I left the sheriff's office.

I stumbled away from the angry mob and down the streets of Burning Mesa. Out of habit, I found myself at The Desert Rose. Maybe I wanted to smell the familiar tingle of whiskey and cigarettes, to hear Eddie's music jingling on the old piano. I fully expected to get a tongue lashing from Mr. Connelly when I came through the swinging doors, but he wasn't there. It struck me as strange—not that I was crying any tears about it.

A small crowd of men sat at the bar, talking with intense, nervous tones. Most of the girls were mulling around the saloon as well, wearing their robes and frightened looks. When I spotted Adelaide's familiar face, the weight of my troubles rushed down on me all at once. My throat swelled. Tears burned in my eyes.

Adelaide rushed over and linked her arm in mine.

"Land's sake, Maggie. It feels like the world's gone crazy."

She pulled me aside to an empty corner of the saloon and sat me down at a table. I pressed a fist against the wood surface, breathing hard, wishing I could smash a hole through it.

Adelaide considered me for a moment, and then waved at Eddie. "A scotch," she said, pointing at me.

"I don't want it."

"Want and need are two separate things." She sat down beside me, setting her hand on mine. "I'm real sorry, Maggie," she said. "Those razers have gotta be out there somewhere. Someone's bound to find them sooner or later."

"Maybe." I shrugged. "But it will be too late for the Apaches."

Eddie came back with three shot glasses and a bottle. "I thought we could all use one."

"Amen to that." Adelaide poured a drink, but it stayed untouched on the table in front of me. For a long moment, we were all silent.

Then Eddie spoke. "Adelaide here has told me what you're trying to do. And I believe you."

I met his warm gaze. "About the Apaches?"

He nodded. "Doesn't seem right that they're doing it. I think someone's hiding something."

"Darn right about that."

"But who?" Adelaide said, pouring herself another shot. "And why?"

I had mulled this question over so many times. Why wasn't it any clearer? The dark thought needled in me that the real culprits might be far away, impossible to find, impossible to track down. But I cast that idea away. I wasn't about to give up—not yet. Not when there were solid suspects afoot.

"We need to look into Emerson Bolger," I said, casting a glance around to make sure no listening ears were close. Adelaide and Eddie leaned in conspiratorially.

"He's up to something," I whispered. "I overheard him talking about Álvar last night. Nothing to directly incriminate him, mind you, but it made me mighty suspicious."

Eddie tapped his lips. "He *does* want Mr. Castilla's mining territory. Everyone knows that."

"But why burn the other towns?" Adelaide asked.

"Maybe they were other competitors. Maybe that's what he does when they don't give him what he wants."

Adelaide twisted her glass on the table in front of her. "Seems hard to believe they'd be so evil."

I shook my head. "Men murder for relics all the time. Imagine what a powerful man like Bolger would do for an entire mining area."

I set my hand on the table. "I'm going to the miner's camp to ask around. Maybe they've heard something about Mr. Bolger or his methods."

"The mining camp?" Adelaide snorted. "Are you crazy?"

"Why not?"

"You've never been there, have you?"

"It's awful dangerous, Miss Maggie," Eddie agreed. "No place for a nice girl like you. Besides, I've heard there's some strange stuff goin' on over there."

I frowned. "What do you mean?"

"Not sure, to be honest. But I hear things. All I know is the miners from Burning Mesa have been on edge for months."

I pondered this for a moment. "All the more reason I need to check it out."

Eddie shook his head. "I don't know…"

I gave an imploring look to Adelaide, and she sighed. "Well, if you got your mind made up, I guess I have to go with you."

"Thanks. I'll owe you one."

Eddie ran a hand through his hair, and then shrugged. "I still say don't go, but if you have to, talk to a man named Gibbs. He's the most decent of any of the miners I've met."

"Thanks, Eddie."

"Thank me when you're back here safe."

I smiled a little. "We'll be careful."

The next morning, I slipped away from the Hacienda once more. It took some fancy maneuvers to get Adelaide out of The Desert Rose, but she pulled it off, as she always did. Since I'd come in a carriage, we decided stealth required us to go on foot to the mining camp.

The sun beat down with extra vengeance, and a thin cloud of red dust hung on the air. Adelaide and I stuck to the covered walkways outside the buildings on Main Street. As we approached the Cooper Hotel, I saw him.

Landon.

He was coming out of the front doors, setting his cowboy hat over his tousled blond hair. I froze in my tracks, but it was too late. He looked up and spotted me at once.

"Hiya, Landon," Adelaide said brightly. "What are you up to?"

"Nothing much." He shifted awkwardly, tossing me a glance. "I have some business in town."

I couldn't tell if he was still mad at me. I didn't know if I was mad at *him*. I avoided his gaze, wishing I could be anywhere else. Adelaide seemed to notice the tension but tried to continue as if she hadn't. "Me and Maggie are just headed—"

"Out," I said quickly. "Out of town. We'll see you around, Landon."

I grabbed Adelaide's arm and started to pull her away. Landon's voice came, soft and pained. "Maggie."

Was it pride that stuck my feet in the ground, refusing to turn around? Either way, I didn't face him. "We've gotta go," I said.

I pulled Adelaide down the walkway. I could feel Landon standing there, staring as we moved on, and the awareness shot me in the back like an arrow.

When we were far enough away, Adelaide gave me a look. "You mind telling me what that was about? I thought you were sweet on Landon."

"I *am*." My head was pounding. I wanted to tell Adelaide about our argument at the party the other night, but the words hung in the air, unspoken. I lowered my gaze away from her, scraping a line in the dust with my toe.

"Is it Connelly?" Adelaide asked, touching my arm. "Tryin' to keep you away from Landon the way he tries to keep me away from Bobby?"

"He *did* say something like that, but—"

"The bastard," Adelaide said, her voice tight with anger. "I swear, one of these days, I'm gonna give that man what he's got comin' to him."

I'd never seen such darkness in her eyes. "Don't you go doing anything crazy," I said. "He's mad enough at you as it is."

Adelaide sighed. "Don't worry; I won't do anything. That's the problem."

I touched her hand, but I knew I was in no position to pass out advice.

We passed out of the main area of Burning Mesa and into the open desert, drawing closer to the red-rock at the base of the Alkali Mountains. A column of thick black smoke rose up from a cluster of sagebrush and desert trees—the miners' camp. Adelaide held my hand as we drew closer.

"You stick right by me, you hear? Trust me when I say that these types ain't no gentlemen."

"Don't worry," I said, pulling out one of my siren relic vials. "I came prepared."

Adelaide stared at the vial and then at me. "Where'd you get that?"

"Moon John."

I uncorked the tube and sniffed cautiously. There wasn't any strong scent. Maybe a hint of sweetness.

"Here goes nothing." I drew in a quick breath and tipped the liquid down my throat.

It burned like ice and warmth all at once. Like pleasure and pain. For a single moment, the sensation was almost unbearable, but then it subsided with an involuntary shudder, leaving me with only the calm residue of water magic.

"Well?" Adelaide asked, analyzing me. "Did it work?"

"Only one way to find out."

The camp consisted of four rows of tents that looked like they used to be white. A fire smoldered in the center, with a cast-iron pot hanging over the heat, the smell of bad chili bubbling out of it. Most of the miners were gone up to the mountains, but a few stragglers—wounded or sick—lay about in their tents, whittling at wood blocks or smoking hand-rolled cigarettes. Every one of them watched us as we entered the camp.

"We're looking for Gibbs," I said to the nearest miner, who was shuffling a worn deck of cards over and over.

The miner scratched his head and pointed to the left with his foot. "He's over there in that last tent. Says he got a bum leg from a shaft cart bumpin' him. I think he's a ruddy liar. Man's been dodging work three days in five lately."

As we approached the end tent, I expected to see a crusty, rough-looking codger like all the others in that camp, but instead, a smooth-faced man in his forties with slicked blond hair and a lazy eye sat on a stool at the entrance to his tent, leaning back against the tent pole. He was tuning a worn violin, plucking the strings and turning the black pegs a bit.

When he saw us coming, a smile spread over his face. "Afternoon, ladies," he said, his voice thick with a strange accent.

"You Gibbs?" I asked.

The man smiled. "I am Nikolai Giboroskov. These men think my name hard to say, so they call me Gibbs."

He said Gibbs long and funny, like *Geebs*.

I smiled. "Nice to meet you, Mr. Gibbs."

"So, what can Gibbs do for two lovely ladies?"

"We got some questions for you," Adelaide said, her arms crossed.

Gibbs blinked. "But of course."

"What do you know about Emerson Bolger?" I asked.

A blank look crossed Gibb's face. "Bolger? I never hear of him."

He sounded utterly genuine. I exchanged a look with Adelaide.

"You ain't heard anything about how he wants to buy out your territory?" she asked. "Maybe you've seen some men around? Had some threats?"

Gibbs shook his head. "I am sorry. Nothing out of usual has happened."

I frowned, remembering Eddie's words. "Well, that can't be true. We heard there's been some strange things going on around here."

The smile tightened on Gibbs's face. "I don't know what you mean."

Adelaide narrowed her eyes. "We hear that you all are acting like you have something to hide."

Gibbs paled. "I know nothing."

"But—"

"Sorry. I know nothing." He stood. His hands shook as he set his violin back in its case and closed the lid. "I must go now."

"Hold on a minute," I said. "We didn't come all this way to get shut down like this."

"I'm sorry," Gibbs said again. "You girls leave now. Do not come back to camp."

"We only want to ask you a few questions."

"No. No, you must leave." He pushed the violin case into his tent, kicked his boots through the opening. "You go. I—I know nothing."

I jumped in his way before he could duck into the tent himself. His lazy eye looked even wilder in his distress. "I know nothing!"

I refused to budge. "I think you do."

CHAPTER TWENTY-SIX

Gibbs looked about as pale as a whitewashed wall. He wouldn't meet my gaze. His hands trembled. "I will not talk."

"You will," I said firmly, focusing all of my energy on the siren elixir that coursed through my veins. "Maybe you don't realize who you're dealing with. I am the personal relic expert for Álvar Castilla, and you will do as I say."

Gibbs swallowed hard. "Please. I have done nothing wrong."

"You'd better start talking," Adelaide said, narrowing her eyes.

"I work hard. I must send money to wife and child in home country."

"You don't have to be afraid," I said, softening my tone. "It's not *you* we're after. We need information about this camp. About what's been going on."

I picked up Gibbs's stool and motioned for him to sit, which he did, shakily.

"Please," I said gently. "Your words are safe with us. But it's very important that we know."

He leaned against his thighs and rubbed his face hard. A sheen of sweat glistened on his temples. He didn't want to talk, but he had to. The magic left him no choice.

"All started one year ago. Boss say we have to work double shifts. We have to work nights. We have to work days off. No time to relax. Boss keep pushing us, and we start to run out of places to dig. So boss say go deeper into mountain. And we do. We dig and dig. We find many, many relic. But we still have to dig.

"But then we hit one layer, and the relics stop. Only stone. Boss mad. He say, keep digging. Like he looking for something but not finding it. He work us day and night. Many men sick and injured. But we keep going. Until…"

Gibbs fell quiet. His gaze was far away, in some dark hole in the mountain. Fear flickered in his eyes like candlelight.

"Until what?" Adelaide asked. "What happened?"

With a shaky hand, Gibbs pulled a little brown glass bottle from his inner vest pocket. He uncorked it and took a quick swig. His body wriggled as the hot liquor rippled through him. "One day, the stone starts coming up dark as night sky. And then we find it."

"What?" I asked softly.

"A relic. A full skeleton. Bigger than dragon. Bigger than behemoth."

"What was it?"

Gibbs shook his head slowly, rubbing his arms as if he were cold. "I do not know. But something about it made me feel cold and dark and angry inside."

Adelaide and I exchanged a significant glance.

"We call in Chinese excavators to extract bones," Gibbs went on. "But they refuse to touch them. Boss spitting mad, but they won't. So boss say we have to do it. No one wants to. We all vote and agree to leave relic alone and bury tunnel. Then Boss says he fire us all and not pay us our wages for that year, which we had been soon to receive. So we have no other choice. We carve out relic and bring it up to surface."

He shook his head. "We send it to refinery. I do not see it again."

Something in the way his good eye shifted made me sense a lie.

"Or maybe you did," I said. "My gut tells me you aren't giving us the full story."

Gibbs stared at me, horrified.

I went on, his fear emboldening me. "Maybe a few men in this camp held onto it. Maybe you did?"

He shook his head, eyes wide,.

"Maybe some of you miners thought you'd use it to clean out your competition," I pressed. "Since the miner boss was working you so hard to find more relics, maybe the easiest solution was to kill off the other mining camps and take their territories!"

"No!" Gibbs cried. "No! Nothing like that."

"You're lying!"

"No!" He fell to his knees. Tears sprang from his eyes. "You are right that I kept some. You are right about that. But I did not hurt anyone with it. I swear to you!"

Adelaide and I looked at each other again, but she seemed equally unsure.

"Please," Gibbs begged. "Please not tell boss I keep a piece. He will not pay me. I must have money to send back to wife and son. Please!"

"Take it easy," Adelaide said. "We're not tellin' anyone. We're just trying to understand what you're talking about."

I knelt down beside him and put my hand on his shoulder to try and calm him. "Who else kept a piece of the relic?"

Gibbs winced. "Only me."

"No one else took any? You sure of this?"

He nodded. "I do not know why I did. I was in charge of seeing that all of relic went into carts and up the shaft. This was my job. And as I check last cart, I…I take small piece."

"What did you do with it?" I asked.

"Nothing. Once I get it back to camp, I become very afraid of it. It fills me with that same cold feeling. I do not want this. I fear it. So I bury it."

His eyes trail to a gnarled, dead tree on the horizon.

"Did you bury it there?" I asked.

Gibbs nodded shakily. "I do not want it close, but I want no one else to find it, to have it. So I bury where I can keep eye on it."

The tree, all bent and sinister looking, made an eerie black outline in the white sunshine. A cold shiver trilled through me. "Will you show us?"

He shook his head. "No. *No.* It must stay in earth forever."

Adelaide set her hand on his arm. "Please. It's very important that we see."

"Very well." He sighed, and with a strained limp, he led us to the shadow of the tree.

He worked slowly, his breath growing more and more labored with every inch he excavated. My heart beat harder as well, though I tried not to show it. I watched the silver shovel cut deeper and deeper into the red dirt. Finally, the edge clanked against something, and a shudder seemed to pass through Gibbs's body. But then, slowly, he bent. With his hands he cut along the edges of a small cylinder. Shaking, he pulled it up from the earth.

It was a regular old pickle jar, but inside I could see a small object wrapped in a red handkerchief. Gibbs pushed the jar into my hands suddenly, startling me.

"I will not touch it again. You want to see it, you see it." He shook his head. "I do not want it there anymore, watching me from the roots of this tree. You take it. Take it from me. Please."

I frowned, twisting the jar at various angles. I certainly couldn't see what all the fuss was about. "All right," I said, shrugging. "We'll take it off your hands."

"You will?"

"Sure."

Adelaide eyed the jar warily. "Maybe we shouldn't."

"Why not? Look at this thing. It's no bigger than an acorn."

She shrugged, and I turned to Gibbs. "Thanks very much for all your help."

"You not tell boss?"

"We swear it. Your secret is safe with us."

He nodded, but he didn't look even a drop more relaxed.

"Be careful with it," he said, his voice low. "Take it to refinery and never look back."

I nodded, having no intention to do so. "We surely will. Thanks again."

We left the camp, but Gibbs stayed by the dead tree, staring at the hole in the earth.

The jar sat on the pale grass beside the Salt Wash, sunlight reflecting off the water sparkling against the glass surface. Adelaide and I had hardly spoken since leaving Gibbs. But as we rested by the river for a minute, the subject couldn't be avoided.

"I'm going to open it," I said.

"I don't know, Maggie."

"Why not? It could be important."

Not looking to her for approval, I grabbed the jar and twisted at the lid, but something jammed it in place. Pursing my lips, I twisted harder, then harder still. And finally, it popped open with a scrape.

"Maggie, don't!"

"I want to see."

"Don't touch it."

I snorted. "Why? You worried I'm going to feel cold and angry and dark inside?"

"Well, that's what Gibbs said."

"Obviously the man was a little unstable, Adelaide. He's been trapped in a mine for a year. I bet he sees and hears and feels all kinds of things that aren't real. Besides, this could be an important clue."

"I don't see how. It's pretty obvious those miners don't know anything about Bolger *or* the town burnings."

"Even so."

I pulled on the handkerchief and it unrolled, leaving a small, dark stone the size of an almond at the bottom of the jar.

"Not polished yet," I said, examining it through the glass. "I wonder what it could be."

Suddenly, my pulse seemed louder in my ears. Everything but that dark piece blurred away around me, leaving only the strange relic and my heartbeat. And then, the faint sound of breathing, ancient and deep. As if the relic itself were alive.

With hands that trembled ever so slightly, I tilted the jar toward my fingers. The relic slid along the glass side with a gentle *clink*. I could almost feel the heat of it on my palm. The ancient breath grew louder in my ears.

And suddenly, Adelaide ripped the jar from my hands.

"Hey!" I snapped, my arms tight at my sides. "What do you think you're doing?"

She twisted the lid back on firmly. "We don't have time for this. I gotta get back before Connelly explodes."

I grimaced, my pulse still beating hard. And yet I knew she was right. We'd probably been gone two hours. Adelaide had feigned a nap, but Connelly could surely mount the stairs and pound on her door at any moment. And there could be someone pounding at my door as well. Esperanza, perhaps. She'd seemed on edge lately, like she was hiding something. I had the strangest feeling that she was spying for Connelly. It certainly wouldn't surprise me.

"Right," I said. I stuffed the jar into my apron pocket. "Let's hurry, then."

Sure enough, when I returned to the Hacienda, Esperanza was waiting in my suite. I did my best to hide the jar from her, but it made me awful uneasy.

All that night and the next day, as I was whisked from one Hacienda amusement to the next, my mind stayed on that relic, now tucked deep in my bureau drawer.

What was it? Did it really have strange powers over the

emotions? Some relics could control the mind, like sphinx or siren, but they were rare and illegal in most countries. Was this one like them? If so, could it possibly have anything to do with the razings? The more I stewed over these questions, the more I had to know the answers.

That evening, a group of traveling performers was set to entertain the Hacienda. All through supper, Ella had talked of nothing else but the beautiful puppets she'd seen in the performers' wagon. Figuring she'd be happily occupied for a few hours, I took the chance to make a quick trip into Burning Mesa and headed straight to the relic refinery.

Grace, the tall, sharp-eyed expert I recognized from when I occasionally dropped by the refinery in my free time, frowned as she took the piece in the palm of her hand. "Where'd you say you got this again?"

"Traded with a miner. He got it in a trade, too. Back East, a few years ago."

"Curious." She turned the relic a few times, examining it from all angles. "Well, tell you what. I'll get this polished up so I can identify it better, and we'll see if we can't find out what this thing is."

When Grace brought the relic back from her steam-polish machine, I had to stifle a gasp. It was red. Deep red, with shadowy traces of black within the bone, like wisps of smoke. And it glowed faintly black.

A red relic that glowed black? I'd read that description before. In the papers in Mr. Bolger's suite.

My thoughts raced like wild birds, faster than I could put in a cage.

"Quite a puzzler, ain't she?" Grace said, startling me back to reality.

"You don't know what it is?"

She shook her head. "I can honestly say I've never seen anything like it in my ten years here at the refinery."

"Can you tell its power? Is it fire?"

"Hard to say. Doesn't look like it after my initial examination, but I'd have to run a few more serious tests to be sure. Sometimes, when a new relic is discovered, it takes years before we can realize its magical properties. Not saying this is a new relic, of course. That's very rare. It's probably just from another country. Europe, perhaps, or the Orient."

For some reason, I didn't want to tell her that the relic had been found right here in the Alkalies. The words burned in my throat, but I swallowed them down. Such information could be downright dangerous in these times.

Grace tapped her chin, then turned to the back rooms of the refinery. "Hey, Moon John. Can you come out here a sec?"

I perked up. "Moon John's here?"

"Yes, ma'am. You're in luck."

The wizened old man smiled warmly as he limped up to the counter where I stood. "Good evening, Maggie. How nice to see you. How have your studies at the Hacienda been coming?"

"Fine," I said, hoping none of my nerves showed. "Just fine."

Moon John nodded, but I could see a glint of doubt in his eyes.

Grace held up my newly polished little relic. "In the meantime, why don't you help us with an identification. We got us a real mystery here. Take a peek at that, and tell me if it's not the strangest thing you ever saw."

Moon John's aged body bent slowly to the lens. He pressed his eye to the scope and stayed there for a long time. So long, I started to wonder if he had dozed off. But then, slowly, he stood. He wore the same puzzlement Grace had, but an inscrutable intensity trembled in his eyes.

I could scarcely breathe. "You know what it is?"

He shook his head slowly.

Grace sighed. "Aw, darn it."

Moon John's gaze was fixed on me. "Perhaps we should keep it for the night. Just so I might look over my books and study it better."

"That's a good idea," Grace said.

But something in Moon John's eyes set off a warning in my heart. And something about that red, black-glowing stone made me want to grab it and not let anyone else even touch it. I needed that relic. There was no way I'd allow them to keep it all night. Somehow, I knew I'd never see it again if I did.

"Actually," I said carefully, "the relic's not all mine, see. It belongs to Señor Castilla. A gift from that sheik. Álvar let me borrow it for the day, to see if I could identify it. He'd be pretty worried if I didn't bring it right back."

Grace frowned. "I thought you said you traded with a miner."

I froze in place. Moon John's eyes shot to mine, now brimming with suspicion.

"N-no," I stammered. "I must have been confusing this for another."

"I see," Grace said, eyeing me now like Moon John.

A charged silence fell. Swallowing a hard gulp, I snatched the relic from beneath the gazing lens. "I'd better be off."

"You sure?" Grace asked. "I'm positive we can identify it if we had a little more time to—"

"No. Thank you. I should take it back to Señor Castilla."

I backed toward the doors, but Moon John's voice sliced through the room. "Maggie. Does this have anything to do with the gift I gave you?"

I avoided turning to meet his gaze, though I could feel it on me. "No. It's nothing you need to concern yourself with."

His voice hardened slightly. "Maggie…"

"Thanks again," I said to Grace. "You all have a nice night."

My heart was pounding as I closed the door. I looked down at the strange, gorgeous relic in my palm. That was close. Too close. Moon John had better be careful with those greedy eyes. I slipped the relic back into the jar and tucked it in my apron pocket.

I hopped back on my horse and rode down Main Street, positive that every passerby on the street was staring at me. That they somehow knew about the relic. A tickle crawled up the back of my neck. I was so preoccupied, I nearly collided with a carriage that had stopped in front of the Cooper Hotel.

I scowled. "Hey—"

A twitter of woman's laughter rang on the air. Another laugh, and then a male voice all too familiar to me. "Thanks for the joyride, Adam," he said to the driver.

More laughter from both. And then, slowly, like it was happening in a dream, Landon stepped out of the carriage. He wore a drunken grin and had lipstick smudges on his cheek And on his arm: Dora.

Her hands were hooked around Landon's elbow. Her auburn hair looked mussed, her cheeks pink.

Landon's eyes clicked to mine. The smile slid from his face.

I didn't move.

Dora followed Landon's gaze to me, then back to him. Landon untwined her arm from his abruptly, and she looked as if she'd been slapped. Landon's mouth opened to speak, but no words came out. Not that I gave him any time to find his tongue. I felt like the sky had crashed down on me, like the ground had collapsed beneath my feet. I had to get away as fast as my body could manage.

My legs finally complied, and I kicked my horse to move. Landon ran after me, sounding frustrated. "Maggie, wait a minute!"

I didn't. I lashed the reins and rode away into the darkness, the stallion galloping in the darkening twilight. His hard-beating hooves pounding in my head, like the pounding of my broken heart.

CHAPTER TWENTY-SEVEN

Late that night, after the swank dinner and mindless chatter, I sat alone at my dressing desk, staring at my reflection in the mirror. A fine mess I'd gotten myself into. Now I'd lost Landon forever. And for what? Because I couldn't let myself admit that he was right?

Meanwhile, I had Sheriff Leander *and* Moon John mad at me, Yahn had lost hope, and my last-chance theory that Emerson Bolger was burning the towns seemed more confusing than ever. I'd managed to ruin everything I'd set my hand to. And I couldn't think of any way to make it right. I was starting to realize that there wasn't a relic on earth that could get me out of this mess.

Or was there?

Almost as if it were acting on its own, my hand tugged open the bureau drawer and slipped into the soft underclothes. The feel of the cool, smooth pickle jar sent a chill through me. I pulled it out and set it on the desk in front of me. The sight of the relic with its deep red hue filled me with a strange power.

I spilled the gem-like stone onto the wood of my desk; my fingers hesitated for only a moment before scooping it up. Sitting in my palm, it almost felt alive. As before, my pulse filled my ears with slow, firm beats. And then the breathing, so deep and faint, like a distant wind.

"What are you?" I whispered to the relic.

It seemed strange that Gibbs had been so afraid of it. I didn't feel any cold or anger. In fact, I was drawn to the relic. Surely I had something wonderful in my hands, something worthy of more than hiding away in a pickle jar. A piece this special should be displayed for all to see.

There were many ways to wear relics. Some people had them embedded into clothes, some wore them on rings. Our phony kraken relic had been set on a chain, like an amulet. Frowning, I rummaged through the wooden box of jewelry Álvar had seen placed in my room. The only thing that could possibly work was a thin silver chain. Maybe if I took it to the refinery they'd drill a hole to string the chain through. Of course, then I'd have to face Moon John and his probing, greedy looks again.

As I studied the chain and the relic, they both became hot as a branding iron. I winced, and they clattered to the desktop, but they didn't stop moving. The relic had begun to change, to bend ever so slightly to the chain. Wrapping itself around it. Making itself into an amulet. I picked it back up, watching in breathless amazement as it settled into its new shape. It must have been the magic, sensing my will to make it a proper, wearable piece, though I'd never heard of a relic that could do such a thing. Within a minute, the piece hung sturdily from the chain. My lips pulled into a smile as I hooked the clasp behind my neck.

The relic lay just between my breasts, warm against my echoing heartbeat. I stroked it slowly, staring at my reflection in the mirror. The sight of it, so powerful and beautiful against my bare skin, filled my insides with a tight, fierce fire.

Let Landon see me this way, and he'd never so much as *look* at that cheap whore Dora again.

I swept to my wardrobe and flung open the doors. The row of dresses hung in quiet splendor, waiting for me, and I examined each one. The occasion called for something as sensual and powerful as my new accessory. I pushed the dresses past me, one by one, until I came to the most vulgar of them all: a sleek black satin. The bodice laced tightly in a corset with a neckline that plunged deep, and it hugged the curves of my body as I pulled it on. Exactly what I wanted.

I stood in front of the mirror. The dress would have made even Adelaide blush. I laughed a little and swept my dark hair freely over my shoulders. Then, pulling my new velvet cloak around me, I slipped out into the hallway.

The empty, dark mansion didn't stall me in the slightest. The knowledge that Mr. Connelly's spies could hear me or see me seemed laughable. He was an old fool. An idiot watchdog for a more powerful man.

My own agonizing and fretting over the past few days seemed laughable as well. Why had I wasted so much time trying to talk to people? If I wanted something, all I had to do was ride out and *take it.*

With a smile, I brought Álvar's sky steed out from her fancy stable. The animal took me across the moon-bathed desert with breathtaking speed, only adding to the trembling feeling of power that coursed through me.

Burning Mesa was mostly deserted, as one would imagine in the middle of the night. I rode right down the center of the street with my back straight and chin jutted out until I reached my destination: the Cooper Hotel. With a slap, I sent the sky steed galloping back to the Hacienda. I would be staying here from now on.

The concierge sat dozing behind the counter. I breezed past him without so much as a blink, choosing what I wanted from the wall of hanging keys behind his head. I knew the room I needed. I'd heard Bobby mention it to Adelaide once. I knew where to find Landon.

My heart started to beat loud and strong within me as I walked through the wallpapered hallway. The wood door marked 134 stood out like a beacon from the others. Smiling, I slipped the key into the latch. It clicked with a *snap*, and I pushed open the door.

Landon sat up with a start, blinking sleep from his eyes. "Who's there?"

The lamp on the nightstand behind him still carried a dim glow. The longer I looked at it, the more the light beamed out, until it was a blast of white. Landon shielded his eyes with his arm.

"Good evening, Landon," I said, stepping into the center of his small room.

"Maggie?"

"Of course. Who'd you expect, Dora? I'm glad to see she didn't stay."

He rubbed his eyes. "What are you doing here?"

"I came to pay a little call. Any crime in that?"

He seemed more conscious now. "I thought you were mad at me."

"I was." With a smile, I pulled the string of my cloak; it dropped to a velvet arc at my feet. "But I've decided to forgive you."

Landon's eyes widened at the sight of me in the dress. I laughed and sat beside him on his bed. "You like it?"

He swallowed hard. "Yes."

"I thought you might."

A tingling silence filled the air, and then I grabbed Landon by the collar of his pajamas.

"If you like it so much, why don't you put your hands on me?"

He sounded shocked. "Maggie, I— "

I didn't give him time to finish. Instead, I pressed my lips to his and drank deeply. Landon hesitated for a moment but then surrendered to the desire I knew boiled inside him. His arms hooked around me. I climbed onto his lap, straddling him with my legs. His hot breath flashed my cheek as he kissed me hungrily.

I tore my fingers through his hair; I arched my neck and pressed his face to my throat. My body pulsed with a surge of desire. His every touch made it rage like a blacksmith's forge.

Suddenly he pulled back, gripping my upper arms. "Wait," he said, breathing hard. "What's goin' on here?"

"I think it's pretty obvious," I said with a smirk.

"What about Connelly?"

"Connelly?"

"Adelaide told me about him tonight." Landon tightened his grip but looked away from me. "When you saw me with Dora, I came runnin' after you, but you were too quick. I went to The Desert Rose to talk to Adelaide about it, to see if there was any way to patch things up. She told me how Connelly's got his guards watching you day and night."

I smiled, not bothering to correct him. Adelaide's little story would serve for tonight.

"I'm sorry about what I said the other night," he added, scraping for words. "And I'm real sorry about Dora. It didn't mean anything. And nothing really happened, I swear. I was just mad at you. I was hurt, and so I— "

I put my finger on his lips. "It doesn't matter. Dora's a cheap, used-up whore. I know it's me you want."

Landon's brow lowered. "You're acting different, Maggie."

"I *am* different." I slid my arms around him and clutched his lower back.

Enough talk. I wanted to taste him. I wanted him to drink of me. He kissed me, but I could feel his resistance. Angrily, I pushed him to his back on the bed. My hands curled at his shirt, and I ripped the buttons open. The sight of his firm, bare chest made my insides burn. I kissed him again, pressing myself against his body. Landon moaned softly, but I could still feel him pulling back.

"I know you want me," I said between kisses. "Don't fight it."

He tried to push me away. "Seriously, what's gotten into you?"

"I'm tired of being weak," I said, running my hands down his chest. "I'm ready to be strong. I'm going to have everything I want now."

"But what about Connelly?"

I tossed my head back and laughed. "He's a fool."

"A fool with power and spies and men with guns. A man who the law turns a blind eye to."

I pushed my fingers through Landon's hair again, kissed his cheek, his neck, his earlobe. "Let's kill him, then," I whispered into his ear.

He pushed me away, sitting up. "What?"

"We'll kill him. It would be simple. I know where he sleeps. We could do the job right now."

Landon looked at me like I was a stranger. "Listen to yourself, Maggie."

"No," I said, shoving him back down on the bed. "Enough talk. I didn't come here for that. You know what I came for."

I started to undo the front laces on the corset of my dress. Landon's eyes widened. "Maggie."

Another pull. My heart was hammering in my chest, and I couldn't breathe. I was reaching to untie the final lace and expose myself fully, when Landon's hand shot forward. He grabbed the relic that hung around my neck.

"What in the—?"

A jolt ran through me. I grabbed for the relic. His eyes linked with mine…and he seemed to understand. "Take this off," he said.

"No!"

But it was too late. Landon ripped the relic away from my throat. The chain snapped. As the tension broke, the relic flew to the ground.

"NO!"

I made a lunge for it, but Landon's arms hooked around me. He tackled me to the bed, pinning my arms at my sides.

"Let go of me!" I screamed.

"It's not you, Maggie," he said, pressing his cheek to mine. "Whatever that thing did to you, it's not you. It's not your mind."

I was panting, my pulse throbbing in my throat. I screamed and struggled in vain. And with each breath, the darkness seeped out of me, seemed to exit with every beat of my heart. Landon held me to the bed until he could feel my body relax.

He slowly let go of me. Breathing hard, we stared at each other for a long moment. Then I became aware of my dress hanging open in the front. I pulled the blanket up to cover me as shame burned over my face. I blinked hard, trying to grasp what on earth had just happened.

"The relic," I said, still trying to catch my breath. "It was the relic."

"I know," he said softly.

I turned away from him, overcome with humiliation for how I'd acted, for what I'd said. "I—"

"Don't apologize. I know it wasn't you. I only want to know what that thing is and how on earth it got around your neck. Is that some gift from Álvar?"

I shook my head, trembling.

"Did you buy it?"

"Adelaide and I got it from the miners' camp yesterday. We were investigating the razings. The miner gave it to us, and I put it in my room. Tonight something made me want to use it."

Landon looked pale. "What is it?"

I shook my head. "I took it to the refinery today. Even *they* didn't know."

"Well, from now on, stay away from it."

I used my cloak to wrap up the relic. I knew the farther away from my touch, the better. Landon didn't look happy about me taking it again, but he said nothing.

"I'll bury it like that miner did," I promised.

I sat back beside him on the bed. Our eyes met, and warmth gripped my heart. I'd missed being with him so much. And as crazy as it had been to come here and attack him like I had, I knew it wasn't anything I hadn't secretly longed to do. Even now, I wished I could kiss him again. If only for a moment longer.

But I wasn't safe here. If someone had seen me leave, riding through town, or stalking into the hotel, word was certain to get back to Álvar. I sat up and hurriedly tightened the laces of my dress. "I've got to get out of here. I've got to go back to the Hacienda."

"No," Landon said, grabbing my hand. "It's not safe this late at night. Someone might notice you."

"If I wasn't already noticed coming here."

Landon ground his teeth in thought. He then turned to rummage in his things. He pulled out the goblin relic belt.

"Take this," he said.

"Landon, no. I can't ask you to— "

"You aren't asking—I'm giving it to you. Please. Take this belt and sneak into The Desert Rose. Adelaide will hide you in her room for the night. Just keep wearing that belt. And then, in the afternoon sometime, when there's plenty of noise and commotion, sneak on back out. Will you do that for me, Maggie? I won't be able to sleep tonight if you tried to go back to that place."

I set my hand to his cheek. "I'm not sure I'll be able to sleep tonight either way."

He sighed deeply. "What are we gonna do about this?"

"I don't know."

Landon cupped my face gently in his hands and pulled me in for a kiss. My eyes closed, and I tried to savor the warm sweetness of it.

"We'll find a way to be together again soon," he said. "I promise."

I nodded, but inwardly, I wasn't so sure.

"Good-bye," I whispered.

I kissed his cheek one last time and slipped from his room. Putting on the goblin relic belt, it wasn't hard to concentrate on the invisibility spreading over me. I knew my life depended on it.

As I slipped through the dark streets to The Desert Rose, the feeling of power was long gone.

CHAPTER TWENTY-EIGHT

"I don't like it," Adelaide said, eyeing the relic on her vanity tabletop. "You should never have taken that thing in the first place."

It was late morning, and thankfully a slow day for Adelaide, so we were able to talk awhile in her room. Given my unexpected, middle-of-the-night visit last night, I had to explain everything, though I left out a few of the less than savory details. Didn't see the point in making myself feel any more foolish.

"I'm going to give it to Moon John later," I said as she braided my hair. "He'll know what to do with it."

"Well, the sooner the better."

"Don't worry. In the meantime, I'll keep it well hidden in my bureau."

Adelaide finished my hair and examined our reflections in her mirror for a moment. "Be careful, Maggie. You're playing a dangerous game. And you got your baby sister to think about."

"I know."

Suddenly, I remembered that I had arranged to spend some time with Ella that afternoon. The long-suffering Señora Duarte somehow managed to carve an hour out of Ella's busy schedule.

"I'd better go," I said, rising to give Adelaide a hug.

"I'll see you soon?" she asked.

"I hope so. I really do."

I raced back to the Hacienda to quickly change out of the vulgar dress and hide the relic again in my bureau. When I came down to the main hall, Ella and Señora Duarte were waiting for me.

"Maggie!"

Ella looked pretty as a painting in her yellow frock and curls. As she ran into my embrace, the feel of her little arms around me wiped away all the stress and worry and madness of the last few days. This was all that mattered. This girl, right here.

I kissed her head and hugged her close. "Hey there, baby girl. How've you been?"

"Good. I'm having lots of fun with my new friend Carmiana, and I'm doing real good at readin'. But I'm glad I get to see you today, Mags. We gonna go fishing like you promised?"

"You bet."

Beside me, the severe Señora Duarte let out a sigh. She had a long, pinched face and pale skin that rarely saw sunshine. Outdoor activities clearly held little joy for her.

"I suppose," she said wearily, as if I had asked her permission. I certainly hadn't, and the intrusion made me bristle.

The more time I spent around this Señora Duarte, the more I could see that she clearly fancied herself the true guardian of

Ella and saw me as some young tart whose presence had to be endured. She watched over my every step at the river, as if she were sure any moment I would somehow compromise Ella's well-being. I tried to enjoy my time with my sister, anyway. Ella and I sat by the riverbank and cast lines into the cool, clay-colored water. As we waited for the fish to bite, we formed mud pies in a sun-baked row. It felt real nice, her and I getting along so well like this. For the first time, I started to wonder if maybe I could be as dear to her as Jeb had been.

I'd only finished a third pie, however, when Señora Duarte approached. She stood by me and cleared her throat. "Miss Ella must go now," she said.

"What?"

"She has her studies, and her siesta to take."

My jaw tightened. "But we just got here."

"On the contrary, it has been exactly one hour. That is what I agreed to. Nothing more."

I stood up and pointed a muddy finger at her. "Listen, ma'am—"

"I am sorry if this does not please you, but I have this child's welfare to think about."

"Are you suggesting I don't think about that? She's my family."

"But she is *my* responsibility."

I opened my mouth to contradict her, but she turned to Ella with a brisk spin. "Come now, *niña*. Rinse your hands. We must go."

It surprised me to see my spirited, fiery Ella obey immediately upon command. This señora clearly ran a tight ship. For some reason, that made me even madder. I had half a mind to tell her where to go, but I knew that would be foolish. I didn't need any more trouble, and she obviously cared about my sister.

I knelt and held out my arms for Ella. "Come here, you."

She hugged me and whispered in my ear. "We'll have some time together again soon, Maggie."

"I know, baby girl," I whispered back, holding her tighter. "I know."

Señora Duarte and Ella rode in the carriage back to the Hacienda, but I stayed behind. I just couldn't bring myself to return yet. I needed time to think. Sitting by the river in the warm sun, I tried to figure out what I was going to do about the mess I'd created. But the more I thought about it, the more confused I became. Nothing added up. I felt tired and overwhelmed. I wanted to see Landon again, to rest in his arms and be safe.

Heavy-hearted, I wandered back to The Desert Rose; I didn't care if Connelly saw me. I needed someone to talk to. I needed Landon. But as I approached the entrance to the saloon, Adelaide burst through the doors toward me.

"Oh Maggie!"

Her face was red from crying, her eyes glassy. She stumbled forward, and I had to catch her to keep her from falling to her knees.

"What is it?" I asked, pulling her up. "What's wrong?"

She drew in a sob and shook her head. "I can't… I can't go on."

My mind was racing with any number of horrible scenarios. I led Adelaide into the saloon and sat her at one of the tables. She pressed her hands to her face on the tabletop, and her shoulders trembled with a sob.

I stroked her back. "Adelaide, please. Talk to me. Tell me what's wrong. You're scaring me."

"They're gone," she finally said, not looking up. "They're gone,

Maggie."

"Who's gone?"

She sniffed and looked up at me with red, watery eyes. Something in her expression made a sliver of ice cut through my heart.

"Who, Adelaide?" I said forcefully, grabbing her arms. "Tell me."

"Bobby and Landon."

Speaking the names broke her again, and she sobbed into my shoulder. I was frozen in my seat, numb. "They're gone?"

She shook her head, wiping the tears on her cheek. "They were sent away suddenly this morning on a job. Their furlough's over early. Which means…"

"They won't be back till next spring," I finished, my throat feeling dry as paper.

Adelaide nodded and started to cry again. I tried to collect my thoughts, but it all seemed impossible. Only the night before, Landon had held me in his arms, kissed my mouth. And now he was gone until next spring. I blinked hard.

"This has to be some kind of mistake. They weren't supposed to go until June."

"It's no mistake," Adelaide said, fire in her tone. "It's all Connelly's doing, I swear it. He knew I loved Bobby, and so he told Señor Castilla to send them away." She slammed her fist on the table. "He did it on purpose." But then, her rage dissolved into sadness again. "Oh, Maggie. What am I gonna do? I can't go on without Bobby; I can't. I just can't."

Her voice broke off in a fit of sobs, and I took her into my arms. It wasn't right that a man like Connelly could control us and take away every piece of happiness we had. It wasn't right.

The last thing on earth either of us wanted to hear at the moment was that man's voice. But Mr. Connelly had remarkably bad timing.

"What's going on down here?" he snarled. "You tryin' to make the whole place sour with all this bawlin' and moping?"

A Creole man, probably one of Álvar's entourage, stood with him, though he maintained a cool distance. I shot an angry glare at both of them. "We're allowed to have feelings, aren't we?"

"Not when you're puttin' our customers at ill ease, you ain't."

None of the men at the bar or any of the surrounding tables seemed to care two straws about us women crying at the corner table.

I set my jaw. "We have the right to be here."

"You don't have any rights unless I *say* you have 'em." He jabbed his thumb at the upstairs. "Adelaide, you get to your room. You have a show tonight to prepare for."

When she didn't move, he took a tense step closer, his eyes bulging. She flinched and rose slowly to her feet.

Connelly snorted. "Get."

We both watched her move up the stairs. Something in her walk was different, broken. It hurt my heart to see it.

Connelly turned to me. "And you. Álvar's people have been looking all over for you this afternoon."

My rage cooled with a thread of fear. "I was spending time with my sister."

"Yeah, two hours ago." Connelly snorted. He nodded his head at the Creole standing beside him. "She's all yours."

The Creole approached silently behind me, and I spun around. "Who are you?"

"I am one of Señor Castilla's men, señorita."

I stepped back. “I was just about to return.”

“As well you should,” he said. “The señor has requested your company this evening.”

“Another party?”

“No. Tonight the señor wishes for a private audience.” The tone in his voice, the subtle emphasis in his words, sent a chill through me. “He has something very *special* in store for you.”

CHAPTER TWENTY-NINE

The dead, glazed eyes of the roast pig on the table fixed me with an accusing stare. I tried not to look at it, but even when I focused on pretending to listen to the musicians or admiring the sun-painted scenery of the desert cliff top where our table had been set up, I could still feel its gaze out of the corner of my eye.

There it lay on a silver serving tray, surrounded with candied fruits, sugared nuts, maple leaves, and bright sprigs of chokecherries for show. A shining, polished apple had been placed in the animal's mouth. I could understand how it felt.

Something had changed. Everything was off. I'd sensed it the moment I arrived back at the Hacienda. Esperanza was there as usual, but this time Flora also waited for me, and instead of helping me into a dress of my choosing as before, Flora commanded that I be put through a full beauty regimen. Bathed, scrubbed, lotioned, and perfumed. And squeezed into a dress she'd created herself "at señor's request."

It was blood red, low necked, and bore only the thinnest strip of material to pass for a sleeve. The maids laced me into an even tighter corset than before and pulled the rich taffeta fabric onto me. They curled the ends of my hair but only pulled half of it up in a jeweled clip. The rest hung in loose curls around my bare shoulders.

To finish the look, a garish ruby necklace with cherry-sized gems had been placed around my neck. As I sat across the table from Álvar, his eyes kept going to the necklace resting against my bosom, which was surely the point of the design. I shuddered deep down and felt very much like that pig on the platter—proudly on display until the master grew hungry.

What was going on? Just when I thought I had it all figured out, that I was nothing more than a young protégée, he'd ordered me to be dressed up and whisked away to a secluded desert spot, as if I were a prize he intended to savor in secret. I battled with myself, certain I must be misinterpreting the situation. I was overreacting, surely.

"How do you like the view?" Álvar asked, drawing me out of my thoughts.

I fumbled for a reply. "It's beautiful."

A sunset supper on a cliff top. Of course, this was no simple basket with bread and cheese. The grand table where we sat seemed bizarrely out of place there, on the windy red-rock. The plates of sumptuous dishes and crystal vases of flowers contrasted with the wild desert spreading out beyond us. Álvar had said he wanted to take us some place quiet, away from the busy comings and goings of the Hacienda. Thankfully, we weren't completely alone. A butler, two serving men, and a four-piece group of musicians joined us, though they kept their distance.

"It's the fanciest picnic *I've* ever been to," I said.

Álvar laughed. "I thought you might enjoy it."

I tried to smile and sipped a bit of my water.

"Are you sure you would not care for some of this excellent champagne?"

"No, thank you."

One of the serving men quietly removed my barely touched plate of food. I turned to thank him, but he had already moved away to the serving area they'd set up behind the carriage. Álvar was watching me when I turned back.

He smiled, swirling his glass. "Would you like to take a little stroll? The ridge beyond that brush there offers an excellent view of the mountains."

My nerves were still on high alert, even though Álvar had behaved like nothing but a gentleman throughout our meal. I shot a glance at the carriage, but the servants remained well hidden. Even the musicians had retired, clearly noticing some secret sign from Álvar to leave us alone.

"Come," he said, holding out his arm. "It is a glorious view."

I stood, managing a weak smile. Álvar didn't move his arm, and I knew what he expected, what any well-bred lady would do. Swallowing a dry gulp, I intertwined my arm in his.

We followed a trail along the edge of the cliff, up an uneven hill covered with rocks and the bright orange flowers of ocotillo cactus. Finally we reached the highest point of the ledge.

"Here we are," Álvar said, planting his fists on his hips.

The view that spread before us made me slow to a stop—a vast, sprawling expanse of red and orange and tiny brush strokes of deep green, all lit with the trembling golden light of sunset. The clouds and sky were painted like a massive rainbow: pink, orange, purple, and blue. Before us, the red-rock cliff fell down in a sheer drop of a hundred feet. And on the near horizon, closer than I'd ever seen them, the huge, dark outline of the Alkali Mountains rose like the backs of enormous sleeping dragons.

"Beautiful, isn't it?" Álvar asked, walking to the very edge of the cliff to take it all in.

I drew in a deep breath of the dry, floral-scented wind. "It's incredible."

He sat on a cropping of smooth red-rock boulders nearby, the perfect place to appreciate the view. "I come here often," he said. "To be alone. To think."

Emerson Bolger's warning about Álvar's catastrophic debts flashed in my mind. It didn't surprise me that my benefactor needed a place to escape from it all. Surely every silver candelabra and velvet curtain and lavishly dressed footman in the Hacienda only reminded him of how quickly he could lose everything.

I sat on the rocks beside Álvar, feeling a little sorry for him. "It must be difficult."

He shot me a quick look. "Difficult?"

I realized my slip and scrambled to cover it up. "To run such a huge estate, with so many things to keep track of. So many things to go wrong."

Álvar smiled a little, though I saw a glint of sadness in his eyes. "It *is* difficult."

We looked out over the desert, which grew more blue-hued with the falling twilight. Maybe I had been too quick to judge Álvar. Everyone faced his or her own challenges. And we all did what we must to survive.

"Are you enjoying yourself at my Hacienda, Maggie?" Álvar

asked.

I wasn't sure what to say. "Yes."

He nodded. His next words were spoken with caution. "I hope you will be happy here, with me. I hope you and I might come to an understanding."

An *understanding?* My whole body tensed. Álvar pursed his lips with caution. "I have learned of some very important developments in recent days. And I will need you."

I relaxed slightly at the mention of my talents. "I don't understand."

"You will in time," he said carefully.

His avoidance only brought the tension back to my chest. "I wish you'd tell me now. I've never understood what you want from me. You must be honest with me, Álvar. I beg of you."

Álvar was quiet for a long moment, then looked up at me, the hint of a smile on his lips.

"As you wish. Do you know what I saw when I used the Djinn relic the other day?" He set his hand lightly to my chin. "I saw you."

My stomach turned to lead at his touch. He traced his finger down the line of my throat. I felt faint. "Please," I said, moving away from him.

Álvar nodded slowly. "I understand your hesitation, Maggie. You're young. Perhaps afraid. But think of what I'm offering you."

My heart was racing. I didn't tell him that I'd given it quite a bit of thought, more than I even liked to admit to myself. All my life I dreamed of more, so much more than I could do or see in my dusty old desert town. Álvar could give that to me. Once again, a vision of him and me, traveling the world together, discovering relics we'd never dreamed of seeing, sprang to my mind.

Álvar brushed my hair over my shoulder, then slid my sleeve down. "Such beautiful skin," he whispered. "Like silk." His lips grazed my bare shoulder, then my throat. His arm slipped behind me, around my waist. The other hand pressed softly at the base of my collarbone.

I couldn't breathe. I backed away from his touch again. "I've offered my talents freely. I see no reason to…confuse our relationship."

Álvar's lips turned ever so slightly up in a smile. "Ah yes. Your *talents*." He spoke the words with a hint of irony that sent a ripple of alarm through me. Then he pulled me back into his arms, this time with force. "That's not what I'm after at this moment, now is it?"

He pressed his lips to my skin firmly. His hands gripped my waist and the back of my neck. He tilted my head back so his lips could travel down my throat, along my collarbone.

A new vision came to me. One of a used-up mistress, cast aside to live in shame and doubt. Perhaps Álvar did think I had a talent with relics, but what would that matter in a few weeks, when my charms had grown tiresome to him? I'd have no grand future, no traveling the world. I'd be left alone, penniless, and with a mark on my reputation I could never remove.

As Álvar's hand slid up to undo the laces of my corset, a swell of shame rose in me. I had been a fool. A fool to convince myself that he was after anything more than the conquest. This talk of talents and studying relic almanacs, it was just part of the game for him. I'd known it all along, only I'd been too swept up with the dream to admit it to myself. That dream was now shattered on the rocks like glass.

Gasping, I broke from Álvar's grip and jumped to my feet.

Álvar was breathing heavily, his face flushed. "What's wrong?"

"I can't do this."

Álvar straightened. For a moment, he said nothing, just brushed a lock of black hair from his brow. "You must pardon me," he said finally, "if I made you uncomfortable at all. I would certainly never want you to feel anything but willing." His words were polite enough, but a strained note of frustration tightened his voice.

"I want to go back now," I said, turning away from him.

There was a crackling silence. My mouth felt dry as sand.

Finally he spoke again. "But of course." He stood and brushed off his coat. "We should head back to the Hacienda before it grows too dark."

"Yes."

We walked in silence down the hill, back to the carriage, where the servants were playing a game of poker on the rocks. They looked surprised to see us returning so soon. How many other women had Álvar brought up to this place to seduce? I was clearly one more petty conquest—just like everyone had known all along. I felt so ashamed, I could have cried, but I swallowed back the tears, refusing to look any more foolish.

Trembling, I stepped inside the plush burgundy interior of Álvar's carriage while outside, he spoke to his servants tersely in Spanish. My hands twisted a piece of my dress in my lap until it formed a tight ball as I struggled to get ahold of myself. I'd clearly angered Álvar by rejecting him. Broke or not, he was still the most powerful man in Burning Mesa, and I needed to try to end things as pleasantly as possible.

But when Álvar finally came in, he didn't even look in my direction. The silence as we started to move pressed down upon me, each second building like a pile of stones on my chest. I tried to look out the window, but night had fallen, and the sky was black as tar.

I drew in a slow, shaky breath. "Álvar, please understand. While I respect you very much as a friend and teacher—"

Álvar's eyes, dark as the sky beyond the window, flashed at me. "Please. Spare me your forced sweetness."

"I wasn't—"

He raised a hand to silence me, and I clenched my jaw.

"Perhaps you are a bit tired this evening?" Álvar asked, his eyes needling me. "Tired after your midnight tryst with my cowboy?"

Ice cut through my veins.

"Do not bother to deny it. Señor Connelly reported it to me first thing this morning. He saw you enter the Cooper Hotel himself."

I could now see exactly how close to the edge of my own cliff I was treading. Álvar knew about my visiting Landon. And if he truly only wanted me as a mistress, there could now be no doubt that he'd sent the boys away on purpose. Was he attempting to cut off any ties I still had to the world outside the Hacienda? My face felt hot.

I met Álvar's gaze now with equal fierceness. "And am I not allowed to speak with my friends without you shipping them off on some concocted task in a far-flung nowhere? I didn't do anything wrong; you don't need to treat me like I'm some kind of criminal."

"Do I not? You certainly act like one, sneaking around in the dead of night on my horses, in the clothes I gave you."

"And you've been so honest?" I asked, furious. "Filling my head with all sorts of lies about talents and relics and training, when all along, all you wanted was..." I couldn't speak it. Shame and anger tore through me. "You took advantage of my youth," I said, tears welling in my eyes in spite of myself. "You betrayed my trust."

Álvar stared at me, thoughts racing behind his eyes. "Maggie...I didn't lie to you."

"You *did*, even if you don't think so now. It was all one big game for you." I pressed a tight fist to my lap. "I may be an insignificant nobody, but I'm not going to become your mistress of the moment. My sister and I will be leaving first thing in the morning."

Álvar laughed, indignant. "Oh, indeed?"

"Yes. *Indeed.*"

Suddenly Álvar was directly in front of me in the little cab of the carriage, one hand pressed against the back wall, right beside my head. His face was no more than a breath away from mine, and his eyes burned with an almost unnatural intensity that made my pulse race.

"You listen to me, Maggie. *I* will be the one to say when this arrangement is over. Not you. You cannot bring your family to my estate, accept my help, and then tell me you are on your way. It doesn't work like that. Do you understand? You owe me, Maggie. And I *will* collect on that debt."

I couldn't speak. Álvar drew in a breath and sat back on his side of the cab. He turned his gaze to the window for a moment, to compose himself. "Forgive me," he said after a pause, his voice stiff, "if I spoke too boldly."

He kept his gaze on the dark landscape rushing past us. "You would be wise, however, not to upset me as you did tonight. For your sister's sake, if not your own."

My heart was racing, but I said nothing. There was nothing

further to discuss. His meaning couldn't have been clearer: I was a fool to think I could play this game on my terms. Álvar Castilla would have what he wanted…or I would never see Ella again.

CHAPTER THIRTY

I concealed my distress as best I could when we arrived back at the Hacienda. Álvar left the carriage without a word, but his servant led me to my room as if nothing had changed. I let Esperanza help me out of the gown, but after she left my room, instead of changing into sleeping clothes, I hurriedly dressed in my own old burgundy dress. I then sat on the edge of Ella's bed, watching her sleep, my mind awhirl.

We needed to escape. Now. Tonight. I could get out of the Hacienda easily enough, but would that be the end of it? With Álvar's men everywhere, I could hardly try and make a different life here in Burning Mesa. No, the more I thought about it, the clearer it became that my only option was to escape as far away as possible, as soon as possible.

I tried to breathe slowly and stay calm, but my heart pounded at the thought of leaving. I didn't know where we'd go, but maybe it didn't matter. We'd make it through somehow. Of course, I had to be smart about it, because Álvar's and Connelly's eyes watched from every direction.

I paced my room, deep in thought, watching my candle grow smaller and smaller. The comings and goings of the Hacienda softened to silence. I had just packed a small bag when the muffled sound of men's voices drifted in from the other side of my door. Men's voices and footsteps—a lot of them.

I tiptoed closer and listened. It was a group. The glow from their lanterns stretched in beneath the crease of the doorframe, and my heart froze. Was Emerson Bolger finally making his attack on Álvar? Was the Hacienda about to burn to the ground like Haydenville?

Trembling, I opened the door and peered down the hallway. The orange light of the lanterns had just rounded the corner. My pulse throbbing, I slipped out after them. I wouldn't stay there to die in my bed. If Ella and I needed to run for our lives yet again, I wanted to know.

I slid down the darkened hall, knowing that if I were seen, it would mean the end of me.

I followed the glow of the men's lanterns until they stopped. They stood just around a second corner, their low voices rumbling the surface of the wall I was pressed against.

Álvar's voice drifted through the murmur like silk. My face snapped up in surprise. *Álvar?* An irresistible force compelled me to look, to confirm if he really was there. I slid my face past the wall a fraction of an inch, then another.

The light of the lanterns gleamed at me. Down the hallway, the men crammed into a small, decorative anteroom, no more than a dead end with some art on the walls and a small marble vase of flowers. Álvar stood at the inner edge. He lifted his lantern, scanned behind their group, and then set his hand against the wall. A hidden panel slid open like a door. Quietly, the men filed into the dark hallway that the panel had been hiding.

I didn't move until long after they'd gone. What on earth were they up to? It seemed dangerous and stupid, but I found myself walking to the little anteroom. The wall completely concealed the place where the panel had opened. I smoothed my hand over, but nothing stood out from the smooth stone. Perhaps Álvar had used a relic to release a trap door. It was dark; I might have not noticed.

As I stared at the enigmatic wall, a dark feeling gripped my heart. I thought of the razings with a cold shiver, but I cast the notion away. Impossible. Álvar was a deeply flawed man, but the kind of man who would burn entire towns full of innocent people to the ground? He wasn't evil, that much I knew. In another life, if he'd been raised on a farm, working and having the simple things of life like I had, he might have been a lot like Landon.

I rubbed a shiver from my arms and turned away from the anteroom. Whatever Álvar was up to, I wanted nothing to do with it. By the next sunset, Ella and I would be on a train, traveling farther from Burning Mesa and Álvar Castilla every moment.

I sat on a stallion from the Hacienda, watching the door to the sheriff's office. It was a bright, windy morning, with a brilliant blue sky. I wished it were raining. I stared at the office and didn't move.

Yahn, I've failed you.

Part of me longed to go in, to see him one last time. To say good-bye and ask his forgiveness. But I knew I didn't deserve closure. I had failed to help Yahn, and I would carry the guilt the rest of my life.

My heart felt like a stone in my chest as I pulled the reins to urge my horse away. I didn't look back as I rode. For Ella's sake, I had to move forward.

And I had to hurry. Train tickets needed to be purchased, and I had a single good-bye on my list: Adelaide. The thought alone made my heart break. When I came to her door, however, she was packing her own trunk. I halted in surprise.

She was smoothing out one of her gowns, but she quickly caught sight of me. "Maggie!" she cried. "Good Lord, am I happy to see you!" She rushed over and flung her arms around me.

"You're leaving?" I asked.

She broke from our embrace. Her blue eyes shone with a happiness that confused me even more. "What's going on, Adelaide? Tell me!"

"Oh, it's so wonderful. I can hardly believe it." She grabbed something from her dresser. "Look, a telegraph from Bobby. He's in a town called Green Springs. He says he can't live without me anymore. He wants to marry me, Maggie. Soon as possible."

"Marry?"

"Yes!"

I hugged her again. "Oh, Adelaide, I'm so happy for you!"

"Isn't it the most wonderful news?"

"What about Connelly? Are you going to sneak away?"

"Don't have to. Bobby sent his entire savings by wire. Five thousand dollars! He says that ought to cover any contract I have."

"What did Connelly say about that?"

"Well, he seemed real resistant at first. And for a minute there, I swore he was gonna rip that money up and lock me in my room.

But then he cooled off and said all right!"

"You don't say."

She nodded. "Can you believe it? He said I just had to see one last big-money client, and then I'd be done forever. I tell you, I feel so happy I could bust."

I smiled, but a nagging thought tugged at me. It didn't seem much like Connelly. Even if Bobby had wired a hundred thousand dollars, anyone with any reasonable business sense could see that Adelaide could and would bring in more money by staying, with her performances and high roller clientele. I didn't say anything, though—maybe I was wrong. Maybe Connelly had some other girl in mind to take her place. Some sad, poor new recruit from the depot.

"I'm finally leavin' this dump," Adelaide said, going back to her packing. "I swear, I thought this day would never come."

"I'm thrilled for you, I really am. I hope you two are very happy."

"Why don't you come with me, Maggie? Landon's there in Green Springs. Maybe you and him could get married, too!"

I laughed. "Well, actually, it's funny you should mention me coming with you."

Adelaide raised an eyebrow, and I told her my plan. When I was finished, she cheered and hugged me again.

"This is perfect! We'll go together! It'll be a new life, Maggie. Me and you and Bobby and Landon."

"And Ella?"

She laughed. "Sure, why not? We'll all live together in one big house and be happy as a bunch of rabbits."

I had to smile at the dream, though a part of me almost didn't dare imagine it. To have a family again. To stop hurting. Was it possible?

"What do you think?" Adelaide asked, holding up a beautiful cream-colored gown. "Make a good wedding dress?"

"Perfect," Connelly said.

Adelaide and I both spun around. He stood in the doorway, his arms folded across his chest, an ugly smirk on his face. Tom hovered behind him in the shadows of the hallway.

"What do you want?" Adelaide asked.

"Looks like you're all ready to go, ain't ya?" he said, ignoring her question. "Well, well, well, guess my little bird is finally ready to leave the nest."

"What do you *want*?" she asked again, more pointedly.

"Your last client's here."

"Oh." Adelaide paused, but then laughed once with a forced air of indifference. "Well, he's an eager fella, isn't he? It's not even noon."

Connelly shrugged.

"All right." Adelaide sighed. "Send him in, I guess. I won't have time to primp, so he'll have to take me as I am."

"That'll be fine."

Connelly stepped into the room with this strange little smile, and a surge of warning splashed over me. Adelaide must have felt the same, by the way she stared at him. Slowly, he reached into the breast pocket of his vest and drew out a wad of bills. He waved the cash in the air.

Adelaide's voice sounded very small. "What's that for?"

"Payment," Connelly said. "I've been saving up for some time for this."

Adelaide's face drained of color. He stepped closer to her, slowly, like a spider approaching his prey.

"Did you honestly think I would let my most valuable commodity go for five thousand lousy dollars?"

She was silent, paralyzed.

"Did you think I'd let you flit off to some worthless cowboy, just because you fancy you've *fallen in love*?"

He grabbed her by the arm, and horror filled me. I made a move for her, but Tom caught me by the wrist.

"Let go!" I glared at Connelly. "Don't you touch her."

But he didn't pay any attention to me. Holding Adelaide close by the arm, he pressed the wad of cash to her cheek. She winced but didn't move. Connelly dragged the cash down her face, her neck. "You belong to me. You will *always* belong to me."

"Let go of her!" I shouted, furious. "Take your dirty hands off—"

"Get that brat out of here," Connelly snarled.

"No!" I fought hard, but Tom pinned my arms behind my back.

"You can't do this!" I yelled. "Leave her alone, Connelly, you bastard!"

But Tom was dragging me out of the room. I kicked and fought with everything in me, screaming, but Tom was too strong. The last thing I saw before he pulled me through the doorframe was Adelaide. Connelly's hand was wrapped around her throat, but she was looking at me.

I expected to see fear or anger or sadness in her eyes. But there was only broken, worn-down submission.

"Adelaide!" I called as Tom dragged me down the hall.

The other girls' doors were cracked open. Fearful eyes watched from the shadows.

"Help her!" I screamed. But no one moved.

Tom threw me into one of the empty rooms at the end of the

hall and slammed the door shut. The lock clicked into place. I pounded hard, hammering my fists on the cruel wood.

"Adelaide!"

I sank to my knees on the floor, my fist pressed to the door. "I'm so sorry."

Three days they kept me in that room. But no matter how long I pounded or how loud I screamed, no one let me out. Tom slid food in without a word, and that was the only contact with others I had. They even locked the window to keep me from screaming out to the people on the streets. I was trapped like an animal.

In desperation, I tried to invoke my importance to Álvar, but Tom let me know in no uncertain terms that Álvar knew I was there. I had nothing. In despair, I thought to use the relic in the jar—evil or not, if I could use it, I'd be free—but it was probably long gone. Esperanza had probably snatched it up first thing when she heard I was gone and proudly delivered it to Connelly. No relic could save me.

As the sky outside my window darkened on the third day, I slumped on the floor against my bed, holding my arms around my knees. I was exhausted, though I knew I couldn't sleep. Worn down, though I still burned with rage.

A draft of cold wind tossed my curtains in a ripple over my bed. I rubbed my arms and turned to see if the window had a crack or something, when I noticed a wisp of white shadow drifting in through the glass. A coil of lightness, almost like smoke, except it carried a faint glow. My eyes widened. I staggered backward to my feet.

The shadow spread and curled in with the wind. It drifted to the center of my room, rippling. Breathless, I stared as it expanded and stretched upward until it formed a vague shape.

The shape of a man.

My back was to the vanity table. I groped behind me, my eyes fixed on the shadow, and grabbed for something to hit it with. Whatever it was, whoever had sent it, I wasn't going to stand there like a sitting duck if it meant me harm. But then, like the tremor of a morning wind, a voice drifted out of the shadow.

"Maggie. We must talk."

"Who are you?" I asked, sounding far more forceful than I felt.

The features of the shadow began to sharpen. A face formed and I recognized it immediately.

"Moon John? How are you doing this?"

"Wraith relic. Another one of those illegal shadow relics no one is supposed to have. But in this case, it had to be used."

An arrow of hope cut through me. "Can you get me out of here?"

"I cannot. I have tried, but Mr. Connelly has locked off the entire upstairs floor, and all of the girls in it."

My breath caught. "Adelaide. Is Adelaide all right?"

"I do not know."

"What about my sister? Please tell me she's safe."

"I'm sorry," he said. "I know nothing."

The past three days had been consumed with worry for Adelaide and Ella. And now I finally had word from the outside, but still no information about either of them.

"I have very little time," Moon John said, his image flickering.

"Why did you come?"

"Another town has burned."

My heart sank, and then fear gripped me. I ran up to the shadowy form of Moon John. I'd have shaken him by the shoulders if I could. "The Apaches. What about the Apaches? Have they hanged them?"

"Not yet."

I sank down with relief, catching myself on the edge of my bed. "Thank God."

"Listen to me carefully, Maggie. I have studied these razings, and I believe that if we find which relic is being used, we can find who is responsible."

"You don't believe the Apaches are involved?"

"No. Whoever is burning those towns is using a very powerful fire relic. The Apaches shun the use of such things."

"Exactly," I said. "That's what I've been trying to tell people, but no one believes me!"

"People believe what is easy to believe. They wish for someone to blame, and so they reach for the fastest answer."

"You've got that right. So who do you think *is* to blame? I have a few ideas."

"As do I." The shadowy image of Moon John moved closer. "But listen to me. The reason I have risked visiting you tonight is to talk with you about the relic you brought in to the registry. You must give it to me. I believe it has powerful fire magic, such as might be used in the razings."

The image of that red, shadowy relic flashed in my mind. So beautiful, so powerful, so dark. It had warmed in my hand to form a necklace and brightened the lamp in Landon's room. A fire relic. A fire relic that could burn an entire town. Chills ran up the back of my neck, followed by a flash of panic. "I don't have it anymore."

Moon John was silent.

"I'm so sorry," I said. "I tried to hide it. But I think that dog Mr. Connelly had my room searched. I'd bet anything he had his spy steal it."

"This is very bad. Very bad."

Lightning shot through me. "Do you think he knows what it is? Do you think he might be involved with the razings?"

Even as I spoke them, the words rang darkly true. How could I have not seen it before? If I knew of any person evil enough to burn an entire town, it would be Connelly.

"He has to be involved," I said. "Somehow."

Moon John's image nodded slowly "But Mr. Connelly could not do this alone."

"Emerson Bolger."

The pieces slowly clicked together in my mind. I remembered Mr. Bolger and Mr. Connelly sneaking through the shadows of the Hacienda, whispering hushed threats. And the papers I'd read on Bolger's desk with an exact description of the dark red relic.

"The two of them are in it together. They're blackmailing Álvar Castilla for his lands. They're trying to scare him into cooperating!"

Moon John's silence betrayed doubt.

"You don't think Álvar's actually part of it, do you?" I said. "Look, he's far from perfect, but he's not a murderer."

"He is the most powerful man for miles. And he has many men working for him, men who *may* be evil, such as Mr. Connelly."

"But he wouldn't let anyone do that under his nose."

Moon John's gaze was sharp. "Indeed not. Surely a man of his position is no less than the leader of such an undertaking."

In my mind I could see the group of men slipping quietly

through the secret passageway in the Hacienda, with Álvar in the lead. I sank into the chair by the vanity, my mind running like a wild stallion. I thought of the raging debts, the miners—his miners—working their fingers to the bone to find him relics that would solve his problems. And what had they found? A fire relic of terrible power.

His words echoed in my mind. *You owe me, Maggie. And I will collect on that debt.* He'd said he needed my talents to help him. But to help him save the towns or destroy them?

"But why? Why would he do such a thing?"

An answer sat before me in the darkness. His debts. Perhaps Álvar thought the only way to clear out all that debt was to eliminate his creditors.

"I can't believe it," I said, my voice hoarse. "I can't believe he would do it."

"Even a decent man can be capable of great evil when he wishes to hold onto great power."

It felt like the walls were closing in, like I couldn't catch one good breath. "But what about Emerson Bolger? He knew about the relic. I found a letter describing it in his room."

Moon John shook his head. "I do not know what this means."

"It means maybe you got the wrong man!"

"No. There are many things that do not add up, Maggie. Something vast and dark has taken hold here, and nothing makes perfect sense."

"Well, what if it's neither man? What if the real culprit is someone completely different?"

"Anything is possible." After a pause, Moon John spoke again, his voice soft. "If I were you, I would forget this matter. I would get out of this town while you still can. Take your sister and go. And do not look back."

I scoffed. "Well, I have to get out of this room first, don't I?"

"You will. Mr. Connelly will let you out to serve the men who are already pouring into Burning Mesa."

"What men?"

"Men from other counties and towns. Word of the new razing has already spread. This time, they will not wait to act."

"What do you mean?"

"A mob has formed to attack the Apaches."

I'd heard the threats so many times, yet the certainty in Moon John's voice made my blood run cold. "But they can't. They don't know where the camp is."

"They will find a way. Álvar Castilla is helping them to cover up his own evil deeds. If he can convince the people of Burning Mesa and this state that the true culprits have been killed, then all will agree that justice has been done, and he will be free."

"It could just as well be Emerson Bolger." I wasn't ready to give up on my theory, not when that dark, nagging feeling refused to go away. "He's helping the mob, too, isn't he? He was there the day they met in The Desert Rose."

Moon John shook his head. "Yes, but that could mean anything."

"It doesn't matter. Whoever's behind it has to be stopped. I'll tell everyone the truth."

"You should do no such thing," Moon John warned. "If you care about the welfare of your sister, you must leave as soon as you can."

I hugged my arms around me, feeling dizzy and sick in the heart. "I was planning to leave. I was going to take her with me to Green Springs. Start fresh. I have a good friend there."

Moon John was silent, but I could see his expression fall.

"What?" I asked, rising out of the chair. "What's wrong?"

"Maggie, my child, Green Springs was the town that was burned two days ago. It's gone. No one survived."

CHAPTER THIRTY-ONE

Grief has a way of consuming even the smallest things in life. Color, sound, smell. I couldn't sense any of it as I mindlessly wiped the tables down in the saloon, poured more coffee, and cleared away plates. Just as Moon John predicted, Tom had let me out of my room the next morning, tossed an apron at me, and ordered me to serve the influx of customers. Men and women clustered at the tables, eating, drinking, and talking in low, nervous tones about their desire to attack the Apache camp. I served them without hearing or seeing them.

I'd gone to check on Adelaide soon as Tom let me out. I tapped on her door, and when she didn't say anything, I opened it. She lay on her bed, silent, staring at the wall. I recognized the look of eyes that had cried every last tear in them. Only then did I know she'd heard about Green Springs.

It hurt my heart to see her so desolate. Part of me wanted

to say, "Maybe Bobby and Landon survived. They're strong boys. They're fighters! If I could survive, maybe they did." But I loved her enough to not tug at that thread of irrational hope, a thread that would inevitably release a surge of even deeper sorrow. So I said nothing and went downstairs to drown out the ringing in my ears with mindless work.

Late that afternoon, as I swept along the side of a table, one of the men grabbed my apron. "You better get on out of here," he said, a slur in his voice.

I jerked my apron from his fingertips and kept moving past him, but this only made him speak louder.

"War's comin'. This town's gonna be turned upside down before it's through. A young kid like you outta get out of here quick as you can."

I still didn't look at him. What difference did it make if war came? Let it.

"The mob's goin' in to get those Apaches at first light tomorrow morning. They're goin' soon as they get the lynching taken care of."

My feet froze in place. I whipped my head around to him. "Lynching?"

"Ain't you heard? They're hangin' those three Injuns tonight. At sunset. The sheriff's finally given the go-ahead."

I stared at him. "Impossible."

"It's gonna be the first shot fired in the war. Gonna get the crowd good and riled up for when they march on them Apaches."

My legs felt numb, tingling. "No one knows where they are."

The man sniffed. "They do now. That Injun bouncer you got workin' here spilled the beans. He told Señor Castilla where to find that camp. So now this crew in here's fixin' to ride first thing tomorrow. Soon as they get them hangin's out of the way."

Standing there, listening to that man, something snapped inside me, something deep inside the layers of numbness I'd tried so hard to build up. All at once, my calm started to crumble. The waves of rage and sorrow burst through those glass walls like a flash flood, and the broom slipped from my hands. My eyes fixed on Tom, standing at the bar, counting money in the till.

I flew at him. He saw me coming, and the frown of concentration dropped from his face. But by the time he could see the fury in my eyes, I had my hands around his collar.

"Traitor!" I screamed. "Murderer!"

"Hey!" He pried my hands from his neck and pulled me away from him. "What in the hell are you doing?"

"How could you betray your own people?" I shouted, my face hot as a red coal. "When you *know* they haven't done a thing!"

Tom's face paled, but he kept a scowl. "You calm yourself down right now."

But I couldn't. My rage surged on, fueled by the sorrow I'd been trying so hard not to face, the sorrow of losing Landon and Bobby and Adelaide, and the dream of living together as a family in some new place. Sorrow at the unspeakable injustice of Yahn hanging to cover up an evil man's lies. The tempest inside engulfed me. I was swept away in the sudden, furious current of it.

"I won't calm down!"

The men around us stared. They cast looks at Tom, wondering if he was going to do something about the crazed female raising such a ruckus. Scowling, Tom dragged me behind the bar.

"Take your dirty hands off me," I shouted, punching him with my free arm. "I don't want to be anywhere near you!"

"Then don't be," he barked. He flung me into the back room. "You stay in here and cool the hell off. I don't want to see you out there until you're calm."

"Innocent people will die because of you, Tom. *Your* people."

His face was stone. "They ain't my people anymore."

"They are! And you've sentenced them to death for something they didn't do."

Tom's eyes blazed. "You don't understand. It's easy for you to get all high and mighty. You never had to…" He choked back his words. "You'd be different if you knew."

"If I knew what?"

He said nothing, and his cryptic behavior only made me more furious.

I glared at him. "I don't know how you can stand here with not even the decency to care."

"Caring won't stop it, Maggie. People are mad as hellfire, and this war is gonna come one way or another. Innocent people will die no matter how you slice it. If you were smart, you'd know what side to be standing on when it all starts. On the side that's gonna win."

With that, he stomped out of the back room, the door swinging shut behind him, leaving me alone in the darkness. I was fit to explode. I wanted to scream at the top of my lungs. I wanted to chase after Tom and pound him with my fists. I wanted to sob and shout and let the whole world shatter at the sound of my rage.

Fierce tears burned down my cheeks. I knew it wasn't really Tom I was angry at. It was the sheer, unavoidable failure my life had become in spite of everything I'd done. Lord knows how hard I'd tried to make something out of the ashes the Haydenville fire had left me in. And yet somehow, there I sat with nothing. Landon dead. Adelaide broken. Ella trapped in the gilded grip of Álvar Castilla, possibly in real danger. And now Yahn, the one person who gave me hope, set to hang at sunset. I gripped my face in my hands, sobbing into the dust and sand. Why? Why didn't I let the fire burn me that night? Wouldn't it have been better?

Feeling dizzy, I sat up and leaned my head against the wall. Wiping my eyes, I held my hand in front of my face. Tears glistened on my fingertips. So many tears. I stared at my hand, and a strange feeling started to flicker inside me. A flame in the center of my heart.

No more tears. I was sick to death of tears. I knew right then and there that I was done being sad and angry. I was through mourning. My troubles hadn't gone anywhere—they were still as bad as ever—but in that moment I knew I was going to *do* something about it. That was my mistake from the beginning—I'd been trying to avoid problems at every turn. I'd been too busy trying to keep my head down and survive and hope the troubles wouldn't find me.

But they had. And now it was time to turn and face them head on.

I rose to my feet, a strong, fierce pulse beating through my body. Landon might be dead, but Ella was still very much alive. And Yahn hadn't hung yet. He *wouldn't* hang. He couldn't. I wouldn't let it happen.

My breath came fast and hard. I needed a plan. Something miraculous. Something magical. I thought of the powerful red relic and cursed myself for allowing Connelly to steal it. It was the only magic I could get my hands on.

But then, like a shot of lightning, I realized that wasn't true. Landon's goblin belt: I'd left it in Adelaide's room. It should still be there under her bed. Unless Connelly had gotten to that, too.

I bolted into the saloon. The men around me, the chaos, all blended into nothing. I could only see the stairs, the hallway, and then Adelaide's room. Panting, I flung open the doors. She was nowhere to be seen, but there wasn't time to look for her. Diving for the bed, I ran my hands over the cool wood floor beneath it. There it was, the thick leather belt with the gleaming gray-green relic on the buckle. Emotion choked my throat as I pressed it to my heart.

Thank you, Landon.

Sunset.

The streets of Burning Mesa stood eerily empty in the golden light. A low wind whistled over the open spaces, tossing a brittle tumbleweed across the road. If I listened hard enough, I could hear the distant murmur of the mob. They rallied around the gallows, waiting, hungry for their first taste of revenge.

I moved unseen along the walkways, keeping one hand on the goblin relic, just in case. My chest clamped up with tension, making it hard to breathe. At least my legs felt strong, thanks to the earth magic of the goblin piece. I headed to the sheriff's office with a determined step, the road spreading before me in a sure path.

The door to the office stood open, and I had exactly what I needed for my plan to work. I had to try. I *had* to.

Drawing in a trembling breath, I slipped the shoes from my feet to move more quietly and stepped forward. The rangers were planning the transportation of the prisoners to the gallows.

The bald ranger who had been so rude to me led the group. "Mitch and Avery, you two watch this north ridge here. We don't want any chance of an ambush. Cobbs, Delgado, you're gonna be on East Street."

"Who's driving the prisoners?"

"Jake and me."

“That’s not many rangers.”

“It’ll be enough, if you men do your jobs. We got six men with the sheriff at the gallows right now, keepin’ a handle on the crowd.”

I stepped closer. Sweat beaded on my temples, on my upper lip, and my legs shook so hard I was afraid I’d fall down. But as I silently edged past the men, no one looked up. I eyed the open door, knowing the hardest part was yet to come.

The rangers started talking about crowd control during the hanging. I stood right by the door, my back to the wood face of the building, my pulse racing. The cluster of men was so close, I could feel their body heat. If one of them had stretched, he would have touched me. I closed my eyes as sweat streaked down my face, tickling my skin. But I was so close. If they would stay out on the deck for a few more minutes, my crazy plan might actually work.

Holding my breath, I slipped into the office. A tense glance around revealed a bit of luck: the office was empty. Trembling, I rushed to Sheriff Leander’s desk—I knew he kept important items there. Sure enough, three dark iron keys lay in the top drawer. I grabbed all of them and held them tightly in my fist. Then, shooting a look to the men out front, I steeled my courage and tiptoed down the hallway to the holding cell.

Yahn and the other Apaches sat stone still on the benches in the cell, eyes closed. At first I thought they might be sleeping, but then I heard the low murmur of their voices. They were praying to the Sacred Ones. Preparing for death.

My heart aching, I pulled the goblin belt from my waist. “Yahn.”

He looked up with a start. Seeing me, his eyes widened with confusion and shock. “Maggie?”

The other two Apaches eyed me with mistrust.

"We don't have much time," I whispered, rushing forward. I pressed the keys into Yahn's hand. "Take these. But don't use them right now. Wait until they're transporting you in the prisoners' wagon. I can buy you one, maybe two minutes to get out."

Yahn blinked, looking even more confused than before. I squeezed his hand in mine. The act filled me with a pulsing, fierce surge of emotion. He had to live. I needed him to live.

"Please trust me. I'll have horses waiting for you by the river. Near the stables. They should take you right past them on the way to the gallows."

"Maggie—"

"There's no time. Keep those keys hidden. Your life depends on it."

Yahn's eyes burned with intensity. "Thank you."

"Thank me when the plan actually works." I shot a look down the hall, sure one of the rangers would appear any second. "I have to go. Remember, don't try to get out of the carriage until you hear me. I'll buy you as much time as I can."

I pulled the belt back around my waist. My throat swelled, and I could barely speak. "Be careful, Yahn."

As much as I wanted to stay longer, I knew I had to hightail it out of there. The rangers would be coming for their prisoners any minute. As I rushed back down the hall, my heart pounded, but this time from exhilaration.

I spun around the corner, into the office. Two men stood by Sheriff Leander's desk—Jake and the bald ranger. They were both staring at the open drawer. The drawer I had left open after taking the keys.

I stifled a gasp, and the bald ranger's face shot up. His eyes went right to me.

CHAPTER THIRTY-TWO

"You hear that?"

I pressed my hand over my mouth, shaking like a leaf. *They can't see me,* I told myself. *They can't see me.* But the bald ranger looked awfully suspicious.

"Probably them Apaches," Jake said, shrugging. "They've been prayin' to their gods all day."

The bald ranger narrowed his eyes but then slammed the desk drawer shut. "Anyway, guess Leander took the keys," he said. "We'll have to use the other set."

"Want me to bring the wagon around?"

The bald ranger nodded. When Jake left, he opened the drawer again, frowning. I pressed my back to the wall, sidestepping to the door slowly as possible. I wanted to get out of there quickly as I could. But I knew I had to move silent, slow and still. Everything depended on it.

I could hardly believe it as my bare feet came down on the hot sand of the open street. Somehow I'd made it. Air rushed back in my lungs, and I clutched my chest as I ran down the road. The first part of my plan had worked. Now for the next phase. I ran to Mr. Connelly's personal stables fast as my feet could carry me.

Connelly had assigned me the task of grooming his horses many times when I worked at The Desert Rose. I'd resented the extra jobs, but now I was grateful as I pulled the key to the stables from under the hidden rock. I nearly scared the horses half to death while approaching, but once I'd stashed the goblin relic belt in my apron pocket, saddling and stealing three of Connelly's stallions went off without a hitch.

After tying them to a mesquite tree by the river, I rushed to my hiding spot back in town. The wagon would drive by any moment. If the plan was going to work, I'd need to have perfect timing. And the perfect distraction.

I looked down at my dress, wrinkled and damp with sweat. My hair was a wild tangle of a braid. I grimaced and smoothed my skirt best as I could, then I pulled my hair free and long. And since this was no time to be prim, I unfastened the top two buttons of my blouse. If Adelaide had taught me anything, it was that a man didn't think too clearly when he had the sight of a woman's bosom. Biting my lip, I undid one more button.

The tromp of horse hooves shot me to attention. After a moment, I could hear the creak of a wood wagon. Trembling, I closed my eyes and forced myself to think about Landon, about Ella and Bobby and Adelaide. I had to succeed.

The prison wagon rolled into sight. Jake and the bald ranger sat on the front bench, scanning the landscape. I drew in a breath and jumped to my feet.

"Help!" I ran out into the road, waving my arms like a crazed woman and screaming. "Someone help!"

The horses reared up on their hind legs, whinnying as I stumbled right into their path.

"Help me! Please!"

Jake jerked on the reins. "Whoa! Easy there!"

The horses stamped their feet to a stop. Gasping for breath, I threw myself at the rangers' feet. "Help me."

Jake frowned. "Maggie? What's wrong?"

"It's too horrible," I said, covering my face and trying to catch my breath. "It's just too horrible."

Through the sliver of space between my fingers, I glanced at the ground beneath the wagon. I saw the feet of Yahn and the other warriors creeping away from the carriage, and a dual jolt of terror and triumph cut through me. Luckily, the crazed look on my face played well into my plan.

I grabbed Jake's hands. "Some men at The Desert Rose, they're planning to kill the sheriff!"

The bald ranger tensed. "What?"

"I heard them talking. They're gonna kill him so he doesn't get in the way of their attack on the Apache camp. I didn't know what to do!"

Jake and the bald ranger exchanged a serious look.

"Who was it?" Jake said. "Did you know them, Maggie?"

Acting like I was trying to remember, I cast a swift glance beneath the wagon again. Yahn and the others were running, getting farther and farther away. A cry of relief threatened to escape, but I swallowed it down.

"I don't remember. I was so afraid."

The bald ranger frowned. He tossed a casual look behind him, perhaps out of habit, or maybe the man had eyes in the back of his head. He turned back to me, but then tensed like he'd been shot. He spun around again and surely spotted them.

"What in the hell?" He shot to his feet.

Horror nailed me to the ground. I glanced at the escaping prisoners, then the rangers. I must have looked like a woman caught in the act, because comprehension washed over the bald ranger's face. "Did you—?"

I ran.

I knew I didn't stand a chance of escaping, but I wasn't going to throw up my hands and turn myself in, either. Besides, if I could distract their attention from Yahn and the other Apaches' getaway, it would be worth it.

The rangers shouted behind me. I could hear them scrambling to turn the carriage around, though the horses were screaming again, spooked by the sudden commotion.

"You get the girl!" the bald ranger screamed to Jake. Jake jumped from the carriage, and his heavy footsteps pounded behind me.

Tiny rocks and burs cut my feet as I ran, but I kept going. I'd never run so hard in my entire life. It felt as if my heart would explode out of my chest.

"Maggie!" Jake shouted behind me. He was winded, but so close. So close. "Stop!" He lunged forward to tackle me, but he was a few inches too far behind, so his hands only fastened around my skirt and apron. With a shout, he went tumbling forward. The skirt tore, and the apron ripped from my waist, but I somehow managed to stay on my feet.

Still running at full speed, I dared a look behind me. Jake growled with frustration and struggled to get back up. My apron lay limp in his clenched fist. The goblin relic belt—it was still in the pocket. The sharp impulse to turn back and get it surged through me, but I shook the thought away. I had to keep running.

"Maggie!" Jake called. "What in the hell are you doing?"

The wind in my eyes blurred my vision, but I kept running. I didn't know what I was doing. Hopefully, buying Yahn more time to escape.

"I don't want to have to shoot you!" Jake shouted. He was running again, drawing closer and closer.

My lungs burned like a cattle brander in my chest. My head pounded, and the muscles in my legs started to lock up. I flailed down a narrow alleyway crowded with empty wood crates. Ahead of me, a four-foot wall glared in the late sunlight. The end of the road. My heart sank. *I tried, Yahn.*

Jake tromped into the alley, gasping for breath.

"Dammit, Maggie." He sighed, and I heard the dragon claw relic on his rifle click into place. "Put your hands up where I can see them."

My head dropped, and I lifted my arms into the air.

Suddenly, the whinny of a horse sounded behind me, and a row of crates crashed in a spectacular burst of splinters. I whirled around. Yahn, on a midnight-black horse, dashed past Jake, smashing the rows of crates as he went. Before I had time to even tell myself the sight was real, Yahn swooped his arms around my waist and pulled me onto the horse behind him.

Jake, who had been knocked backward by the falling crates, shouted with rage. And then an earsplitting explosion of fire blasted behind us.

"Get down!" Yahn cried.

Squeezing my eyes shut, I clamped my arms around his strong

waist. The flames from Jake's dragon-claw rifle filled the entire alleyway with light and heat, and fire slashed over my bare feet, singeing the ends of my hair and my dress. Every crate in that alley burst into flames.

The horse screamed with terror, but Yahn jabbed his ankles into the animal's haunches and pulled back on the reins.

In slow motion, the horse leaped at the four-foot wall ahead of us. It kicked into the air, flailing with all its might. The wall sped toward us. We were going to hit. I screamed and buried my face against Yahn's back.

But then we were airborne.

For a single glistening moment, we soared through the air on unseen falcon wings. We flew over the wall, beyond the mass of flames, beyond Jake's yells as he ran from the burning alleyway. The horse landed on the other side with a *thud*. It whinnied once and thrashed its head, but Yahn smacked the animal's side and made a strange, fierce cry. With that, the stallion galloped forward. I clung to Yahn as we raced into the desert beyond Burning Mesa. To the Alkali Mountains. To safety.

I didn't let go of Yahn until we could see the firelight of the Apache camp glowing through the darkness ahead. We'd ridden deep into the pine forest of the Alkali Mountains on a winding path no one could follow. As we rode, I told him about the attack, but he already knew. One of the guards had taunted them with the information, to ensure their final moments were ones of torment.

When we drew near the camp, Yahn fell quiet. I gazed at the mysterious trees around us, teeming with unseen life. The air was cool and rich with the smell of pine and greenery. It was dark as pitch, and I couldn't shake the feeling that we were about to be ambushed, so I kept my arms laced around Yahn, grateful for his protection.

Finally he spoke. "My people might not trust you right away, Maggie. You must not let that discourage you. I will tell them of all you've done for me, for all of us."

"I understand."

Three scouts moved out of the dark silence of the forest. Who knew how long they had been watching us?

Yahn hopped down from the horse and spoke to them in the Apache language. They cast dubious looks at me, but then motioned us to enter their camp. Yahn gently lifted me from the horse. I could have gotten down on my own, but I was exhausted and saddle sore, and it filled me with a deep comfort to feel the strength of his arms. If only for a moment.

Most of the Apaches had gathered around a huge central fire in the camp. I noticed war paint on the young men and weapons being prepared. The other two Apaches Yahn had been imprisoned with had surely arrived and told them about the impending attack.

The group parted as Yahn and I approached the fire. A gray-haired woman in an elaborate robe approached us, her arms open. Yahn dropped to his knees before her, but she bent to lift him, to take him in her arms, a sheen of tears glinting on her cheeks. For a long time, Yahn and the woman embraced. She had the same liquid brown eyes, and I realized she must be his mother.

When they broke, her glance turned to me, and silence fell over the camp. All watched, their faces lit with wavering shadows from the fire. Yahn began to speak with her in their native tongue. The older woman listened, but her eyes didn't leave me the entire time.

When Yahn had finished, she continued to study me. For what seemed like forever, the only sound to break the silence was the gentle crackle of the fire and the distant music of crickets. I tried to hold her gaze, my heart beating hard in my chest.

Finally, Yahn's mother spoke a few words. As if responding to her call, several of the oldest members of the tribe stepped forward, and together, they approached me. I took an instinctive step back, but Yahn's face was calm. He nodded once, as if to say that everything was all right. I held still, trembling on the inside as they examined me up close, touching my cheek, feeling a piece of my hair.

They spoke together softly, and then stepped back. Yahn's mother turned to the tribe. She raised her hands in the air for their attention and then motioned to me.

"Sitsi."

The elders all nodded, murmuring the word. "Sitsi."

A ripple of reaction passed through the tribe, some surprised, some wary. I looked to Yahn. He stared at me, a stunned expression on his face.

"What are they saying?" I asked, shakily. "What is Sitsi?"

Only in speaking the word did I remember where I had heard it. It was what the Apaches had called to me in my vision with the Djinn relic. "What does it mean, Yahn?"

Yahn looked to his mother, who nodded. He blinked slowly. "Sitsi. It means daughter."

I could hardly form words. "Why are they calling me that?"

"Because they can see who you are. They can see you are Apache."

CHAPTER THIRTY-THREE

Yahn's mother came forward and set her hands on my face. "Ya ta say, sitsi."

"She welcomes you," Yahn said softly.

I shook my head. "I don't understand. You're saying *I'm* Apache?"

Yahn nodded.

"I'm not. I couldn't be. My mother…"

Her face drifted into my mind. I pictured her long black hair worn back in a braid. Her soft copper-hued skin and elegant, high cheekbones. She looked… Well, she looked a lot like the women who watched me from the flickering shadows of this camp.

Perhaps seeing the confusion scratched across my face, one of the elders spoke, and Yahn nodded in agreement. "Come," he said. "They offer us warm food and drink by the fire. I can try to explain, though I am as surprised as you."

The tribe took their places around the blaze. Pipes were lit, and the painted warriors addressed the elders with serious, tense words. I didn't have to understand their language to know they were talking about the attack.

I glanced beside me to Yahn. He was watching me already. My face flushed.

"I'm trying to understand this all," I said, looking absently at the warm but untouched corn cake they'd placed in my hands.

"It must be difficult to grasp."

All my life, I'd never thought much of Mama's darker complexion. She only ever talked about her Swedish father, and even as a young child, I understood that she carried a certain measure of shame about her mother's heritage. But I figured she was simply part Italian or Mexican. I would never have imagined Apache in a hundred years.

"Are these elders certain?" I asked. "How can they tell?"

"They felt the Legacy within you."

"Legacy?"

Yahn seemed to be searching for the right words. "It is a common spirit within all of our people. A power. A way to communicate with the Sacred Ones. Have you ever felt it? When you held a relic, have you heard the faintest whispers of their souls, still dwelling in the remnants of their bodies?"

His words made my breath catch in my throat. I stared at him in awe. "I have felt it," I said, my voice barely above a whisper.

"It was the power of the Sacred Ones, reaching out to you from beyond death."

Was it possible? Surely there was some other explanation. But as I sat there, staring at the warm, shivering flames, the bare truth of it grabbed me. Thoughts came together in my mind like a shattered pot, joined at last by the crucial but long-missing glue. The voices I'd heard when I was near relics. My enduring fascination with the creatures they once were. The reason Mama hated me wanting to use them. Why I'd never met my maternal grandmother. And why Tom had so quickly taken a liking to me when I started at The Desert Rose—he must have sensed the Legacy within me. It also clarified why he seemed so defensive about betraying his people. Because he was betraying mine as well. Even my vision with the Djinn relic now made sense. Closing my eyes, I could still see the mass of Apaches standing in the flames, calling for me. Daughter. How could it all be a coincidence?

Not only did I, in fact, have a talent with relics, it was clearly a deeper connection than I could ever have imagined.

"It's strange," I breathed. "But I believe you."

"You can feel it, as I do now. It is the Legacy, showing us the truth."

Our eyes met, and indeed something did pass between us. I just wasn't sure if it was the Legacy, or something even deeper hidden in my heart. I cast my gaze down into my lap as heat rushed to my cheeks. "This Legacy," I said, "it's a bond with other Apaches as well as relics?"

"We are all connected. And not just the Apaches, but also our brothers the Navajo and the Jicarilla. The Chiricahua. All people native to these lands have the Legacy."

"And that's why you don't like the relics being mined out of the mountains."

"It is the greatest desecration. You have seen what happens when humans try to harness the power of the Sacred Ones."

"The razings."

"Yes."

“Is that why your tribe attacked the excavators’ camp?”

Yahn nodded. “The call for fiercer resistance began last year, when our scouts brought back word of something happening in the mining tunnels near our land. Something evil. Our men sensed the darkness before they had even laid eyes upon the place. It was brought from deep, deep within the earth.”

Comprehension struck me. “The red relic.”

Yahn looked surprised. “You know of it?”

I could almost feel the shadowy bone in my hand, with its eerie black glow and pulsing power. A shudder crawled through me. “I think so.”

“The moment we heard of the first whole town burning, our elders began to fear that this relic was something different. Something ancient—a creature that existed long before the dragon or the griffin or the mermaid. From a time when the Earth was just a sapling, and magic was in its purest elemental state. A fire relic capable of consuming not only the land, but the mind as well.”

“How does it consume the mind?”

“By digging for the most destructive, darkest thoughts of the user and feeding them until those evil impulses take over completely.”

I remembered how, when I wore the relic, my hatred of Mr. Connelly had transformed into an active plan to murder him. How my attraction to Landon turned into a forceful seduction. For so long, I’d been unable to imagine someone evil enough to burn an entire town. But now I could see that with the power of this relic to corrupt, over time, anyone could be that evil.

“We call it Ko Zhin,” Yahn said. “Dark fire.”

“So you know for sure what it is, then? This Ko Zhin?”

His face shadowed. “No. That information has been taken

away."

"What do you mean?"

He sighed. "Some truth is so sacred that only a few may know it. Over the centuries, our tribe has honored only two of the elders with that privilege: one man and one woman. The Vessels. Carriers of our sacred stories and the secrets of the Legacy."

I frowned. "And they won't tell you what's going on? Even if your lives depend on it?"

"They cannot tell us now. They are dead, murdered long before the razings began. They sliced the Father Vessel's throat while he hunted. And the Mother Vessel was killed in the mountains." His eyes went back to the flames, lost in painful memories.

"My betrothed was the Mother Vessel's granddaughter, and soon to inherit her honored role. They were together that day. We never found their bodies, only their bags. And my Sika's dress, torn and covered with blood."

I stared at him, horrified, and deeply saddened for him. "Who would do such a thing?"

"We do not know. Some suspect the miners. The Mother Vessel was very near their territory. Perhaps they wished to make an example of her."

Emotion choked my throat like smoke. I thought of Landon, and Mama and Papa and Jeb. No one should have to lose someone they love.

"I'm so sorry," I whispered.

Yahn said nothing for a while, only stared at the fire, as if his fiancée's ghost were flickering there in the yellow light. Finally he spoke again. "My heart tells me that their murders had a greater significance. That they were somehow related to the discovery of the Ko Zhin. I believe someone killed them to prevent us from discovering the truth."

"It must be another Apache. Who else would know about Vessels?"

"There are some," Yahn said darkly.

A shiver crept over my skin. It seemed no one was safe.

My mind went to Ella with a pang of fear. She was still at the Hacienda, and more vulnerable than ever. If I was part Apache, than so was Ella, and the Legacy would give her increased power with relics as well. It wouldn't be long before Álvar figured that out. And worse, he now had the perfect way to punish me for my meddling with his plan. Cold panic clawed at me. "I have to go back to the Hacienda. I need to get my sister."

"It is dangerous."

"No more dangerous than for you. That mob wants blood."

"Let them come. We are prepared to face them."

"You're outnumbered. And besides, they'll use relic weapons."

"We will fight," Yahn said. "They wish to cast us from these mountains forever, and this is simply their latest justification for doing so. This is a battle that will find us no matter where we run."

"Well, I won't let my sister get caught up in it. I have to go back and find her."

Yahn frowned at the fire, thoughts flickering behind his eyes. Then he looked up. "We will help you. We will go with you."

"No. I appreciate the offer, but it's *definitely* too dangerous for you."

"At least let me accompany you to the border of the Hacienda. I wish to see you safe, Maggie."

My face warmed. "I would appreciate that."

Standing at the edge of camp, Yahn's mother kissed my forehead, thanking me in the Apache tongue for saving Yahn and the others. She told me I was always welcome in their midst, and I prayed silently that they would somehow survive the onslaught that was about to befall them.

The entire tribe saw us off, standing on the edge of the dark forest. They looked as strong and certain as the trees themselves, even though they knew they faced death in the morning. A cold hand tightened around my heart as Yahn and I rode away. I couldn't take my eyes off the Apaches. My people. After losing so much, the sensation of gaining a family seemed almost too good to be true. I watched the tribe until the glow from their fire was a faint shimmer in the distance.

We rode swiftly down the mountain. I shared the horse with Yahn again, so he wouldn't be slowed down with two horses on the ride back. Before long, we'd left the cool, wooded darkness of the Alkali Mountains and returned to the familiar red-rock of the desert. It seemed we'd barely started when Yahn pulled the mare to a stop near a cluster of yucca trees, shadowed by the walls of the Hacienda.

As I dismounted, I hesitated, absently adjusting the saddle. I knew a speedy farewell would be best, but the words halted in my throat. I wasn't ready for this moment of peace to end. I wasn't ready to be parted from Yahn again.

"Well," I said, dusting off my skirt, "I guess this is it."

Yahn nodded. "Find your sister quickly and take her some place hidden."

"I'll be careful."

He fell quiet, his gaze lowered. "I wish I could do more to make sure you are safe."

"I feel the same."

"You have done more than I ever imagined. I owe you my life, Maggie."

"Guess we're even, then."

Our eyes met, and neither of us looked away. A soft breeze cut past. Standing there in the moonlight together, with the gentle song of crickets beyond, a warmth spread within me, from my toes to the crown of my head. Both of us were about to face danger, greater danger than we'd ever known, but in that moment, everything felt safe. And I needed that safety. I'd craved it for so long, and there was something about Yahn that brought it, deep in my soul. I'd felt it all those years ago, when we were two outcast kids at the mission school. I felt it when he saved my sister and me from the fire. I didn't want to lose it.

"I should go," he said.

"Yes."

But I didn't move, and neither did he. I stared at the dark ground and listened to the rhythm of his breathing. Standing this close to him, I was certain I could feel the Legacy that bonded us together. It was what I'd felt all along with him: a closeness. A need to be with him, to see him safe.

"Yahn, did you sense I was Apache? Why didn't you tell me before?"

"I did sense a bond to you, but I didn't recognize it as the Legacy at first."

My voice was little more than a whisper. "What did you think it was?"

"I was confused," he said.

"So was I."

His eyes swept over my face. My body moved closer, as if

pulled by an invisible thread.

"But we know now that we are as brother and sister," he said. "No matter what happens tomorrow."

"Yes." I swallowed hard. A brother. Was that what he was to me? Somehow my connection to him felt different…stronger. I pushed away the question. Yahn's words had reminded me of what mattered most when all was said and done: my sister. I could not lose sight of that.

"Good-bye, Yahn," I said, keeping my face turned from him. I wasn't sure I had the strength to look into his eyes.

"Good-bye, Maggie. I will always remember you."

It sounded so permanent. I closed my eyes to keep myself together but then darted a single look over my shoulder. I had to. If this was the last time I would ever be near him, I wanted to see his face, his beautiful, dark eyes.

There were more words I wanted to say. Words that seared my heart. But I said nothing. I held Yahn's gaze for a brief moment, then left.

CHAPTER THIRTY-FOUR

I ran, trying to pound away further thoughts of Yahn with my feet. I had to focus on the task at hand. Before I knew it, before I was ready, I was standing a few feet away from the high stone wall of the Hacienda.

The guard behind the gate held up his lantern. "Who goes there?"

"Maggie Davis," I said, striving to sound more confident than I felt. "I am Señor Castilla's mistress, come to see him at once."

The guard seemed to recognize me. He looked surprised, but as I analyzed his expression, I could see that it was merely surprise to see me arrive on foot at such an hour. He hadn't been briefed yet about my part in the failure of the hanging. Luck was on my side.

"Señor Castilla is waiting for me, you fool," I snapped with feigned haughtiness. "Now let me in at once, or he shall hear of this."

The guard fumbled for the lock. "Of course, señorita. Of course."

He swung the gate open and motioned for me to enter. I looked at the shining mansion ahead, and a coil of fear wrapped around me. But I had come this far, and there was no turning back now. I knew what needed to be done.

All I could think of was that hidden passage Álvar and his men had slipped into. What if Moon John was right? What if Álvar had taken the Ko Zhin skeleton for his own and become a slave to its evil?

I had to at least check. I was closer than ever to finally solving the mystery that had plagued me all this time. Closer than ever to having closure, to knowing who had killed my parents and why. And if Moon John was right, and the Ko Zhin was here, maybe I could take it somehow and prevent the slaughter of an innocent people.

When I got to the door to my room, I felt a momentary flash of despair. Surely Señora Duarte would be sleeping in my place to keep an eye on Ella. Did she know about my fall from Álvar's grace? I set my jaw. It was a risk I'd have to take.

I clicked open my door as softly as possible. Señora Duarte, her hair all tied up in rag curls, snored softly in my bed. I bit my lip and tried to peer across the suite into Ella's chamber. As quietly as possible, I padded to her bedside.

Ella's eyes fluttered open groggily as I shook her shoulder, and I immediately put a finger to my lips as I motioned with my eyes to Señora Duarte. Ella blinked a few times. She probably wasn't entirely sure if this was a dream or not, but she nodded once. Kissing her cheek, I lifted her into my arms.

We were nearly to the door when I realized the key piece I would need for my plan to work. The siren relic elixir. It was still tucked in the drawer to my nightstand—right next to Señora Duarte's face. My mind raced. I had to fetch it, if I could.

I set Ella down and once again motioned for her to be as quiet as possible. Each footstep I made toward the nightstand seemed to creak unbearably. My gaze stayed fixed on Señora Duarte, focused on any shift in her soft, rhythmic breathing. I slid closer, one slow step at a time. Finally my fingertips rested against the nightstand.

With eyes squeezed shut and a prayer in my heart, I pulled at the little drawer. It creaked. Señora Duarte inhaled sharply, but then let out a deep breath. Still asleep. Squeezing my breath, I tugged the drawer the rest of the way open. The blue vial of siren elixir rolled out, glinting in the lamplight. Safe and untampered with. My plan became a shade less crazy.

Ella padded groggily beside me, grasping my hand as we followed Señor Torres, the Captain of the Guard, down the dark corridor.

Waking him in the middle of the night had actually turned out to work in my favor. His mind was softer, more susceptible to the siren relic's magic. He showed reasonable resistance to the idea of taking me to the hidden chamber, but when I insisted that Álvar had summoned me there in an angry rage, he relented.

I kept a hand firmly on Ella's as we neared the passage. My eyes switched left to right at the closed, silent doors. The slightest creak sent stabs of fear through me, even with the calming coolness of the siren magic in my veins. I could feel the power waning within me every second. There certainly wasn't enough left to influence anyone else. To be stopped and challenged right now would be a disaster. But thankfully, the hallways remained empty. The Hacienda slept.

When we reached the little anteroom, Señor Torres shot me another hesitant glance. I gazed back earnestly. "I do hope Álvar isn't furious that I've taken so long. I hate to think who he'd blame."

The hint was clear. Gritting his teeth a little, Señor Torres set a hand on a seemingly blank piece of the wall. His fingers pressed down, and five indents sank into the stone. With a gentle rumble, the panel of wall slid open. Ella breathed a little gasp of surprise. I squeezed her shoulder.

The shadowy corridor spread out before us, dark as pitch. I hesitated. Álvar could be in there at that moment. Or his men. Even if he didn't have the Ko Zhin, he clearly didn't want people seeing whatever he concealed behind that wall.

But I had to try. I had to know.

A thought came to me. Summoning every final ounce of the siren magic that I could, I turned to Señor Torres. "You had better go in and announce us. I want to make sure he is ready to receive me."

The Captain pursed his lips, but the magic still held sway over his mind, and he bowed. "If you wish."

I breathlessly watched him enter the dark corridor. As soon as he vanished in the shadows, I grabbed Ella's shoulders, kneeling in front of her.

"You listen to me," I said firmly. "There's something I have to check in there. But I can't let that man know I'm checking, understand? You wait right here for me."

Ella shifted nervously. "Maggie…"

"It'll be okay. I promise. I'll sneak in there real quiet. And if

I hear Señor Castilla's voice, I'll come right back out, and we'll make a run for it together. But you need to stay right here until I get back, okay?"

"Okay," she said, nodding.

I kissed her forehead and, drawing in a deep breath, slipped into the shadow of the tunnel. I'd have given anything for Landon's goblin relic right then. The corridor wound down, deep into the bowels of the Hacienda, dark and silent. And empty. But just when I was starting to think I'd better cut my losses and turn back, the corridor ended in a vast, round chamber.

I pressed my back against the tunnel wall to hide. But after a moment of holding my breath, I realized I didn't hear the sound of anyone talking or even walking about in the chamber. Was there perhaps some other passage connected to the tunnel that I'd missed? I gathered my courage and peered into the large chamber.

Empty.

Except…in the center of the chamber, bathed in a column of moonlight that cut in from some distant grate above us, stood a pedestal of stone. And on the pedestal was a red staff. A red staff that emanated a faint black glow. A staff that filled my heart with hot, pulsing wind.

The Ko Zhin.

It *had* been Álvar all along.

The realization struck me like lightning on a pond. Álvar had killed my parents. And Jeb. And Landon and Bobby. He'd burned all those towns. He would have watched Yahn hang. And now he led the siege against an entire group of innocent people.

My people.

Nausea burned through me. My entire body trembled; my legs felt like jelly. In spite of all I'd seen, everything I'd had to face, I had never been more afraid in my entire life. I knew immediately that I had to get Ella, and I had to get her that instant.

The sound of scraping stone tore through the chamber. Startled, I spun around. Just behind the Ko Zhin, a hidden doorway opened in the wall. Fear cut through me. I turned to run, but then a strange, small sound, like a muffled shout, froze me in my tracks.

I turned back around, breathless. And then I heard a voice I recognized, a voice that sent ice shooting through my veins.

"My, my, my. If it isn't Maggie, my little lost lamb."

Percy Connelly stepped into the chamber. He held a struggling Ella in his arms, with one hand pressed firmly over her mouth.

"Look who I found," he said, motioning to her as he stepped into the moonlight.

Rage burned through me. "Get your hands off my sister," I roared, lunging for them.

Ella tore her face free from Connelly's hand and screamed. "Maggie! Look out!"

But at the same moment, a harsh pair of arms locked around my waist. I shot a look over my shoulder. Señor Torres smashed one hand around my throat, glaring.

"Let go of me," I shouted, gasping through his grip.

Connelly laughed. "I must say, it's a bit of a surprise to see *you* here. Thought you'd caused all the trouble possible this evenin'." He grinned, satisfied. "When I volunteered to guard the staff tonight, I just thought I was making myself useful to Álvar; I didn't know I'd get this little surprise. But I don't mind. I've been waiting a long time to give you what you got comin' to you."

He pulled a strange sand-colored relic from inside his pocket. Something about it filled me with fear and made me fight his grip with renewed fury.

"First the brat," he said.

"Don't you touch her," I screamed, boiling with rage, fighting Señor Torres's grip with all my might.

But Connelly pressed the relic against Ella's forehead. In an instant, she went limp as a rag doll.

"No! Ella!"

He set her on the ground and started to walk toward me. I fought as I'd never fought before. Tears burned my eyes. "You'll pay for this, Connelly!" I kicked Señor Torres with all my strength.

"Hold her still," Connelly barked.

"No!" I shouted, tossing my head up, hoping against hope that I'd wake someone in the rooms above us. "Help me! *Someone hel—"*

Connelly jammed the relic against my forehead. I went stiff as stone, and everything turned dark.

When my eyes cracked open next, I felt as if my head were submerged in a bucket of water. Everything blurred and swam around me and a dull hum filled my ears. I squeezed my eyes closed, then opened them several times. Only then did a semblance of color return, and only then did I start to recognize my surroundings.

The first thing I noticed was that I was standing, but something held my arms above my head. I looked up, blinking groggily. Dark iron bands enclosed my wrists. Chains. They hooked firmly to the wall, holding my arms up tightly. I looked down to see similar shackles locked around my ankles. My limbs could move a few inches at best.

The fog in my head pulled back slowly as I looked around me. Dark, damp stone. A single torch burning on the far wall. Empty sets of chains hanging at other places along the walls around me. And ahead, a thick wood door with a single, barred window. Like some kind of cell.

Blinking hard, I forced myself to piece together the events that had preceded this moment. I remembered the relic staff. The Ko Zhin. Connelly. Ella being dragged away screaming. A coldness clenched around my chest. Prison. I was in *prison.* I tugged my arms hard, but the chain only pulled taut.

"Hello?" I called. My voice echoed off the gray stone of the cell. "Is anyone out there?"

The yellow light of a lantern glowed through the tiny window on the door.

"Hello?"

Something clicked, and the door slowly swung open.

"Why, hello, Maggie," Connelly said, strolling into the cell with a casual and insufferably self-satisfied air. "Sleep well?"

"You have no right to keep me here, Connelly. Let me go this minute."

"I think not."

I pulled at the chains on my arms. "Where's my sister? Tell me right now."

"Maybe she's dead," Connelly said, shrugging.

His words took my breath for a moment, but then I reminded myself that Connelly was lower than a snake. I couldn't trust a word he said. "You're lying."

He snorted. "Guess you'll never know."

"If you hurt her, I'll kill you!"

"How're you gonna do that, huh? You look a little tied up at the moment."

His tone sent a chill through me. No one but Yahn knew I had come back to the Hacienda. No one would know where to look for me. And besides, people disappeared every day in these parts. With no family but Ella, and my only living friend, Adelaide, catatonic in her room, it could be weeks and weeks before someone even noticed I was missing.

"What are you planning to do to me?" I asked, though to my dismay, I sounded more afraid than defiant.

A mean smile pulled at Connelly's mouth. "Oh, there's plenty I'm gonna do."

"Álvar wouldn't let you lay a hand on me."

"Wouldn't he?" Connelly chuckled. "If I were you, I wouldn't trust anything Álvar said or did lately." He tapped his skull firmly. "That relic got into his brain and made him think all kinds of strange stuff."

I glared at him, but if Yahn had been right about the nature of the Ko Zhin, I knew it was true.

"He never *really* wanted you like that; you ain't his type. It was just that relic grabbing hold of his head, making him obsessed with you. Hell if I know why—you're nothing but a worthless little whore in my book."

My mind was too swept up in his claim about the Ko Zhin to care about the insult. Why would the magic make Álvar obsessed with me?

"At any rate," Connelly continued, moving closer, "he's not worried about you now. Not when he's gone to fight the Apaches."

I tensed. "It's morning? They've left already?"

"Yes, indeed. They headed off while you were sleepin' in your cozy new room here. Good thing I kept that staff safe for Álvar.

He's got it right where he needs it now."

Words died in my throat. Seeing this, Connelly chuckled. "I 'spect they'll be back by lunch. Shouldn't take them long to wipe those dirty Injuns out."

I wanted to tear that smile off his face. "You have innocent blood on your hands, and I hope it haunts you the rest of your life."

"*I* have blood on my hands? Do you see me off killing Apaches?"

"Please. Don't act like you aren't part of it. You're probably the one giving Álvar all the ideas."

Connelly laughed. "Oh, I see how it is. You don't think your precious patron could possibly be capable of coming up with such an evil plan." He snorted. "Well, think again. I do as I'm told, and I make myself useful to the rich little bastard. But *he* is the one with the hankering to torch this whole valley to the ground. Maybe you don't know it, but the kid's drowning in debt."

I said nothing.

"Yes, ma'am. Every property he owns has been sold out to someone else. 'Course he got himself in *real* trouble when he started sellin' out properties twice. Three times, even. It was just a matter of time before them creditors came to collect. Lucky for him, right about that time he found the fire relic."

Connelly seemed to be enjoying every moment of this. "You oughta see your little lover boy out there. He makes sure we get the job done. Yes, he does." He laughed. "The night we burned Green Springs, there was this one little cabin up on the hill. As we rode up, a man comes runnin' out, screamin' and beggin' us to spare his six kids."

"Stop," I said, trembling.

"Álvar has him shot in the head. Then he raises that staff, and the fire comes out like nothing you've ever seen. Like a pillar of pure lightning. Well, the cabin goes up in flames like a wisp of cotton."

"*Stop*."

"We could hear them kids inside, screamin' and—"

"*STOP!*" I shouted, thrashing my arms. "Stop! Stop it!"

Connelly quieted. I could see his smirk from the corner of my gaze. I clenched my jaw, hating that he'd gotten to me, hating that he'd found my most vulnerable place, hating the despair that surged into my soul.

"Sheesh," Connelly said, folding his arms with satisfaction. "What's eatin' you? Not like he killed your family. Oh, shoot. I forgot. He did."

"Leave me *alone*."

"Why should I? I'm having so much fun."

A woman's voice echoed against the stone walls. "Now it's my turn for some fun."

I snapped my head up, and Connelly whirled around. We both stared, speechless, as Adelaide walked into the prison cell.

She looked different. She was barefoot and dressed only in her underclothes: a camisole and petticoat with a red corset. Her pale hair flowed wild and free around her. The blank grief in her eyes had changed to a fierce gleam. And around her neck, a relic amulet that made my pulse freeze.

"Adelaide," I breathed. "What are you doing here?"

"I have a little business to tend to," she said. She held up the almond-sized piece of Ko Zhin, still on the chain I had fastened it to, and gave it a kiss. "Look familiar, Connelly?" She smiled. "Bet you thought I didn't know the code to that safe in your room. Tsk. You always did underestimate me."

Connelly set his jaw. "You thievin' whore."

"Look who's talking, sugar. If I recall correctly, you stole it from Maggie in the first place."

"Listen to me, Adelaide," I said, my voice shaking. "Take it off. Please. It's *very* dangerous."

A dark smile flashed in her eyes. "I know."

"You have no idea what you're dealing with," Connelly growled. "Hand it over. Now."

"What makes you think I don't know how to deal with it, Percy?"

"You have no clue the kind of fire power that thing's capable of."

"Well, sure, I do. This lovely Hacienda's burnin' to the ground as we speak. I guess it's so nice and quiet down here that you didn't notice all the screaming."

The color drained from Connelly's face. I thought immediately of Ella, scared, alone, and terrorized yet again by fire. *Dear Lord, let Adelaide be exaggerating to scare Connelly.*

"You didn't," he said.

She shrugged. "It took a little *persuasion* to find you. But we do *so* need to talk."

He took a step backward. "Stay away from me."

"Now is that any way to speak to an old friend?"

Like a striking rattler, Connelly leaped for me. His arm clamped around my waist, pulling himself halfway behind me. His other hand squeezed my throat.

"Don't come any closer, or your friend here dies."

As if for emphasis, his fingers smashed against my windpipe. Gasping, I tried to fight his grip, but he held me against him, a human shield.

Adelaide's smile faded. "Not wise, Percy."

"I said *get back*."

I thrashed with all my might, but that only made him squeeze harder. My lungs burned like hot iron in my chest as the world around me started to go fuzzy and dark. I could hear my own gagging and nothing else. All I could think of was Ella, alone in the world.

Adelaide's voice rang in my ears. "Stop! Don't hurt her."

"You gonna get back?"

She obeyed, her voice suddenly small and afraid. "Please. I—I'll do anything you say. Just let her go."

Connelly glared but slowly released his grip on my throat. Air rushed in, and I coughed and gasped huge gulps of it.

"That's more like it," he said. He stepped from behind me and jabbed out an open palm. "Now give that relic to me this instant."

Adelaide pulled the relic slowly from around her bare neck. As much as I wanted to see the thing far away from her, I knew it would be worse in the hands of Mr. Connelly. I kept my eyes on Adelaide, trying to silently communicate some other plan, any other plan. But she didn't look at me as she stepped forward with the relic in her fist.

Impatient, Connelly stomped forward. "I said, give it to me."

Adelaide held the relic out over his open palm.

But then, like the flick of a match against wood, her eyes snapped up, burning.

Fast, so fast I almost didn't see it, her hand jabbed forward, and a flash of flame illuminated the entire room. I winced, turning my face away from the heat. Connelly's scream echoed over the stone. The smell of smoke and singed flesh choked my lungs. When I opened my eyes, Connelly was lying on the ground. The left side of his body was charred and bleeding, but he was alive. He panted as he stared up at Adelaide.

I swallowed back the bile that rose in my throat.

"Please," Connelly rasped. "Please. Don't kill me."

Adelaide laughed. "Don't you think that's what Bobby said as he died in your fires? Don't you think he wanted to live?"

"I didn't kill your cowboy. It was Álvar!"

"Spare me your lies." She swung the relic over him like a pendulum. "You're going to get everything you deserve tonight, Percy. And I'm going to have a good time giving it to you."

My heart was pounding. "Adelaide—"

"Stay out of it, Maggie."

"Don't do this. You don't really want to kill him. You don't want blood on your hands."

She whirled around to me, her face ablaze. "I do. And I will, so don't you dare try to stop me."

"He's a bad man," I said. "He deserves to stand trial for everything he's done and then rot in prison for the rest of his life. Don't give him an easy out by killing him."

The slightest hint of doubt flickered behind her eyes, and I grasped for it. "Get the keys from him. Let me out of these chains, and we'll chain *him* up. We'll leave him to think about everything he's done to you."

Connelly's breath rattled heavily. His gaze snapped from Adelaide to me and back.

"Please, Adelaide," I said. "Go on and let me out of here."

She turned to Connelly, her relic aimed at him like a gun. "The keys."

"Right here," he said shakily. With his unburned arm, he pulled the iron ring from his pocket.

Adelaide pointed to me. "Get her out right now."

He nodded. His body was bloody as a butcher's block, but he managed to drag himself over to me. I cringed as his shaking, charred hand unlocked the chains at my feet. He tried to stand to get my arms but doubled over in pain. Adelaide kicked him aside, and he balled up with a groan of pain. Not even glancing down at him, she unlatched my hands herself.

The moment I was freed, I grabbed her in my arms. It was part hug, part restraint, though I hoped she wouldn't notice the latter.

"Now let's get out of here," I said, holding her close. "Come on. We'll leave him to rot."

Adelaide was staring at Connelly. Her chest rose and fell with tense breaths. I guided her ever so slowly toward the door. We took one step. Then another.

"He'll suffer real good in here," I said, in a soothing whisper. "Real good."

We reached the door. "Come on now," I added.

Suddenly, Adelaide tore away from my grip. Her eyes flashed. "No."

"Adelaide—"

"No!" she shouted. "He's going to pay for what he took from me!"

I reached for her, but she'd already thrust out her hand. With a cry, she sent a beam of white fire shooting right into Connelly's stomach. His body arched backward, and his scream filled the room.

I threw my arms around her. "Stop! Please!"

"Get back," she roared, shoving me off her.

I flew backward, slamming into the wall. My vision blurred with pain.

"You took everything that mattered to me!" Adelaide cried, sending another beam of fire into Connelly. He didn't move this time or even cry out. The damp straw scattered on the floor now smoldered with flames. Smoke darkened the air, burning my eyes.

Adelaide raised the Ko Zhin relic with a trembling fist. She was panting heavily. Charges of fire and power surged around her, gathering for a final blaze. I staggered to my feet.

"Adelaide, don't! You'll kill us all!"

"Time to send you to hell where you belong, Percy Connelly." She raised her hands over her head.

I jumped for her. My hands wrapped around hers, around the relic. It felt as if I were pressing my palm against a hearth, but I held on. The night in Landon's hotel room flashed through my mind, how he'd held me and talked me out of the madness. It was my only chance.

"This isn't you, Adelaide," I cried. "You're not a murderer."

"Let go!"

I pulled her hands closer, hugging them to me, though they felt like hot coals on my skin. The flames grew around us. Heat melted against our faces.

"You're a good person," I cried. "A loving, kind person. This relic is making you think evil things, but it isn't you. It isn't you!"

There were tears in Adelaide's eyes. "Stop!"

"Think about Bobby. He loved you so much. He wanted to marry you, to start a life with you. He died loving you, Adelaide."

She shook her head fiercely, the tears now streaming down her face. Her hands were shaking. I took the risk of prying her fingers open. She sobbed, but she released the relic into my palm. I flung it into the flames fast as I could.

"No," she moaned. "No! He has to pay."

"He's dead," I said, holding her in my arms. "He's dead, Adelaide."

She shook with sobs. The fire around us raged, and I guided her to the door. Right before we left, she looked back. The orange of fire reflected in her flooded eyes, along with a pang of horror at what she'd just done.

"It's over," I said softly.

Her face dropped down. Keeping one arm around her, I pulled the prison door shut, leaving the evil of Percy Connelly behind it.

CHAPTER THIRTY-FIVE

As we ran up the spiral stone stairs to the main level of the Hacienda, we were greeted with more fire. My breath caught in my chest. So Adelaide *had* been telling the truth.

People ran in all directions, servants carrying armfuls of expensive curtains and the good china. Guards shouted out to one another, trying to make some semblance of order. Haciendellas lifted their elaborate skirts to run at full speed. Dense black columns of smoke twisted and spread over the ceiling. And everywhere fire trembled in thick fans of light and heat.

Adelaide's face was ashen as she ran beside me. "I did this."

"It wasn't you." I squeezed her hand.

She said nothing.

I hated seeing the raw guilt and horror in her eyes, but I had a bigger problem on my hands. Ella was somewhere in that fire and chaos. I ran down the burning hallways, pulling Adelaide along, and tried my best to keep the panic that shook inside me from exploding.

Then a familiar face rounded the corner—the long, pointed face of Señora Duarte. Only she was alone. When she saw me, her eyes widened, and she spun around to make a run for it. I lunged, grabbing her arms, and slammed her against the wall.

"Let go of me!" she cried. "I have done nothing!"

"Calm down."

"I have done nothing wrong!"

I held her firm and looked into her eyes. "I only want to find my sister."

Señora Duarte shook her head, her eyes squeezed shut. I gripped her shoulders. "Where is she? I know you know."

She was trembling but remained silent. I shook her once, hard, startling her eyes open. "You *will* tell me where she is," I said.

She was silent for a breathless moment, and then her body melted in my arms. Sorrow splashed over her face. "I could not stop him. He took her, and I could not stop him."

Ice rushed through my veins. "Who took her? Álvar?"

Señora Duarte nodded, sniffling woefully. "He took her with him to the mountains. To the battle. I begged him not to. I told him it was far too dangerous for one so young. But he did not listen. Why would he do such a thing?"

I didn't answer her, but I knew. If Álvar couldn't have my Legacy to use for his dark purposes, he would use Ella's instead. The thought of my poor sister, scared and confused and witnessing the horrors of battle filled me with a rage I had never known before. That rage coursed through me with a power stronger than any relic could offer. Stronger even than the evil bones of the Ko Zhin. All at once, any fear or danger we might face seemed inconsequential. I was going to get my sister, and I was going to do it right now.

Getting horses proved easy enough thanks to the chaos that gripped the Hacienda. It was a free-for-all anyway, so two women taking a horse hardly drew any attention. Adelaide followed me without question; she was still too stunned by the things she'd done while possessed by the Ko Zhin. As we rode together toward the mountains, I tried to explain everything I'd heard at the Apache camp, but she seemed so shaken by the day's events that she only nodded, and I wondered if she'd even heard me.

I wasn't prepared for the scene I found near the red-rock cliffs that stood at the base of the Alkali range.

Fire. Smoke. Towers of blackness billowed to the heavens, blocking out the sun. Everywhere men blasted guns and shot arrows. In the chaos of battle, I could hardly tell who stood on what side. Hacienda, Apache, townsfolk—they all blurred together in the smoke and noise. The only thing that punctured the mayhem was the stark brightness of the blood splashed over rocks and sand and sagebrush.

A flash of red light lit the smoky fog in the distance—relic magic. I could see signs of it everywhere. To my far left, a man fell to his knees, gripping his head and thrashing about, his mind filled with some dark illusion. Ahead, a floating bowie knife held by an invisible attacker slashed at an Apache warrior. And all around me, the fireballs of dragon claw rifles soared like comets, exploding against trees or the cliff face or a ground of men.

Adelaide and I had to get out of there. Fast. I scanned every direction, searching for Yahn, searching for Álvar. Part of me knew it was pointless. The battle stretched over a huge expanse of land. They could be anywhere.

An earsplitting blast of sound tore through the air. A flash of light, bright as the sun, and then *fire*. I whirled around. From somewhere high on the cliff, I caught sight of a column of fire that seemed to come from the Devil himself. When the flames hit the earth below, they ricocheted up in a fifteen-foot wall, and steaming hot wind from the impact blasted over the land. Men scattered in all directions away from the massive blaze. Those who didn't get killed instantly, that is. As I watched, a cold, fierce terror gripped my heart, and I knew. That fire came from the Ko Zhin. And Álvar Castilla.

I grabbed Adelaide's hand and started to pull her toward our horse. The flames had spooked the animal into the safe shadow of a cluster of shrub trees. We ran up to her, but as I came closer, I noticed the reins tied to one of the branches. My feet slammed to a stop. I certainly hadn't tied her there. Frowning, I turned to look around and spotted two strange men. They walked side by side, heading directly toward us in a way that raised the hairs on the back of my neck. When I spun back the other way, I saw another man coming out from behind the Joshua trees.

Three men, neither Hacienda nor Apache, with ragged clothes and unkempt beards. Probably just angry, out-of-work members of the mob, relishing the chance to legally spill blood. They spread out a little, trying to surround us as they closed in.

"Stay away," I called, pulling Adelaide close to my side. "I'll shoot you if you get any closer."

"Easy, girlie. We just want to have a chat."

"I'm warning you. Stay back."

But they kept moving closer. Adelaide breathed hard at my side. I squeezed her hand. "Get ready to run," I said under my breath.

One of the men pulled a rusted knife from his inner coat pocket. "You girlies better play nice, or we'll have to cut you up real bad."

"Hand us over your relics," another demanded. "We know you got 'em."

"Don't hurt us," I said. "We'll give you everything." Mind racing, I bent to the ground. "Here, take it!"

I flung two fistfuls of dirt in the face of the closest attacker. The man whipped back, smashing his fists into his eyes with a roar.

I grabbed Adelaide's hand. *"Run!"*

We tore off, tripping over rocks and cactus and scrub brush to get away. A dark stabbing in my heart told me we couldn't possibly outrun all three of them, but I pushed forward anyway, hoping for another group of fighters to get in the way, another blast of fire from above—anything to give us a chance to escape.

The men shouted behind us, closing in. I screamed for help, but it was a bad situation any way you looked at it. With the chaos of battle all around us, no one would be able to stop those men if we were attacked. Likely no one would even notice.

And then, through the smoke and heat and noise of the battle came a horrible and haunting sound, like a ghostly scream. Beside me, Adelaide dropped like a rock. She tumbled to the ground, rolling twice.

"Adelaide!"

I spun around to get her, but she was lying on the dirt, shaking, an expression of horror twisting her face. She stared at something no one else could see, paralyzed with fear. I'd read about such symptoms: a terror that froze a person's body, made them lost in a nightmare until they died from not eating or drinking.

Banshee relic.

This couldn't be happening. Not now. Not to Adelaide. I wouldn't believe it.

"Adelaide!" I said, shaking her hard. "Get up!"

But she didn't move. The three no-accounts tramped up, grinning cruelly.

"Don't touch her!" I screamed, falling over her trembling body.

"Take it easy, girlie. You play your cards right, and we won't have to use the banshee on you as well."

I swung my arm through the air. "Get away! Get back!"

One of the men swooped up behind me, jerking me to my feet. He pinned my arms behind me and, in the same action, brought the blade of a knife against my throat. The edge pressed into my skin, slicing the first few layers. "Didn't we say to calm down?"

His rank breath turned my stomach. I tried to look away, but the knife pushed harder on my throat, forcing me to stay still.

The apparent leader of the group pointed a dirty finger in my face. "Now you listen. We know you got relics. Two women wouldn't be prancin' around in battle without 'em. So pass 'em over."

"We don't have anything," I said, my voice choked. "I swear it."

"You're a bad liar," the knife wielder whispered into my ears, slicing the blade against my skin. It felt like a red-hot brander. Blood slid silently down my neck.

The third man crouched by Adelaide. "Want me to search this one?"

The leader opened his mouth to respond, but his body suddenly went rigid. His eyes bulged, and a strange, choking gasp escaped his lips. And the lean shaft of an arrow protruded from his throat.

Eyes filled with shock, the leader gripped the arrow and tried to pull, but it was deeply embedded in his flesh. He drew his hand away; it dripped with bright red blood. A strange, sad look passed across his face, like a man suddenly woken to a terrible truth. He fell to his knees, gasping in a strained way. And then, all at once, he was facedown in the dirt.

We all stared at his body, motionless, speechless. I thought a rogue arrow must have hit him, but then I heard a horse whinny. Every other sound evaporated from my ears. The smoke ahead seemed to part. I watched in amazement as a painted stallion galloped toward us, with Yahnuiyo strong in the saddle.

CHAPTER THIRTY-SIX

Yahn fired two more arrows as he rode up, but they landed intentionally to the side of either man. Warning shots. Another horse followed a ways behind him. I recognized that rider as well. Sheriff Leander.

Yahn came up in front of the roughnecks, and his horse reared on its hind legs with a furious and terrifying whinny. Yahn drew back his arrow with cool intensity.

"Let them go, or I put the next shots into your brains."

Both men complied immediately. They ran off faster than I'd ever seen men run. Yahn jumped down from his horse, as did Sheriff Leander, going right to Adelaide's crumpled body.

Yahn came toward me, and I ran to close in the distance. We came together in a fierce, colliding embrace. I pressed my face to him, squeezing my eyes shut with intense relief. No words needed to be spoken. The warmth of the Legacy coursed through both of us, and the moment couldn't have felt more right.

I might have stayed there forever if awareness hadn't shot through me. "Adelaide," I said, my eyes snapping open.

Yahn and I both ran to her side. Sheriff Leander held her in his arms, patting her face gently, but she didn't rouse. She still gazed up at unseen terrors. The only movement came from slight twitches and a general trembling.

"What's wrong with her?" Sheriff Leander asked.

"Banshee relic," I said, my voice tight.

He swore under his breath. Yahn's brow lowered. "Such evil."

I nodded grimly. "We need to get her treatment fast."

Sheriff Leander passed Adelaide carefully into Yahn's arms. "Take her to Moon John quick as you can. But be careful. This fire's spread to Burning Mesa, and all hell's broken loose over there."

Only then did I process what an unexpected team they made, Yahn and the sheriff. "You're not…trying to hang him anymore?" I asked the sheriff.

He shook his head. "We know Álvar Castilla is responsible. At least my rangers and I know it. Last night, I got a two A.M. visit from Emerson Bolger. Turns out he's had his suspicions of Señor Castilla for some time. Well, for the past week, he's been coaxing information out of Mr. Connelly at The Desert Rose, pretending that it was in regard to a mining operation. When Bolger finally offered Connelly a high-ranking position in his new company once he took over in Burning Mesa, Connelly betrayed Castilla, told Bolger everything. And Bolger promptly reported it all to me."

I shook my head, dazed. "All this time, I thought he was responsible for the razings."

Sheriff Leander nodded. "And he thought *you* were a spy for

Castilla."

"I guess that would explain why he was always such a bear to me."

"Who can blame either of you? It's hard to know whom to trust in times like these. I might have suspected Bolger myself if I hadn't known him since we were kids. Anyway, once we knew the truth, I tried my best to stop the mob, but they were too worked up. The fool thing is, they're all so fired up about the people burning towns down that now they're about to do it themselves."

"You can't go into Burning Mesa," I said to Yahn. "It's not safe."

"It's more dangerous to stay here," he said. "Your friend needs help at once."

Sheriff Leander nodded and clapped a hand on Yahn's shoulder. "Ride hard, son."

"I will. Come, Maggie."

I started to follow, but my feet slowed to a stop. Around me, the battle still raged. The fire still burned. And somewhere out there, Álvar Castilla still had my sister. I knew what I had to do, and it wasn't riding off with Yahn.

I watched him as he carried Adelaide gently toward his horse, and my heart burst. There was so much I wanted to say. To do. Everything in me wanted to be near him. But I knew I couldn't follow. Not without my sister.

"Hurry," Yahn said, glancing over his shoulder at me.

It felt like two boulders crushing me on either side. I stepped forward and grabbed his hand tightly. "I can't go," I said, filling the charged silence.

"What do you mean?"

"Álvar has Ella. I can't leave without her."

Sheriff Leander came closer, frowning deeply. "We'll find her, Maggie, I swear to you. We'll find Castilla and bring him down."

I shook my head, the pain compounding within me. "You can't. He'll kill Ella if you try to take him in. That's why he brought her into battle—as a shield, can't you see?"

Yahn's face was dark. "You cannot reason with him. You know what he possesses."

"I agree," Sheriff Leander said. "He could burn you like a scrap of paper."

I knew it was probably impossible to convince them, but I tried. "I know him. I'm sure I can find a way through to him."

Sheriff Leander shook his head at my reasoning. "We don't even know where Señor Castilla is. He's probably well hidden. And well guarded."

I knew where Álvar was. The moment I'd seen that huge column of fire, I knew. He was on the cliff where he'd taken me for dinner. I was about to tell Sheriff Leander this when, in a flash, I saw a way to keep him off my trail.

I tried to look thoughtful as I crafted the lie. "You know, when I was at the Hacienda, I heard them talk a lot about a cave hidden in the forest just beyond the grounds. A safe place, they called it."

Sheriff Leander brightened. "Do you know exactly where it might be?"

"Not sure."

He nodded. "That's a good lead, Maggie. Well done." He set his hand on Yahn's shoulder. "I'd better go inform the rangers. If we get Castilla, we can put this whole thing to an end."

We all nodded in agreement, but as we watched Sheriff Leander ride off, Yahn half turned his face to me. "You sent him astray."

"You know why I had to."

He was quiet for a long moment, staring at the burning red-rock cliffs before us. "My mind trusts that you know what you are doing, but my heart fears for you."

Closing my eyes, I grabbed his hand. His warm, strong touch was like a pillar of strength cutting through the chaos in my soul. "I can do this," I said.

His voice was soft. "I know. I only wish I could come with you."

"You have to help Adelaide. She needs treatment *now.*"

Yahn drew in a slow breath. "Promise me you will be careful."

I hoped he couldn't see the fear that shook my very core. "I promise. Now go. Hurry."

Once he was mounted in his saddle, with Adelaide secure against his chest, he cast a final look at me. I nodded, pulling the bravest face I could manage under such conditions. Watching him ride away broke me into pieces, but I knew I'd done the right thing. Ahead of me, the high red-rock cliff stood like the castle of some ancient giant. Álvar was up there, so that was where I needed to be.

Drawing in a shaky breath, I walked into the fire.

CHAPTER THIRTY-SEVEN

The cliff top looked different as I climbed the final stretch of hill. Heat from the fires below rippled up in baking waves. Smoke covered the sun, creating a shadowy, red-tinted dimness and filling the air with its oppressive smell. When Álvar's outline came into sight, standing against the edge of the cliff, I ducked down behind a boulder.

Heart pounding, I peered over the edge, searching for Ella. When I spotted her sitting against a clump of rocks with her arms tight around her knees, so scared and small and quiet, it took everything in me not to run to her.

As I moved closer, Ella spotted me. Her little face lit up, then dimmed. She was worried Álvar would hurt me. I wanted to tell her it would be okay, but instead, I motioned for her to stay where she was. I knew I had to play this smart. I had to play the only angle I had, if it still existed. Exhaling once, I stood and stepped forward.

Álvar snapped around at the rustle of my feet over the dry grasses on the cliff top. Right away, I noticed the strange fierceness in his eyes, the pale rage hanging on his countenance. He held the Ko Zhin staff in his hand, though in a way it looked as if *it* held *him*. Even now, I could feel its power reaching for me, its dark, alluring whisper in my ears. Even knowing what I knew, I still wanted to take the staff in *my* hand. I wanted to possess just a flicker of that strength.

"Ah, Maggie," Álvar said, a cold smile crawling over his lips. "I knew you would come."

It took every ounce of strength for me not to tremble under his gaze. "I'm here for my sister. Let her go."

He gave a single, sharp laugh.

"She's innocent in this," I said, fighting with everything in me to keep calm. "I'm the one you want."

His eyes flicked with darkness. "Indeed. You are."

"Then let her go, and I'll do as you say."

"It doesn't work like that, Maggie. You'll do as I say, and that is the only thing that will keep me from burning your sister to ash."

Ella whimpered. Though my own insides were shaking with fear, I dared to move closer to the edge of the cliff. "Álvar, please. Don't do this."

He slammed his staff to the ground. "Enough!" A snap of fire lashed out of the Ko Zhin. The dry, wind-blown patches of shrubbery ignited on the cliff top around us. I jumped back, but Álvar pointed the gleaming relic at me.

"Did you think you'd get something for nothing? Healing your sister. Your fine room. And all those pretty dresses—those were given with a price."

"And what do you demand?" I asked, shaking inside, fearing the answer, now that I knew it had *indeed* been my talent he was after.

"You, Maggie. You shall be my greatest, most valuable relic." He stepped closer, his eyes bright with the reflection of white flames. "I have realized what makes you so special. It is alchemy. You've somehow internalized the magic. It is part of you."

"Listen to yourself, Álvar!" I cried. "I barely know what alchemy is. How could I possibly have performed it?"

His smile was wild, crazed. "Ah, but you have, whether you intended to do so or not. And I will find out how. I will study you, and you will teach me, and with our new powers, we will make everything right again. We shall wipe out the Apache people. We shall wipe out those who would seek to destroy everything I've built, everything my family has built. Let them all burn, and from their ashes, you and I will create a new, better world."

"These aren't your thoughts, Álvar. You have to see that. It's the relic. It's got ahold of you."

"You understand *nothing* of this relic."

"It only wants you to use me like it is using you. You have to fight it."

"Silence!" he shouted, plumes of fire curling out of the Ko Zhin.

I knew my words fell as meaningless on his ears as the hot wind. As long as Álvar held the Ko Zhin, his rage would only grow. The evil would continue to push him further and further. I had to separate him from that staff.

My mind raced back to the prison cell this morning with Adelaide. I had subdued her by forcing her to see the good in herself. Maybe, just maybe, I could do the same with Álvar.

"I know you don't want to kill all those people," I began, switching tactics. "Innocent people. Even your own men are down there."

"Necessary sacrifices."

"I *know* you don't mean that."

"You know nothing!" he said. The flames shot from his staff like angry hands, reaching for my little sister. I held up an arm to block my face from the blaze. Álvar took the moment to yank me toward him.

"I won't help you," I shouted, struggling to pull from his grip.

"You *will.* Or I will burn you where you stand."

"No!" Ella ran up to us, sobbing frantically. She threw her arms around my legs, trying to pull me away with all her strength. "Don't kill her," she sobbed. "Please don't kill her, Mr. Castilla."

I stared at Ella, my heart bursting. Suddenly, seeing she cared for me this much, I felt strong and even more determined to fight for our lives.

Her tenderness seemed to affect Álvar as well. The rage in his eyes wavered slightly—a tiny crack in the steel wall of blind anger. His grip loosened enough for me to free my arm. I shot Ella a glance, and she backed away. Only the smallest window had opened. But I had to try and take it.

With our faces close, I dared to touch Álvar's hand. He looked there, then back at me, the conflict and confusion blossoming on his face.

"I understand why you feel trapped," I said, my voice soft. "I've heard about the debts."

"How dare you mention that…" But his voice trailed off into silence.

"I understand, Álvar. You know I do. I know what it feels like to be put in charge of something so important. I know what it feels like to fail."

His eyes flashed, but I tightened my grip.

"You think this is the answer, but I promise you, it will only make things worse. There is another way. A way back, out of this. If you stop right now, you can save yourself from doing something that would destroy your soul forever."

He was breathing hard, staring fiercely into my eyes.

"You don't have to do this. Walk away, Álvar. I know it's what you really want."

"Don't," he said, his voice not angry but confused, seething with conflict.

Swallowing the hitch in my throat, I reached up and touched his face. He flinched but didn't recoil from my hand. As I searched the rich brown of his eyes, a strange, startling thought caught me. He wasn't evil. In fact, deep down, he wasn't so different from me. I would do anything to protect Ella, just as he would do anything to protect his family's honor. If I'd kept my tiny piece of Ko Zhin, wouldn't I have resorted to equally dark ends?

"No matter what you've done," I said, "I know you're a good person."

His voice was strained, stricken. "That part of me is lost."

"Not lost. Taken. By the Ko Zhin."

It was the Ko Zhin that had killed my family. All those towns. And now, it sought to kill this man's soul—and mine with it. I could see the fierce red staff from the corner of my eye. A glittering darkness. An evil beauty. And something pulsed within me. I knew what I had to do.

"I will save you," I whispered.

And with a surge of adrenaline, I lunged for the staff.

Unbearable flames flared as my arms wrapped around that relic. The momentum of grabbing it, and ripping it from Álvar's distracted grip, sent me tumbling to the ground. I could hear Álvar's cry, but it was muted in my head with the raging fury of the Ko Zhin.

Evil, thick and dark as tar, burst through me. This Ko Zhin bore a hundred times the power of that little sliver I'd gotten from the miner. And with my gift, with the Legacy, that power blazed tenfold stronger. It pulsated in my mind with deafening fury.

When I rose to my feet and saw Álvar standing there, stunned, all I wanted to do was burn him forever. He deserved to pay for everything he'd done. He was weak, and he'd let the magic control him like a puppet. He let it kill my parents, my brother. He let it burn my home. A man like him deserved to be nothing more than ash on the wind.

I would control this power. As the white-hot staff burned in my grip, I could see it all like a vision. A vision of my right and destiny.

I would wipe him out, then obliterate every one of his evil underlings. With my fire, I would bring to justice every man who had murdered an innocent. They would all pay. Their ashes would be recompense for the ashes they created. And I would build the world anew. A just world. A right world. A world I would rule with my benevolent power.

A scream pierced the roaring fire of my mind. Looking to the side, I saw the smallest flash of a little face. Surrounded by the tongues of flames that spread over the cliff top—flames I was creating—a pair of brown eyes, so like Papa's, pleaded with me silently.

Ella.

It was as if a beam of light cut into the darkness inside me. I had to stop this.

The Ko Zhin was taking over my mind. It was filling me with evil, with hatred. If I didn't stop, I would burn the entire cliff top, with Ella and Álvar as well as myself.

But justice had to be done. Think of all the innocent people who died by his hand. He had to be punished. He had to pay. I would make him pay. Fire for fire. Death for death.

NO! With a cry, I fell to my knees. It was destroying me, every second that I could feel the Ko Zhin tighten its hold on my heart. Trembling, I saw the drop-off of the cliff, falling to the abyss below. I only needed the strength.

The Ko Zhin seemed to sense my resistance, and it blazed harder in my mind, a quaking rage so intense, I could only see flames in my eyes.

Think about Ella, I screamed to myself. I called up her face in my mind. Then Mama and Papa and Jeb. Then Adelaide. Landon. Yahn. For them, I had to end this. I had to do it.

Over the pain and fire and blackness of despair, my own roar rang in my ears. I had the power to overcome this. I had Apache blood in me. A Legacy stronger than this evil.

A surge of strength, like hot white light, tore through me. I lifted the Ko Zhin staff over my head. It burned my hands, melted onto them like liquid metal.

With a cry, I flung the staff over the edge of the cliff. But as I did, a final surge of will from the Ko Zhin pulled through me. I lost my balance and slipped forward, my body hurtling into the smoky, burning abyss below.

CHAPTER THIRTY-EIGHT

For a blinding moment, there was only the whistle of wind in my ears and the sensation of falling.

Then, with a blast of pain, my body struck a boulder jutting out on a lower ledge, and I flipped over. Gravity and inertia dragged me to the edge, but a sudden, overpowering surge of desperation threw my arms out in front of me, and my fingers latched onto the rock.

Lying on my stomach on the tiny ledge, I held on for my life, trembling with the shock of the fall. Flames flickered far below, and smoke plumed skyward. Panting, I looked up. The top of the cliff cut through the shadows above, so close.

I lifted a shaking hand to try and reach for it but felt myself slipping, so I stayed clinging to the rock. Sweat beaded on my forehead. My pulse pounded so hard, I felt as if I were only a beating heart. I couldn't reach safety.

A shadow fell over the smoke-shrouded sun above. Álvar stared down at me with a face of stone. I stared back, speechless.

"You destroyed my staff," he said.

"It had to be done," I said, trembling as I struggled to hold my body on the sandy little ledge. "The world is rid of it now."

He shook his head slowly. "No."

"It's burning in its own flames as we speak."

Álvar gripped his head and dropped to his knees at the edge of the cliff. "You're *wrong*," he cried, a desperate roar in his voice.

I shook my head, but he spoke over my protest.

"There is more, so much more. The entire skeleton. That staff was just a trifle."

Cold spread over my whole body. "Where have you hidden the rest? It has to be destroyed, Álvar."

"I don't have it," he said fiercely. "That's what I'm trying to tell you. The man from back East I told you about—the expert, the relic scholar! He was the one who told me where and how to dig for the relic in the first place. He put me up to it. He told me it would solve all my problems, but he just wanted it for himself. He used me!"

My head whirled with the strange information. But there were more pressing matters. The sand and grit beneath my body seemed to be pulling me closer and closer to the edge. My sweaty hands trembled at the exertion of gripping for dear life.

"You have to get me up," I said, shaking. "I can help you if you get me up."

"He is the cause of all this," Álvar said frantically, as if he hadn't heard me.

"Álvar!" I cried. "I can't hold on much longer."

He turned to me, looking dazed and wild and afraid all at

once. "We have to find him. His power is greater than you know, Maggie. *He* is the alchemist I spoke of. It's not just a myth; it's real. And with this evil relic, he will have unimaginable power."

I stared up at him. Álvar's prolonged use of the Ko Zhin must have come at the cost of his own sanity.

"Do you *swear* to help me find him?" Álvar pressed. "To clear my name?"

The sand scraped against my palm, pulling, tugging me down.

"I swear it," I said, desperation taking over. "Now help me!"

For a moment Álvar's eyes blazed with thoughts, but then his hand jabbed down to me. Trembling, I tried to reach for it, and once again, my body started to slip. It seemed certain that if I let go of the rock, I'd plunge to my death. I looked up at Álvar, and the terror must have been bright in my eyes.

"Reach, Maggie," he said. "You can do it. You are stronger than any other person I know."

My entire body was shaking. My throat was tight as a clenched fist. I hadn't come this far to die. And Álvar was right, I was strong, stronger than I'd realized.

Drawing in a sharp, determined breath, I stretched out and grasped Álvar's hand. My body dropped down, but then I felt a strong grip on my wrist.

"I've got you," Álvar shouted.

"Don't let me fall!"

I kicked and scraped my feet against the wall of the cliff, sending cascades of dirt and rocks plunging down. With the adrenaline of the moment, I found the strength to reach up with my other hand. Álvar grabbed it.

"I've got you!" he cried in a strained voice.

Before my blurred eyes could focus, my chest was passing

over the top of the cliff. I kicked my feet off the rock, propelling myself even more. Ella ran up, shouting my name, and she flung her arms around Álvar and pulled. With a heave, the three of us tumbled forward to the dry, blessedly flat surface of the cliff top.

Before I even processed what had happened, Ella had her arms around me, weeping. "Maggie, Maggie."

I held her to me and gasped huge, sobbing breaths of air. My arms couldn't hold her tight enough. We wept and hugged.

Álvar stood shakily beside me. He was breathing hard, but he didn't look relieved. He stared at me, ashen. "You must believe me, Maggie," he said, his voice strained. "That scholar is far more dangerous than I. He has the rest of that relic, and he will take its power. You think I should hang for what I have done; I know this. And perhaps I should. But my actions will be nothing compared to his."

"Who is he?"

Álvar started to back away slowly. He looked more afraid than I'd ever seen him. "I will find you," he said. "When the time is right. And you must help me."

Ella seemed to sense the darkness in his tone. She grabbed onto me tighter. "Maggie, make him go," she whispered.

I hugged her, shushing softly. But my eyes went back to Álvar. I knew I should detain him; I should keep him there on the cliff top until Sheriff Leander came. He was a guilty man who deserved punishment.

And yet as Álvar backed away, I didn't try to stop him. Somehow I couldn't send him to the gallows—not when I'd felt the overpowering evil of the Ko Zhin for myself. Wasn't Álvar just a desperate young man who had been in far over his head?

As he turned to go, Álvar passed a final look back at me, and something unreadable burned in his eyes. It sent a strange shiver through me. He held my gaze for a few more moments, then disappeared into the smoke.

I gazed at the space where he had gone, unsure of what to think. Pushing away the feeling, I kissed Ella on her soft hair.

"It's over, baby girl," I whispered. "It's all over now."

CHAPTER THIRTY-NINE

In the cool forest of the Alkalies, the Apaches' memorial for their dead lasted two days and nights. I attended but clung to the fringes. I might have Apache blood, but I still didn't feel like I fully belonged. The keening and wailing from the tribal women rang into the clear mountain air, nearly drowning out the endless beating of the drums. Yahn's mother spoke in the Apache tongue, praising the actions of the many brave warriors who'd fallen.

I couldn't help but think of Landon. In my heart, this was his funeral, too.

The event left me drained, body and soul. I stayed up through the night, but as dawn started to crest, I could feel myself fading. I'd come mostly in the hopes of seeing Yahn, but the crowd was so dense that I hadn't even caught a glimpse of him.

I walked my horse through the thick trees, breathing in the cool smell of pine and morning. I was ready to go home and sleep until the heaviness in my heart faded.

A twig snapped to my left. I froze, alert to the possibility of danger. But then Yahn stepped out from behind a wide tree trunk. At the sight of him, something inexpressible swelled in my chest. I couldn't stop myself from rushing to his side, from throwing my arms around him.

I had so many feelings but no words. It was probably just as well. Speaking would have only released the tears I was trying so hard to hold in.

"It brings me joy to see you safe," Yahn said. We parted, but his gaze stayed connected to mine. "You did a great thing, Maggie. You saved many, *many* lives."

I shook my head, filled with sorrow. "If only I could have done more."

Yahn was quiet in mournful agreement. He stroked my horse's mane. "What will you do now? Will you have a place to stay in the town? And a way to care for your sister?"

I nodded. When I'd made it back to town, the day of the battle, I immediately went to Adelaide. I helped Moon John until late into the night, searching his books for possible relic cures, then grinding and mixing the right elixir. It was worth all the work to simply see Adelaide okay, but then, as Moon John and I cleaned up, he made an unexpected offer, asking if I would like to be his apprentice. He told me he would provide for Ella and me while I trained, and one day, I'd repay him when I was working in a relic refinery of my own. Even days later, it almost seemed too wonderful to believe.

"I've found good work," I said. "And we have a place to stay for a while. We're going to be okay."

Yahn nodded. "I am relieved to hear this. I hope you know

that you are welcome to return to our tribe at any time if you ever need help."

"Thank you."

A silence fell. It was my cue to say farewell, to let him rejoin his tribe and their continuing ceremony. But my feet remained rooted to the ground. How could I leave him after everything that had happened? After everything I'd learned? He was part of me now, and I him, and I didn't want to let that go. Would I ever see him again? We lived in different worlds, worlds that rarely intersected. Would this moment be the last I looked on his face?

"Maggie."

Hearing him say my name only drove the wedge of sorrow deeper into my heart. It was time for me to leave. I knew that it was time.

Choking back emotion, I turned my eyes to the ground. "I don't want to say good-bye."

"Then do not."

If only it could be true. I blinked hard, but two tears escaped, anyway. I kept my face down so he wouldn't see. "Then what *do* we say, Yahn?"

He set his hand beneath my chin and gently turned my face forward. His eyes were warm and sad and beautiful.

"We say *egogahan*," he whispered, wiping the tears from my cheeks. "In our tongue, it means 'until we meet again.'"

I knew I shouldn't, but the words tumbled out in a trembling murmur. "And will we?"

A small smile brightened his face. "Perhaps, Maggie Davis. Perhaps."

Like a phoenix, the town of Burning Mesa rose out of the ashes. After the funerals and memorials had been held, we all did what tough desert folk have to do. We picked ourselves up and started again.

The weeks after the battle brought a flurry of rebuilding. A long, fresh rain had passed over the land, cleaning away the ash and heat, and by the time the sun came out again, the whole town seemed ready to press on. You couldn't throw a stone without hearing the hum of a saw or smelling the fresh pine of new wood or hearing the clang of hammers on nails.

And more than buildings were coming up. Our hope returned. Word came of towns rebuilding everywhere, of fresh groups of settlers coming out West to make a life in this desert. Sheriff Leander promised that Álvar Castilla would be found and brought to justice, that new peace treaties would be made with the Apaches. It was like Burning Mesa had come alive again.

True, I still had unanswered questions deep in my heart. And the faintest hint of shadow still lingered over all that had occurred, but I decided not to focus on that. For now, we were safe. And that was all that mattered.

One of the biggest rebuilding projects was to raise up The Desert Rose again. With Connelly dead and Álvar gone, the half-burned saloon might have been torn down completely. But Eddie rallied a group of the weekend regulars to take up their hammers and nails and bring back The Rose.

The sound of their work in the air on a bright, warm morning did my heart good. I'd helped Adelaide into the large wheeled chair the town doctor had lent us, and we walked to the bustling site. Men worked in every corner, carrying long, clean planks of wood and handfuls of nails. The dancer girls scurried around with pails of water, laughing and flirting with the workers to lift their spirits. And on the streets, townspeople watched the progress with parasols and curiosity unfurled.

As we approached, Eddie, who was busy framing, waved at us and shouted out a greeting. Ella ran ahead, grinning. She'd taken quite a shine to him lately.

"Let me help, Eddie!" she cried. "I can help!"

"Come on over, pretty girl," he called. "You and me will build this place good."

I wheeled Adelaide to a shady spot, away from the crowds. "Comfortable?" I asked, arranging the blanket that was draped over her lap.

She nodded, smiling weakly. I turned to go, but she grabbed my hand.

"What's wrong?"

"Nothing," she said. Her eyes searched my face, and I saw the faintest gleam of tears on them.

"What is it?" I asked, kneeling by her. "What's wrong?"

"Nothing's wrong," she said. "I just wish Bobby could be here."

I set my hand over hers. "I know."

"No, listen to me. I wish Bobby could be here to see that I'm gonna be all right. If this old saloon can be built again, well...so can I."

"I think he knows," I said softly. "I think he's here right now, with Landon and my mama and papa and Jeb. All of 'em watching over us."

She smiled at the thought and nestled back in her chair. I squeezed her hand. Even after all the good that had happened, my throat still choked up at the thought of those I'd lost. I was going to be all right, too, though their absence left a hole in me I suspected would never close up.

But I aimed to see that their deaths wouldn't be in vain. The rest of the Ko Zhin was out there, and I intended to learn everything I possibly could about it. And for the first time, it wasn't out of any abiding curiosity about relics but out of a sense of duty. A determination that not one more innocent life would be touched by dark magic.

I saw Moon John waiting at one of the intact tables. He'd asked me to meet him that morning to discuss the very matter of the Ko Zhin.

I took a seat beside him, and he lifted a small silver pitcher. "Have some lemonade?"

"Sure," I said, smiling. I reached for a few folded sheets of paper in my apron pocket. "I copied down a bit more information on rare fire relics. Nothing about the Ko Zhin, of course, but it's good background information."

"Excellent," he said, pouring me a drink. "Keep reading that text. There is still much we can learn."

"And you said you have something for me?" I asked.

"Indeed." Moon John set down the pitcher. "You know the sheriff has been interrogating some Hacienda deserters. One of them talked. Leander wouldn't tell me much, but he did mention that Álvar had a special interest in the Harpy Caverns. Apparently, there was something in them that he was *very* interested in. Something relic related. Only a few of his closest inner circle knew the details."

The hairs on my arms prickled up. I remembered the strange mining shaft that night we hunted ghost coyotes, the dark, bent tunnel that had called to me so powerfully.

"And there is more," Moon John went on. "A relic scholar from back East was planning to come out and stay at the Hacienda. They think it had something to do with whatever was in the caves. Word is, he was bringing his own specialized team of relic extractors."

My throat felt dry. "Is the sheriff going to investigate the caverns?"

Moon John nodded slowly. "We would hope, but in the meantime, we must be vigilant. I doubt the razing of the Hacienda will keep such a man away forever."

"Right," I murmured.

Perhaps reading the look of concern on my face, Moon John set his hand on my shoulder. "Do not be troubled, Maggie. Our town is well protected. Especially now, considering the new friendly terms with the Apaches. If anyone tries to come for us again, we will be ready." His confidence made me feel a little better, and I managed a smile.

At that moment, Ella skipped up to us, her cheeks pink from helping Eddie. "Hi, Moon John," she chirped.

"Good morning to you, Miss Davis," he said, smiling widely. "Are you having a good time this morning?"

"Oh, yes, sir." Ella grabbed my hand. "Come here, Maggie. I want to show you the wood I nailed up."

"And I want to see it."

I stood, and Moon John nodded warmly for me to run along. Ella grabbed my hand, pulling me out into the street so we could get a full view of the slowly growing structure.

"That plank right there," she said, pointing with a proud smile. "I put the nails in all by myself."

I scooped her into a sideways hug. "Well, would you look at that! I'm real proud of you, baby girl."

She beamed, and we stood for a moment, arm in arm, watching

The Desert Rose in the bright desert sunshine.

Ella rested her head on my side. "Is this gonna be our new home, Maggie?"

"I think so. Does that sound good to you?"

"I want to be wherever you are."

A tremor of emotion gripped my throat, and I knelt in front of her, holding her shoulders in my hands. "You will be, Ella. We're a family, no matter what. And I promise, we'll never be apart again." I touched her chin. "Sound like a plan?"

"Okay, Maggie."

A smile grew on her face, and she looked so much like Jeb, it almost hurt. I knew I could never make things exactly like they were before, but for Ella, I had every intention to try.

"Can we have lunch now?" she asked, grabbing my hand. "All that hard work made me so hungry, I could eat a dragon."

I laughed. "Well, I don't know about a dragon, but I think we have some fried chicken left."

I turned to get Adelaide when I noticed a man running down the street, heading toward us. Straining for a better look, I recognized Sheriff Leander. For a moment, my heart froze to see him looking so intense, and a flourish of fear ran through my brain. After all we'd been through, I didn't think I could bear more trouble. I gripped Ella's shoulder, but as Sheriff Leander approached, I noticed he was beaming.

"I came as soon as I heard," he cried, running up to me. He was red-faced from his sprint and sweaty, but he was smiling.

"Heard what?" I asked.

He bent over for a moment to catch his breath. Then he looked up, once again smiling. "Come on," he said. "There's something you need to see."

I followed him to the town infirmary, my heart inexplicably pounding. Sheriff Leander led me to the hospital room. Patients from the battle lay in the row of beds in varying states of recovery. A worn-looking nurse bustled around with medicine and relic elixirs for the pain. I couldn't understand why the sheriff had brought me here, until my eyes fell on the last bed, tucked beneath the far window, resting in a beam of bright sunshine.

The patient slowly turned his face to me. In an instant, the room blurred. There was only my pounding heart, only this sharp ringing in my ears. The light streaming in the window glinted off a pair of sky-blue eyes.

His face badly cut and half covered with white bandages, Landon Black managed his usual, charming smile.

ACKNOWLEDGMENTS

So many people helped make this dream come true for me. I wish I could give you all a hug, but we can settle for a shout out.

First, I want to thank my spectacular agent, Mollie Glick. You're a true pro. *Relic* wouldn't be what it is without your fantastic insights and hard work. Thanks also to Kathleen Hamblin and Brandy Rivers.

I'll always have a special place in my heart for Stacy Abrams, my outstanding, brilliant editor. Thank you for loving and believing in my story. It's truly been a dream working with you.

Thanks to all the lovely people at Entangled: Tara Gonzales, Alycia Tornetta, Kari Bradley, J.J. Bonds, Heather Riccio, Annette Macias and Alexandra Shostak. You've all helped make this experience perfect for me.

I feel beyond lucky to have made such generous, funny and talented writer friends over the years. Natalie Whipple, Kasie

West, Jenn Johansson, Candice Kennington, Michelle D. Argyle and Sara Raasch. Thank you for guiding me through my many Philosophical Journeys, for making me laugh my head off, for letting me read your incredible books, and for helping to make me the writer I am today. I love you all!

And thank you to the many other fabulous writers I've come to know who have read for me, helped me and been there for me. Kiersten White, Kristen L. Martin, Chantele Sedgwick and Sara Larson, to name a few.

Love to all my Colorado peeps! The Best Book Club Ever: Jenn, Betsy, Darcy, Celeste, Mindy, Cheyanna, Suzy, Melissa, Amy and Kendra—you all really are the best. And thank you to my beautiful friends, Natalie and Lisa. This moment wouldn't be as fun without my CC.

I have so much gratitude for my family. Mom and Dad, you taught me to believe in myself, to push myself. You showed me so many amazing new places. You nurtured my creativity and gave me a happy, adventurous childhood. I'll never be able to thank you enough. Jared, Sarah, Becca, Diana, Rachel and Amy, you're the best siblings ever, and I thank you for all the love and support over the years.

Becca, thank you for that one awesome lunch at Cafe Rio, when we said, "Why not me?" That started everything. Diana, thank you for the countless talks and advice, not just about *Relic*, but everything else. Thank you for always completely believing that I'd reach this point one day. I hope you know I most certainly could not have without you.

And finally, I want to express my love to my own little family. Amber, Logan and Ella, you kids are truly my proudest creation. And my wonderful husband, Ben, I wish I could show you how much your love and support has meant to me. Thanks for being there even when it wasn't easy. You've helped me live my dreams, and I'll always love you for that. I'm so happy to share this moment with you.

Read on for a sneak peek at Cindi Madsen's chilling

ALL THE BROKEN PIECES

What if your life wasn't your own?

Liv comes out of a coma with no memory of her past and two distinct, warring voices inside her head. Nothing, not even her reflection, seems familiar. As she stumbles through her junior year, the voices get louder, insisting she please the popular group while simultaneously despising them. But when Liv starts hanging around with Spencer, whose own mysterious past also has him on the fringe, life feels complete for the first time in, well, as long as she can remember.

Liv knows the details of the car accident that put her in the coma, but as the voices invade her dreams, and her dreams start feeling like memories, she and Spencer seek out answers. Yet the deeper they dig, the less things make sense. Can Liv rebuild the pieces of her broken past, when it means questioning not just who she is, but what she is?

Available online and in stores now!

1

White ceiling, a fuzzy face hovering over hers. Gloved fingers against her skin. A steady chirping noise mixed in with words she couldn't quite catch hold of.

Opening her eyes took so much effort. And they kept closing before she got a good look. One prick, another. Tugging at her skin. A blurry arm moved up and down in time with the pinpricks.

I think I'm going to puke.

Strange, dreamlike voices floated over her. "I think she's waking up."

"She's not ready yet."

Cold liquid shot into her arm at her elbow and wound up to her shoulder, through her chest, until it spread into her entire body. Then blackness sucked her back under.

• • •

Her leg twitched. Then an arm. She wasn't telling them to move; they kept doing it on their own. Her eyes flickered open and she caught a flash of a white ceiling. The chirping noise sounded out, steady and loud.

With a gasp, she shot up.

Hands eased her back down into the soft pillows. "Take it easy," a blurry form said.

She blinked a couple times and her vision cleared.

A woman stood over her, a warm smile on her face. Her dark hair fell from behind her ear as she moved closer. "How are you feeling?"

Confusion filled her. She felt lost, scared. She wanted…she wasn't sure what. "I'm…" Her throat burned as she tried to form a sentence. "I don't…" The words didn't sound right. They were thick and slurred. Frustration added to the confusion as she tried again. "What's…going…am I?"

The woman reached down and cupped her cheek. "Shh. You were in an accident. But everything will be fine."

She searched her memory. There was nothing. Nothing but flashes of being in this room. "I feel…strange."

"But you're talking. That's an excellent sign." The woman sat on the edge of the bed. "Do you remember anything? The accident? Your name?"

Pain shot across her head as she searched through the fuzziness. Tears pricked her eyes. "I don't remember…anything."

"Olivia, honey, it's me. Your name is Olivia, and I'm…" Her smile widened and unshed tears glistened in her eyes. "I'm your mother. Victoria Stein."

Olivia tried to put the images together, tried to make sense of it all. But it didn't fit. Or she couldn't remember if it did. A tear escaped and ran down her cheek.

The woman—*Mom*—leaned down and hugged her. "It's okay. You were in a bad car accident and had to have several surgeries, but you're going to be just fine. Because I'm going to take such good care of you."

Mom squeezed Olivia's hand. "Let me go get Henry—your father. He'll be so glad to see that you're finally awake."

When Dad stepped into the room, he didn't look familiar, either. Olivia saw the concern in his eyes, but there was something else. He seemed reluctant.

Mom pointed at the chirping monitor. "Look at her heart rate. She can understand me, and she can talk."

Why is she saying it like that? Like it's a big surprise. Olivia licked her lips and forced the question from her dry throat. "Why wouldn't I be able to talk?"

Mom sat on the foot of the bed. "Because, dear, your injuries were so severe. The brain trauma, and your heart…" She shook her head, then placed her hands over her own heart, looking like she might start crying. "You're our little miracle."

Olivia reached up, feeling the tender spots on her head. Her fingers brushed across a row of—were those little ridges made of metal?

"Careful. The staples are almost ready to come out, but it's still going to be sore for a while."

Staples?! Her stomach rolled. *I have* staples *in my head?* She lowered her now-shaking hand. "Can I get a mirror?"

Mom looked at Dad, then back at her. "I don't think that's a good idea. Not until you've healed a little more."

Olivia gave two slow nods. If only everything weren't so strange. If she could just remember something. Anything.

"You're healing very well," Dad said. "And your heartbeat is strong. That's good."

Mom smiled at her. "That's because you're amazing."

Dad grabbed Mom's hand. "Darling, I need to talk to you about something. In the other room."

Mom patted Olivia's leg. "You just relax. I'll be back in a few minutes."

The two of them left the room, but when Mom swung the door closed, it didn't latch. Olivia could hear their voices in the hall.

"I still think we should…" She couldn't make out the rest of Dad's muffled words. "…know if I can do this."

"…late for that," Mom said. "We'd lose everything, including…" Her voice faded as they got farther away. "…have to move."

She could tell the conversation was tense, but the words were impossible to decipher now. Holding a hand in front of her face, she turned it back and forth. A plastic tube ran from her arm to a machine next to her bed.

Weird. Everything was weird. She pulled a strand of her hair forward. Dark brown—like Mom's. But it didn't help her remember how she looked or who exactly she was. She kicked off her covers and stared at her legs. Running her gaze up and down, she assessed the damage: a few bruises and cuts. Her chest felt tight. She peeked into her nightgown and stared in horror at the long red stripe running down her chest.

Gross.

You're alive. You shouldn't be thinking about looks.

She dropped the nightgown, then put a palm over her heart. *Ouch.*

Lowering her hand, she scanned the room. *I wonder how my*

face looks. From the way Dad stared at me, plus the fact that Mom won't let me see a mirror, it must be bad.

Brains are more important than looks.

That's what ugly people say.

Olivia put her hands on her head and squeezed. "Stop it," she whispered to her arguing thoughts, hysteria bubbling up and squeezing the air from her lungs. What was happening to her? Why didn't she recognize her parents or know where she was? *Who* she was? Tears ran warm trails down her cheeks. "Just make it all stop."

Mom swung open the door and walked into the room. "What was that, dear?"

Olivia swiped the tears off her face. "Nothing. Is everything okay?"

Mom nodded. "Of course. I'm going to take some time off from work to help you heal. As soon as we get you recovered enough, we're moving. After everything that's happened, I think we could use a fresh start."

Olivia was still too hazy to think about a fresh start. All she knew was that something seemed wrong. Make that *everything* seemed wrong. So she clung to the hope that she would recover quickly. And that when she did, all the wrongness would go away.

Read on for a sneak peek at Lea Rae Miller's adorkable teen romance

THE SUMMER I BECAME A NERD

On the outside, seventeen-year-old Madelyne Summers looks like your typical blond cheerleader—perky, popular, and dating the star quarterback. But inside, Maddie spends more time agonizing over what will happen in the next issue of her favorite comic book than planning pep rallies with her squad. That she's a nerd hiding in a popular girl's body isn't just unknown, it's anti-known. And she needs to keep it that way.

Summer is the only time Maddie lets her real self out to play, but when she slips up and the adorkable guy behind the local comic shop's counter uncovers her secret, she's busted. Before she can shake a pom-pom, Maddie's whisked into Logan's world of comic conventions, live-action role-playing, and first-person-shooter video games. And she loves it. But the more she denies who she really is, the deeper her lies become, and the more she risks losing Logan forever.

prologue

When I was in junior high, the school I went to held a Halloween festival every year in the gym. There were all these little booths where we could bob for apples or throw darts at balloons for crappy little prizes like plastic spider rings and whistles that didn't work. There was a "jailhouse" that was really just a big cardboard box with a door and a window with black spray-painted PVC pipes as the bars. We could pay a dollar to send someone to "jail" for one minute. For some reason this turned into a declaration of love if a boy sent a girl to jail.

The biggest part of this festival was always the costume contest, probably because the winner actually won cash. In sixth grade, I was determined to win this contest. I spent weeks before the festival making my costume. I figured if I went as something the judges—who were just the softball coach, the head of the cafeteria, and the principal—had never seen before, I was sure to win.

At the time, I was really into this comic book series called The Pigments. My favorite character was Spectrum Girl. She had a pink afro and this awesome cape. The cape was what I spent most of my time on. I got these long, wide strips of fabric in every shade of the rainbow, then lined the edges of each strip with bendable wire so the strips would stick out behind me and be all wavy so it would look like I was flying.

On the night of the festival I was so pumped I almost threw up as I waited in the wings of the stage. The other competitors had all chosen the same old costumes: witch, robot, the main character of whatever the most recent animated movie was. I could feel it in my very core that I had this thing wrapped up.

Then, Mrs. Birdhill announced me.

"Our next trick-or-treater is Maddie Jean Summers. She's dressed as"—and here's where I started to doubt myself because when she said this last part, it sounded like she was reading words she had never heard before—"the leader of the superhero team The Pigments, Spectrum Girl?"

Yep, she ended it like she was asking a question.

I stepped onto the stage, expecting a wave of *ooh*s and *ahh*s, but what I got was complete silence. I swear I heard a cricket chirp somewhere in the back of the room when I stepped up to the microphone.

"Hi. I spent two weeks working on my costume. I chose Spectrum Girl because she's the strongest of all the Pigments, and I think she sets a great example for young women today," I said and took a few giant steps back so I could make a slow turn.

When I made the complete 360, I stopped and looked out at the audience. It was a sea of my peers, everyone I went to school with, everyone I wanted desperately to impress. In the front row was my best friend, who shall remain nameless. She would always rag on me when I mentioned anything comic related, so I had learned not to talk about it.

I remember looking down at her in her cheerleader costume. I'm sure my eyes were pleading with her to break the silence, to help me—even if she didn't like comics, we were best friends. Surely she'd support me.

Instead, she leaned over to the girl next to her and whispered something in her ear. They both giggled before she-who-shall-not-be-named yelled, "Where did you get your costume idea?"

I stepped up to the microphone, thinking my answer would help. Everyone loves Superman and Batman, how could they not like a costume based on a comic character?

"The Pigments is a comic book I like a lot," I said.

"A comic book? What a dork!"

I don't know if everyone agreed with her, but they all laughed with her. Laughed me right off the stage. Thank goodness no one was hanging out by the back exit because it would have been even more embarrassing if someone had caught me bawling my eyes out in a dark corner.

Later, as I tore my excellently crafted cape to shreds and stuffed it into a garbage bag, I vowed no one would ever get the chance to hurt me like that again.

And that's when my double life began.